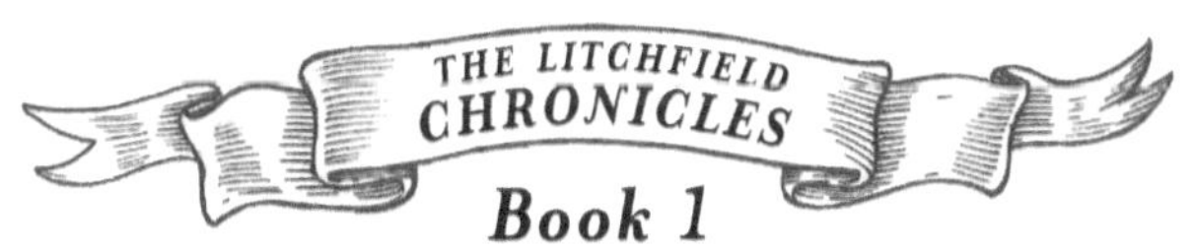

THE EDUCATION OF EBENEZER WELLS

LOUISE HARMON

Copyright © 2024 by Louise Harmon

All rights reserved.

No part of this publication may be reproduced, distributed, or transmitted in any form or by any means, including photocopying, recording, or other electronic or mechanical methods, without the prior written permission of the publisher, except as permitted by U.S. copyright law. For permission requests, contact Hot Brick Books, PO Box 15, New Hartford, CT 06057.

The Education of Ebenezer Wells is a work of fiction. All incidents and dialogue, and all characters, with the exception of some historical figures, are products of the author's imagination. Where real-life historical figures appear, the situations, incidents, and dialogues concerning those persons are entirely fictional and are not intended to depict actual events. In other respects, any resemblance to actual persons (living or deceased), events, or locales is entirely coincidental.

ISBN: 979-8-9915313-1-3

Cover and interior design by David Provolo
Silhouettes by Lauren Muney, after William Bache (1771-1845)
Map by Owen Bruce McKenzie
Author Website: louiseharmon.com

TABLE OF CONTENTS

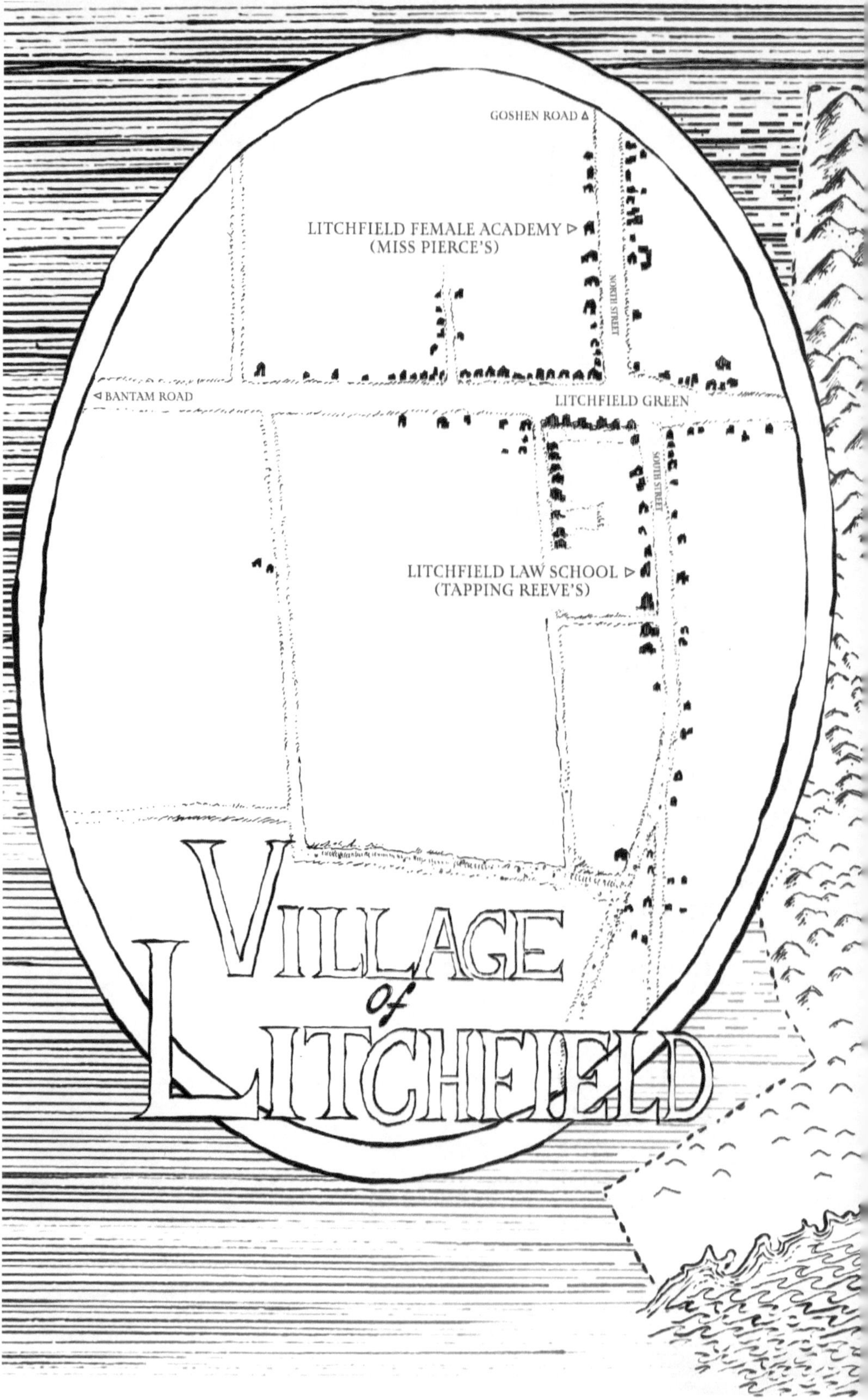

GOSHEN ROAD
LITCHFIELD FEMALE ACADEMY
(MISS PIERCE'S)
NORTH STREET
BANTAM ROAD
LITCHFIELD GREEN
SOUTH STREET
LITCHFIELD LAW SCHOOL
(TAPPING REEVE'S)
VILLAGE of LITCHFIELD

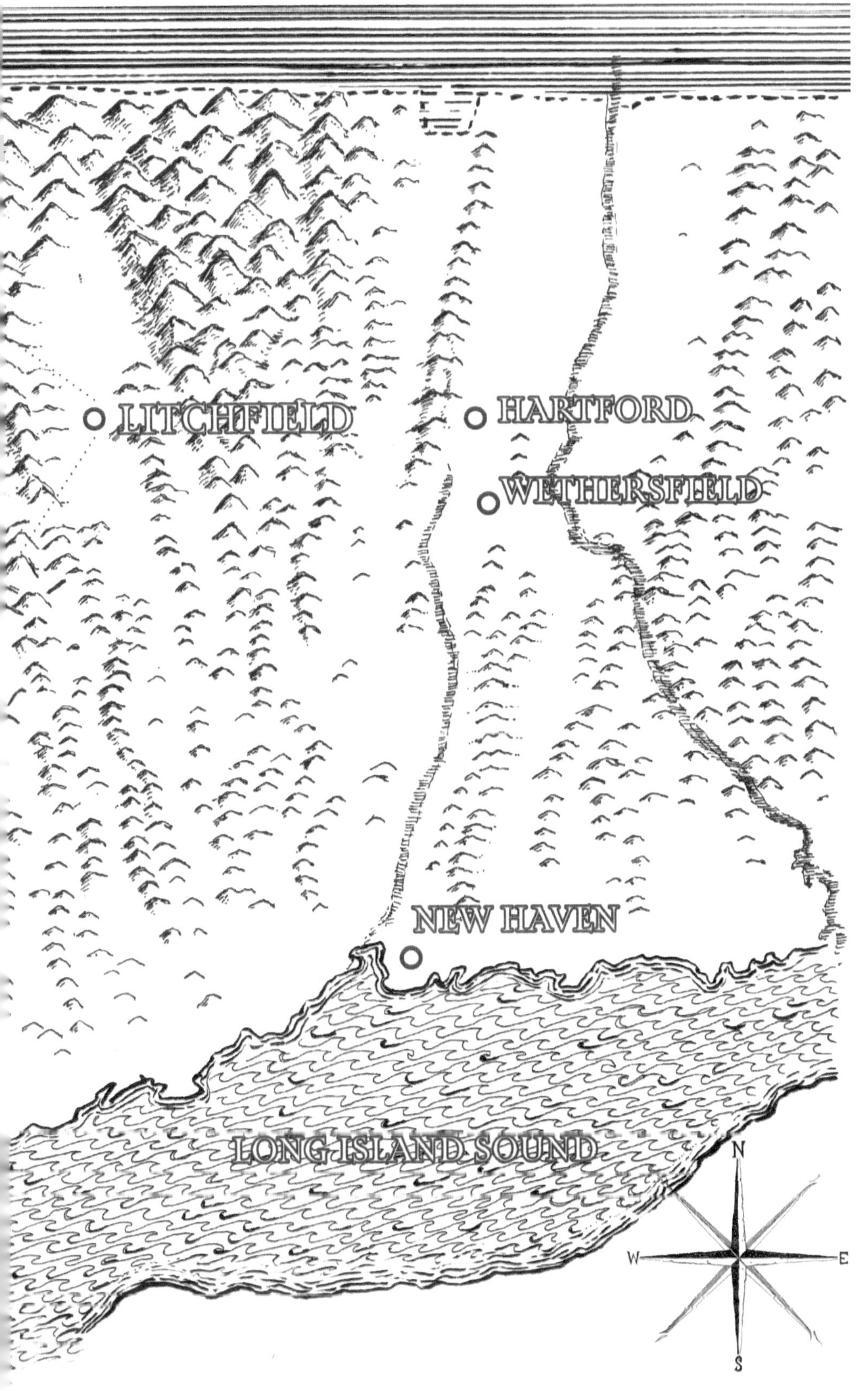

LITCHFIELD
HARTFORD
WETHERSFIELD
NEW HAVEN
LONG ISLAND SOUND
N
W
E
S

CHAPTER 1

Promenading on the Green

"Will Miss Pierce let me attend the winter ball?" Her question sounded more like a command. Her accent was thick and languid—from the South, Eb surmised.

Eb Wells had propped himself up against the wall of the stagecoach, first asleep, and now pretending to be. The stagecoach traveled on the turnpike from Hartford to Litchfield. Lashed down to the metal top railings, trunks were piled high on its roof, full of clothes, shoes, coats, writing supplies, books—all the accoutrements for a year away at school. Eb opened his eyes just a crack to look out the window. An inky blue sky, dark leaves, and black branches flew by. It was an early September evening in 1819, and a chill was in the air. In Connecticut, the sun and the temperature went down together.

Eb and his traveling companion, Thomas Bradford, had journeyed by sea from Savannah, Georgia, and boarded the stagecoach in Boston. They were on their way to the Litchfield Law School in the northwest corner of Connecticut where both would study law. Eb's older brother was the lawyer for Thomas's father, a wealthy planter. Their families had arranged for them to travel together, but now at the journey's end, Eb was thoroughly sick of Thomas Bradford. Fifteen days with him was fourteen days too many. Over the squeaks and groans of the stagecoach, Eb listened to the lulling voices of the two women across the aisle from him, happy for the diversion. His liaison with Thomas Bradford was one of convenience, not affinity.

"It depends on how old you are when she schedules the ball." Eb peeked to see who was speaking. The reply came from the slight young woman who had boarded the stagecoach in Hartford. She had a pale, angular face and brown eyes, her dark hair pulled back in a bun. Wrapped in a long black woolen cloak with a hood, it was difficult to tell much more about her. Eb guessed her age to be about twenty. She was a Yankee, her voice bearing the nasal twang of New England.

"I'll be sixteen the second week of January." This declaration was made by the young woman who had boarded the stagecoach in Boston with Eb and Thomas—the one from the South. Eb had observed her then and could tell she was out of his league. Dressed in a pale blue coat with mutton sleeves, her blonde curls escaped from her matching bonnet in a calculated display of rebellion. Her face was perfectly symmetrical and heart shaped.

"If the ball is scheduled before your birthday, I wouldn't count on it," the dark-haired woman said. "The rule is no balls until you're sixteen. No exceptions."

"That's ridiculous." The woman from the South tossed her head. "I won't be any more mature the day after my sixteenth birthday than the day before. Miss Pierce will surely bend the rule." This she said with the certainty of someone accustomed to having rules bent for her. "It's a silly and arbitrary rule."

"It may be arbitrary. I'll grant you that." The smaller woman shivered and pulled her cloak around her more tightly. "But it isn't silly. The law sometimes needs sharp lines like that. It eases administration. I'm just letting you know. Miss Pierce loves a rule."

A snort of slumber ripped through the air. Thomas Bradford leaned into the corner of the stagecoach, sleeping in earnest. His long legs were crossed, his elbow buried in a leather bag placed in the middle of the bench to mark his jurisdiction. Quarters were cramped. Eb did not want Thomas to wake up—or for the two women to compare them. Thomas was classically good-looking with thick brown hair brushed studiously off his face—and tall. Eb was short, had scruffy auburn hair, and wore glasses that were chronically falling down his nose. Thomas dressed well and tried to present his right profile whenever he could, his mother having told him his right side favored a Roman coin. Eb's clothes were plain and pedestrian, and to his knowledge, no one side of his face favored the other.

Eb Wells leaned over and whispered, "Are you ladies headed for the Litchfield Female Academy?"

"We are." The dark-haired woman gathered her hood tighter around her neck. "This is my fourth year. I'll be an assistant teacher this year." She gestured to the vision in light blue wool beside her. "Miss Montgomery's just starting at Miss Pierce's."

"Do I detect a Southern accent?" Waking from his slumber, Thomas Bradford stretched his hands over his head in an exaggerated effort to rouse himself. "From one of you?" Thomas gazed across the aisle at the two young women.

"I'm from Charleston. Can't you tell?" Peering out from her pale blue bonnet, the woman from the South gave him a flirtatious, appraising look, assessing the cut of his coat and quality of his shoes.

"I had my suspicions, miss." Thomas made a bow. "My name's Thomas Bradford." He nodded toward Eb. "And this is Mr. Ebenezer Wells. We're both from Savannah, although my father's plantation is further north in Georgia." Eb gave a stiff little bow in imitation of Thomas.

"I'm Katherine Montgomery." She put out her gloved hand for them to press her fingers, before turning to her traveling companion. "I'm so sorry, but I don't remember your name. I know you told me in Hartford."

"Rebecca." She did not offer her hand. "Rebecca Harding."

"And you're headed for the Litchfield Law School?" Katherine asked.

"Yes," Eb replied. "We're both starting the course with Judge Reeve and Judge Gould."

Thomas was now wide awake. He leaned over in the direction of Katherine, who sat directly across from him, trying to present his right profile, a difficult task in a lurching stagecoach. "Montgomery?" Thomas rolled the name around in his mouth like he was tasting an unknown wine. "Are you any relation to the Montgomery family of Beaufort? On Orange Street?"

"Why, of course. That would be our Uncle James's house." Katherine gave a coquettish toss of her head. "I've been there many times. Would you be the Bradfords of Washington, Georgia? Mary Mount?"

"Yes, that's right," Thomas said demurely. "We had a home in Beaufort, but we let it go. My father is now building a summer home in the mountains. In the northern part of the state." Thomas shook his head sadly. "I didn't approve of the Beaufort sale, but I was up at Yale at the time, and couldn't voice my dissent."

Eb bristled at Thomas's glib expression 'let it go.' He wondered how much money had been exchanged in that land transaction. Had his brother represented the Bradfords? And how did Thomas Bradford manage to get Yale into any conversation?

"And you?" Katherine turned her attention to Eb. "Did you go to Yale as well?"

"No." Eb pushed his glasses up his nose. "I went to Franklin College. But my older brother's a Yale grad. My father too." He immediately regretted what he had said. What was he trying to do?

Impress this woman who was way too tall for him that his family could afford Yale? Besides, it was an accolade that belonged to his brother and father, not to him. Eb could kick himself.

"I see," Katherine replied with a dismissive sniff—one that signaled an end to the conversation.

"Where's Franklin College?" Rebecca Harding came to Eb's rescue, sensing he was at a disadvantage, that he was being judged poorly for his plain clothes, his scruffy hair, his migrating glasses, his alma mater—and his short stature.

"In Athens, Georgia." Eb perked up. "A public institution. My father thought I wasn't diligent enough about my studies, so Yale was out for me."

"Did you like Franklin College?"

"I loved it." Eb's four years at Franklin College had been the best years of his life, expansive in every way. "The school's been struggling a bit. It's new, you see, and small. We only had five in our graduating class. But Athens is lovely." Eb wondered if he was babbling. His older sister Malinda always told him: if you think you are babbling, you probably are. Undaunted, he finished his monologue. "And the flowers in Athens are quite different from Savannah's. Less tropical. Higher elevation, the red soil, you know."

"I know nothing of Georgia's soil." Rebecca Harding cocked her head inquisitively. "But what did you study?"

Eb's face lit up. No one outside of his family had ever asked about his studies before. "Latin mostly, and a little Greek. But mathematics too, theology, and philosophy."

"And why are you studying law?"

"Why? Well, let's see, well, I . . ."

Eb's family expected him to join his brother John's law practice in Savannah, but he did not want to say so, having done enough gratuitous bragging for one day. "It was my brother's idea. He went to the Litchfield Law School too."

"But your brother went to Yale, and you didn't," Rebecca pointed out. "You've already broken with precedent."

"The answer is quite simple." Thomas Bradford interrupted. His guard was down. For a few seconds, he gave the impression of a man still hungover from the night before, a man impatient with a conversation that did not revolve around him. "Judge Reeve's law school is the best. Eb's brother—John Wells—he's our lawyer. John went there, and he represents some of the finest people in Savannah. My father's one of them. Eb will study with Judge Reeve so that he can return to Savannah and practice law with his brother."

"I might do so." Eb stiffened, annoyed at Thomas's speaking for him. "At least that's the plan." He turned again to Rebecca, and his tone softened. "To answer your question, I'm not sure why I'm studying law." Eb took a longer look at Rebecca Harding. Yes, her face has sharp lines, Eb thought, but she possesses a beauty of her own. Subtle and interesting. "Livelihood, I suppose, and an opportunity to see the world. I've got family in New Haven. But as for the law?" Eb shrugged. "I'm not sure why I should study it."

"I'll be curious to hear how you find it." Rebecca settled back into her black cloak which enveloped her like a cocoon.

"Do you know William Hurley from Charleston?" Katherine Montgomery interjected, directing her question to Thomas Bradford. "He'd have been in your class at Yale?"

"Of course, I know Will. He's from the Hurleys of Summerville." Katherine and Thomas continued to discuss their mutual friends in low conspiratorial tones. For them, this conversation was not inconsequential as they wove themselves into the mythical tapestry of Southern aristocracy. Eb Wells and Rebecca Harding fell silent, having nothing further to contribute. Darkness had descended. The stagecoach squeaked, creaked, and swayed, careening over the unpaved road, avoiding the potholes in the turnpike.

In Eb's father's day, there was no such thing as a 'law school.' William Wells had 'read for the law,' apprenticing with Rufus Henderson, Esquire, in New Haven, copying contracts, examining land titles, and filing papers at the courthouse. William and his fellow apprentice, Ned Haines, read *Blackstone* to each other at night. But both had attended Yale. Yale had shown them what an education should look like: brick buildings, a curriculum, books, professors, lectures, exams. Their experience with Rufus Henderson did not measure up. He barked orders to his apprentices but made little effort to educate them.

During his apprenticeship, William Wells courted his wife, Abigail Cabot. Abigail was the younger sister of a colleague from Yale, Dr. Ebenezer Cabot, and a student at a female academy. Her parents would only consent to the match if William was an established professional. After the War of Independence, New England was glutted with lawyers, so Eb's father moved to Savannah, Georgia, to start his law practice. After their marriage, Abigail joined him. In their modest saltbox house on East York Street, she gave birth to five children. Their first child, John, was born in 1789; the second, Malinda, came in 1791. Two more girls followed but died in infancy. Eb arrived in 1798.

The sons of William Wells had a different legal education from their father. John was the first in the family to go to the Litchfield Law School in northwest Connecticut. The idea of a 'law school' was an innovation—a sea change from their father's haphazard apprenticeship. Judge Tapping Reeve, the founder of the school, had systematized the study of law. He built a small school building in his side yard, gathered students, set a curriculum national in scope, lectured, gave oral exams, ran moot courts, and created a community of scholars. The Litchfield Law School represented a revolution in legal education. It was renowned throughout the nation.

While in Litchfield, Eb's brother John became engaged to Miss Eliza Jackson, the daughter of a wealthy Charleston planter. Eliza had been a student at the equally famous Litchfield Female Academy, headed by Miss Sarah Pierce. Miss Pierce too was an innovator, but in female education. At her school, a young woman could study substantive academic subjects, as well as the ornamental arts. John Wells had wanted their father to send his sister Malinda to Miss Pierce's, but William Wells thought the expense too great. Abigail Wells became the teacher of Malinda, Susan, the housekeeper's daughter, and her boys before they attended the academy in Savannah.

Unlike his older brother John, Eb struggled at school. He was a dreamer, wandering the streets of Savannah with his commonplace book tucked under his arm. He called it *The Detritus of the Idle Mind*, or just *The Detritus*. In it, Eb sketched flowers and wrote down observations or phrases that struck his fancy. He knew every flowering bush in Savannah, as well as the Latin names of every bird who migrated through coastal Georgia. His older brother thought no real man should possess such knowledge. His father too was disappointed. Both bemoaned Eb's lack of ambition. William Wells declared that sending Eb to Yale would be a waste of money. Eb would go to Franklin College instead, the new state institution of higher learning in Athens, Georgia.

William Wells died of malaria in Eb's last year at college. It had been his last wish for Eb to attend the Litchfield Law School and join the family law practice with John. While not thrilled, Eb was not opposed. He wanted to see the world. At least the journey to Connecticut began at sea. His mother had regaled him with stories about New England. Finally, Eb could see for himself the New Haven Green, the Long Island Sound, the vibrant colors of fall—maybe snow. How bad could it be to learn some law?

Eb Wells sat poised on a chair in the parlor of Miss Pierce's house on North Street in Litchfield, next door to the female academy. It was a late Tuesday afternoon, a few weeks into law school. Miss Pierce had invited a few of Judge Reeve's students for tea with some of her students. The room was a blur of colorful gowns and well-coifed hair, interspersed with the dark suits of a dozen or so law students. His landlady, Mrs. Edwards, had persuaded Eb to attend the gathering. Eb needed a break from studying, she insisted. Mrs. Edwards, a widow in her sixties, ran a boarding house on North Street with her unmarried daughters. She had taken a shine to Eb who was unlike her other boarder from Georgia, Thomas Bradford. Thomas skipped lectures, frequented the hotel tavern in town, and chafed at her rules.

'Living with that old biddy is like living with my grandmother,' Thomas moaned during their first week in Litchfield. Not knowing anyone else, the two young men had clung to each other for the first few days. But as soon as Thomas found more fashionable Southern law students to spend time with—mostly at the tavern—he left Eb Wells behind. Eb was immensely relieved. He liked Mrs. Edwards.

"Mr. Wells . . ." Eb's chair was next to a sofa on which sat Rebecca Harding and a petite young woman he did not know. "I'd like you to meet one of our new students this year," Rebecca said. "Miss Martha Lewis. She lives on the outskirts of Litchfield but is boarding with us here at Miss Pierce's." Martha Lewis had a mass of coppery red hair that threatened to escape from her giant ebony hairpin. She wore a simple, high-waisted brown cotton dress. Eb tried not to stare at her freckles, lightly sprinkled across her cheeks. He had never seen freckles on a proper young lady before. His older sister Malinda was solicitous of her alabaster skin. In Savannah, freckles on a woman were anathema.

"How do you do, Miss Lewis." Eb bowed to Martha, uncertain what else to say.

"And how are you finding the study of law?" Rebecca broke the awkward silence. Both Martha Lewis and Eb Wells were unaccustomed to parlor banter. It was Rebecca's job, as an assistant teacher, to model appropriate behavior. Miss Pierce regarded the social events in her home as an integral part of her students' education.

"I don't quite know what to say," Eb replied. Rebecca seemed much taller than he remembered. Perhaps she was more imposing seated next to Martha Lewis, whose feet barely touched the floor. Rebecca's dark brown hair was pulled back in a bun at the nape of her neck. She wore a loden green empire waist dress with a tatted ivory lace collar. A gold locket dangled from her neck. Rebecca also possessed a stiff formality he had not seen before.

The tone of the occasion was set by Miss Sarah Pierce, the head mistress, who stood at the end of the narrow room like a smiling statue. Miss Pierce was a diminutive, intense woman in her fifties. Eb thought she looked like a cross between an owl and an eagle, peering out from the edges of her English lace cap. She reminded him of his sister, although Miss Pierce was closer to his mother's age. Eb always teased Malinda that she too had strigine qualities, although there was no hint of an eagle in her kind, round face. After his first few weeks at law school, he was missing his older sister, even her bossy ways.

"Sometimes I can hardly follow what's being said," Eb admitted to Rebecca. "I sit there during the lecture and try to take notes, but it's all Greek to me. Except if it were Greek, I'd understand more of it."

"Studying law is a new endeavor for you, isn't it?"

"It shouldn't be. I'm the son of a lawyer, and the brother of a lawyer. You'd think some of the law might conveniently run in my veins."

"Did you spend much time in your father's law office?"

"No." Eb shook his head. "My brother John did, but not me. My father passed away last year. John took over the practice." These facts he relayed in a matter-of-fact manner. "But I was always much happier upstairs in the schoolroom with my mother, Malinda, and Susan. Or roaming the streets of Savannah. I thought what Father did was boring."

"Ha!" Martha Lewis interjected with an impish grin. "I never find my father's work boring." Rebecca put her hand gently on Martha's arm. Martha had interrupted what the man was saying, what Miss Pierce deemed the most important part of any conversation, although not a rule Rebecca herself always respected. Martha added, more subdued this time, "My father's an artisan. He does portrait likenesses. Miniature cut-outs of profiles. Silhouettes." Eb was about to ask her a question when Rebecca brought the conversation back around to him.

"I'm so sorry to hear about your father's passing. Are Malinda and Susan your sisters?"

"Just Malinda. She's my older sister, but Susan—well, she's like a sister, I suppose. Susan's the daughter of our housekeeper. My mother undertook her education, and mine as well," he added, "until I went to a boys' academy. Now Susan's my sister's companion."

"I envy you, having a brother and a sister." A look of sadness crossed Rebecca Harding's face. "I was an only child."

"Well, I dare say you're still an only child," Eb teased. He was trying desperately to engage in light banter, not something he was adept at. "You haven't yet shuffled off this mortal coil."

"The past tense is appropriate. I lost my two brothers." Rebecca fingered her gold locket. "And my parents are dead. My mother died when I was eight, my father when I was twelve. That made me an orphan. I became the ward of my great-aunt and uncle in Hartford."

"Oh," Eb mumbled.

"I can't presently be an only child. I lack parents to complete the relation." Rebecca thought for a moment, casting her eyes down at the floor. "Then again, because I'm the ward of my great-aunt and uncle, and they're childless, I could be said to be the only child of two people who have no child."

"Yes, well, you might say that." Eb was not certain he followed Miss Harding, and he was embarrassed his jest had dredged up her sad history. "I'm sorry to hear of your tragedy."

"Me as well, Miss Harding." Martha took Rebecca's hand. "I had no idea about your losses." Martha came from a large, fractious household on the outskirts of Litchfield, out toward Goshen. Both parents and her three older brothers were still very much alive.

"No matter." Rebecca looked up at Eb. "But tell me, why are the lectures so hard to follow? Is it Judge Reeve you can't understand or Judge Gould?" This was Rebecca's fourth year at the female academy in Litchfield. She had endured many conversations about the pros and cons of the two law lecturers. Academics were her métier.

"I'm lost with both." Eb pushed his glasses back up his nose. "I really like Judge Reeve. I take my midday meal with Mrs. Reeve. At the table, I've no trouble understanding Judge Reeve, but when he stands behind the lectern, I've got no idea what he's talking about." Eb felt relieved to confess this to someone. He had been hopelessly lost for weeks.

"When you first begin to study the law"—Rebecca assumed the voice of a teacher—"you must master its vocabulary. Write down every unfamiliar word the lecturer utters. Don't go further until you've gained command over it." Eb was listening to her intently. Her dark eyes sparkled in the dim light of the parlor. "That's how you start." Rebecca poked Martha who was dreamily sizing up the other girls' frocks across the room. "You should heed my word too, Miss Lewis." Martha nodded but appeared to have no idea what she was assenting to.

"Go on," Eb urged.

"You can find definitions in *Jacob's* in Judge Reeve's library," Rebecca continued, "and in *Blackstone* as well, I assure you, but they might be hiding out. Maybe in a dependent clause. Consider it a hunting expedition." Rebecca thought for a moment. "Studying law is like learning another language. You must build up your vocabulary, one step at a time, or you'll be lost."

"That's good advice, Miss Harding." Learning another language was something Eb understood. He liked Latin, and Greek to a lesser degree, but had never applied his linguistic skills to law school. Instead, Eb had been floundering in Judge Reeve's library. The more diligent students went there during the afternoon, to study, read cases, and peruse *Blackstone.* Eb labored at length copying over his lecture notes, but he had been writing down the words without comprehension. Judge Reeve and Judge Gould were aiming law in his direction, but no one had instructed him on how to study it. Rebecca Harding had given him a concrete task—one familiar to him. Martha was about to say something amusing about dictionaries when the trio was interrupted.

"Well, if it isn't my fellow refugee from the South," a female voice called out in a silky, Charleston accent—Katherine Montgomery. She landed on the couch next to Martha, her pink damask dress engulfing the rest of the sofa. Katherine's fair hair was parted in the middle, with curls spilling down the sides of her smooth cheeks. Eb stood up from his chair, but Katherine waved him back down. "I say, Mr. Wells, where's your good friend, Thomas Bradford?" Eb noted that at the bottom of her symmetrical, heart-shaped face was a pair of soft, plump lips. They were slightly reddened to the color of strawberries. Eb wondered if the effect was natural or artificial.

"I don't know," Eb stammered. "We're both boarding with Mrs. Edwards. Quite a lot of us are, maybe fifteen law students, but I hardly see Thomas these days." Eb suspected that Thomas Bradford was in the tavern at the United States Hotel, or the tavern on East Street, but did not want to say so. Litchfield was a town much obsessed with temperance due to the influence of the renowned minister of the Congregationalist Church, the Reverend Lyman Beecher. Rumor had it that Miss Pierce also took a dim view of law students who drank. Even Judge Reeve was an advocate of temperance.

"Don't you see him at the law school?" Katherine was becoming versed in the schedule, the teachers, the oral exams, and moot courts of Judge Reeve's law school. The two bastions of education in Litchfield had a symbiotic relationship. All the students at Miss Sarah Pierce's female academy on North Street were knowledgeable about the ways of the Litchfield Law School. The same was true of the law students on South Street about Miss Pierce's. As new students, Katherine and Martha were trying to learn about the law school. That was where all the eligible young men in town could be found, the girls who boarded at Miss Pierce's promised them, as they gossiped around the table after supper. "Doesn't Thomas attend the lectures?" Katherine asked.

"Oh, yes," Eb replied. "Certainly, but Thomas sits up front. I'm in the back." The truth was Thomas Bradford sat as far away from Eb Wells as he could get. Whenever Thomas attended a lecture, he and a cluster of other Southern dandies would saunter in, colonizing the front row of the crowded schoolroom. If the weather was the slightest bit inclement, Thomas Bradford and his crew would not appear at all. Eb knew these things because he never missed a lecture, surveying everything from his perch at the end of the last row.

Katherine Montgomery flashed Eb a smile, showing off her straight white teeth. "Please do send Mr. Bradford my warmest regards, Mr. Wells, won't you?" Her drawl made him homesick for Savannah.

"Yes, yes, I will." Eb gazed up at Katherine Montgomery, reciprocating her smile. She was much taller than he, even sitting down. This was a woman perfect for the likes of Thomas Bradford, Eb thought. She must think me a midget. A bumbler.

Rebecca Harding got up quickly from the couch. "You must

excuse me." She straightened her green dress and prepared to make her way to the other side of the room. "But I have business with Miss Pierce. Miss Lewis, would you like to join me?" Martha took her cue and hastily followed Rebecca Harding, making excuses and fumbling goodbyes to Katherine and Eb. Eb stood up in the flurry of feminine movement. Katherine looked somewhat deflated.

"Goodbye, Miss Harding," Eb called after them, "and Miss Lewis. So nice to have met you." Before he could sit down again, Katherine Montgomery abruptly stood from the couch. Of course, she would leave now, Eb thought. I'm the only one left to talk to.

"Don't forget my message to Mr. Bradford." Katherine Montgomery took off, leaving Eb standing alone. He watched her pink damask skirt float across the room. "Nice to see you again, Mr. Wells," Katherine called over her shoulder in a dismissive fashion.

She left behind a floral scent. Gardenias. Eb had not smelled gardenias since he roamed the streets of Savannah last summer. In the autumnal New England landscape, with the sun low on the horizon, the brooding gray skies, the trees turning an array of colors, a whiff of gardenia seemed wildly tropical and remote.

The clock on the mantel read six thirty. Eb realized he was standing at the end of Miss Pierce's parlor all alone. It was time to walk back to Mrs. Edwards's boarding house. Eb wanted to return to his attic room and make a list of legal terms to master. Tomorrow, he was going on a hunting expedition in Judge Reeve's library. For definitions.

Rebecca Harding grew up in Wethersfield, Connecticut. Her father, a cabinet maker, made furniture in a studio down at the Cove, not far from their saltbox house on Hartford Avenue. Rebecca had not always been an only child. One baby brother died of bloody flux, the other of scarlet fever. When Rebecca was eight years old, her mother died in childbirth—a third baby boy accompanied her to the family's grave on Hungry Hill. There was talk of moving Rebecca to Hartford to live with her Great-Aunt Gertrude, a stern woman married to an insurance man. But James Harding would not hear of it. Rebecca was all he had left.

Until the age of twelve, Rebecca attended an informal dame school in the home of Mrs. Johnson. The Johnsons lived in a grand brick house on Broad Street, with four chimneys and many windows, facing the Wethersfield Green. Mrs. Johnson took on the education of eight-year-old Rebecca Harding and another girl, Elizabeth Stafford, who lived two doors down with her doting grandparents, Captain and Mrs. Cox. Mrs. Johnson wanted to enliven the classroom for her only child, Penny, aged nine, who was lazy and indifferent to her studies. Both Rebecca and Elizabeth read and wrote circles around Penny who saw no reason to do either.

The three girls became fast friends. Rebecca and Elizabeth were the scholars, but Penny Johnson knew how to have fun. Penny was also talented in the garden where she knew all the herbs and their healing powers. She was good at stitchery too. Penny's samplers were perfect, Rebecca's lumpy and ill-conceived, Elizabeth's somewhere in between. Rebecca Harding scoffed at embroidery. Why spend hours squinting inside a wooden hoop when she could be reading?

At age thirteen, Penny Johnson went off to study at Miss Patten's school for painting and embroidery in Hartford. The school was famous for training girls to do heraldic embroideries and painterly scenes in silk threads. Elizabeth Stafford's mother insisted that her daughter attend a female academy in New Hampshire, closer to her family in Boston. Rebecca's father was at a loss about what to do for Rebecca's education.

Then tragedy struck. James Harding sliced his hand in the woodworking shop. This happened from time to time, even to the most experienced craftsman. But his wound would not heal. It became hot and angry, with red streaks moving up his arm. When Rebecca woke up the next morning, her father was burning up with fever, calling out for his dead wife to relieve his pain. The doctor was called, and he administered a tincture of rosehips and echinacea, garlic, and red gloom, but to no avail. James Harding was dead the next day of blood poisoning.

The house and studio in Wethersfield were sold, and the proceeds put into a trust for Rebecca. She now had no choice but to move in with her great-aunt and uncle in Hartford. For over three years, Rebecca rattled around their gloomy old house on Main Street, studying on her own, huddling next to a meager fire, her pathologically frugal great-aunt having rationed her wood. By tiptoeing from room to room, Rebecca managed to avoid her elderly relatives. Obsessed with foreign missions, they hardly took notice of their silent, dark-eyed great-niece who lived in the corners of their house—and their hearts. Rebecca missed Elizabeth and Penny, and the maternal warmth of Mrs. Johnson. She also yearned for her adoring father. For those desolate years in Hartford, Rebecca was homesick, grieving, and lonely.

But Rebecca Harding was resourceful. She applied to the famous Litchfield Female Academy in the northwest corner of the state. This would solve, she argued to her neglectful guardian, the 'what to do with Rebecca' problem. Rebecca could get a diploma at Miss Pierce's and become a teacher. Her small pot of money was more than sufficient to pay for four years of study. Her Great-Aunt Gertrude was convinced—and relieved. At age sixteen, Rebecca Harding had found a new home—at the Litchfield Female Academy.

Letter to Malinda Wells from Eb Wells, Litchfield,
September 23, 1819

Dear Malinda, my favorite old maid,

So glad to hear you and Mother are well. John's moving the law practice from East York Street makes sense. The house on Johnson Square is more elegant, the address more fashionable. I worry he takes on more land law cases. Eliza's father keeps referring clients to him, other slave-owning plantation owners. His meals are cooked and his chamber pot emptied by enslaved people. I know all this upsets Mother and probably you. I don't like it either. (Censor judiciously if you read this to the family.)

You ask if I'm enjoying law school. The word 'enjoy' does not come to mind. Law school is nothing like college. Most mornings I balance myself on a wooden bench for an hour and a half lecture. (Today it was on the Law of Baron and Femme.) I yearn for my days at Franklin when our teacher held classes under a tall oak tree. College was for me a delight. I read widely and studied under the quivering leaves, dappled with sun, discussing ideas with my friends. Law school is not a delight. I read narrowly, have few friends, and when I study, there are so many books, bottles of ink, pen and paper to juggle, quivering leaves are out of the question. And forget the dappled sun. I spend all day inside, either in the dark lecture room or in Judge Reeve's equally dark library

But neither is the law without interest. I both love and hate it. I balk at the law's divorce from history and philosophy. Judge Gould insists the law is a science, but I have my doubts. Once I enter its labyrinthine maze, I stagger around, often down a narrow path of unknown destination. I see no evidence of an overarching plan. Still, hours pass by in its pursuit. John did not prepare me for this fascination.

You and Susan would love our dear Judge Reeve. Next year, he retires. This makes me sad, but I'm grateful to have him now. Judge Reeve is elderly and portly. Some days he walks with a limp—gout, no doubt. His silver hair falls onto his shoulders. His eyes are like orbs, large and wide set. He dresses as if the War of Independence just ended, but he is dignified in his bearing. Judge Reeve takes an interest in all 'his boys,' always asking how we're doing. He remembers John well, referring to him as my 'distinguished brother.' His voice is extraordinary. He seems to have a throat disorder, so he speaks in almost a whisper, even when he lectures. All forty or so of us sit elbow to elbow on our wooden benches, remaining totally silent to hear him. We write down his every word.

Judge Reeve often startles us. An unformed idea will pop into his head, and he'll wander off mid-sentence, inventing a hypothetical to illustrate some dry legal principle. He'll get tangled up in the telling of the story—and can be very funny. I've noticed that when he 'goes off,' most of my fellow law students stop writing. They think him doddering, under the illusion that his dense, complete sentences of law are all that matters. I know better. I have figured this out. Most of what Judge Reeve whispers to us from the lectern comes right out of *Blackstone*—volumes 2 and 3 to be exact. Frankly, Malinda, I don't ascribe much originality to the lectures, only to the man who reads them. His law school is a vast improvement over our father's inadequate apprenticeship.

Susan will love this story. Judge Reeve's absent-mindedness is legendary. He once walked up North Street on his way to visit a friend, hanging onto an empty bridle after his horse had slipped away. Judge Reeve went through all the movements of fastening the bridle to the hitching post before entering the house. He hadn't even noticed that his horse had wandered off.

Some claim Judge Reeve's eccentricity led him to marry his servant not long after the death of his first wife. By all accounts, the first Mrs. Reeve was quite different. Sally Reeve was the only sister of

Aaron Burr, well-educated and refined, but sickly. The second Mrs. Reeve is a large, outgoing woman, probably in her middle forties—much younger than her husband. I take my midday meal with her. She takes an interest in all the law students and has been kind to me. She too has a quick wit. Without her, the law school wouldn't be such a lively place.

Judge Gould is our other master, a Yale man, half the age of Judge Reeve. I suspect our brother John has more respect for Judge Gould. He's a brilliant man with a prodigious memory, and a command of the law's structure I fear Judge Reeve may lack. But Judge Gould's style doesn't suit me. No one's ever known him to have a flight of fancy. He doesn't bother to learn our names—we are too many, he protests. This will interest you and Susan—all the girls think he's swoon-worthy, with flowing hair and a long, pointed chin. James Gould would never fail to notice that the horse he'd been dragging through Litchfield had already taken off.

The hour is late. In my next letter, I'll tell you about my new friend, Rebecca Harding. She reminds me of you, Malinda, in her intelligence. Her dream is to become a teacher. I'll fill you in on the social life here in Litchfield later too. I know you and Susan are far more interested in that than my legal studies or my teachers.

I miss you so very much, all of you, Mother, Susan and Lottie, John and Eliza and the girls, and of course you, my dearest sister. I even miss my hot, steamy Savannah.

All my love,

Your brother Eb

"More porridge, Mr. Wells?" Mrs. Edwards stood over Eb, wielding a wooden spoon. Her face was etched with wrinkles, her gray hair piled loosely on the top of her head. Mrs. Edwards was serving her boarders in shifts. It was Saturday morning with no classes for anyone to scurry to, and a new platter of bacon and scrambled eggs was being prepared by one of her daughters. The boarding house servant, Maggie, was leaning over the fire, making a fresh batch of porridge.

Eb and another young man, also new to the law school, were lingering at the table. Mrs. Edwards had seen hundreds of young men come through the ranks of the law school. These two new students, Eb Wells from Savannah, and Charles Godwin from New Haven, were going to be among her favorites, she was certain, even though both were struggling to fit in. Perhaps because of it.

"No thanks, Mrs. Edwards." Eb secretly wished for more tea but had already consumed his allotted cup. Another shift of hungry students was waiting in the wings. He felt comfortable, sitting near the fire, chatting with Maggie who was full of local gossip, and listening to Mrs. Edwards's unsolicited advice. Eb slipped the boarding house's old orange-and-white cat, Sir Winston, a tidbit of bacon. Eb tolerated dogs, but this was his first exposure to a cat. Sir Winston was a fine mouser, and Mrs. Edwards had given him free range of the kitchen and her larder— the entire house. The old woman spoke to the elderly cat as if he were a person. "I don't need more porridge." Eb leaned over to give Sir Winston a pat.

"And you, Mr. Godwin, more porridge?"

Charles Godwin mumbled a "No, thank you." Charles sat across from Eb, a tall, thin young man with a pale complexion, sandy-colored hair, and the longest, most delicate fingers Eb had ever seen. But Charles Godwin was unbearably shy. So far, he had never uttered a word to anyone beyond the barest pleasantries.

"Would you two boys do me a favor? Walk into town and pick up some things for me at the grocery?" Mrs. Edwards smiled. "I've already put in the order."

"I'd like to, Mrs. Edwards . . ." Eb replied. It was understood that Charles would never answer first. "But I need to study." Eb was eager to hit the books for a few hours before going over to the law school. Saturday was the day for the oral exams, a ritual he had not yet endured, being new to the school. But Rebecca Harding had recommended that he attend 'to get the lay of the land.'

"It would be a great help to me, lad," Mrs. Edwards insisted. Eb gave Sir Winston an under-the-chin rub. The fat old cat was purring, extending his neck in ecstasy. "And you should stretch your legs. You must mind the health of the body, Eb, or you can't perform the work of the mind."

"All right, Mrs. Edwards." Eb grinned at her. His sister Malinda often used similar tactics to get him to run an errand. It was comforting to be manipulated by a kind, older woman. "Charles, shall we walk into town and pick up her order?" Eb wondered if Mrs. Edwards had invented a joint enterprise to throw them together. She was capable of such subterfuge, having recently coaxed Eb into another tea at Miss Pierce's academy.

"Sure." Charles swallowed the last of his tea. Eb bid Sir Winston and the women in the kitchen goodbye, and the two young men took off for the grocery in town. From a distance, they looked like two brothers, the older one tall and spindly, the younger one about twelve. Eb was accustomed to looking up to his own brother. Charles was every bit as tall as John Wells, but he was a much less substantial man, more like a slightly bent sapling. It was a brisk autumn day in Litchfield, and the leaves were beginning to turn. There had been no rain for several weeks, so unpaved North Street, often full of mud in the fall, was blissfully dry, perhaps a little dusty, but easy to navigate.

"So, you're from New Haven?" Eb already knew the answer.

"Yes." Charles did not offer more. They trudged along in uncomfortable silence.

"I'm from Savannah, but my uncle lives in New Haven," Eb continued, as if Charles had asked him something. "My Uncle Ebenezer. I was named after him. Dr. Cabot. He's my mother's older brother, a physician." Drat, Eb thought. Shut up. Malinda always said when someone's shy, give them a chance to talk. Otherwise, you'll end up giving a monologue—a wall of words with no door through which someone can enter. "I've never been to New Haven, or anywhere outside of Georgia." Eb plowed on. "But I'll be going to my uncle's house for the long breaks. It's too far to go home to Savannah."

"So, your name isn't Edward?" That was the first full sentence Charles Godwin had ever uttered in Eb's presence. His eyes were wide with wonder. "I thought your name was Edward. I heard everyone calling you Ed. I must have misheard."

"No, my name's Ebenezer, but my family, friends, well, everyone, have always called me 'Eb.' I never much felt like an Ebenezer."

"What does an 'Ebenezer' feel like?" Charles asked tentatively. "How does it differ from an 'Eb?'"

"Well, an 'Ebenezer' sounds so formal, like someone who ought to sport an admirable set of sideburns, a banker perhaps. Certainly not a name for a baby, or even a young boy. 'Eb' suited me when I was little, but unlike some men, I never outgrew my nursery name." Eb was struck by an idea. "You know how it is. Take my father. He started out as a 'Will.' He goes to college and becomes a 'William.' Or my older sister, Malinda. She was a 'Mimi' as a toddler but grew into her full Malinda-hood." Eb lightly lobbed the ball back to Charles. "So, were you ever called anything but Charles?"

"No. I was born a full Charles. I probably arrived on this earth with a set of sideburns, although I'm not sure they qualify as admirable." Charles did have a full head of sandy, wavy hair, but his sideburns were wispy and under-achieving. "I was never given a nickname to outgrow." Charles seemed sad at this observation. "I suppose I could have been a 'Chas.' That wouldn't be so bad, but what about a 'Charlie'?" Charles pondered this for a moment. "I wonder what being a 'Charlie Godwin' would have been like. How different would my life have been?"

"I feel certain a 'Charlie Godwin' would be the sort of man who strides into taverns with confidence, knows everyone at the bar, slaps all the good fellows on the back. You know, asks how they're faring." Eb thought about a jovial Charlie of yore, a popular boy at Franklin. He looked up and cast Charles a sly look, venturing to tease him. "Just like you, Charles."

"Oh yes." Charles tacitly acknowledged his shyness, his lack of any tendencies—or opportunities—to stride into taverns and slap all the good fellows on the back. "That kind of a 'Charlie Godwin' sounds just like me."

"Here's what I wonder." Eb was pondering his own fate, pleased that Charles had not rejected his gentle ribbing. "What does it say about a man who remains an 'Eb' long after he was supposed to develop into something more manly like an 'Ebenezer'?" Eb furrowed his brow. "Should I be worried about that?"

"I think it says your family and friends like you the way you are," Charles said kindly. "But if you want, I could start to call you 'Ebenezer,' just to try the name on. Or if you don't like the persona, I can go back to 'Ed.'" Charles cast his own sly look back at Eb.

"I don't really want to be an 'Ebenezer,'" Eb admitted. "We already have one in the family. I wouldn't want there to be any confusion at the holidays, although probably everyone calls him Dr. Cabot." They had crossed the Green and entered the town center. Eb opened the door to the grocery, first letting a servant from the Beecher household go through with her parcels. "I don't want to feel compelled to grow sideburns. I'm not even certain I can."

"Sideburns on you might be grand." Charles followed Eb into the grocery. "I'd like to sketch you when you grow your sideburns. A portrait of the great early-nineteenth-century lawyer, Ebenezer Wells."

"Sketch me?" Eb looked over his shoulder. Charles's face seemed relaxed for the first time in this long, lonely first month in Litchfield. Eb was envious. Malinda had begged him not to bring his art supplies to law school. Sketching would only distract him from his studies, and he was not that good. "You have a sketchbook?"

"I do." Charles took a deep breath. "I want to be an artist." The two young men picked up Mrs. Edwards's order of beets, onions, a dozen ears of corn, and two heads of cabbage, and began to make their way back to the boarding house. The town was bustling with people running their own morning errands. Eb sidestepped a snorting pig who was rooting around in the street for anything tasty to eat.

"If you're going to be an artist . . ." Eb juggled the package, so the ears of corn did not slip out. "Then why on earth are you in law school?"

"I ask myself that every morning." Charles shook his head. "My parents want me to have a profession. My father's in shipping. My two older brothers joined the family business, but I'm not interested. I went to Yale for a few years but dropped out. No one in my family takes my being an artist seriously. My parents have decided I'm to study the law." Charles too stopped to reposition the parcels he was carrying, not wanting the beets to roll onto the ground. He seemed invigorated from having strung more than two sentences together. "I guess it's all right. Law will give me a way to support myself and my art. Mother was less enthusiastic than my father. She was raised in the Society of Friends. They aren't so enamored of lawyers or 'going to law.'"

"You're a Friend?" Eb was surprised. Charles wanted to be an artist. The Quakers were renowned for rejecting the arts as vanity and a distraction from the Inner Light. Charles also did not wear the talismanic broad-brim hat, and while he dressed conservatively, he did not adopt plain dress.

"No, my mother was," Charles replied. "She grew up a Friend in Philadelphia, but she married out of the Meeting and was expelled. So, I'm not a true Quaker. But I've been raised in a Quaker home, at least one with Quaker values. For that matter, why are you studying law?" Charles tossed the question back at Eb. "Do you like it?"

"Well, I do, and I don't," Eb replied. The two young men made their way up North Street, deep in conversation. As usual, Mrs. Edwards was right. Eb Wells and Charles Godwin had a lot to talk about.

Charles's mother—Mary Sedgewick Godwin—had grown up in a Quaker family in Philadelphia. Her father, a textile merchant, did business with *Godwin's* of New Haven, a shipping company that transported goods back and forth from New Haven, Boston, Philadelphia, and the West Indies. *Godwin's* shipped all kinds of products—pork and beef, salted and barreled, grain, fur, tobacco, lumber, wax, sugar, rum, and textiles. Its owner, George Godwin, refused to transport human cargo. Many Quaker merchants dealt with him.

Charles's father was on business in Philadelphia when he was invited to dine at the Sedgewick's home. Recently widowed, George Godwin had two boys at home, aged five and seven. Mary Sedgewick, the middle daughter, was only twenty—fifteen years George's junior. She was tall and willowy, with pale skin and a quiet, dignified manner. Mary captured George's heart, but her parents were appalled. George was not a Friend, but a Congregationalist. Marriage outside the Quaker community was not allowed.

In the past, the Connecticut Puritans had persecuted the Quakers. The views of the Quakers were radical. According to the Friends, revelation was accessible to anyone. No one needed the intercession of church elders. Each person had his or her own Inner Light, a sacred illumination present in all human beings. Quakers were staunchly egalitarian. A woman, a native, a Black person, could speak God's word. Quakers adopted plain dress. They were pacifists and abhorred the institution of slavery. The Puritans were threatened by the Quakers for their missionary spirit and the spread of pernicious ideas. The New Haven colony was particularly harsh on the Quakers. Quakers who entered the colony could be whipped, imprisoned, forced into hard labor, or have their hands branded with an H for 'heretic.' A Quaker who offended more than three times might have a hot iron bored through his tongue.

But by the time Charles Godwin's father fell in love with Mary Sedgewick, religious diversity was tolerated within Connecticut. There were the Rogerines in New London, Episcopalians, Baptists in the eastern part of the state, and scattered throughout, in places such as New Milford, Sherman, Darien, and the Western District of Hartford, even some Quakers. No one was going to stop George Godwin from marrying a Quaker woman if he chose to. But upon their marriage, Mary Sedgewick was expelled from the Philadelphia Religious Society of the Friends. She went to live with her new husband in his stately home on Church Street in New Haven, never to see her family again.

Mary Godwin gave birth to a son of her own, Charles. She had no more children, for reasons undiscoverable by the midwife. Mary raised all three boys in the tenets of her former religion. Her two older stepsons dutifully attended Yale and joined the family business. But the youngest son Charles was a rudderless ship. He had failed at Yale, having no flair for theology, the profession his mother had steered him toward. He also had no interest in shipping. Worse yet, Charles wanted to become an artist—an unthinkable prospect, his parents believed.

In desperation, his father enrolled him in Tapping Reeve's law school in Litchfield and paid for the entire program. Charles acquiesced because it was in his nature to do so. Besides, he looked forward to leaving home. Once he was set up in a boarding house in Litchfield, away from the prying eyes of his family, Charles could sketch with impunity.

Letter to Elizabeth Stafford from Rebecca Harding, Litchfield, September 27, 1819

My dearest Elizabeth,

Please forgive my delay in answering. I've been buried in work. Right now, I'm completing the tedious three-month journaling requirement. After writing inanities to myself, it's a delight to write to you.

I'm sorry to hear Miss Fiske's Seminary lacks academic rigor. Her emphasis on the ornamental arts is a fiscal necessity. That's all most parents seek for their girls, I fear, skills in embroidery, painting, music, and French. No reason to bother their pretty heads with Latin or Greek, geography, astronomy, literature, and philosophy. Miss Pierce too needs to placate parents. This year's class is large, with over one hundred and sixty girls. You would have to endure embroidery and plain sewing here too, even at Miss Pierce's, although you might get to paint a map. Miss Pierce and her nephew, Mr. Brace, are both devoted to geography.

I love to hear news of your suitors. Our novels exhort us to fall in love, but we both know your young man must measure up to the Stafford family's standards. You must marry well, Lizzie. I know you worry about me, but I'll be fine. I've inherited enough money to pay for Miss Pierce's. I can't count on more. My Hartford relatives will undoubtedly bequeath their fortune to the foreign missions. I'll support myself by teaching. Other academically inclined young women here share my ambition. Catharine Beecher, for one. She's the oldest daughter of Reverend Lyman Beecher. Catharine talks of starting her own female academy someday. Her younger sister Harriet, nine years old, just started at the school. She too is exceptional. That's what the Beecher family does well—generates exceptional children. Some are even female. Reverend Beecher is unusual for educating his daughters.

At times, I grow weary of female academies being justified by the ideal of Republican motherhood. How we must prepare ourselves to educate our future children. No one ever suggests any inherent value in developing a young woman's mind. Rather, the value of female education inures to the benefit of our future children, our hypothetical sons, even now. But in truth, most of my schoolmates will marry.

I'm just grateful there's now a place in our country for someone like me. An unmarried woman who wants to become a teacher—to earn a livelihood of her own. Who could have imagined such a thing, even a decade ago? I can't count on a brilliant marriage, Lizzie. I lack your beauty and wealth. But I don't need to marry. Having a husband—even a suitable one—would be an encumbrance.

But enough about me. As to your suitors, I reject Mr. Ruggles. He wants you to have a dozen children? How many Ruggles spawn does the country need? Your value to him is as a breeder. But I do like the second contender, Mr. Hathaway. He's chosen medicine and reads widely. Please, Lizzie, choose a man who loves to read as you do—and respects your intelligence. I vote for Mr. Hathaway. But this third contender? Mr. Townsend won't do. He lacks a profession, and I guarantee you, he won't be constant. I'm warning you. You may be swooning over him now, but if you settle on him, you'll regret it.

Here at Miss Pierce's, we have teas, theatrics, upcoming balls, and promises of sleigh rides. For the first time, I've been taking promenades on the Green in the afternoons. I've a new friend, Martha Lewis. She's two years younger, a local girl who makes me laugh.

Like me, she's the daughter of an artisan, and not from a professional family. It's such a pleasure to have a friend again. You would like her, Lizzie. I'm certain.

Both schools in Litchfield have more students from the South this year. I'm morbidly fascinated by a new student, Katherine Montgomery, who complains all the time of 'missing her Lulu.' (I assume Lulu is her personal slave.) She seems like a typical Southern belle. With men, Katherine melts into a simpering pool, eyelashes batting with the innocence of a babe. But as soon as the man disappears, this delicate tropical flower turns into a competent young woman. She's traveled all the way up north to attend a school for its academics. I laud her for that. But whenever there's a man around, Katherine hides her intelligence. Finding a husband seems to be paramount for her. She has set her cap for a cad, a Mr. Thomas Bradford.

I like very much another new law student from Savannah. (His parents came from Connecticut, so to my mind, he doesn't count as a true Southerner.) Mr. Wells is not like most law students from the South. He doesn't dress to accentuate his broad shoulders, which he doesn't possess, or his great height, which he lacks as well. He doesn't swagger or engage in duels. Mr. Wells wears glasses that always fall down his nose, and he dresses poorly. I fear the sharks at the law school will eat him alive, but it's too early to tell. He struggles with his studies. I'm advising him, but he seems lost. Still, I enjoy his company.

Enough of this prattle, my dear friend. Write again soon. Thank you for sending me *The Vicar of Wakefield*. It was a great pleasure to curl up with Goldsmith in the evening, even though the plot seemed contrived. Novels tie up everything in the end. Life does not. I've been sharing the book with some of the other girls who board here with Miss Pierce. I hope you don't mind.

Please send Penny my love in your next letter. Writing to Penny requires a certain energy I lack at present. Writing you a letter, Lizzie, is like talking to my own heart.

Yours affectionately,

Rebecca

"All right, Charles, be serious now." Eb Wells and Charles Godwin were studying up in Eb's tiny third-floor room at Mrs. Edwards's. Because it was in the attic, sausages, dried apples, bags of other small fruits, bunches of herbs, and Mrs. Edwards's daughter's medicinal roots hung from the rafters. Eb paid a lesser rent but liked the privacy and the sweet smell of dried fruit and herbs.

"Put your sketchbook down, won't you?" It was evening, and Eb was trying to decide whether to light a fresh candle. He might need to write to his brother John for more money as candles were expensive. Perhaps it was not worth starting a new one. Light still came through the window, but only a little, and Eb was tired.

"I won't put my sketchbook down," Charles quipped. "I'm working on sketches of Sir Winston. I don't want to stop while I've got the light." Mrs. Edwards also gave the old cat free rein in the attic to catch mice. That was another condition of Eb's tenancy, to tolerate predatory visits from Sir Winston. It was understood the old cat could sleep upstairs. Mrs. Edwards would never put him out in the cold.

Eb looked over at Charles with exasperation. Charles had draped his long body over Eb's one chair, a piece of graphite in hand, a sketchbook in his lap, his head bent in concentration. The two young men studied together in the evenings. The thought was: two legal heads are better than one. But at this moment, Eb felt like the only legal head in the room.

Charles was meditating on the miraculous way a cat's arm ended up in a paw. "I'll talk law with you, if you like, but I won't look at another word tonight." In fact, Charles Godwin had already studied four hours with his friend that afternoon. He knew when enough was enough, whereas Eb did not. He studied all the time, even getting up early in the morning to go over his notes.

"All right." Talking law was a form of studying law, Eb supposed. Besides, Charles had a unique perspective that got Eb thinking. A conversation with Charles Godwin was never a waste of time, although Eb wished Charles would move off the subject of feline paw design. 'A weapon inside an elegant mitt.' Charles too had never spent time with a cat who lived indoors. He was ensorcelled.

"So, what's the definition of a 'master'?" This was Eb's new tactic: to start with a definition. "Think of the Latin term 'magister,' a chief, a head, director or teacher."

"Hmm . . ." Charles lifted his pencil to think. "I know this one. It's a person who, by law, has a right to personal authority over another." He resumed his sketching after this flourishing display of knowledge.

"Very good." This afternoon's study had not been wasted. "And of course, the servant is the person who has the authority rightfully exercised over him—or her." Eb was poring over his notes. "All right, Mr. Godwin, where do wives, minors, and employees fit into the scheme?"

"Well, Judge Reeve says they're all servants. He's obviously never been to our house." Charles smirked. "There's no doubt who's the master at the Godwins', or the mistress, I should say. My mother seems meek, but she always gets her way. My father's her willing servant. Me, my brothers too." He smudged a bit of his pencil mark at the tips of Sir Winston's ears with his long fingers. "I don't see why men and women can't be treated as equals."

"In what sense?" Eb looked up from his commonplace book.

"Take education." Charles squinted at the orange-and-white cat.

"From all you've told me of your sister Malinda, she's every bit as intelligent as you are, or your brother John. He went to Yale, but your father left Malinda to study at home with your mother and a servant girl. How fair was that?"

"She's never complained." Eb frowned, annoyed that Charles had no sister to point out equivalent inequities in the Godwin household. "And we don't really consider Susan a servant. Besides, I didn't get to go to Yale."

"That was due to your own laziness." Charles smiled affectionately at his friend. "And Malinda wasn't sent to a local academy or Franklin College either." He put his sketchbook on his lap and watched Sir Winston who had gone into a frenzy of stomach licking. "Your sister may not recognize her right to be aggrieved. Women are trained to accept their roles in life, as daughter, wife, mother, widow—well, as a servant."

"Sending Malinda to Yale or Franklin was out of the question." Eb was miffed. "It's not as if my father was unique. No young women go to college. That's just the way things are."

He had been too young to remember the heated discussions over whether Malinda could go to Miss Pierce's academy.

"I don't mean to single your parents out. But just because 'that's the way things are,' doesn't mean that's the way they should be." Charles looked at Eb earnestly. "Let me ask you this, Eb Wells. Do you think a woman capable of going to college? What about Malinda? Or this Miss Rebecca Harding? You seem to think she's very smart."

"She is." Eb blushed, as he always did when Rebecca's name was mentioned. "I'm certain she's much smarter than I am." The two were silent for a moment while Eb regained his composure. "Besides, Miss Harding *is* getting an education, at Miss Pierce's. She's learning literature, rhetoric, astronomy, Latin, geography, and math. Almost everything I studied at Franklin, and you at Yale." Eb nodded, satisfied to have pointed this out. "And look at her friend, too, Martha Lewis. She's just a local girl. Her father's merely an artisan, and she's also getting a fine education."

"I'll admit that." Charles returned to his drawing. "But a female academy like Miss Pierce's is only available to a handful of wealthy white women. Still, I'll grant you this. Her female academy is a new idea, and subversive." He put down his pencil with a sigh, irritated with Sir Winston for not sitting still. "But think about this. Both Miss Harding and her friend must embroider pillows and sing songs in Italian, even when they can't sing—in exchange for learning Latin." Charles picked up his pencil again, Sir Winston having resumed his posture of slumber. "The students at Miss Pierce's are even taught how to draw. I envy that. Art was never offered to me as part of *my* education. I might have stuck it out at Yale if I could have studied art. Men and women are not treated the same." Charles tried to erase his last few strokes of graphite. "But the impact's far worse on women. Judge Reeve is right to call them servants."

"You and I both know he didn't invent that idea," Eb blustered. He would not countenance any criticism of Judge Reeve. "He got that law from *Blackstone*, and Judge Reeve has criticized the disparity of treatment between the sexes in his writings. He urges us to look at the agency of married women in real life." Charles was no longer looking at Eb, fixating once again on the old cat. "And look at his own life for a moment," Eb continued. "Mrs. Reeve is strong and smart, maybe not Rebecca Harding kind of smart, but shrewd and capable." Charles also took his midday meal with the Reeves, and like Eb, Charles was a Mrs. Reeve fan. "From what I can tell of Mrs. Reeve, she's formidable. In real life, who could be her master? Not Judge Reeve, I'd wager."

"What is the relationship between real life and the law? I'd like to know," Charles asked off-handedly. "I'd like to paint her."

"Who? Mrs. Reeve?" Eb looked up from his notes. "You want to paint Mrs. Reeve?" Eb considered this. "I don't know, Charles. She's a tall, big-boned woman, with a ruddy complexion, not noted for her beauty. She's always making fun of herself for that."

"I know others don't find her beautiful, but I do," Charles replied. "Take a look at her hands. They're so useful, with their knobby knuckles, and big, glorious, double-jointed thumbs, always doing something—knitting, kneading bread, serving soup, clearing dishes." Charles looked up from his sketch. "I've even seen her outside in the back garden, washing clothes in tin bins. Those hands are never in repose. I'd like to paint her washing clothes."

"You're an odd fellow, Charles Godwin. I like Mrs. Reeve tremendously, but I don't see the beauty in her that you do."

"That's because you aren't looking for it," Charles responded briskly, returning to his sketch. Sometimes Charles exasperated Eb, pretending to see things Eb could not see. Perhaps it was his inherited Quaker Inner Light, but it was annoying.

"All right then, let's go on." Eb returned to his notes. "Besides the big three—wives, children, and employees—name the other six kinds of servants?" Charles rolled his eyes, and Eb could tell Charles was done. "I'll read them then," Eb said. "Slaves, apprentices—that's us at the moment, we serve Judge Reeve—menial servants, day laborers, agents, including lawyers—that would be us, someday, God willing—and debtors assigned in service. Six kinds of servants." Eb spread his hands out before him. Rebecca Harding had taught him this trick. When there is a list of things, assign each category to a finger. The list of other servants took up his left hand and his right thumb.

"Are you going to make the slaves your pinkie finger or your thumb?" Charles asked his friend, who was looking back and forth from his notes to his outspread hands.

"Good question." Eb ruminated. "I'm thinking my pinkie finger. Lately, I've been using my left hand for the beginning of the list and moving toward the center, so I'll start with the left pinkie finger."

"I would choose the right thumb for the slaves." Charles had given up on using the uncooperative cat as a model. From memory, he had started a second sketch of Sir Winston from behind, lapping water. It was not going well. "The thumb is unique, not just one of five fingers."

"Why that order?" Eb peered up from his hands for a moment.

"Well, to my mind, casually adding slaves to the list of servants was a categorical mistake of grand proportions. It's at the crux of the divide between those in the nation who own people, and those who don't." Charles looked up at Eb. "Take Thomas Bradford. His father in Georgia or South Carolina, wherever their plantation is, probably owns a hundred or more human beings."

Eb settled back on his bed. He had learned that when Charles Godwin went off on something, it was impossible to divert him. Like waves on the edge of an ocean, there was no stopping these intermittent, pulsating rushes of words.

"In our grandfathers' time, a slave could move out of his category." Charles barely took a breath. "He could buy his freedom with a sum of money and the master's permission, just like the other servants on the list. But these days, with so many slaves toiling in the fields, picking cotton, manumission in the South is being phased out. There's even talk in South Carolina of making it illegal."

Charles stopped for air. "So, slaves are no longer like the other servants on Judge Reeve's list. They can't escape their status. Apprentices can become masters. Lawyers can quit their practice. A menial servant like Mrs. Reeve can marry the master, although as a wife, I suppose she's just a servant of a different order." Charles paused in the middle of his diatribe. "Maybe women are closer to slaves—there's no escaping her diminished status. She's still washing some man's drawers."

Charles looked down and erased something from his sketch of Sir Winston. Eb said nothing, thinking about what Charles had said. "Anyhow," Charles added in a much softer voice, "make the slaves your thumb is all I'm saying." Perhaps Charles knew he was more likely to win Eb over if he did not criticize his hero. "I'm just saying, Judge Reeve shouldn't have put them on the list of servants. He's the one who said that slavery is contrary to the laws of natural justice—he should know better. Africans engaged in forced labor are not servants, Eb. They're chattel."

Eb decided to rearrange the order of his list of the other six kinds of servants, after the big three, in his notes. He would do so in the morning. Slaves would end up on his right thumb.

"So, how do you feel about being a servant?" Charles asked. "I believe Judge Reeve called us lawyers, servants of 'a higher order.'"

"Yes." Eb looked up from his hands. "He did say that. It works like this. The client or principal has lawful control over the lawyer, but only over the subject matter of the agency. For example, the client could order the lawyer to execute a deed, but not to wear striped trousers."

"I would myself never wear striped trousers." Charles shook his head. "That's not a vestige of my Quaker roots. I just don't like striped trousers. Thomas Bradford has a pair."

"My brother John wears them too." Eb thought of his tall, stately brother, getting ready to go to the Episcopalian church in Savannah, wearing his long gray coat with a tall collar, a black top hat, and a pair of white-and-gray-striped pants with loops inside his boots. "They aren't my style either." Eb could not imagine dressing like his brother or having a stunning, wealthy wife like Eliza on his arm.

"I've got a question about your brother John." Apparently, Charles was not ready to give Eb a rest. "I've heard Thomas say your brother's law firm represents his father. Does John have a lot of plantation owners as clients?"

"He does," Eb admitted, "now that my father has passed away. Remember too, John's wife Eliza grew up on one of those big plantations. She brought three slaves into their marriage. A wedding gift."

Eb wrinkled his brow. "That was a terrible shock for my mother. Our family would never own slaves. My mother grew up in a household in New Haven with abolitionist leanings. She refused to have enslaved domestic help. Lottie, our housekeeper, is Scotch-Irish, a paid servant, a widow whose child was raised in our home."

Eb could not remember how much of this story he had told Charles already. "My father knew my mother didn't approve of slavery. He would only represent merchants who shipped products from the harbor—tobacco, indigo, rice, rum—but not people. He didn't want any direct dealings with slave traders. Sort of like your father, Charles." Eb had closed his notebook and was sprawled on his back on the bed, contemplating the eaves in the ceiling. "When you think about it, with cotton now being the dominant cash crop, and the rise of these huge plantations, my father's position wouldn't be tenable in Savannah." Eb lifted his legs, putting his feet onto the eave's edge to give himself a good stretch, avoiding the herbs hanging over his bed—Santolina, Southern Wood, and Chives. "Maybe it was better my father died last year."

"He probably would disagree with you." Charles ventured a smile. "But your brother? How does he feel about having slave-owning clients? I would find that unbearable. Honestly, I hate the notion of lawyers being agents." Charles shook his head in dismay. "How would that be, if your client was a slave owner, and you hated the institution of slavery?"

"My brother *is* a slave owner himself." Eb was almost upside down on his bed. "He may only own three town slaves, but I suspect he's getting used to the idea." Eb brought his legs down and swung himself to a seated position, carefully avoiding the drying herbs again. "Let's face it, John must at least tolerate, if not condone, the institution of slavery. He wouldn't be able to afford the house on Johnson Square, or support Eliza and the two girls, if he didn't. Not in Savannah. He'd have no law practice at all."

"How does that sit with you?" Charles had returned to his unsuccessful rendering of Sir Winston's backside.

"Not well." Eb shook his head. "My mother and Malinda struggle with it too. Our family's only been in the South for a generation. To our neighbors, my mother is viewed with suspicion because she's a Yankee. At least we were born in Savannah. But Father wouldn't let us utter an anti-slavery word outside of the house." Eb paused. "I don't know how John is regarded these days. I haven't been in Savannah much for the last four years. His law practice was just growing when I left."

"Could you practice law with your brother, knowing you might be facilitating the buying and selling of human beings?" Charles gave Eb a penetrating look. "Even indirectly?"

"I don't know, my friend. It's problematic." Eb felt a sudden wave of exhaustion. He did not feel like tackling the oppression of his sister, the injustice of slavery, and his own complicity in both—all in the same evening. Eb had to laugh to himself. Before he had gotten to know Charles Godwin, Eb imagined him impossible to engage. Instead, here he was, his long, thin legs crossed under his sketchbook, drawing a cat in the attic, and Eb could not get Charles to shut up. It had been a long day. Eb leaned back on his pillow. "Shall we call it a night and go to bed? Otherwise, I'll have to start another candle."

"Good idea." Charles closed his sketchbook and yawned. He lifted his gangly frame out of the chair and looked down at Eb, sprawled on his bed. "To tell you the truth, Eb, I like the front half of Sir Winston much better than his hind end." Charles moved toward the door, tucking his sketchbook under his arm. "And I'd also like to add"—Charles opened the door and said over his shoulder—"Sir Winston is essentially a white cat. The orange splotches are gratuitous ornamentation."

Litchfield in the autumn glowed. The sugar maples were turning a riot of brilliant colors—yellows, oranges, and reds. They pulsated against the dark green of the many pines. In the early morning, a mist rose off the fields. In low spots, small clouds formed, hovering mysteriously in the hidden valleys. The apple harvest was coming in, and hot cider was served from a window in the grocery on the Green. The bees were slow and suicidal, drowning themselves in cups of hot, sweet apple juice. Warm September afternoons beckoned to the students from both schools in Litchfield to put down their books and come outside.

In the late afternoon, after the rigors of classes, the young women from Miss Pierce's strolled around the Litchfield Green. Up and down North and South streets, small groups of female academy students wandered, linked arm in arm, wrapped in cotton shawls and wide brimmed bonnets—hoping to run into students from Judge Reeve's law school. The promenade was an informal way for the young men and women to mingle and flirt. No one would ever dream of taking one of these walks alone.

Rebecca Harding had always stayed in her room and read novels after classes. Now she had Martha Lewis's arm to link in hers. Rebecca had asked Miss Pierce for permission to pursue their friendship, aware of her position as an assistant teacher. Miss Pierce readily assented. Both girls were daughters of artisans, she reasoned, making it difficult to fit in. Besides, Martha made the serious Rebecca laugh, and Rebecca kept the volatile Martha on an even keel. In only a short time, Rebecca and Martha became co-conspirators. They shared secrets, gossiped at night, read books together, borrowed each other's clothes, and on crisp autumn afternoons, went down to the Green.

At first Charles and Martha were the designated 'tag-alongs.' Rebecca was seeking out the company of Eb Wells, and vice versa. But the 'tag-alongs' soon became the courting couple, a status not so clear between Eb and Rebecca. At first, Eb had to beg Charles to walk down to the Green with him. The thought of talking to young women paralyzed Charles Godwin. When Mrs. Edwards urged him to attend a tea at the female academy, he had snorted. He would rather have a tooth extracted without whiskey. About walking down to the Green, Charles feared—justifiably—that Miss Harding and Eb would immerse themselves in conversation, leaving him all alone with her friend. What was her name again?

But Eb was adamant. Charles must join him on the Green. Eb needed to ask Miss Harding about the oral exams. Eventually, Charles agreed to accompany him. He was curious to meet Rebecca Harding and secretly wanted to know what the afternoon promenade was all about. Charles found Miss Harding attractive, although not his cup of tea. Eb was right. Rebecca Harding did resemble a Dark-eyed Junco, with her gray dress and white collar and sharp, dark eyes. Dressed so plainly, Rebecca Harding also resembled a Friend. Charles discerned how smart she was, and why Eb would seek her out. But what about Miss Harding's friend?

Charles could not get over the glory of Martha Lewis, her thick, coppery hair, her high cheekbones, her green eyes, the constellation of light freckles across her cheeks. Her nose wrinkled whenever she laughed, which was frequently and at unexpected intervals. Martha Lewis laughed at things no one else found funny. That she did so alone in no way deterred her hilarity. Charles was struck dumber than usual.

Rebecca and Eb were several steps ahead, deep in conversation. Rebecca was explaining why one must first state the rule before launching into its exceptions. Many law students make that mistake, she warned in a low tone. The rationale for the rule shines light upon the exceptions. Behind them, Charles and Martha were strolling. Charles was so much taller than Martha, he feared he must stoop to speak to her. But Martha Lewis spoke in a confident voice, almost booming, not at all like Rebecca Harding's discreet murmurings.

Charles could stand upright. With no effort on his part, Martha chattered away. Did bees know when they were dying? Why is hot cider so much better than cold? Did Charles understand Miss Pierce's draconian system of debits and credits? Would he like to meet her dog, Lucky? Did Charles's family have a dog?

Martha's three older siblings were brothers so talking to young men in a casual fashion came naturally to her. All Charles had to do was ask a question. "And why is he called 'Lucky'?" He would then have the pleasure of watching Martha's face light up, her lovely orangish, luscious lips parting to display a row of perfect ivory teeth. She would launch off on a long story about Lucky's provenance. Charles was mesmerized. He wanted to paint her.

Later that evening, back in Eb's attic room, Charles announced, "I've met the woman I'm going to marry." Eb's eyes widened. How could this have happened? Eb had been so involved in his conversation with Rebecca Harding, he had failed to notice Charles and Martha behind them. Charles asked Eb if he thought it was improper to fall in love with Martha just because he wanted to paint her. Eb pointed out that Charles also wanted to paint Mrs. Reeve. The two young men discussed the kinds of love a man might have for different women—a mother, a sister, Mrs. Edwards, Mrs. Reeve, and now, Martha Lewis. Eb pointed out the difference seemed to lie in Charles's preoccupation with Mrs. Reeve's knobby, knuckled hands—and in contrast, with Martha Lewis's lovely, orangish, luscious lips.

Charles and Eb also discussed the perversity of nature, why one of the tallest men at the law school would fall for one of the shortest women at Miss Pierce's. With his modest stature, wouldn't Eb have been a better match for Martha? But Eb nixed the idea. He and Martha would look like a set of Carolina Wrens, hopping along together. Better the lovely, diminutive Martha promenade through the streets of Litchfield on the arm of an elegant Blue Heron.

The romance progressed. Within a few afternoon strolls around town, Martha and Charles proved capable of creating a world all their own. Martha was a great lover of plants, shrubs, herbs, and trees. The two people shared their joy of nature. Martha told Charles everything, and he began to confide in her. On these long walks, they were oblivious to anyone else. It suited the quartet well. Rebecca and Eb led the way, Rebecca pontificating, Eb's hands clasped behind his back, absorbing all she said. The four young people met every day until the stunning Connecticut autumn began to taper off.

The weather was getting chilly. By early November, the promenades began to give way to indoor teas, games, amateur theatrics performed at Miss Pierce's, lectures by Lyman Beecher, and going to church. As boarders of Mrs. Edwards, Charles and Eb were required to attend Sabbath services, as was true of Rebecca and Martha. The four sat together in the back rows, endeavoring not to make eye contact for fear of laughing—not always with success. One day, Martha's mother, Ruth Lewis, approached Charles Godwin and asked if he would like to join them at their cottage outside Litchfield for a cold tea. He went.

If their chemistry were not enough to bind them—and it was—Charles's affinity for Martha's family sealed the deal. Her father, Benjamin Lewis, was a portrait artist of the finest caliber. He worked in a variety of media, depending on the patron. For everyday people, Benjamin Lewis would draw the sitter's profile by hand, and cut the portrait from lightweight black cardboard, mounting it on a light background, usually white, sometimes pale pink, or ivory. Commissions for rich people—Litchfield had many of them—he might do by painting on glass, either in black or in grisaille, with filigree highlights in delicate gold. Some of his portraits were small enough to fit inside a locket. Two such portraits of her parents hung from Rebecca Harding's neck, although the artist was from Wethersfield.

Charles Godwin was fascinated by everything about Benjamin Lewis—his large ramshackle studio behind the cottage, his exquisite profiles, his integrity about his work. Martha's father was of medium height, stocky, often sporting a grizzled beard, with short, square hands remarkably fine-tuned in their manipulations. Benjamin Lewis was also a quiet, reticent man who had somehow found himself at the head of a large, raucous family.

His wife was an older version of her daughter. Everyone said they could be taken for sisters—although the mother lacked Martha's freckles and was in possession of a brighter, brasher shade of red hair. Ruth Lewis was cheerful and hardworking. She cooked and cleaned, indulged their four children, and shielded her husband from the clatter and clutter of family life. She sent him out to the studio, every morning, to be an artist and bask in solitude.

None of the Lewis sons inherited their father's artistic talent. The oldest two, Robert and Ben, were already out of the house. Together they ran a grocery store in Kent, not far from Litchfield. The youngest boy, Jack, was undecided about his occupation, and he ended up staying at home to help in the studio. Jack was a wiry young man, restless and red-haired, although his hue too was a brighter red than Martha's, closer to their mother's.

Jack knew how to let his father work. He carved out from the sprawling studio a small office with a door that he could close. Jack discovered the art business was more than making profiles: ordering paper and matting, corresponding, generating commissions, mailing finished work, managing his father's schedule. Jack Lewis also had a flair for advertising. Through church connections, Jack found new patrons for Benjamin Lewis profiles and miniature portraits. The father and son traveled together in the spring and fall when stagecoaches were more dependable. Jack scheduled the sittings, made reservations, and lugged his father's equipment around to the fancy houses in Albany, Poughkeepsie, Hartford, Windsor, and Wethersfield.

Without Jack's astute business sense, Benjamin Lewis would have been hard-pressed to make a living. There was fierce competition from those 'shysters' who worked the harvest fairs and summer revivals. Benjamin Lewis disdained the men who used a mechanical needle to trace their subject's profile onto an engraving plate. They demeaned his art. Jack knew how to market his father as a fine artist, and the studio prospered.

Martha always hung around in the studio to watch her father work. As the youngest and most amusing child, his only daughter, Martha was her father's pet. Benjamin Lewis let Martha assist with the matting, but because she was a girl, he would never consider teaching her his craft. Women did not become artists. Even so, Martha had shown academic promise in other ways. With Jack's shrewd stewardship of the portraiture studio, the family pooled its resources to send their only daughter to the Litchfield Female Academy.

At Miss Pierce's, Martha was adept at depicting botanical subjects. But a new skill was emerging—drawing maps. Geography was much promoted at the female academy and often conjoined with the ornamental arts. Martha had an innate sense of proportion and line. She insisted that came as no surprise, having watched her father in his studio all her life. Drawing the outlines of South America was not far off from drawing a person's profile. Her instructor, Mr. John Brace, had disagreed. "Don't sell yourself short," he said. "Your maps are exceptional." Her teacher had seen Martha Lewis's talent even if her father had missed it.

Once Charles got a feel for Mr. Lewis's work, he was eager to learn how to make profiles, even to do a 'fancy one' by painting directly on glass. Benjamin took one look at Charles's sketchbook and invited him to come over on Saturdays after the oral exams, welcoming him to stay for tea, or even supper. He would show him how things were done. Charles was ecstatic, Martha pleased. She wanted her family to approve of Charles. Even so, her brother Jack was edgy around him, protective of his younger sister. Perhaps too, he was envious of Charles's talent and his father's enthusiasm over Charles's work. The two young men were warily working out their differences, and a future was beginning to reveal itself. Charles Godwin might make a perfect husband for Martha—and a good addition to the Lewis family and portrait studio.

If Charles Godwin had his way, he would have dumped the study of law, proposed to Martha, and apprenticed himself to Benjamin Lewis. But he lacked the courage to tell his parents. They had a lot invested, financially and emotionally, in his becoming a lawyer. How could he disappoint them, once again? How could he casually mention in a letter home that he had fallen in love with a local girl, wanted to apprentice with her father, a renowned profile artist, and oh, yes, by the way, he was also quitting law school? The family pressure to stay the course, and his own tendency to waver, forced Charles to put himself on a schedule.

Here was his plan. He would spend time getting to know Martha Lewis better—as a human being, and not just a beauty. Charles knew he could be rash. He wanted to be deliberate in his intentions toward her. Charles would also spend Saturday afternoons in Benjamin Lewis's studio until the spring break. By then, Mr. Lewis might invite him to spend the month working for him full-time. Regarding law school, at least for now, Charles would ride on Eb's coattails. But he did write to his mother of his tentative plans to stay in Litchfield for the month of May.

Mary Godwin promptly wrote back. She missed her son. Why would Charles not come to New Haven for all his breaks from law school? Was he not coming home for the holidays in December? Mary Godwin wondered why Charles would be lobbying to stay in Litchfield for the month of May. His silence on the matter filled her with dread. She had an intuition—it was not the law that had captured her son's attention.

CHAPTER 2

November Chill

"And how are your studies coming along?" Katherine Montgomery grilled Thomas Bradford in her Charleston drawl. Thomas tried to keep up with Katherine's purposeful stride as they walked back from services at St. Michael's Episcopal Church on West Street, about a mile from the center of Litchfield.

Their meeting at St. Michael's was not quite by happenstance. Several weeks before, Thomas had run into Katherine on North Street. She had mentioned the Episcopal services on Sunday. Thomas replied that he might attend as well. He was missing his Christ Church in Savannah, he complained—disingenuously. The opportunity to walk Katherine Montgomery home from St. Michael's was more on his mind than any spiritual concerns. To be fair, the same was true for Katherine Montgomery.

It was the first week of November, and the fall foliage was still in full color. Neither Katherine nor Thomas had ever experienced a New England fall before. They were enjoying the remaining colorful leaves still clinging to the branches of the trees under an iridescent gray sky. The days were getting shorter and chillier. Winter was on its way.

Katherine had on a light rose-colored wool cloak which she wore with the hood spread out over her shoulders, her blonde hair falling down her back. "Are you liking the law lectures any better?" Katherine looked approvingly over at Thomas's classic profile. He was dressed in his Sunday suit, with white-and-gray striped trousers, and a well-tailored black coat. His thick brown hair had grown longer since their first encounter.

"The lectures are fine, I suppose," Thomas said with a sigh. "I've been trying to go more regularly. You know, after my father's letter." The week before, Thomas had confessed to Katherine about a stern letter from his father in Savannah. Robert Bradford knew Thomas had been lax about going to the law lectures. He also knew Thomas could be found most evenings drinking in the tavern at the United States Hotel. He had made it clear that if Thomas did not straighten up, he should just come home—no need to waste money on law school. Thomas had not relished sharing the contents of this letter with Katherine. His father's concerns reflected poorly upon his character, he knew, but Thomas had no one else to talk to. "I still don't know who snitched on me," Thomas whined. "Probably that dullard Wells."

"I doubt that," Katherine replied. "Eb Wells doesn't go to taverns. He wouldn't know about your carousing." She arranged her hood to put her blonde hair to the most advantage. "Besides, there're plenty of other young men up here from the South. Your father could have asked any one of them to keep an eye on you." She thought for a moment. "Maybe it was Judge Gould."

"Do you think he'd do that? Would he even notice me?" Part of that speculation thrilled Thomas. He admired Judge Gould. Judge Reeve was a bumbler, with his inaudible voice and erratic asides—

certainly past his prime. "I never thought of that." Thomas gave Katherine a sideways glance. "And what do you think about my carousing, as you put it, Katherine? Does that concern you as well?"

From their conversations after church, Thomas had come to understand Katherine was not the coy young woman he had first thought she was. She might wear the façade of Southern coquetry, but once engaged in serious conversation, Katherine Montgomery was more than a Southern belle. She was intelligent—not as intelligent as he was of course, but very smart for a woman. It was not her fault she did not have a Yale education, although he suspected her Latin was better than his.

"What does it matter what I think, Thomas?" Katherine held her head high. Thomas noted her elegant posture, the controlled way Katherine held her upper body, from years of training at her French boarding school. She knew how a refined woman ought to move through the world. His mother would approve.

"Well, it matters to me." Thomas stumbled over his words. "I want you to think well of me." Again, he cast her a sideways glance to see what effect his words might have. Katherine's face was unperturbed.

"If you want me to think well of you . . ." Katherine finally responded, glancing over at Thomas. "You must be more serious about your studies. I don't approve of these boys from the South who come up here to Litchfield to study law and then spend all their time in the tavern. That might be behavior befitting an undergraduate at Yale, but not an aspiring attorney." Katherine said this last sentence with emphasis, almost disdain.

"I see." Thomas thought back on his years at Yale. He had always gone to taverns in the evening and done the bare minimum to pass— anything to avoid his father's ire. He was content with the mark of *Inferiores*, relieved he had not received a *Perjores*. Thomas frowned, not pleased to learn Katherine wanted him to become a more serious student. "You want me to be a worker bee like that drone Eb Wells?"

Thomas groaned. "He just about lives in Judge Reeve's library with that odd bag-of-bones fellow who never speaks."

"That's Charles," Katherine interjected. "Charles Godwin. His father's in shipping in New Haven. He's on the brink of courting someone in my class, Martha Lewis. She's a bit of a country bumpkin, but Miss Pierce's will surely improve her. There's a joke going around school. It's a match made in heaven. She talks, and he listens." Katherine kept her gaze on the remaining leaves, and not on Thomas. "Still, they seem happy together. I think Charles is working with Martha's father. He's some kind of an artisan."

"Yes, that Charles fellow, the shadow of Eb Wells. I remember him from my first year at Yale. He never talked back then either. I don't know what Wells sees in him. Or vice versa." Thomas Bradford had little respect for Eb Wells, who did not come from money or a good Southern family. Eb's parents were Yankees, and he had not even gone to Yale. Besides, Wells wore glasses that kept falling off his nose, and his clothes were pedestrian.

But even Thomas Bradford had to grudgingly admit that, along with another new student, Oliver Hull, Eb Wells was gaining a good reputation at the law school. Both Oliver and Eb were giving stellar performances on the Saturday oral exams. The rivalry between 'Hull and Wells' was talked about in admiring, hushed tones around town, by law students and female academy students alike, even at the tavern in the hotel Thomas frequented. Some of the law students would hang around after their turn at the exam to see who would garner the most praise: Oliver Hull or Eb Wells. Bets were wagered.

Thomas was not surprised—and did not mind—that Oliver Hull was excelling. Thomas had first met Oliver Hull at Yale. Hull came from an old Windsor family and had distinguished himself at college as well. He was known to be hardworking and smart. But Eb Wells? And his sidekick? Thomas was discouraged. Even that mute

Charles Godwin was better at taking exams than he was. Charles's voice was halting, but he still stammered out respectable answers to the questions hurled at him. Thomas kept having to 'take a pass.' He was not alone. Some of his other colleagues from the tavern were in the same boat. None of them had figured out that, unlike college, law school required studying. Above all, Thomas hated the public aspect of his failure.

"Anyhow," Thomas protested, "I don't see how Wells does it. I'll bet it's that woman, Miss Hardwell, he walks out with all the time. She's coaching him. That's what the guys at the tavern all think."

"Rebecca Harding." Katherine corrected him. "You might be right." Katherine pulled her rose-colored cloak tighter around her, feeling a chill. "Rebecca hopes someday to become a teacher. Maybe she's practicing her pedagogy on Eb Wells."

"Do you think they're courting?" Thomas was not the only one in Litchfield who wondered about the relationship between Eb Wells and Rebecca Harding. "I see them together all the time, with Charles and that local girl."

"I'm not certain," Katherine answered. "Whenever I see them together, they seem to be talking about the law."

"Goodness." Thomas let out a low moan. "What could there be about the law to even talk about?" Katherine did not answer but kept her gaze on the horizon, her long stride unabated. "So, that's what you want? You want me to become a pedant like Eb Wells?"

"No, I don't." Katherine turned slightly in Thomas's direction, giving him a sweet smile that completely disarmed him. "I don't want you to be like anyone else, Thomas. I want you to be yourself." This Katherine said with slow deliberation, speaking in an exaggerated Southern accent, her voice dropping an octave. She gave his arm an intimate squeeze. "But it wouldn't hurt you to study more and go to the tavern less. We both want you to do well."

"We do?" Thomas stopped walking for a moment and turned

toward Katherine, pulling her to a halt. His voice cracked, an embarrassing response that happened when he felt a strong emotion. He cleared his throat. "I mean, you do?" This was his first inkling that Katherine Montgomery had any interest in him, aside from being her escort back to town from St. Michael's. His drinking buddies had ranked all the young women at Miss Pierce's, and Katherine Montgomery's rating was among the highest for beauty. It was also rumored she was among the richest, with promise of land in the South. And yes, Thomas admitted grudgingly, she was also intelligent, although that was not part of the package he was pursuing.

"I'm only interested in your doing well, Thomas . . ." Katherine measured her words carefully, locking eyes with him for a few seconds. "What I mean to say is—you must start to take yourself seriously." Katherine resumed walking with confidence toward town. "If your plan is to continue on the carousing course," she added over her shoulder, "to keep going to the tavern every night, skipping lectures, and not studying, I don't care if you do well—or not." Those last two words she uttered like a hammer, tacking down any hopes of further romance. She flashed him another sweet smile. At the same time, the sun came out.

Katherine Montgomery was a pragmatist, despite her youth. Her own future depended on the ambition, abilities, and character of her future husband. She liked Thomas Bradford. Even with his height, his classical profile, he had a lost puppy quality that appealed to her. But she would not be saddled with a man who lacked ambition—or drank. For Katherine Montgomery, Thomas was only a proverbial singular fish in a deep blue sea.

"I see." Thomas tried to catch up with her. "I'll give the matter some thought."

The next day, Thomas showed up on time for Judge Gould's lecture. After the midday meal, he found his way to the library. Eb Wells, Charles Godwin, and Oliver Hull were already there, along with a dozen or so others, furiously copying their notes into their books and consulting the cases Judge Reeve had exhorted them to look up the day before. Eb raised his eyebrows when Thomas walked in. Without saying a word, he scooted his books over, making room for Thomas at the table.

Thomas collapsed on the bench. He stole a glance at Eb who was totally absorbed in thought, bent over his lecture notes. Out of the window, from the dusky light of the library, Thomas could see that it was a beautiful late autumn day. *This could be my last glimpse of the sun before winter,* Thomas thought in despair, casting an eye around the room of silent, dedicated scholars. He put his head in his chin and let out a long, heartfelt sigh. This was not where Thomas Bradford wanted to be.

Letter to Eb Wells from Malinda Wells, Savannah,
November 12, 1819

Dearest Eb,

I hope this letter finds you in good health. We're all fine. I do worry about Mother. Since Father's death, she picks up every illness that blows in. We'll soon be into winter which won't improve her health or spirits. She's still grieving the loss of Father, I believe.

Mother, Susan, and I were invited to tea on Johnson Square last week by Eliza and John. It's really a beautiful home with an elegance we could never aspire to. Eliza used the china set we love. That wedding gift from England with the most beautiful, hand-painted pink roses and gold rims. Later, Mother and I bemoaned how nothing in our china cabinet matches anymore. Still, I'm rather fond of our hodgepodge. Each cup and saucer has its own story. Eliza's set has only one story to tell: a trip across the Atlantic at great expense.

It seems strange to see our older brother against this background of wealth and refinement, but he seems at ease. John has a lot of land cases these days, representing business associates of Eliza's father mostly. He barely mentions his work. He knows it upsets Mother. Even though John does not assist in buying and selling slaves for anyone, the people he represents surely own them. Mother and I try not to talk about it, even between ourselves.

I read your last letter at John's request. (I did censor that one part.) You were right. He did like Judge Gould better. John was surprised you were so intrigued by the law. He thought, with your love of flowers and birds, sketching and wandering, you wouldn't find it compelling.

By the way, John wants you to undertake a moot court, if you are asked. That's how a student gets noticed at the law school—how reputations are made. John knows you aren't fond of public speaking, but he urges you to do a moot anyhow. And, he added, don't forget to do a stellar job. No pressure there, little brother!

John's sending money to Uncle Ebenezer's to procure some new clothes in New Haven when you're there over the holidays. If you do a moot court, John says, you must be properly dressed. You represent the Wells family of Savannah. Don't go to a tailor in Litchfield. John says half the men in Litchfield still think the War of Independence is ongoing—their clothes reflect that. Use the tailor on Grand Avenue in New Haven. Uncle Ebenezer will know. John advises you to try to look more like Judge Gould, not Judge Reeve. At Susan's insistence, John is also sending money for new glasses so that yours won't fall off in the middle of the argument. Susan dislikes the way you push them up your nose. Uncle Ebenezer knows a good instrument maker. Get gold frames, John says. Me, I hope you'll get yourself a proper winter coat and some new boots. I worry about you in the cold. I wish you had heeded my advice.

Uncle Ebenezer is looking forward to your visit. Since our grandmother died, he's been lonely. You will love him. He only came to Savannah once when I was about six years old, and brought me Fanny, my Connecticut doll. Do you remember her? She still sits on my dresser. I remember him as a sweet man and devoted to our mother. He called her his 'baby sister.'

For me, Connecticut is this mysterious place our parents always spoke of with nostalgia. First, John was able to go up to New Haven, then to Litchfield, and now you too are in Connecticut. I'm the only family member who hasn't been. You must write to me more about what you're seeing—the autumn leaves, frost on the blades of grass, frozen ponds, and at some point—perhaps by the time this letter reaches you—snow. I so envy you, living in a boarding house in Litchfield, studying something new, having an adventure. All I know is Savannah. You'll have to see things for me, my dear Eb, and for Susan who misses you as much as I do. She practically memorizes your letters.

I'm happy you're making friends. Charles Godwin sounds like such an interesting fellow. And how is Miss Harding? You know, of course, John found his wife at Miss Pierce's. Perhaps you will as well. I can already see your ears burning at the suggestion, but John says it's one of the main reasons a young man studies in Litchfield. As for your reports about sharing quarters with a cat, I'm amazed. Mother would never countenance that—a cat who comes inside and sleeps on your bed. I too cannot imagine it. Why is he knighted, Eb? What did he do to deserve his title?

I must be off now and tend to Mother. Please be well. Write more news when you have time. Mother, Susan, and Lottie all send their love, as do John and Eliza and the little nieces who appeared at the tea in matching dresses. They looked like angels but did not always act so.

With love,

Malinda, your old maid sister

Thomas Bradford was confused by his feelings for Katherine Montgomery. He already had one unsuccessful courtship under his belt. His parents had planned a match with a distant cousin, Judith Graves. Her father owned a large parcel near Mary Mount, close to Washington, Georgia. A marriage between them would have strengthened ties with a loosely tethered wing of the family. Land would be settled on Judith, that, as her husband, Thomas would have the use of. His father, Robert Bradford, was hungry for more land.

Thomas's older brother Frank was already married. His wife came with her own modicum of wealth, but no land. Frank and his wife lived at Mary Mount and managed the African laborers, working closely with the Irish overseer. His father had recently purchased—in the illegal slave trade—a large group of slaves from the West Indies. This influx of new labor had to be quietly settled and trained. Frank was not only overseeing the construction of new slave cabins, but weighing bags of cotton, determining which slave was sick and needed a doctor, who would live where, which slave family had earned the privilege of its own vegetable patch—all the details of running a plantation.

Meanwhile, Thomas was up at Yale, training for nothing. Primogeniture had been abolished in Georgia, so he was not in the unfavorable position of a British second son. But upon graduation, Frank was emphatic. Thomas was *not* to work at Mary Mount. He was too lazy, drank too much, and was too soft-hearted with the Africans. What else could the second son of Robert Bradford do? Thomas's only assets were that he was tall, handsome, and well-dressed. Robert Bradford's attorney, John Wells, was also tall, handsome, and well-dressed. Maybe Thomas could become a lawyer?

Robert Bradford could not afford to overrule his older son. He needed Frank to run the plantation. Besides, Frank's assessment was on the mark. Thomas would be a liability at Mary Mount. Robert Bradford came up with a two-part plan to put Thomas to good use. First, send him to the Litchfield Law School in the fall, and second, marry him off to Judith Graves. An engagement would do for the present. Thomas was instructed to praise her many charms, discover her interests, and let her know what a fine fellow he was.

The Bradfords invited Judith, along with her brother Dudley, to visit them at Mary Mount. Thomas thought Judith 'not an unpretty woman,' but she had an overbite. Her charms were too few to praise. She also lacked spirit. He could not discover whether she had any interests, expressing opinions about nothing, often murmuring, 'Uh hmmm,' 'I dare say,' and 'No, not really.' Judith must have been bored, exhausted, or inherently phlegmatic. All Thomas had to fall back upon was his father's last instruction—to let her know what a fine fellow he was.

Judith Graves was not impressed. She confided to Dudley, after two interminable days at Mary Mount, that while Thomas Bradford was admittedly tall, handsome, and well-dressed, he drank too much and was full of himself.

And so, the match did not happen. Thomas was chagrined. His brother had nothing but disdain for Thomas who could not even tempt a plain house wren into the cage of matrimony. His father was angry, laying all the blame for the debacle on Thomas. Robert Bradford did admit, within the confines of his wife's bedroom, that Judith Graves was bland. His mother defended Thomas, as she always did, and promised her husband that their son would find a fine Southern girl, preferably one with land, at Miss Pierce's female academy. Everyone said so.

Thomas *had* found one, but becoming her suitor came at a high price. He must give up the tavern, attend lectures, and study like that weasel, Eb Wells. He would have to read the law all day, putting up with that elongated whippet, Charles-what's-his-name, who moved around Judge Reeve's library in silence like a mute monk, filling up ink wells and sharpening quill pens. Katherine wanted him to be like them—obedient drones, good soldiers in the law's army.

Lying in his bed at night, Thomas contemplated his situation. Katherine Montgomery and his father wanted him to do the same things. This confluence of plans for him—independently arrived at—disturbed Thomas. He was accustomed to disappointing his father and comfortable in his role as the family's black sheep. So far, there had been few repercussions. But if he did not meet Katherine's conditions, she would drop him. Worst of all, how could Thomas have the same emotions toward Katherine that he harbored toward his father? Is this how one should feel toward one's beloved? Angry and rebellious? Destined to disappoint? But Katherine would only bestow her favors upon him if he buckled under—if Thomas became the man she wanted him to be.

But then again, Katherine was so lovely, so rich. Her smile melted him. He loved her blonde hair and the way she carried herself. Her father owned a large plantation. Maybe all those things did matter after all. Thomas Bradford was afraid to admit something else. Maybe he wanted to buckle under. Maybe he wanted to become the man Katherine Montgomery wanted him to be. And she smelled of gardenias.

Thomas had no one to talk to. He would never say so, but he envied Eb Wells and Charles Godwin. The mismatched pair came into the schoolroom each morning, chatting idly about this or that, teasing each other in a gentle, aimless fashion. They seemed so comfortable in their alliance, one so tall, the other so short, fitting together like two pieces of a jigsaw puzzle. Thomas pummeled his pillow. "Maybe, what I really need right now is not a wife. Maybe I need a friend."

"And why, Charles, might I ask . . ." Judge Reeve sat across the table from Eb Wells and Charles Godwin, helping himself to a slab of ham. "Why didn't you finish your course at Yale?" At his elbow sat his ten-year-old grandson, Tapping Burr Reeve, just home from classes at the female academy. T.B., as he was called, was being raised by his grandfather and Mrs. Betsey Reeve.

T.B.'s father was Aaron Burr Reeve, Judge Reeve's only son by his first wife. Aaron Burr Reeve had been an attorney in Troy, New York, but had unexpectedly died just sixteen days after T.B.'s birth. T.B. was now studying with Miss Pierce until he was old enough to go to college. The Litchfield Female Academy educated promising young local boys as well as attracting young women from all over the United States. Lyman Beecher's sons had attended Miss Pierce's, as had the sons of Judge Gould.

Betsey Reeve was serving the noontime meal. It was the middle of November, and she was just developing her hot dishes for the season—today was her inaugural potato leek soup. As she bustled around the table, Judge Reeve continued his questioning of Charles Godwin. "Didn't you like Yale?"

"Well . . ." Charles held up his index finger to indicate he had just taken a mouthful. Judge Reeve patiently waited, slathering mustard onto his ham. The late autumn sun was filtering through the window, lighting up the old man's silver hair that fell in curls upon his shoulders. "I wasn't getting much out of my courses." Charles swallowed. "I was supposed to be studying for the ministry, but nothing made any sense to me." Charles had grown quite comfortable in the Reeves's dining room that looked out over the side yard where the law school stood.

"I see." Judge Reeve was persistent. "And what made you decide to study the law?"

"I didn't," Charles said with a wry smile. "My parents decided for me. My father's in shipping in New Haven. That's the family business." Charles delicately picked up a wan tomato slice with his fork from a platter. "But I'm not that interested in shipping. You just count things, weigh them, and move them from one dark place to another. My parents insisted I do something respectable, so they sent me to study with you."

"And how do you like the law?" The old man added some fresh lettuce to his slice of ham. He leaned over and put some lettuce on his grandson's plate, suggesting with his fork that he eat it. T.B. looked up at his grandfather with disdain, not keen on eating anything green.

Tapping Reeve was fond of these two new students, Eb Wells and Charles Godwin. He appreciated how polite and attentive they were to his wife, Betsey. Some of the young men treated her like a common servant. Nothing bothered him more.

"Well, sir, it's not as wretched as I expected, thanks to Eb." Charles gestured to his friend. "We study together. That makes it tolerable." It was true. Without Eb, Charles would have been floundering.

"'Not as wretched as expected,' eh? High praise." Judge Reeve gave a hearty laugh. Charles Godwin was not his first student who felt no calling for the law. A parent himself, Judge Reeve had steered his own son, Aaron, T.B.'s father, toward the legal profession. "And you, Eb?" The judge lowered his gaze, the difference in height between Charles and Eb being substantial. "Why didn't you go to Yale like your brother John?"

Judge Reeve remembered Eb's brother well, even though he had left Litchfield seven years ago. Like Eb, John had excelled at the oral exams. He was also outstanding in moot court. Judge Reeve gave Eb a look of appraisal. John Wells had a more commanding presence than this younger brother. He was tall, had broad shoulders, and a rich baritone voice. Eb possessed none of those things.

But Eb Wells exhibited other qualities his brother lacked—qualities Judge Reeve valued. Eb had an intellectual curiosity about the law—and a passion for it. Judge Reeve also appreciated his most endearing trait—Eb Wells found Judge Reeve amusing. When he took off on a flight of fancy from the lectern—veering from the script *Blackstone* had provided—the judge would scan the rows of dogged law students, perched on their wooden benches, looking for someone in the room to recognize how funny he had just been. The old man would search for the face of Eb Wells in the back row. When he found it, Eb invariably rewarded him with a grin. None of the other dullards in the lecture room knew when to laugh. Sadly, Judge Reeve had observed before, lawyers are not known for their sense of humor.

"I'll be forever known as the Wells boy who didn't go to Yale," Eb said with dejection. Judge Reeve was finally comparing him unfavorably to his brother. "I was an indifferent student when I was young. My father said he wouldn't waste his money on my going to Yale. So, I went to Franklin College instead. In Athens, Georgia." Eb wiped his mouth with his napkin, and added almost apologetically, "I loved my studies at Franklin College. Particularly the classics."

"Then you can join the elite club of those of us who didn't go to Yale." Judge Reeve smiled. "I didn't go to Yale either. My father insisted I go to the College of New Jersey so he could save money by my boarding with relatives."

"Really?" Eb's eyes grew large. It never occurred to him that this distinguished old man, this fragile, ancient old man, to Eb's way of thinking, might once too have had a disappointed, penny-pinching father, who could—or would—not send him to Yale. "Did you like it? Your college that wasn't Yale?"

"Yes, like you, I did." The judge gave his wife a brief 'thank you' as she triumphantly served him a steaming hot bowl of potato leek soup. "I got a fine education there and helped run the college's grammar school. I also tutored the late college president's son, Aaron Burr. That's where I met my first wife, my pupil's older sister, Sally Burr."

Charles and Eb were riveted. They knew Judge Reeve had once been married to Aaron Burr's sister. Everyone knew that, but it was another thing for the old man himself to tell the story. "Aaron and Sally were orphaned and became wards of their uncle. I was beneath her in station. Sally and I couldn't marry until I made something of myself. You understand. I had to provide for her properly. So, I suppose you'd say, I became a lawyer for love." Judge Reeve beamed at the two rapt young men. This was not the first time he had told this story.

"The law school was erected out there in the yard because my first wife Sally was never well," the old judge continued, not needing to be prompted. "She couldn't abide having her house overrun with law students. Some of them, like her brother Aaron, slept in the attic. We had classes in the parlor. The moot courts were held in the gathering room. My law office was on the first floor too. She felt banished to her room." Judge Reeve stopped to blow on his hot soup. "My poor wife had no peace and quiet in her own home. But my current wife, Betsey, took excellent care of her." Judge Reeve took a tentative spoonful of soup and looked across the room at his wife approvingly. "So, we built the law school out there on the side yard. Then we added this room so that Sally could stay downstairs and watch what was going on. The stairs were difficult for her. She was never very well," he added again with a tinge of sadness.

"So, that's why you put up the law school building?" Eb was fascinated. The idea of having a free-standing building in which to educate forty or fifty apprentices at one time, on national principles of law, according to a set curriculum, was revolutionary. It was unheard of in Eb's father's day. Eb assumed that Judge Reeve had spontaneously, brilliantly come up with the idea of a free-standing law school and a standardized legal education. Instead, Tapping Reeve had built the law school because the first, infirm Mrs. Reeve was frazzled in her own home. "Because your wife wasn't well?"

"Yes, more or less," the judge admitted. "What I'm trying to say to you, Eb, is this . . ." He gazed kindly at the young man with his large, orb-like eyes. "Don't let yourself be defined as the Wells boy who didn't go to Yale. I wouldn't be where I am today if I'd gone to Yale."

"I suppose you're right." Eb looked across the table at the boy, T.B. Reeve. "Where did you send your son to college?"

"To Yale, of course," Judge Reeve answered. "My grandson will be going there too." He leaned over and gave the ten-year-old a gentle hug. "And why not, Eb? It's the best college around." As Judge Reeve winked at Eb, he gestured to his wife, who was across the room tending to a few of the stragglers. He wanted a refresher on the soup. Eb lifted his empty bowl as well, as did Charles Godwin. Betsey Reeve gave them a hearty smile. Her potato leek soup was a success.

"The general rule is this." Miss Pierce gestured before her. "Utensils are placed in their order of use, from the outside in. Forks on the left of the plate. Knives and spoons to the right." Miss Pierce was seated at the head of the table in her formal dining room. She wore a plain, navy empire waist dress, white linen around her neck, and a matching cap tied under her chin, trimmed with bobbin lace, framing her face.

The female academy was located next door, consisting of a large room, capable of being partitioned, with two fireplaces at either end, and a piano against the wall. The students took their academic lessons in the school, sitting on backless, wooden benches. Some classes, however, such as etiquette and ornamental arts, took place on the first floor of Miss Pierce's home. This was a session on table manners.

In front of Miss Pierce was a full place setting. A small group of students were gathered around the table. Each had an individual bread plate and butter knife in front of her, slightly to the left. A basket of warm rolls sat on the table, along with a dish of butter in its center. It was late morning. Hunger had overtaken a few of the students who were already busily buttering. Miss Pierce's pedagogical goal of the day was to cover the niceties of eating bread.

Miss Pierce promoted a holistic education. Her girls would learn literature, rhetoric, writing, mathematics, and geography, but at the same time, proper manners, and comportment. Most of these young women hoped to marry well. If some of the autumn romances bloomed into more formal courtships, her students would marry future congressmen, judges, or successful attorneys. Association with the Litchfield Law School launched its graduates into the highest orbits of government and society. A young man's future might depend on the impression he made in the elite dining rooms of the fledgling Republic. It was expected his wife too would know how to eat bread properly in a formal setting.

"Note," Miss Pierce continued, "the knife blades are always placed with the cutting edge toward the plate." Katherine Montgomery was seated to her left, Rebecca Harding and Martha Lewis to her right, with six or seven other girls spaced out around the table.

Katherine Montgomery rolled her eyes. Her mother had taught her these lessons in their Charleston dining room years ago, and her etiquette was later honed at her French boarding school. Rebecca Harding had put off the study of table manners until the very end of her academic training. Rebecca was not unschooled in how to eat bread, having been drilled by Mrs. Johnson in Wethersfield, but she was insecure about the finer points. Rebecca was taking notes in her small commonplace book while Martha Lewis was listening with a mixture of fascination and dismay. Her own mother did not possess more than one kind of fork or knife, so all of this was news to her.

"Katherine," Miss Pierce asked, "perhaps you could tell the other girls where the butter knife can be found."

"Yes, of course." Katherine gestured with her well-manicured hand to the butter plate. "The butter plate is placed above the forks, at the left of the place setting. There you'll find what Miss Pierce calls your 'butter knife,' placed diagonally across the plate, handle on the right, and the blade facing you."

"Are there any rules about the butter knife?" Miss Pierce queried.

"Well," Katherine said, "there's the master butter knife . . ."

"Surely you jest." Martha Lewis interrupted, giggling. "That's the master butter knife? How do we know it's a man?" She pointed to the larger, saber-shaped, dull-edged knife that perched on the edge of the central butter dish. "And what does that make these little ones on our plates with the round tips—his servants? Are they males or females?" Miss Pierce raised an eyebrow at Martha Lewis who was prone to small explosions of humor, as unexpected as they were irrepressible.

"No, Martha." Katherine saw no cause for amusement—Martha Lewis could be so infuriating. Still, she considered Martha's question. While oddly put, it had merit. "I suppose you could think of the individual butter knives as servants. Each guest uses her own knife to 'serve' the butter onto her piece of bread. That's why they have a curved tip—so as not to tear the bread." Katherine ran her finger over the curved end of her little knife. She considered that these smaller, individual knives must be female. Martha Lewis had made her see it in a new way. "Anyhow, the master butter knife is never used to spread butter on the bread. Its sole purpose is to transfer butter from the central butter plate to the individual butter plates. That eliminates the risk of contamination."

"Oh, I see." Martha seemed deflated.

"In the South," Katherine continued in a condescending manner, "we refer to the small individual utensil that each person uses on her bread as a 'butter spreader.' That avoids confusion with the master butter knife." Some of the girls locked eyes across the table with discomfort. Katherine seemed to be contradicting Miss Pierce.

Miss Pierce did not seem to mind, any more than she minded Martha's risible interruptions. "And what other rule might a young lady in society want to know?" Miss Pierce was an experienced teacher. She was strategically using Katherine Montgomery's accomplishments to keep her from deriding others. From her many years of teaching, Miss Pierce knew better than to assume all her students were as knowledgeable about table etiquette as Katherine Montgomery. Martha Lewis might not be the only young woman sitting at the dining table who did not understand the function of the master butter knife. "About bread and buttering, I mean."

"About eating bread generally," Katherine said with authority, "you should only take bread when there's a course on the table already. That means no bread is eaten by itself, either before a course, or in between. Bread's always an accompaniment to a course." Katherine seemed to be enjoying her role as purveyor of knowledge. "Plus," she continued, "my mother insists that it's only proper to butter one bite at a time."

Katherine picked up her roll and tore off a small portion. She transferred some butter from the central butter dish with the master butter knife. She then used her own butter knife—spreader—and delicately put some butter on that one piece. "Only ill-bred people butter the entire piece of bread at one time." This Katherine said with a sniff, looking down the table at the two inseparable sisters from Albany who had already buttered their entire rolls. "It makes for greasy fingers, and butter on your cheeks."

"My father does that—butters the whole slice of bread. On my mother's baking day." Martha interrupted again. "Mother will call him in from the studio for hot bread, and he slathers the whole piece with huge dollops of freshly churned butter. Does that make him ill-bred?" For once, Martha was not laughing.

"I don't mean to suggest your father is ill-bred," Katherine replied. "But I believe your father's an artisan. Perhaps your household hasn't abided by the rules of higher society." The statement was true but stinging. Martha Lewis held herself erect, her freckled cheeks beginning to turn splotchy, her green eyes glowering.

"And what's wrong with being an artisan?" Rebecca jumped into the fray to defend Martha. This was not the first snide remark she had heard at Miss Pierce's about fathers who were artisans, or worse yet, 'in trade.' Rebecca did not give Katherine a chance to recover. "My own father was an artisan too, a cabinet maker. He had wonderful manners. That is, if you believe—as I do—that at the heart of good manners is consideration of others."

Katherine felt the rebuke, understanding she had overstepped her bounds. She had offended a classmate, and worse yet, one of the assistant teachers. Rebecca Harding was someone she both feared and admired. Katherine Montgomery also did not know that Miss Sarah Pierce's own father was a farmer and a potter who had made red earthen pots, jars, and milk pans for everyday use in rural households. An artisan if that.

"I feel certain Katherine didn't mean to cast aspersions on your father, Rebecca, or on yours either, Martha." Miss Pierce tried to defuse the situation. "But it's not proper in polite society, Katherine, to refer to the background of another person, certainly not someone you're breaking bread with. Or of anyone, really." Miss Pierce raised her eyebrows at Katherine who shifted uncomfortably in her chair, aware she had offended Miss Pierce too. "Not everyone has had the privilege of an education like yours. I would ban the expression 'ill-bred' from your vocabulary." The older woman continued with quiet emphasis, casting a discerning glance down at the other end of the dining table. "Even if you think it might apply to your colleagues from Albany who've already demolished their bread." Miss Pierce smiled at the two hungry young sisters who had buttered their entire rolls and consumed them. Sarah Pierce too remembered a time in her life when she did not know the proper way to butter her bread.

"I'm sorry to offend," Katherine murmured. "I just meant to suggest these are the rules for gatherings in polite society, that's all." She looked apologetically at Martha and the two sisters at the end of the table, but she could not bring herself to make eye contact with Rebecca Harding who was still fuming. "It's just useful to know the proper rules, even if you don't use them at home."

"Precisely." Miss Pierce looked around the table at the girls who hung on her every word. "You must master these rules to maneuver in polite society. It will be expected that as a refined, educated woman, you'll know how to approach a bread plate, a roll, and a master butter knife with aplomb." She nodded at her young charges. "And Katherine makes a good point, Martha." Miss Pierce looked over at this lively local girl from Litchfield, reminding herself what a good idea it had been to admit her. "At home, in our intimate settings—on baking day in our own kitchens—the rules get broken all the time. And when our beloved fathers break them," she added with a warm smile, "we have permission to break them too."

Miss Pierce had dissipated the tension in the room. Katherine Montgomery had been somewhat rehabilitated. Martha was permitted to adore her father, with his warm whole piece of bread, inappropriately slathered with butter. Even Rebecca Harding had calmed down and was taking notes, not about the master butter knife, but about Miss Pierce's strategies as a teacher. Rebecca could not have defused the powder keg between Katherine and Martha once Martha's fuse had been lit. Worse yet, Rebecca herself had escalated the situation. Rebecca aspired to be like Miss Pierce, who intuitively knew how to manage tense exchanges. But Rebecca's tongue was sharper.

"I know you girls are hungry." Miss Pierce gestured to the clock on the mantel. "But we have a few more minutes. Which direction do we pass the bread around the table? Katherine?"

The week after Katherine Montgomery's eighth birthday, her father and younger brother died. Travis, only five years old, fell ill with terrible stomach cramps, a high fever, and frequent liquid, bloody stools. Unfortunately, Katherine's father too came down with the 'bloody flux.' Within three days, Travis was dead, and Katherine's father died a few days later. Katherine and her mother were on their own.

Three years later, Katherine's mother remarried, a wealthy planter and widower, Mr. Randall Montgomery, also of Charleston. He had two sons from his first marriage, James, aged sixteen, and Morris, almost thirteen. Upon their marriage, Katherine and her mother moved into Randall Montgomery's grand house on Wentworth Street.

In a gesture of magnanimity, her new stepfather let Katherine take the name of 'Montgomery,' but no formal adoption took place. Katherine was only eleven years old, a tall, awkward child, with her nose always in a book. Randall Montgomery had little use for a girl child until it came time to marry her off. In the meantime, he allowed Katherine to sit in the boys' schoolroom, but not take up the tutor's time. In the summer, when he took the boys to their plantation on a sea island, Isle Pines, Katherine could use the tutor then. The tutor expected a year-long contract. Teaching Katherine would fill up his time—better than giving the tutor a holiday.

Katherine never missed a day in the classroom. Pervis Mitchell was a fine teacher, a skinny fortyish bald man with protruding teeth. Mr. Mitchell welcomed Katherine into the classroom. She was bright and eager to learn, but Morris was a problem. He took an instant dislike to his stepsister who was already a far better reader than he was. He did not like to be outdone by a girl. Morris would taunt her and throw small objects in Katherine's corner. She had to sit behind a screen.

James, the older boy, was studious, preparing to go to college at William & Mary. Katherine would scoot her desk as close as she could when James was learning Latin, a subject she excelled at. Katherine and James competed on either side of the screen for accurate declensions. Katherine almost always won. James treated her with the affection of a much older brother.

The tutor had to walk a fine line. His employer, Randall Montgomery, had no interest in educating another man's daughter. But James, his prize pupil, benefited from having a second sharp student in the room. Katherine would rattle her screen if she had a question, and Mr. Mitchell would let James try to answer it. The tutor never asked Morris to contribute. He was too busy throwing things at Katherine.

For the summers of her twelfth and thirteenth years, Katherine had Mr. Mitchell's full attention when Morris and James went to Isle Pines. Randall Montgomery wanted his boys to know how indigo and cotton were grown, how slaves were managed, how overseers were to be overseen. James hated the summers. The sea island was miserable, buggy, and hot. James was morbidly afraid of miasma and falling ill, a warranted fear during the summer off coastal South Carolina. But Morris loved his hands-on agricultural education. He roamed the island at will, lording it over the overseer and ordering the slaves around as well.

Mr. Mitchell and Katherine enjoyed those two golden summers. Both missed James, but not Morris. The schoolroom had cross ventilation, and the sea breezes kept them cool. The third floor was too high for mosquitoes. The two sat comfortably at the large desk in the dark room, with Lulu, Katherine's personal slave, sitting in the corner. (Even at her young age, Katherine's mother insisted on a chaperone.) Mr. Mitchell taught Katherine how to write. She developed a distinctive, flowing cursive, and loved to engage in fine knotting. She was happy with a pen in hand, not so much for what she had to say, but for its pure physicality. For fun, Katherine taught Lulu her letters, making Pervis Mitchell acutely uncomfortable. He could get in a lot of trouble, with his employer and the law, for teaching a slave how to read.

After the second summer, Mr. Mitchell found a better paying position, and James went off to college. Katherine wept bitterly over both departures. Morris shed no tears. Over the summer, Morris's voice had deepened, and he had sprouted a fledgling beard. Morris found himself unexpectedly interested in his stepsister, Katherine. Her body too had changed, filling out with curves where none had been before. Katherine surprised everyone, including herself, by emerging from a chrysalis of awkward childhood into a statuesque beauty. Morris began to pursue her with predatory intent. His father had let him spend a few nights with a couple of slave women on the plantation that summer. Morris now understood what women were for.

A day or two after his brother's departure, Morris lay in wait for Katherine in the hallway upstairs. When she appeared, Morris jumped out from behind his door, grabbed her by the arm, and pulled her into his bedroom. He tried to kiss her. She struggled, but he jammed her up against the wall, pressing his body urgently against hers. Katherine started to scream, and Morris put his hand over her mouth. She bit down on the fleshy inside of his middle finger, so hard he howled and let her go, clutching his injured hand to his chest, cursing Katherine who had turned in a panic and dashed out of his room.

The doctor was called to treat Morris's finger. At supper, Randall Montgomery dressed Katherine down for her brutal attack, never thinking to ask how his younger son's finger had ended up in Katherine's mouth. But her mother did think to ask. That evening, Katherine confided everything to her. Her mother considered telling her husband but decided against it. Randall would just shrug and say, 'Boys will be boys.' Instead, Katherine's mother enrolled her daughter in a new French boarding school on Broad Street. Madame Talvande had fled Haiti after the slave revolt in Saint-Domingue and had started a school for girls. Katherine would become a boarder at her school.

When Katherine's mother presented her husband with the bill from Madame Talvande's, Randall Montgomery roared. But he grudgingly paid the bill. Katherine would learn to speak French with the *crème* de la crème of Charleston society, bearing the Montgomery name. Randall Montgomery too had noticed Katherine's metamorphosis. Who knows, he said to his wife, chewing on a piece of tough mutton, Katherine might yet become an asset. Her mother promised Katherine she would never have to live under the same roof as Morris. Morris kept a sulky distance from Katherine during the holidays and bore a permanent scar on his finger.

After three years at Madame Talvande's, Katherine wanted a more rigorous academic education. Several of her schoolmates had traveled north to study at the Litchfield Female Academy. There Katherine could study history, literature, geography, math, astronomy, Latin—the same subjects James was offered at William & Mary. Again, Randall Montgomery balked at the price. He saw no need for educating Katherine any further. She already knew all that she needed to ornament a front parlor.

But Katherine's mother convinced him. Several other young women from Charleston had studied with Miss Pierce and returned engaged to wealthy planters' sons. These tales of marital success persuaded Randall Montgomery. Paying for the Litchfield Female Academy might be a sound investment if Katherine could lure a wealthy Southern gentleman, preferably one with land, into matrimony. Besides, she was too young to marry now. A female academy was a good place to park her until she got older—until she was ripe for the picking. But Randall Montgomery made it clear. She had two years to find a suitable match.

If Katherine failed in her quest up north, Randall Montgomery would find someone else for her to marry. His younger son, Morris, had expressed an interest. Katherine, and her mother, recoiled at the suggestion, but Randall Montgomery waved away their protestations. Katherine and Morris were not related by blood. No formal adoption had ever taken place. His lawyer assured him—he had already asked—no legal impediments existed to such a marriage. And 'Morris wouldn't make such a bad husband,' Randall Montgomery had insisted, 'if Katherine couldn't find one on her own.'

"That was a splendid meal, Martha," Eb said over his shoulder. He and Rebecca Harding walked in front of Charles and Martha. The romantic couple lagged behind, deep in conversation, analyzing Martha's mother's apple butter, comparing it to that of the Godwins' cook in New Haven. Rebecca was wrapped in her long black cloak with the hood pulled up over her head. Wearing only a light jacket, Eb was beginning to feel the cold.

It was late November, and the Lewis family had invited Eb, Rebecca, and Charles over for a Saturday afternoon feast to give thanks for the harvest. Ruth Lewis had cooked for several days— baked ham, mashed potatoes, sweet potatoes, peas, onions, cranberries, hot fresh bread, and an apple tart for dessert, drizzled with fresh cream. There was honey and apple butter to smear on the bread, along with a huge jar of freshly churned butter. It was late afternoon, and the four were walking back into town, Martha and Rebecca to Miss Pierce's, and Eb and Charles to Mrs. Edwards's. The days were growing shorter and shorter. Nightfall would soon be upon them.

"I'm so glad you could both come." Martha had prattled on to her parents about Rebecca Harding and Eb Wells. Charles had become a regular at the Lewis cottage, and the whole family had heard all about his study partner, Eb Wells. Martha had told them all about her new best friend, the smartest girl at school, Rebecca Harding. Rebecca and Eb had been introduced to them at church, but Martha's family was curious to know them better. It had been a festive occasion, with lively conversation, delicious food, all lubricated with hard cider.

"It's all in the quality of the apples at your disposal," said Martha. Martha and Charles were trying to decide why the New Haven apple butter was so thin. The couple was walking with Charles's arm tucked under Martha's, a maneuver they were now accustomed to. Charles towered over Martha, but he had discovered a way to place his hand and forearm beneath her elbow that satisfied the physical closeness they both craved. "Our apples up here are just superior." Martha spoke with authority, even though she had never been out of Litchfield or tasted New Haven's fruit.

"You know what clothes you are to order at Dr. Cabot's," Rebecca Harding said, letting the apple butter conversation meander along without their input. Rebecca had gone over the list of things Eb needed to acquire over the upcoming holidays in New Haven. His brother John had sent a sum of money to their uncle's home to outfit Eb with new clothes. Three shirts, two pairs of pants (long enough, Rebecca chided), two ties, two new pairs of boots, one regular pair and another thicker, taller pair for the snow, better suited for the unpaved wintry streets of Litchfield, a black suit for more formal attire—for a moot court performance—and two vests, one matching, the other a contrast. The list went on and on.

"I suggest you select a brown for the second pair of pants, and make sure the second vest can be worn with black or brown, a brocade would be nice, perhaps a soft brown, maybe camel colored." Rebecca had clearly given this some thought. "Nothing too severe. You don't want to look like Judge Gould. He always looks so funereal." Rebecca was peering out from the hood of her cloak. The sun was low in the sky. Eb's lips were blue. "And you already know how I feel about a proper winter coat. Let's not argue about that again."

"I agree," Eb conceded. "Let's not." The two walked on, listening to Charles and Martha prattle cheerfully about the old dog Lucky, stealing scraps from under the table. "And Rebecca?" Eb pushed his glasses back up his nose. "Do you really think I need new glasses? I see fine with these."

"Yes, you need them, and I agree with your brother, gold ones, but have those adjusted for a backup pair." Rebecca gave Eb an affectionate look. "We need to break you of the habit of pushing your glasses up your nose. It isn't dignified, Eb. As for your handkerchiefs, you'll need a dozen of those. You keep using the same two over and over. They're quite ratty."

"All right." Eb sighed. Rebecca sounded like his sister Malinda, who was always on him about his handkerchiefs, making sure his pants and sleeves were long enough, the need to adopt a color scheme. The habit of pushing his glasses up his nose was a new complaint. Well, perhaps not. Susan Graham had harped on that before. More than once. "I really don't see the reason for all this fuss about what I'm to wear."

"You and Oliver Hull are probably going to argue in a moot court. Chances are, you'll become a renowned attorney one day, maybe even a judge." Rebecca gave Eb's arm a squeeze. "Don't you want to start looking the part?"

"I suppose so." Eb was not certain he did. His rapid rise at the law school had taken him by surprise. It had not been his intent to excel. Eb had never imagined the law would appeal to him, yet he was fascinated by it, amused by it, infuriated by it. The more he studied the law, the more he fell under its spell. The hours spent in Judge Reeve's law library, the hours spent studying with Charles at night, the hours spent cramming by himself in his attic room—all this effort had the collateral effect of unprecedented academic success.

This threw Eb off. His performance in college had been inconsistent. At Franklin College, Eb had finally mustered enough discipline to avoid flunking subjects of no interest to him. His high marks in Greek and Latin kept his average up. But overall, Eb was comfortable in the middle of his small class at Franklin where no one knew John Wells. Unfortunately, here at the Litchfield Law School, his older brother's reputation as 'distinguished' lingered on. Worse yet, Eb now had to live up to his own reputation. He was touted as one of two new law students with 'brilliant' answers on the oral exams. His rival, Oliver Hull, a tall young man from Windsor with a long, equine face, was always in the law library, looking over his shoulder, trying to outdo him. It was a lot of pressure. Eb felt an obligation to keep up, but mostly he felt like an imposter.

"I just don't see why all this sudden fuss about my clothes."

"You have to trust me on this." Again, Rebecca reminded Eb of Malinda. "If you're going to have an outstanding legal career, you'll have to dress better."

"That seems so superficial." Eb blew into his hands to warm them.

"It may seem superficial, but it's not. Being well-dressed and neat in one's appearance sends a message of competence and self-assurance. Those are important traits in a lawyer."

"But I'm not that self-assured," Eb protested softly, not wanting Charles and Martha to hear. "You know that already."

"Yes, I know, Eb." Rebecca lowered her voice and took his arm. "And I love your honesty about that." After a pause, she added, "But if you force yourself to act more self-assured, you'll soon *feel* more self-assured. It's sort of like fooling yourself."

"Have you ever done that?" Most of their discussions about self-improvement focused on Eb. He was curious to hear what she had to say.

"Yes." Rebecca was frank. "This year, on my first day of assistant teaching, right before I went into the classroom, I felt dizzy and nauseous. Through the crack in the partition, I could see the eight new rhetoric students, sitting on the benches, all waiting for me. I panicked. My heart was pounding, my palms damp. I thought—what if I can't answer their questions? What if I stammer and feel woozy and have to leave the room?"

"Really? You felt like that?" Rebecca had just described how Eb felt every Saturday morning right before the oral exams. "You always seem so confident, Rebecca."

"Well, I'm not always," she said bluntly. "And certainly not that first day. I took some deep breaths and told myself sternly that I knew more than they did. I forced myself to walk into the classroom, smile at the girls, and act self-assured." Eb was listening intently. This was the closest he had ever come to learning of a chink in Rebecca Harding's armor. "Once I got started, everything was fine. I fooled myself into thinking I could do it, and I could. I still get a flutter of it, right before I go into a classroom to teach. Even now after all these months. Preparation is the key to everything."

"How so?" Eb asked, fascinated to hear Rebecca Harding was not always in full command of herself.

"I find the more prepared I am, the less my nerves undermine me. Where I really get into trouble," she added hastily, "is when I don't know the material. My nerves unmask my ignorance. I lose self-confidence. I sink."

"You sink?" Eb was marveling at this revelation. "Even Rebecca Harding can have an off day?"

"Oh, yes," Rebecca said with a smile. "The thing of it is—when you have an off day, you must run back to your room, make a cup of tea, and throw yourself into a fit of self-pity and doubt. You deserve it. Later that day—or maybe later that week—when you're feeling less bruised, you stop beating yourself up. Try to learn from the experience."

"And what do you learn?"

"For me, at least," Rebecca answered, "I was almost always ill-prepared. If I'd truly mastered the material, I wouldn't have faltered. Even then, some bright student might pounce on me with a question I never considered before." Rebecca thought a moment. "The truth is having a case of nerves is just part and parcel of any kind of public presentation—teaching, arguing a moot court, being in a play, giving a sermon." Rebecca rearranged her hood back up on her head—it tended to fall onto her shoulders when she was walking. "Now I expect some heart pounding and clammy hands on my teaching days. But when I'm well-prepared, my nerves disappear once I get going."

"I get like that before the oral exams on Saturday," Eb confessed in a low voice.

"Of course you do. It's a very public arena. If you don't know the answer, everyone at the law school is there to witness you stumble." She gave him a wicked smile. "Perhaps hoping you'll stumble. Someone might even be laying bets on whether or when the Great Eb Wells will fall flat on his face."

"So, what I've been doing"—Eb ignored her comment, continuing with excitement—"is before the exam, Charles and I make up questions from the week's material and write out complete answers. Then we memorize them. Charles says it's cheating, but I keep telling him it's not. I used to do that for Latin exams. If you listen closely to the teachers, you can pretty much figure out what they're going to ask you. You know, by what they emphasize in their lectures." Rebecca smiled. This was an academic trick she already knew. "And Judge Gould practically blows a trumpet when it's a concept he wants you to know," Eb went on. "He'll even state the principle two times over in the lecture. So, I make a note to myself: 'Memorize this.'"

"That's good, Eb. You thought that up all by yourself—making up answers to predictable questions?"

"I did." Eb was proud. It may have been the sole study technique he had acquired so far, not suggested by Rebecca Harding.

"You're coming along nicely." Rebecca gave him a warm smile. "But you still need some new clothes and a pair of glasses that will stay on your nose."

Eb did not hear her, having been swept into the conversation behind them. Charles and Martha were arguing over whether yams were better with butter and salt, or butter and molasses. This was a subject upon which Eb had a firm opinion. The quartet made their way down the upper reaches of North Street.

Night had fallen. It was already dark. Candles and oil lamps were being lit on kitchen tables, desks, and in windows throughout the town. Winter was more than on its way. Winter had already arrived. All right, Eb Wells admitted to himself, shivering. I really do need a warmer coat.

CHAPTER 3

The Holidays

"I had no idea it could be so cold." It was the second week of his winter holidays in New Haven. Eb and his uncle were eating breakfast at the mahogany table. The dining room on Elm Street was decorated in the federal style by Eb's grandmother, who had died a few years ago.

Her son, Dr. Ebenezer Cabot, was the only Cabot now left in the large house. His housekeeper, Esmeralda, had quarters on the third floor. He had two other free Black servants, a cook and her husband who performed a wide range of tasks—Mr. and Mrs. Potts. They lived in their own home on State Street. Nothing in the house had changed since Ebenezer Cabot and his 'baby sister' Abigail had grown up in it, except for the expansion of the medical office on the first floor. Dr. Cabot ran a clinic for the poor, three mornings a week, and needed a waiting room.

In the dining room, Esmeralda hovered over the matching mahogany sideboard, replenishing hot water in the teapot. She was an elderly woman who had worked for the family for over forty years. Wearing a white starched apron and a gray dress that matched her wiry gray hair, Esmeralda moved about the room with authority. She was light skinned, of mixed-race origin.

"I couldn't imagine being this cold back in Savannah, no matter what John tried to tell me." Eb could not stop shivering.

"And this is nothing, Eb," the older man said. "It's just nippy out. Wait for our first snowstorm." The day before, Eb had walked back and forth from the house on Elm Street to the tailor's shop on Grand Avenue. It was only a few blocks away, across the New Haven Green, but the sharp wind off the Long Island Sound had penetrated his light wool coat. He had felt uncomfortably cold.

"It's a good thing you're having a heavier coat made up." Esmeralda had no problem inserting herself into any conversation. She had known Ebenezer Cabot since he was an adolescent. "I never saw a young man so ill-prepared for a Connecticut winter," she said, pouring Eb some more tea. He enjoyed having limitless cups of tea, unlike his rationed share at Mrs. Edwards's.

"I see the need now." Eb agreed. "A friend in Litchfield has been urging the same thing, but I didn't believe her."

"Your mother's probably been in the South so long, she can't remember how brutal the New England winters can be. And Miss Abigail never did have her head screwed on tight." Esmeralda shook her head. "I suspect your sister, Malinda, is more practical. I don't see why she didn't send you off better prepared."

"She may have tried," Eb mumbled with a hint of apology. He and Malinda had argued bitterly over what he was going to pack for Connecticut. Eb hated that his older sister was always right. She could be overbearing and bossy. Eb had exerted his independence by failing to bring appropriate boots, enough shirts, or handkerchiefs— and no heavy woolen coat. The price of his autonomy was a woeful lack of preparation for the winter.

"Perhaps you're just a hothouse flower," Dr. Ebenezer Cabot

teased. He was a bald man of sixty, with a thick middle, graying hair at the temples, and a slightly stooped posture. No one would ever call Dr. Cabot handsome. Like Eb, he wore glasses, and his ears were a bit too protruding, a bit too large, but he had a gentleness about him. "John had more meat on him when he was here."

Eb's older brother had also spent his holidays while at Yale, and later at the Litchfield Law School, in their grandmother's house on Elm Street.

"He grew accustomed to the cold during his years at Yale, but he always swore the winter was far harsher up in the Litchfield Hills. Certainly, they get more snow." Dr. Cabot picked up the weekly newspaper that Esmeralda had brought him. "It's the elevation, I suppose."

"Would you mind if I used the library again?" Eb had packed his commonplace books—for there were now several, representing distinct phases of preparation. He was compiling the final edition of the past three months of work. Seated at the large French writing table in his grandfather's library, Eb loved to spread his materials far and wide. It was such a luxury to have an entire month with nothing on his schedule—no lectures, no oral exams, no new *Blackstone* rolling in, no teas at Miss Pierce's. He was missing Mrs. Edwards, his friends, and the cat, Sir Winston, but it was a relief to be away from the pressures of law school.

Eb was looking forward to hours alone in his grandfather's library—refining his notes, culling, and expanding them. His goal was to crystallize the law mastered so far into a systematic, legible final book, *Volume I.* It made him happy to sit in the dark room with its bookcases on either side of the fireplace. He had the use of one of his uncle's oil lamps, with a limitless supply of whale oil. No rationing of candles here. The library served a different purpose in the evening. After supper, he and his uncle retired there. The two of them would sit together before the fire, on the matching gold chinoiserie wingback chairs, first to drink a little tea and later some whiskey, to read and talk. But it was morning, and Eb wanted to get to work.

"You don't need to ask." His uncle looked up briefly from the newspaper. "You're welcome to any corner of the house that suits you."

Dr. Cabot was pleased to see how his younger nephew had taken to the study of law. In this, Eb was unlike his older brother, who had always declared himself on holiday in New Haven whenever on break from law school. John Wells had taken off each day and most evenings to meet up with old friends from Yale, spending little time with his uncle and grandmother. He was an excellent student, both at Yale and at the Litchfield Law School, but also enjoyed an active social life.

An active social life was foreign to Dr. Cabot. He had always been more comfortable in the evening, sitting by the fire with his mother in the library, a fat book of history in hand. Dr. Cabot was no misanthrope. He was fond of people. As a physician, he treated many patients every day, peering down raw throats, listening to congested lungs, palpating abdomens, setting limbs, lancing boils, making diagnoses, dispensing medication. But by evening, Ebenezer Cabot was done with humanity. He always opted to stay in, a much lonelier proposition since his mother had died. This habit may have accounted for why he had never married.

It was unfair to compare his two nephews—but Dr. Cabot could not help himself. John Wells was more of everything. John was more confident. He had more stature. He was more concerned with wearing the right clothes, going to the right schools, and associating with the right people. He effortlessly claimed the privileges that were his—and there were many. John Wells was a white male from an affluent family, educated at elite institutions. But he did not even recognize these attributes as privileges. Rather, John assumed they were his birthright.

Eb Wells, the younger nephew, was a much smaller version of his brother, and nearsighted like Dr. Cabot. He seemed indifferent to his clothes and had not attended Yale. He lacked self-assurance and the sense of entitlement that his older brother exuded. Indeed, Eb seemed altogether tentative about his right to inhabit the world. All things considered, Dr. Cabot liked him better. He enjoyed talking to Eb about the law. Eb was passionate about his studies. He reminded Dr. Cabot of how he had felt during the two years he had studied medicine at Columbia College. Ebenezer Cabot knew what it was like to pore over the books for hours on end—and not notice the time passing. Even now, when Dr. Cabot was stumped, he could spend long evenings in the library with his medical books, in pursuit of a diagnosis.

Furthermore, Eb was respectful of Esmeralda, about whom Dr. Cabot was very protective. John Wells had displayed an irritating tendency to order her around. But this younger boy was attentive to all the members of his household. Eb had the good sense and tact to pretend to take Esmeralda's unsolicited advice. He also drifted back to the kitchen mid-morning each day to visit the affable Mrs. Potts. Mrs. Potts had a soft spot for Eb. He would sit at the kitchen table and share a cup of tea with her, and sometimes Mr. Potts, and sample whatever was coming out of the oven. During all his holiday visits to his Uncle Ebenezer, John Wells never once set foot in the kitchen on Elm Street. Gentlemen did not enter the kitchen in John's world, but Eb was drawn to its warmth.

"Grandfather's library is a great place to work," Eb commented to his uncle. Eb's family never had a library. His uncle's home in New Haven was far grander than their house in Savannah, as were its furnishings. The address on Elm Street was also in a fashionable location, right on the New Haven Green. Eb wondered if John had learned to aspire to this more elevated lifestyle from his frequent visits to Elm Street. Their clapboard house on East York Street in

Savannah was large and comfortable, but modest in comparison. Eb also now realized how much his mother had sacrificed when she moved to Savannah to be with his father.

"I see here your Lyman Beecher is taking on the Unitarians in Boston." Eb's uncle peered up from the newspaper. "He's defending the orthodox views of the Congregationalist Church against the Unitarians. They unaccountably find Calvinism gloomy and harsh." Dr. Cabot shook his head. "I get the Universalists up in Danbury and the Harvard Unitarians all mixed up. They both reject the Trinity, if I'm not wrong, and believe everyone can achieve salvation. But how they differ, I can't say. Their theological distinctions are impossible to follow."

"I've heard Reverend Beecher preach in Litchfield," Eb replied. "The mistress of my boarding house makes us attend services. But I wouldn't call him 'my' Lyman Beecher, even though everyone in Litchfield admires him." Eb knew Judge Reeve thought Lyman Beecher was Litchfield's most important citizen. Rebecca too was in awe of him, and of his sprawling, accomplished family.

"Well, I suppose now that Connecticut has gotten rid of our state religion, Beecher can attend to lesser battles." Dr. Cabot was not really listening to his nephew. "I heard the other day Beecher's been advocating for the American Colonization Society." Eb's uncle looked over at Eb. "Do you know about those people? The ACS?"

"A little bit." Eb would not have known about the ACS at all were it not for Rebecca Harding. She was acquainted with Lyman Beecher's oldest daughter, Catharine, who had also been an assistant teacher at Miss Pierce's. Lyman Beecher's ideas about the 'Back to Africa' movement had flowed downstream from Catharine to Rebecca to Eb, in bits and pieces. "I don't know much," Eb admitted. "I think the idea is to send free Blacks back to Africa. They say free Black people will be much happier there. It's their homeland and all." Eb did not feel on solid ground. "At least that's what I've heard."

"Much happier?" Eb's uncle lifted an eyebrow. "Who told you that?"

"Well, that's what I heard from a friend who was talking to Lyman Beecher's daughter," Eb stammered. He had just relayed the sum of what he knew about the American Colonization Society. "I guess it makes sense. They would be among their own people in Africa and wouldn't have to worry about becoming a slave again. Or being discriminated against."

"How long do you think Black people have been here in New Haven?" His uncle needled him gently. "Do you have any idea?"

"Well, no." Eb's mother had told him about Connecticut's slaves—all the thirteen original colonies had them. At the time of the War of Independence, Connecticut had more enslaved Africans than any other state in New England. Eb also knew that slavery was being phased out in Connecticut by the Gradual Emancipation Act. Judge Reeve had covered that in a lecture. Connecticut had taken a slow approach to eradicating slavery, so as not to threaten the social order. The law had freed children born to an enslaved mother after 1784, but only after he had reached age twenty-five, or for a girl, age twenty-one. The statute had not freed the mother, father, or any other adults. There were still slaves in Connecticut, although with each passing year, fewer and fewer.

"Make a guess." His uncle nudged him again. "How long do you think Black people have been here in New Haven?"

"Maybe quite a while?" Eb's voice was tentative. His reservoir of knowledge was only inches deep.

"Connecticut has had Africans here since the mid-1600s," Dr. Cabot said patiently. "Many of them, once slaves, like the ancestors of Harriet and Anthony Potts, became emancipated. Their descendants now live as free Blacks. Esmeralda too. She and her mother were emancipated by their master's will." He peered at Eb again over the top of his newspaper. "The Dixwell Avenue area has been home to free Blacks for many generations. Some of them have been in Connecticut as long as our ancestors, the family of Mr. and Mrs. Potts, for one."

Esmeralda was tidying up the sideboard so she could eavesdrop on this conversation.

"Some of those free Blacks own homes, run businesses," Dr. Cabot continued. "They've built a life here. Some fought in the War of Independence and the War of 1812." He put down his paper, resting it on the table. "So, they might not take kindly to being forced back to Africa. They're Americans, just as you and I are." Dr. Cabot took off his glasses and closed his eyes, rubbing the bridge of his nose. "Anyhow, I'd be careful about saying how 'much happier' American free Blacks would be in Africa. The ACS claims their emigration will be voluntary, but I fear it won't be. It's a bad business, Eb, even if well-intended by some." Dr. Cabot let out a sigh. He had not meant to sound so didactic.

"I didn't know all that, Uncle." Eb's ears were red. He felt ashamed of his ignorance. "Ever since I left Savannah, I've been trying to sort out my feelings about slavery." His uncle put his glasses back on, picked up his newspaper, and hid behind it. Esmeralda remained at the sideboard, polishing the teapot over and over. "And I don't know much about free Blacks here in the North." Eb tried to recall if he had ever met one in Savannah. "But things look very different from up here, I'll say that."

Eb began to butter his third piece of toast in a distracted way, wondering if he was talking to himself. His uncle seemed absorbed in reading the paper. "Judge Reeve doesn't support the institution of slavery. He and Theodore Sedgwick represented Elizabeth Freeman in Massachusetts—Mumbet. She was one of the first slaves to win her freedom in court. Also, my friend Charles Godwin—he's from here in New Haven, his father is in shipping—well, Charles believes in outright abolition." Eb was addressing no one in particular. "I guess that's because he's a Quaker. Or his mother was, which is about the same."

"Godwin?" Dr. Cabot lowered his paper for a second and tried to recall the name. He had been listening after all. "I don't believe I know them."

"Charles is my best friend at law school. His family lives over on Church Street. We're getting together next week at The Beers Tavern." Eb reached for the jam pot and put a large glob of blackberry preserves on his piece of toast. "You know, a break from our studies. Charles has very progressive ideas about almost everything."

"The Quakers usually do. But back to the business of slavery . . ." Dr. Cabot peered at Eb through his glasses. "What about your brother John? Where does he stand on these matters?"

"I'm not sure." Eb was uncertain whether their uncle knew that John's wife had brought three slaves into their marriage.

"I believe his wife's father owns a plantation." Dr. Cabot spoke cautiously. "Eliza's father must use slaves for labor in his cotton fields."

"Yes, sir, he does."

"And John's clients? Do they also own slaves?" Uncle Ebenezer probed further. "Malinda writes that John's law practice has started to focus more on land transactions. Are his clients also elite Southern planters? Friends of Eliza's father?"

"Yes, I believe they are. It does seem likely many do own slaves." Eb tried to explain the history of the law practice. "Back in the day, our father's clients were more mercantile. He was down at the wharf all the time, doing contract work between shippers and merchants. But John's practice is moving away from all that."

"What does my sister think about all this?"

"She worries that John's becoming more embedded in the planter society. Mother doesn't approve of slavery, as you know." Eb stopped to savor his preserves and toast. "There was always a tension in our house over the issue. Mother refused to have enslaved labor.

Father didn't approve of slavery either, but he had a law practice to protect. His compromise with our mother was not to represent any clients who transported slaves or used them." Eb hesitated. "That was an easier proposition back then, before the rise of the big cotton plantations."

"I see." Dr. Cabot's forehead creased. "And your sister, Malinda?"

"Malinda doesn't approve of slavery either. But when we were growing up, we weren't permitted to say anything about it outside the house. The Wells family was already suspect because Father and Mother came from up north. And now? There's no doubt about it. If someone in the family took a public anti-slavery stance, it would hurt John's law practice."

"That's a difficult position to be in." Dr. Cabot shook his head. "I feared this might happen when John became engaged to Eliza. She's a lovely young woman, I'm sure," he added. "I hold nothing personally against her, but a marriage like that—to a woman who comes from a slave-owning family? Well, it could rip a family apart."

"It could." Eb was glum. He too had been worrying about this for the last few months. Charles frequently brought up the injustice of slavery. Recently, Charles had brought some pamphlets to Eb with anti-slavery articles by a Rhode Island Quaker named Moses Brown. Eb had read them with great interest.

"We'll talk about this some more, Eb." His uncle stood up. "But I've got to go to the clinic right now. Good luck with your studies."

The two men went their separate ways, leaving the table to be cleared by Esmeralda.

"So, that's the story." Charles Godwin was in his mother's sunny morning room in their house on Church Street. This is where Mary

Godwin took her tea after breakfast, wrote her correspondence, embroidered, and read.

Charles's father and older brothers had already left for the shipping office on New Haven's wharf. They were loading agricultural products onto a ship sailing to New York and Philadelphia. The wagons were already assembled, full of bags of wheat, flour, rye, animal feed, and some lumber—cargo packed for shipping. It was a big operation, with the lumber going into the hull first. All three men of Godwin & Sons were needed. Charles had been invited but declined. He was going to study, a dull proposition without Eb.

"This isn't good news, Charles." Charles's mother had put her embroidery down. She was wearing a plain gray morning dress, with a white linen kerchief tucked in around her neck, and a triangular olive woolen shawl around her shoulders to cut the chill in the room. A small fire was going. Both Charles and his mother faced the flames.

Mary Godwin possessed an innate elegance, a tall, slender woman with a long, delicate face, and pale, almost transparent skin. Normally of tranquil disposition, this morning Mary Godwin was distressed. Her youngest son—her only biological child—had just informed her that he wanted to court, and eventually marry, the only daughter of some portrait artist up in Litchfield. She'd had an inkling something like this had happened when Charles had announced his intention to spend the spring break in Litchfield, but Charles's news was far worse than she had imagined. Charles also wanted to give up law school and become a full-time apprentice to this girl's father—to throw away his legal career and become a common artisan.

"How old is this young woman?" Mary Godwin asked, attempting to calculate how much time they had for the romance to fizzle out.

"Eighteen. Four years younger than I am. She's just started at the Litchfield Female Academy, and she excels at drawing maps. Martha's working directly with Miss Pierce's nephew, Mr. John Brace."

Charles tried to portray Martha Lewis as a serious student—and about her maps, at least, she was serious, despite her giddy demeanor.

"And how long does she intend to study with Miss Pierce?"

"Maybe a couple of years." Charles was vague about Martha's aspirations. The couple had spent more time talking about Charles's future than Martha's. "I'm not proposing we marry right now, although I'd like to." Charles felt embarrassed but did not shy away from sharing his feelings with his mother. In the past few months, he had grown even fonder of Martha Lewis. Charles Godwin was no fool. He knew the value of a smart, beautiful woman who found humor in everything—and who adored him.

But the circumstances between Charles and Martha had altered with no input from Martha. One day, before the holiday break, without saying a word to Martha, Charles had approached Benjamin Lewis in the portrait studio about whether he could seriously court his daughter. Benjamin Lewis said he would be happy to consider Charles as a suitor for Martha, on two conditions.

First, Charles must seek—and obtain—permission from his parents in New Haven to court Martha, with the intention of marrying her. Second, Charles must never tell Martha of their conversation, nor reveal that Mr. Lewis had imposed the first condition, regardless of the outcome with his parents. If his parents refused to consent, Charles would desist from seeing Martha with no explanation. This negotiation was to remain solely between the two of them.

Benjamin Lewis was behaving like a protective father. Regarding the first condition, he wanted to avoid disapproving parents from discovering the liaison too late and intervening at the last minute. Charles came from a wealthy New Haven family, one of higher social standing than his own. Objectively, marriage to his daughter was a 'step down.' If Charles's parents prohibited the union, it was better the courtship did not proceed. Benjamin Lewis could not bear to see his darling daughter's heart broken. Even now, she would be crushed if Charles withdrew his affections.

The second condition was more complicated. Part of it was self-protective. Benjamin Lewis did not want Martha to discover that he had imposed these conditions. She would not approve of his paternal meddling. But he also wanted to keep Martha from hearing the harsh news that she had been deemed unworthy by Charles's parents. He would not have her hurt.

"I don't feel ready for matrimony at present." Charles looked sheepishly at his mother. "Not until I've developed more skill at cutting profiles."

"But aren't your legal studies going well?" Mary Godwin was unable to hide her distress. "You're doing so well and getting over your shyness too. I thought you told your father that you'd passed every one of the Saturday oral exams."

"I did," Charles admitted. "Eb and I studied for them, four or five hours a day. I went to all the lectures. It's not like my time at Yale. I'm trying harder than ever before. But my efforts pale compared to Eb's. It's no wonder he's the best student in our class."

"But we don't need you to be the best student in your class, Charles," Mary exclaimed. "Your father and I are just pleased to learn you're studying hard, passing all your exams." Charles's mother picked up her small embroidery hoop again. "The law's a good profession for a young man of your social standing."

"But you used to tell me our nation was too litigious, Mother," Charles insisted. "That if people treated each other with the respect all creatures of God deserve, we wouldn't need the law—or lawyers."

"I know I did," Mary conceded. "Those are the Quaker values I grew up with. But as a mother, I want my son to do well. I can appreciate why you might not be interested in the shipping business. Who cares about whether they load the logs on first or at the end?" She shook her head, referring to the tedious conversation at the breakfast table that morning. "But you still need to make a living."

"I would be making a living. I'd be working in the studio of Benjamin Lewis."

"That's not very lucrative," Mary Godwin said disapprovingly. "Or socially productive."

"What's not socially productive about art? People like to have miniature pictures of their loved ones around their necks, or portraits hanging on their walls. They bring pleasure." Charles looked around his mother's morning room. Not for the first time, he observed the walls were bare. Like her plainness in dress, this too was part of her Quaker background, a simplicity in décor, avoiding the representation of God's creatures. Charles crossed his long arms against his chest. "I don't see why I have to become a lawyer if I don't like it," he said with petulance. "It's my life, not yours." Charles felt acutely uncomfortable. His heart was pounding. He loved his gentle mother dearly and did not want to be at odds with her.

"Well, cutting silhouettes isn't going to afford you the lifestyle you're accustomed to." Mary looked over at Charles, stricken. "I can't imagine their cottage in Litchfield compares favorably to our home here on Church Street."

"I don't need this lifestyle," Charles insisted, waving his hand around the large, understated room, with its high ceilings, pale, yellow walls, and double-hung windows, with muntins separating the panels, six below and six above. "The Lewis cottage is warm and cozy. The family eats simply, but the food is delicious. Mrs. Lewis is a great cook. Litchfield is a thriving, prosperous town. There's a good doctor there, two of the best schools in the country, and a wonderful church. Lyman Beecher is their minister." Charles was beginning to sputter. "And the fact is I don't want to be a lawyer, Mother." This last sentence he uttered at a decibel level far louder than was appropriate for polite, morning room conversation.

"And I don't want my only son to be an artisan," Mary retorted with equal determination, although she did not raise her voice. "You will regret this decision, Charles. It won't do."

"Just like you regret having married Father?" Charles played the one card he knew might weaken his mother's opposition.

"That was totally different." Mary Godwin pulled herself up stiffly. "Now, I don't want to discuss this anymore." She looked down at her hoop and stabbed at a stalk in need of a flower. "And please don't bring up this matter with your father either." She did not look up at Charles but stared fiercely at her embroidery. "Not right now. The holidays are such a busy time. Your father's mired in work. Let's move the subject off the agenda for the time being."

Charles's mother was counting on enforced silence, the passage of time, and her own disapproval to extinguish the glowing embers of her son's ardor.

Charles left the morning room in a huff. He had been looking forward to writing Martha his daily letter, but now he did not feel like it. He had miscalculated his mother's response. She had summarily rejected Martha Lewis and turned up her nose at his apprenticeship with a fine artisan. For a hot second, Charles was relieved. He had promised Benjamin Lewis that he would not tell Martha about these conversations—with his parents, or with her father. At least now, he did not need to inform Martha that his mother had found her wanting. Martha would not be waiting for word.

That relief was short-lived. The only thing Charles Godwin wanted to do was to go to the hardware store. He needed some painting supplies.

It was a cold, gray December in Litchfield. Rebecca Harding had stayed at Miss Pierce's over the month-long break. Her great-aunt and uncle had invited her for the holidays, but she had declined.

She did not want to travel the distance to hide out in a big, old, freezing house in Hartford where she knew no one. The prospect was disheartening.

Miss Pierce had offered her a stipend for the month to stay at school. Rebecca would assist with correspondence and help supervise the hold-over students when the Pierce sisters were traveling. This time of year, many inquiries from parents needed to be answered, including questions about tuition, boarding opportunities, curriculum, transportation, and extra charges for music lessons, painting, French, and Latin. Miss Mary Pierce, Sarah Pierce's younger half-sister, would dictate the letters to Rebecca. The subject matter of the letter and the date would be entered into a logbook alphabetized by the last name of the student. That way, a record was made of what the female academy had represented.

Miss Pierce placed high value on the administration of the school. Keeping track of admissions was vital. 'Without students, the school would not exist,' Miss Pierce would say cheerfully, peering in the doorway to the administration office. She meant to egg on Rebecca and her sister who were slugging their way through mind-numbing correspondence. 'Keep up the good work,' the older Miss Pierce would add over her shoulder, as she moved on to more interesting tasks.

It was a dreary two weeks of repetitive, boring work. The female academy on North Street was locked up. Miss Pierce's house was cold and almost empty. Rebecca was lonely. Eb Wells and Charles Godwin had gone to New Haven. Martha was with her family out at the Lewis cottage, although Mrs. Lewis had invited Rebecca over for Christmas Eve—something she looked forward to. Rebecca Harding and a few disconsolate boarders of Miss Pierce's were left behind to rattle around in the large vacant house. By the middle of the month, even the Miss Pierces were gone, with only their nephew, Mr. Brace, remaining in Litchfield, nominally in charge of the school.

But at meals, it was Rebecca who sat at the head of the table with the students who could not go home for the holidays—a couple of girls from Ohio, and several others from the South. For a while, it had looked as if Katherine Montgomery would be among them, but at the last minute, another student from the South, with a cousin in Boston, had issued Katherine an invitation. Rebecca was relieved. She and Katherine had developed an edgy, uncomfortable relationship.

Rebecca was looking forward to her solitude. In the morning, she worked in the office, but during the afternoon and evening, her plan was to finish her journaling project, and study for her general exams. To qualify for the diploma, she would be assessed on geography, English grammar, American and European history, modern Europe, arithmetic, natural and moral philosophy, chemistry, logic, and rhetoric. As an assistant teacher, Rebecca was given board and a tiny room on the third floor. She also received an allotment of tallow and beeswax candles by which she was supposed to—and did—study.

But Rebecca's secret pleasure was to read a novel at night. Miss Pierce disapproved of fiction unless it had some Christian bent. Rebecca took books out from the circulating library in town, smuggling them into the house. Presently, she was reading a book called *Waverley* by an unknown British author. Her friend, Elizabeth Stafford, had sent her the book for Christmas. Miss Pierce need never know that a portion of Rebecca's study candle was devoted to reading *Waverley*. If found out, Rebecca would argue she was learning about Jacobite history. During the break, when things became dull in the office, writing the same letter to anxious parents, over and over again, Rebecca would cheer herself up with the joy of secret anticipation. When it became dark—time to retire—she would light her candle by the kitchen fire and ascend the two sets of stairs. Once ready for bed, Rebecca would crawl between the sheets and read her novel. She was no longer required to be Rebecca Harding. Warming up under two layers of woolen blankets, a hot brick at her feet, she could travel to the Scottish Highlands with Edward Waverley, into the misty mountain lair of the clan Mac-Ivor. Romance and adventure waited for them there. Reading her novel at night, snug in her bed, was the best part of her day.

But over the holiday break, Rebecca felt a sense of unease. She had endured an awkward conversation the first week of December with Miss Mary Pierce. The two were seated in the school's administrative office. Rebecca was readying the ink for the morning's correspondence when Miss Mary said amiably, "I expect you'll be lonely this month without your young man around."

"My young man?" Rebecca raised her eyebrows in surprise. She wiped her fingers on the apron she wore specially for the messy task of writing.

"Yes, that nice young man with the glasses. The one who's getting such a good reputation down at the law school. With the Southern accent." Mary scrutinized the first piece of correspondence, not looking up at Rebecca. "I hear his answers at the Saturday oral exams are outstanding. Even Judge Reeve says so."

"Eb Wells." Rebecca had been surprised when Eb excelled at law school, but she was pleased for him. "Yes, he's proving to be very talented, but I wouldn't really call him my 'young man,'" she added hastily.

"Oh?" Mary looked up at Rebecca. Like her older sister, Mary Pierce had large brown eyes. "I thought perhaps you were contemplating a courtship. I see you with him all the time, walking around town, going to church. The four of you sit in the back pew of the church each Sunday, Martha Lewis and her young man, and you and Mr. Wells, is it?" Mary put down the letter. "I just assumed this was someone you might be developing a romantic attachment to."

"Not at all." Rebecca felt her neck and ears turn red. "We're just friends, that's all. He was a little lost at first. I helped him with some study techniques."

"Well, that's good then." Mary sounded dubious. "What exactly are your plans, Rebecca, upon finishing the course?"

"I want to be a teacher like Miss Pierce," Rebecca responded with alacrity. "That's always been my ambition. To find an entry-level position in a female academy."

"You'd be an excellent teacher. I know my sister has a lot of faith in you. When you get your diploma, I'm sure she'll assist you in finding a situation." Miss Pierce was known for mentoring young women who wanted to pursue teaching careers. "But matrimony will put an end to that ambition." Mary said this softly, picking up the piece of correspondence again. "I'm certain you know that already." Rebecca made no response. "But really, Rebecca, there's nothing wrong with getting married." Mary Pierce was not finished. "Most of our young women here do marry. We educate them so they in turn can educate their children to play their role in society as responsible citizens."

"Yes, Miss Pierce." Rebecca hoped to stave off another ode to the glories of Republican motherhood.

"So," Mary Pierce continued, "I just wanted to say that if you found yourself forming a romantic attachment to this young man, or any suitable young man, your education would never go to waste." Mary smiled across the desk at Rebecca. "You'd still be a teacher, but of your own children and grandchildren."

"Yes, Miss Pierce," Rebecca repeated. She did not want to linger any more on the subject. "I appreciate your saying that, but I would rather be a teacher in a female academy."

"And is Mr. Wells aware of that, I wonder?" Mary would not let her off the hook. "That you're determined not to marry?" She shuffled around the stack of letters, not looking up at Rebecca.

"Certainly, he is," Rebecca answered, almost curtly. Mary took the hint and let the matter drop, having accomplished her mission. Picking up the first letter in the stack again, Mary Pierce started to dictate a letter, this one to a fretful mother from New Hampshire who wanted to rent the pianoforte in the parlor for her daughter to practice on. The clunky classroom piano would not do.

Later that night, after Rebecca finished her chapter of *Waverley*, she lay in her narrow bed in the dark, thinking over her conversation with Mary Pierce. Rebecca had more clarity about her own aspirations than Eb Wells's expectations. Did he want something more from her than friendship and educational guidance? She hoped not. At least she thought she hoped not. But then again, she wasn't certain of anything. That night, Rebecca Harding experienced her first bout of insomnia over Eb Wells. It would not be her last.

Letter to James Montgomery from Katherine Montgomery, Boston, December 15, 1819

Dearest James,

Thank you for your letter. You'll be home for the holidays. Sadly, for me, the distance is prohibitive. A friend from Miss Pierce's, Lucy Bailey, has invited me to Boston for the month. We're staying in her cousin's townhouse on Beacon Street, right on the Boston Common in a most fashionable neighborhood.

Boston seems much grander than Charleston. It's such a pleasure to wear a different frock every day, instead of wearing the same drab one, over and over. I'm having a new woolen coat stitched. I also bought some fur-lined boots and gloves. You simply can't fathom, my dear brother, how cold it is up north. I don't know how they stand it. Remind me to never complain of winter in Charleston again.

I'm glad your studies are going well. So, you've decided to study law? It's not too late to change directions. Father will let you stay longer at college, I feel certain. William & Mary has an excellent reputation. You need not travel to Litchfield for a better education. It's true. The Litchfield Law School produces many judges, legislators, and educators. But you're well-situated in Virginia. Honestly, you'll be more comfortable in the South. It's become clear to me, James, that people up north don't understand our ways.

You ask about my studies. I'm not disappointed in my education. A small group of us at Miss Pierce's study Latin after hours. Mr. Brace, Miss Pierce's nephew, attended Williams College. He teaches us math and science, and a course he calls 'Natural Philosophy,' in which we study mechanics, hydrostatics, pneumatics, meteorology, electricity, magnetism, even chemistry. Mr. Brace has a passion for entomology. After the break, he'll bring his bug collection to school, including two from China, supposedly quite beautiful, if such a thing can be said of a bug. Miss Pierce's is in every way superior to Madame Talvande's. Here no one makes me sing 'The Bay of Biscay O!' to the reed organ. Still, I credit Madame Talvande for my excellent French. I speak far better French than even Miss Pierce. No one up north understands the subjunctive.

Speaking of the subjunctive, you inquire about my romances. I've been attending church each week with a law student from Savannah, Thomas Bradford. His family know your Uncle James from a Beaufort connection. Thomas is a Yale graduate, tall, well-turned-out. His family has large landholdings in Georgia. In short, my dear brother, this is the young man our father has sent me to ambush. Thomas has much to offer, but I worry about his maturity. He's not a serious student and spends too much time in taverns.

Another law student also hails from Savannah, a Mr. Eb Wells. While of short stature, he is good-looking enough, on the scruffy side, but he could be cleaned up. Mr. Wells is one of the best students at the law school. If a girl were to set her cap for him, it would be for his potential, his future earnings and status. Eb Wells will become a prominent attorney, no doubt a judge someday. He has no land, nor much money, I suspect, although his brother, a Yale graduate, has a law practice in Savannah. At present, our father would not consider Mr. Wells suitable, but with the right guidance, he could go far. Finding a husband presses on me, my dear brother. I will not have Morris forced upon me.

I must go. Study hard and send my love to everyone. Happy Christmas. Give Mother a special warm hug. I'm missing you all.

Yours affectionately,

Katherine

Thomas Bradford sat at a rough wooden table across from his new friend, Richard McKenzie. A warm fire roared in the center of the room. Around the stone hearth, several dozen men were drinking and eating. The innkeeper, his wife and daughter, bustled around the smoky room, carrying tankards of ale and slabs of wood, bearing bread and cheese and slices of sausage. Thomas was cold. Even though he wore a pair of tall boots, their soles were slim, and he was trying to position his feet closer to the fire. This was Thomas's fifth visit to Bradley's Tavern in the Bantam section of the Litchfield area.

Richard McKenzie was a red-faced, beefy young man from Charleston, a fellow law student from the South who was also sitting out the holidays in Connecticut. Richard had promised Thomas that Bradley's was a better place to drink than any tavern in Litchfield. What constituted 'better' was its distance from Lyman Beecher, Judges Reeve and Gould, and Miss Pierce at the female academy— the luminaries of Litchfield who advocated temperance. Both Richard McKenzie and Thomas Bradford were fond of their drink.

"It's more than just liking my drink. I like the masculine atmosphere of the tavern," Richard said. "A place where a man can be himself. With no female academy ladies lurking outside, making you feel like a criminal for having a wee drink." Richard's face was flushed. He was already tipsy.

Thomas took a nervous look around the room. As had been true on the other evenings at Bradley's, no one else from the law school was there. His favorite tavern in Litchfield was always packed with law students. Thomas's every move might be reported back to Katherine Montgomery. She seemed to know when he crossed its threshold, even when she was in Boston. On the other hand, the risk of a Thomas Bradford sighting at Bradley's Tavern was low.

But Bradley's Tavern was far away from Litchfield. Getting home was problematic. Earlier in the evening, Thomas and Richard had hitched a ride out along the Bantam Road on a cart of hay. Now it was dark and getting late. Commercial carts back to Litchfield were going to be scarce. Both Richard and Thomas agreed—it was too far and too frigid to walk back to town.

Richard and Thomas could spend the night at Bradley's, the innkeeper told them, for a fee. He had unheated rooms upstairs. They would have to share a bed, something they had done the night before. Richard's girth had claimed most of the bed. He was also a blanket hog.

Thomas worried that his allowance for the month of December was going to run out. Lodgings cost money—and he still had to pay for his room at Mrs. Edward's. He had also discovered a New England drink called a 'Stone Fence,' a blend of hard cider and dark rum. Unfortunately, rum in New England was more expensive than in Savannah.

"Do your parents put pressure on you to marry?" Thomas wondered aloud. Richard McKenzie was a recent acquaintance. The two had been thrown together during the lonely month of December.

"No," Richard said. "I'm a lucky man. Once I'm done here, I'm going to apprentice with my uncle's law practice in Charleston. The family will introduce me to suitable young women at that time." Richard's father was a merchant, a cotton broker of good standing, although his family did not own land, except for their well-appointed house on Thomas Street. "I had to promise my mother not to fall in love with a girl from the female academy." Richard took a long swig of ale, sounding cheerful. "She wants a hand in selecting my wife. I don't mind. My mother has impeccable taste. And how about you and Miss Montgomery?"

"Ah, yes, well," Thomas stammered. "She and I go to church together each week. We've become friends."

"Perhaps more than friends?" Richard raised his eyebrows. "Not having a love life of my own, I could at least fantasize about yours." He chuckled. "Only a romance could convince me to go to church— at least while I'm out of my mother's sphere of influence."

"No, we're just friends for now. It might progress romantically," Thomas added with hesitation, "except Katherine wants me to become a more serious student. Like Oliver Hull or that Eb Wells."

"Oh, well, those fellows—Hull and Wells—they study all the time." Richard had stayed the extra hour during last week's round of oral exams to hear Eb Wells and Oliver Hull recite on the law of municipalities. Richard had laid a bet on Wells. "That's how that happens. But I'm grateful. At least Wells has a Southern accent. It's good for the likes of you and me. Judge Reeve and Judge Gould don't always take seriously law students from the South." Richard belched. "They think we're empty-headed dandies, sent here by our rich fathers to get a quick and prestigious legal education. And to marry well."

Thomas blanched. Richard had just described Thomas and his situation.

"Yes." Thomas pretended to agree, but it shocked him that any-one would consider Eb Wells in the same class of people as himself and Richard McKenzie. "Do you think that's all it takes to do well? To study all the time?"

"No." Richard thought over the question for a moment. "I knew the law as much as Wells last week, at least the basic principles. Somehow Wells has a knack for laying it out, making it all sound clear and simple. He's just more confident with the law than mere mortals like us." Richard scratched the back of his head with his ham-like hand in a gesture of rare introspection. "I suspect, although I hate to say this—after all, he's a dullard socially," Richard ventured tentatively, "but Eb Wells has talent."

"Oh." Thomas did not want to learn that even if he studied all the time, he could not surpass Eb Wells. "And Richard, how do you manage to keep up at the law school?" Richard McKenzie had arrived in Litchfield several months before Thomas. While far from being a brilliant scholar, Richard performed adequately on his oral exams—or at least well enough to squeak by. Thomas had never seen Richard frequent the law library or crack a book. Neither did Richard attend lectures. Thomas had not realized this until recently when he had started to show up for lectures himself, trying to appease Katherine Montgomery.

"Not by studying hard, that's for sure." Richard leaned forward in a conspiratorial whisper. "I have access to a full set of notes from Judge Reeve and Judge Gould's lectures from two years back. They contain every single word the judges have ever uttered. Five volumes of them. We pass them around, take turns, those of us in our study group. That's how I manage to pass—barely." Richard looked furtively around the room, worried he might have been overheard. He continued in an even lower whisper. "The author of the notes has underlined what portions showed up on the exams in the past. I just memorize those."

"Really?" Thomas's eyes were wide. The prospect of having access to a full set of lecture notes and the questions on the exams was tantalizing. He could stop going to lectures. "How might one get access to a set of those notes?"

"You've got to be in the right study group." Richard gave him a drunken smile. "And swear an oath of secrecy. Judge Gould must never know. He considers any copy of his lectures to be his property. That is, if someone has placed them in the marketplace and is making a profit off them." Richard looked at Thomas with gravity, not a demeanor he often assumed. "We could get in deep trouble if he found out."

"How does one join this study group?" This would be a way to show Katherine Montgomery that he was serious about the law, without expending much effort.

"You have to know the right person." Richard resumed his ease, giving Thomas the same inebriated smile. "And contribute some money for the use of the notes. It's a cooperative effort, although you'll never truly know the identity of your partners."

Thomas Bradford put up his hand to indicate he would like another Stone Fence, while mulling over how to ask his father for a larger allowance. Thomas could claim he was running into 'unanticipated law school expenses'—that what they had budgeted for this enterprise was not enough. Thomas looked across the table at Richard who was beginning to look quite drunk. The writing is on the wall, Thomas thought, moving a little closer to the fire. They weren't going to make it back to Litchfield tonight. Perhaps Thomas could ask the tavern keeper for a second blanket. He would be willing to pay for one, if necessary.

On a pewter platter, Esmeralda carried a note to Dr. Cabot into the dining room. A young Black man had come to the back door to deliver a message as Eb and his uncle were just finishing supper. Dr. Cabot quickly read the note while Esmeralda waited for a response. She stood by the table like an imposing statue, a red-flowered printed turban wrapped around her head. "You may tell the gentleman I'll be coming out back in a few minutes." Dr. Cabot wiped his mouth with his napkin. "And Esmeralda, please ask him if I might bring my nephew along."

Eb wondered why he was being invited, having volunteered in the clinic waiting room just that morning. He had greeted patients, taken down their names, pulled medical files, and entered new appointments in a leather book. Just think, I'm twenty-two years old, Eb had said to himself, looking around the waiting room with apprehension. These are my first poor people. At least, I think that's what they are. His brother John always referred to 'the unwashed poor,' but to Eb, the people in Dr. Cabot's waiting room looked clean enough. He watched the ruddy-cheeked mother, perched on the wooden bench with her restless boys, smoothing down their rebellious cowlicks. Two old men were sitting in the corner, comparing the pitiful state of their boot heels. One of them flashed a pair of empty gums when he smiled, but Eb was used to that, even among the affluent elderly. Eb had noticed something else with chagrin. Even these 'poor people' wore winter coats superior to his.

"Why should I go with you?" Eb asked his uncle after Esmeralda left the dining room. "Is it an emergency?"

"I doubt it, but a patient to look in on. I'd like you to come along and meet Mr. Lanson."

"Who's Mr. Lanson?"

"William Lanson. He's a free Black man here in New Haven. He operates a company over on Fleet Street. They hire out carriages and stable horses. Mr. Lanson is an important man in our city. He was responsible for extending the Long Wharf almost ten years ago, allowing large boats to dock in our port." Dr. Cabot was finishing the last of his pork chops. "Without William Lanson, New Haven couldn't have competed with other harbors, including New York. One of his drivers is waiting out back now." Esmeralda reappeared, indicating to Dr. Cabot that Eb could accompany him. "I think you'll find Lanson interesting."

Within fifteen minutes, Eb and his uncle arrived at the carriage company on Fleet Street. William Lanson was a confident, stocky Black man in his early forties, dressed in beautifully tailored gentleman's clothes—made of fabrics far finer than Eb was wearing and even finer than the garments he had ordered last week. Lanson greeted Dr. Cabot at the front door.

"I appreciate your coming so promptly, Dr. Cabot." Lanson shook Eb's hand with a firm grip. "Nice to meet you."

"What's on your mind, William?" Dr. Cabot reached into the carriage for his medical bag. "Do you have a patient for me?"

"Yes, I do." William Lanson led them through the carriage house where over a dozen elegant carriages were parked. Eb was amazed by what he saw in that dark, cavernous room. So many types of conveyances—gigs, a covered wagon, smaller wagons, hackneys, and a small fleet of shiny black carriages—all parked side by side, empty, polished, and poised for the morning's work of transportation. William Lanson waved greetings to the night watchman who was sitting by the backdoor, keeping vigil against theft and chicanery. The three men exited the carriage house, made their way stealthily across the yard in the dark, and entered the stable.

"We have a young man here. Arrived yesterday. A traveler who's under the weather," William Lanson said as they made their way to the end of the stable. Twenty or more horses were snorting contentedly after a long day's work. Eb took in the sweet smell of hay and horses at rest. Eb was deathly afraid of riding horses, but he loved to be around them—if they were tied up and stationary. Lanson called out some of the horses' names as they walked through the dark room, slapping a few gently on their backsides.

When they arrived at the end of the stable, William Lanson surprised Eb by pressing on a portion of the back wall, which pivoted and gave way. It seemed to be a secret panel. Behind it was a small room with a cot, a chair, and a small table. On the table was a Bible, a candle, a cup, and a pitcher of water. Under the cot was a chamber pot, and on the cot, huddling under a blanket, was the shape of a man.

"This is Percy," William Lanson said to Dr. Cabot. "Percy, are you awake?" He shook the shoulders of the man who opened a wary eye, peering up at the strangers from underneath the blanket. "It's all right. This is Dr. Cabot. He's come to look after you." Percy looked dubious, but Dr. Cabot did not seem to mind. He sat down on the chair and placed his medicine bag on the table.

"Good evening, Percy." Dr. Cabot reached for his tongue depressor. "This is my nephew, Eb. He's accompanying me this evening. I understand you've been traveling." Percy did not reply. To Eb, he looked like a terrified boy. "How long have you been on the road?"

"Weeks," Percy croaked in an almost inaudible whisper. "I'm not sure how long, but a long time."

"Percy came to us on a ship from New York yesterday morning," William Lanson said. "From one of our regular carriers. He's headed up north to find his mother's sister who lives in Pittsfield." Lanson shook his head. "But I'm worried about his health. I hate to send him on to Waterbury like this." Eb wanted to ask a question but decided to wait. His uncle could fill him in later. Dr. Cabot scooted the chair closer to the cot.

"Percy," Dr. Cabot said gently, "would you mind if I examined you?" Percy looked to William Lanson for reassurance, and Lanson gave him an encouraging nod. Percy slowly brought down the blanket, revealing the face of a dark-skinned, young man with a scar above his right eye. He appeared to be in his twenties. Dr. Cabot felt the area around his neck, peered into his eyes, and looked inside his mouth, pressing down on his tongue. "Would you mind sitting up and taking off your shirt? I'd like to tap your chest." Percy sat up and removed his shirt. Dr. Cabot leaned over and put his ear on Percy's chest. "If you could turn the other way," Dr. Cabot continued, "and let me listen to your breathing from the back."

Percy pulled the blanket off and did as he was instructed. Eb stared at the expanse of black skin on Percy's back and stifled a gasp. The young man's back was crisscrossed dozens of times with scars and ancient welts, a latticework of shiny, raised skin, lighter in color than the velvet smoothness of the rest of his ebony back.

"When was the last time you were whipped?" Dr. Cabot's tone was matter of fact, as if he were asking the young man when he had last eaten.

"Last summer," Percy responded in a low, rasping voice, followed by a wet cough.

"Some time ago then." Dr. Cabot leaned over again to listen to Percy breathe. "And where have you come from, young man?"

"The Carolinas." Percy did not make eye contact with Dr. Cabot.

"Near the coast?" Dr. Cabot continued his interview with quiet equanimity. Percy nodded. Dr. Cabot shifted in his seat and took another look at the young man's eyes. "And have you had any fever with this illness?"

"No, sir, I don't think so," Percy answered in a hoarse whisper. "Not this time. I'm fine. I just want to get up to Pittsfield."

"What do you think?" William Lanson was peering over Eb's shoulder. Dr. Cabot handed Percy back his shirt, and those terrible scars disappeared from view. Percy lay back down. "Is he fit for travel up north?"

"Certainly not." Dr. Cabot maneuvered the blanket up around Percy's shoulders and gave him a gentle pat. "He's not gravely ill, but if he doesn't get some rest, eat some good food, drink a lot of fluids, and stop moving around for a while, his cough may develop into Winter Fever. That could become serious."

Lanson stood silently, waiting for instructions.

"Can you keep him here for at least a week?" Dr. Cabot turned to Lanson. "He ought to stay in bed, drink hot liquids, gargle, eat three meals a day, and above all—rest. He's thoroughly depleted. If he builds up his strength, in a week or two, you can arrange his transport."

"Of course," William Lanson said. "No one else is coming this week, but you never know. Still, we've got the attic for backup."

"The attic is free? Isn't that bed right next to the chimney? It would be much better for him to be in a warm room."

"We can move him," William said. "That's easier on our housekeeper anyhow. She doesn't like to walk through the stables. She says the horses make her sneeze. That way, we won't have to listen to Anna complain all week." He smiled. "There's virtue in that."

"But I want to go to my aunt in Pittsfield," Percy croaked from the cot, his eyes filling up with tears. "Now."

"And you *will* go to Pittsfield," Dr. Cabot replied. "But not until you're feeling better. We can't have you arriving at your aunt's home on death's door." He looked down at Percy who had disappeared under the blanket once again. "How about I come back in a week's time? We'll see what wonders Mr. Lanson's housekeeper can work. She's a wonderful healer." Dr. Cabot looked over at William Lanson. "Ask Anna to have him gargle with warm water and salt every hour. Then hot tea with honey and lemon. She should also apply her plaster of sweet almond oil and syrup of violets to his chest. She knows what to do."

"Thank you, sir." Muffled sounds came from beneath the blanket.

"And when you're much better, Percy, Mr. Lanson will arrange your transport up to Waterbury." Dr. Cabot gave his arm under the blanket another reassuring pat. "You may leave New Haven either next week, or the week after."

"Yes, sir." Percy capitulated. He did not have the strength, or courage, to argue with this white doctor. His protector, William Lanson, seemed to be on his side as well.

"We'll move you up to the attic room after they've gone." William Lanson leaned over to give the young man's foot a reassuring squeeze. "You'll be warmer up there and closer at hand."

Dr. Cabot stuffed his medical supplies back into the bag. "That's it then. Percy's a strong young man. He'll be fine. But listen, you must call me immediately if he starts to run a fever. He's been laboring in the swamp miasma, and in this weakened state, we might see an attack of Ague. No need for quinine right now if there's no evidence of fever. But either way," Dr. Cabot said with emphasis, "Winter Fever or Ague—any fever at all, I want you to send word."

The three men left the secret chamber and walked quietly through the dark stable. Dr. Cabot called after William Lanson as they made their way past the sleeping horses. "Remember now, William, food, fluids, and rest for this young man. He's exhausted and ill. I don't want to hear you've got him back down here in the stables, brushing the horses," Dr. Cabot said, ribbing William Lanson. "At least not for a week."

"I'll do my best, Dr. Cabot," William called out over his shoulder, "but some men are hard to keep down." At the front of the building, before crawling back into the carriage, Dr. Cabot and Eb shook William Lanson's hand and said goodbye. Within half an hour, they were back on Elm Street, warming themselves by the fire in the library.

Eb had so many questions. Why was Mr. Lanson going to transport Percy to Waterbury if he was trying to get to Pittsfield? How had Percy gotten from the coast of the Carolinas to New Haven? Why had they made the visit in the dark of night? And what was with the hidden room at the back of the stable? Was the attic a hiding place as well? What would happen if they got caught?

More than anything, Eb needed an explanation for those scars on Percy's back—the smooth, crisscrossing latticework of raised welts. They evidenced unspeakable cruelty. Without asking, Eb already knew the answer. That night, lying in bed, he could not get the sight of those deep scars on that young man's back out of his mind.

Eb Wells had his own fitful night of sleep.

"So that's the situation." Charles looked glumly across the table from Eb. The two had met at The Beers Tavern in New Haven, at the corner of College and Chapel Streets, to catch up on their holidays. Eb was ebullient. He had been studying hard, helping out in the clinic, savoring Mrs. Potts's excellent cooking, and drinking all the tea he wanted. Charles was miserable.

Charles had just told Eb about the talk with his mother. She had rejected outright his courtship with Martha Lewis, his proposal to quit law school and become a profile artist. None of his plans had gone over well. Worse yet, he could not approach his father who was 'too busy with work.' Charles did not know what to do. He continued to write Martha daily but felt a sense of impending doom.

"I wonder if it was such a good thing Martha wasn't privy to your conversation with her father." Eb stared into his tankard of ale. Charles and Eb had traveled down from Litchfield on the same stagecoach. When Charles revealed his negotiation with Benjamin Lewis, Eb had balked. "You remember? I mentioned that on our way down from school."

"Yes, I do remember." Charles drilled his long, thin fingers on the wooden table, in no mood for Eb to be right. "I see that now, in hindsight. But I never thought my mother would react this way. Her own parents were so harsh when she wanted to marry, I thought she could be persuaded. That I could meet Mr. Lewis's conditions."

Eb gave him a sympathetic look. "But now Martha's going to know something's up." Charles looked dolefully across the table. "What am I to do? I can't now honorably court Martha. I didn't get my parents' permission, as I said I would. It doesn't seem likely my parents are going to bend." Charles let out a sigh, and his eyebrows pinched together. "And I can't tell her why I can't court her. So, how can I proceed without breaking my promises? Or hurting her feelings?" He put his elbows on the table, placing his chin in his right hand. "More to the point, I don't want to stop courting Martha. I don't want to lose her. I love Martha."

"Maybe you'll just have to tell Martha what happened." Eb was beginning to hurl himself at a solution. "Go back to Mr. Lewis. Tell him you must be released from your promises. Otherwise, you and Martha can never be together." Eb wished Rebecca Harding was there. She would know how to analyze the situation. It was clearly an issue of contract law. Charles was doubly obliged by having accepted Mr. Lewis's condition of his parents' approval as binding, and then by promising Mr. Lewis not to tell Martha that he had imposed the condition. "Mr. Lewis was motivated by love for his daughter," Eb suggested. "In his mind, he was protecting her from disappointment."

"You're right." Charles was sullen. "I don't doubt his good intentions. I think highly of Mr. Lewis. You know that. But his good intentions have deprived me of any chance of being with Martha." He gave a deep sigh. "Still, it's my own fault. I painted myself into this sorry corner with my own glib promises." It was Charles's turn to stare into his tankard of ale. "I'm going back to Litchfield early. I can't bear to be at home anymore." He shook his head. "I thought my mother would be more sympathetic."

"You know, if you do tell Martha what's happened, she's going to be frightfully angry— with both you and her father." Eb could just imagine Martha Lewis's green eyes widening with disapproval, her skin growing blotchy with feminine outrage. "Martha's not going to take kindly to being excluded from the negotiation. You know what I mean," Eb went on. "The two men in her life, going behind her back, exchanging promises about how the rest of her life is going to work out—without any input from her."

"I know." Charles groaned. "I'm sure you're right." The prospect of a furious Martha frightened him. "That too has crossed my mind."

"You may just have to tell her." Eb saw no other way.

"I can't, Eb. She'd be so hurt by my mother's rejection of her. And I did make those foolish promises to her father, under no duress." Charles slumped down in his chair. "I'm not a promise breaker. It's my Quaker upbringing, I suppose."

"Forget about any promises for a moment." Eb was crafting a hypothetical, just as Judge Reeve liked to do from the law school lectern. "Would you marry Martha Lewis—without the approval of your parents?" Eb thought he knew the answer but wanted to hear it for himself. "Assuming she forgave you for these improvident negotiations."

"I would," Charles said without hesitation. "I honor my parents and would want them to approve of my marriage, but if they didn't, I would still marry Martha." He paused. "If she'd have me."

"Then Martha would have to feel the same," Eb continued. "Remember, her father won't give his approval for you to court unless you have *your* parents' permission. That means there'd be bilateral disapproval—on both sides." Eb was thinking about going back to Elm Street and charting out all the permutations in his commonplace book. The problem of Charles and Martha's derailed courtship was just the sort of puzzle Eb liked to tackle. "So, it isn't really like your mother's situation," Eb pointed out. "In your parents' case, they only had one set of disapproving parents to appease. Your father was much older—no parents to disapprove of the marriage. No one's affection or support to lose." Eb realized he was about to enter murky waters. "The facts are different, Charles. At the time, your father already had his shipping business—a good livelihood to support a wife. And two boys who needed a mother."

"Ah yes, the problem of livelihood." Charles sank his lanky frame further down into his seat. "I'm at a loss for a profession either way. If I married Martha against her father's wishes, he'd find me unworthy of his trust—and I couldn't apprentice with him. I'd have to become a lawyer after all. But my parents would cut me off financially if I insisted on marrying Martha. So, no more law school."

"But maybe you could still apprentice in the traditional way," Eb suggested. "Like Judge Reeve did when he wanted to marry Sally Burr. He had to 'read for the law,' apprentice, start his practice—to show he could support her." Eb thought for a few seconds. William Wells had to prove his mettle in the same way. "My own father too. My Cabot grandparents wouldn't let my mother marry my father until he'd established his law practice."

"Oh, my goodness, what a disaster." Charles grabbed his head between his hands. "I hate any scenario that ends up with my being a lawyer. I know you can't imagine it, Eb, but I don't like the law. It's great that you do. You love it. You're good at it. But for me, I can only endure as much law as I need to pass my exams." Charles reached for his tankard, took a gulp, and brought it down with such a crash that ale spilled onto the table. "I don't want to be a lawyer. I want to be an artist and marry Martha Lewis."

The two young men looked across the table at each other. From their vantage point at The Beers Tavern in New Haven, in the middle of December 1819, none of Charles Godwin's dreams would ever come true.

Letter to Martha Lewis from Charles Godwin, New Haven,
December 20, 1819

My dearest Martha,

I write this letter with a heavy heart. Its contents will come as a surprise. You will be distressed. This I know. Worse yet, you will not understand my motivations. I have decided that it would be best if you and I were not to walk out with one another anymore. I do not want to mislead you or waste your precious time. While we have not embarked on a formal courtship, we had an understanding that we might do so. We had even talked of marriage.

I hereby relieve you of any commitment to me in this regard. If you feel obliged to me in any fashion, I release you from any promises, expressed or implied. That way, you may pursue someone more suitable. I am heartbroken about this, Martha, but I have no choice in the matter. I hope we may remain friends when we see each other in Litchfield. My regards to your family.

With deep affection,

Charles Godwin

Letter to Malinda Wells from Eb Wells, New Haven,
December 25, 1819

Dearest Malinda,

I wanted to say Happy Christmas. I'm missing you all today. I'm glad you all are going to Johnson Square. Don't forget to feed Monroe tidbits of meat under the table for me, and to dote upon the nieces, even if they're not well-behaved.

People up here in Connecticut don't make much fuss over

Christmas—except with food. Mrs. Potts made an amazing feast today. Turkey, hot biscuits, cranberry sauce, sweet potatoes, yellow corn, green beans, and one of her apple pies. I keep trying to get her recipe, but she's tight-lipped about her ingredients—she hints at extra cinnamon. My friend Charles Godwin claims such a pie is impossible in Savannah. Our apples are wanting. Charles is in a foul mood these days, having quarreled with his mother over law school and Martha Lewis. I don't envy him. I would hate to ever have a falling out with Mother, or with you. It would tear me apart.

I've been distilling my notes in Grandfather's library. I love these long hours studying the law. It's like wandering inside a vast, medieval structure, a castle perhaps. I wind my way down narrow hallways, leading this way and that, trying to make out what the architect planned, wondering if there was an architect at all. So far, I see no evidence of any architectural drawings—but I keep hoping.

Our Uncle Ebenezer is a wonderful person. You were right to remember him so. He has me reading Dr. Benjamin Rush, a Philadelphia physician. Rush took a scientific view of the African race, arguing they didn't differ from white people in their natural abilities. Rush was also an advocate for female education. I'll have to tell my friend Rebecca Harding about him. Uncle Ebenezer admires Dr. Rush and his ideas immensely, although I don't believe he adopts his medical practices. I wonder why I never heard of Rush. An oversight of Franklin College.

I've been working in our uncle's clinic two mornings a week. He took me recently to meet a Mr. Lanson, a prosperous free Black man here in New Haven. Lanson does very well, but others not so much. Our uncle has shown me the plight of some of the free Black people here. Their community is strong and vibrant, but their homes are more than modest. I understand better now where Mother's abolitionist views come from. Her attitudes toward slavery did not arise from the miasma of Savannah, but from her family on Elm Street.

In hindsight, Abigail Cabot was a poor candidate for transplantation to the South. Still, she had to follow our father. We both know that. (As always, censor judiciously.)

I'll write more later. Please send John thanks for the clothes and glasses. All procured and a new haircut too. Tell him the barber Mr. Grimes sends his greetings. Mr. Grimes talks of moving up to Litchfield. I'll be back at school the first week of January. It will be sad to say goodbye to everyone here on Elm Street. They've made me feel very welcome. I'm looking forward to coming back in May. I only feel sad about missing you all in Savannah on this Christmas Day. Please send all my love to Mother, Susan, Lottie, John, Eliza, the girls, and to yourself.

With love,

Your younger brother, Eb.

"You don't have to undertake this, Eb, if it makes you uncomfortable in any way." Dr. Cabot and Eb were sitting in the library on Elm Street after supper. Mr. Potts, a tall, thin, dark-skinned man with a white beard, had made a fire before leaving for home. Eb and Dr. Cabot were ensconced in the gold brocaded wingback chairs, designed to capture and retain the heat from the fire. The oil lamp had been extinguished, and the fire's flickering light lit up the bookcases on either side.

Esmeralda had brought in a tray with a porcelain tea service on it and placed it on the small table between them. She busied herself around the room, trying to make the two men more comfortable. From the cabinet, she pulled out shearling slippers for Dr. Cabot, placing them beside his chair. From the sofa in the corner, she picked up a linen pillow decorated with yellow coreopsis flowers, embroidered years ago by Eb's grandmother. Esmeralda gave out a low whistle and tossed the pillow at Eb from across the room.

Eb had just shed his shoes. He caught the pillow midair, and Esmeralda clapped her hands in approval. Now he could put the pillow under his feet. It was a bitterly cold night in late December. Even basking in the warmth of the fire, Eb shivered. How was he going to survive the rest of the Connecticut winter?

"There are risks involved. You need to be aware of that." Dr. Cabot tried to ignore the flying pillow that had whizzed past his ear. He shot Esmeralda a warning glance. She returned an irrepressible grin, her white turban glowing in the fire's light.

"Yes, I know, Uncle." That evening before supper, Dr. Cabot and Eb had made a second visit to see Percy. During his two-week stay in the attic at William Lanson's, he had fully recovered. Over protests about doctor's orders, Percy had insisted on grooming the horses. He wanted to earn his keep. That night, Dr. Cabot, William Lanson, and Eb had met him in the stable. Percy was cleaning the mud off a dappled mare's hind legs.

Percy bowed awkwardly and gave them a crooked smile. He turned out to be a slight, ebony-colored young man around Eb's age, more comfortable with the mare than with his visitors. Still, his bearing was in sharp contrast to the last time Eb had seen him. Just two weeks before, Percy had been a frightened, sick boy, cowering under a blanket. Now, standing in the dark barn, stroking the horse's sloping gray shoulder, shushing her and bidding her to stay calm, Percy seemed shy, but self-possessed and erect. He was also well-spoken.

Percy expressed his gratitude to Dr. Cabot and wanted to know when he could travel, eager to go to Pittsfield. Someone had sent word to his aunt that Percy was staying in New Haven for a couple of weeks but was expected in western Massachusetts soon. Dr. Cabot declared him fit for travel, and William Lanson had a proposal. If he were willing, Lanson would like Eb to assist on the first leg of Percy's journey.

"All I have to do is accompany Percy by stagecoach from New Haven to Waterbury?" Eb wanted to be certain he understood the mission. Esmeralda had left the room and returned, carrying a plate of warm molasses cookies which Mrs. Potts had left cooling in the kitchen before she left for home. Dr. Cabot immediately reached for a cookie. "And pretend he's my servant? I mean, my slave?"

"That's right." Dr. Cabot savored his molasses cookie. "It was Lanson's idea. Percy will sit on top of the coach with the driver. They've made other arrangements for his transport up to Pittsfield, but he needs to get to Waterbury first." Dr. Cabot had taken his shoes off too, stretching his stockinged feet close to the fire to warm his toes. "Since you've just bought a new trunk, no one will think twice if you have Percy to help you on the journey." Dr. Cabot smiled. "That's where your new haircut, well-tailored suit, and Southern accent will come in handy. People will naturally assume you own Percy." He wiggled his toes dangerously close to the fire. "Just think, you came down to New Haven a ragged law student, but now you're traveling north, looking every bit the Southern gentleman."

"I don't feel like one." Eb automatically moved his hand to push up his glasses, only to find the new gold-rimmed glasses sitting snugly on his nose. It was taking some time to shed the habit.

"No matter." Dr. Cabot stretched his hands out to warm them. "On this occasion, you're a wealthy young man from Savannah, visiting relatives in Waterbury. You shouldn't mention the law school in Litchfield. In Waterbury, you and Percy will get off the stagecoach. Lanson has arranged for a clergyman to pick you up. You'll spend the night in Waterbury with the Reverend Whitson's family. The next day, you'll don your old clothes, and the Whitsons will put you on the morning stagecoach to Litchfield—restored to the lowly status of law student. The driver will be a different one. No one will put two and two together—that the day before you had an African slave in tow, and the next morning, you don't." Dr. Cabot reached for a second cookie. "Esmeralda, tell Mrs. Potts she'll make me fat." He wiped a crumb from the corner of his mouth.

"And what about Percy?" Eb was still mystified about how these travel arrangements were made. "How will he get up to Pittsfield?"

"He'll leave the same day you arrive in Waterbury. Lanson has it arranged already. We don't need to know anything more about it. Better we don't. All you need to do is to play your part. It would help this young man out a lot." Dr. Cabot looked gravely at his nephew for a moment. "Remember, in the eyes of the law, you're smuggling another man's property. You need to understand that. There could be consequences should you be caught."

"I do understand." For the last two weeks, Eb had been haunted by the image of Percy's ruined back. The raised crisscrossing scars that formed a lattice across his torso kept appearing in his mind's eye. This image arose uninvited on the pages of his book while he studied during the day, and it invaded his dreams at night. Sometimes Eb saw blood running from the lash marks in bright red rivulets or settling more solidly into aubergine carved crevices. Sometimes Eb even imagined he heard the crack of the whip.

In Eb's mind's eye, this assault took place on the back of someone he knew, a young man his own age, a person with a name who was gentle with horses, who had a crooked smile, and a worried aunt in Pittsfield. Growing up in Savannah, within the walls of the house on East York Street, Eb had always maintained a half-hearted stance against slavery, mostly to please his mother and sister, perhaps to rebel against his father and brother. But now? Now slavery had a name, a face, a mauled back.

"I don't mind bending the law in this instance. The laws supporting slavery are morally corrupt." This Eb announced with solemnity, avoiding eye contact with Esmeralda.

"Listen, Eb." Dr. Cabot said, determined to emphasize how

serious the endeavor could be. "If you were found out, it might impact your ability to practice law."

"It might. I know." Eb was thinking of Judge Reeve. It was rumored that runaway slaves had found their way to Judge Reeve's house, looking for shelter as they traveled north. Eb was willing to take the risk if Judge Reeve was. More than that, he knew what his friend Charles Godwin would do.

Ever since his arrival in Connecticut, Eb's abolitionism had been crystallizing. Charles and Eb had engaged in long conversations in his attic room, and Charles had brought him abolitionist pamphlets to read. Besides the writings of Benjamin Rush, his uncle had lent him his copy of the narrative of Venture Smith. Eb had now spent time in New Haven near a thriving free Black community. His tailor and maybe his barber had been free Blacks, as were William Lanson, Mr. and Mrs. Potts, and Esmeralda. These were all people Eb knew, liked, and trusted.

"And you can't tell others what you've done. Not anyone up at the law school, or anywhere," Dr. Cabot said, his face serious. "It would not only put Percy at risk, but also William Lanson, Reverend Whitson, even myself." Eb was listening intently to his uncle. "That means you can't tell Malinda either—certainly not your mother." Dr. Cabot shuddered involuntarily. "If anything happened to you, or jeopardized your future, Abigail would have my head on a platter."

"Don't worry." Eb reached over for a molasses cookie. If he did not claim his share, his Uncle Ebenezer would eat them all. "My mother will never find out. No one will."

"That's good, Eb." Dr. Cabot reached down for his slippers and wedged his long stockinged feet into them. "We're all set then."

Eb closed his eyes. He wanted to relish the first bite of Mrs. Potts's molasses cookie. When it melted in his mouth, Eb could taste the butter and sugar and dark molasses dissolving into their constituent parts. Could it be Eb detected salt? This needed his full attention.

Eb was often the first to arrive for a meal in the dining room on Elm Street. In those moments of privacy, he would take a lingering look at himself in front of the round, gilded federal mirror that hung above the mahogany sideboard. The mirror was convex, a bull's eye, distorting the viewer and his environs. From the top of the mirror, an elegant golden eagle perched on her pedestal, her wings spread. She peered down on Eb. Toward the end of the visit, the observant eagle was about to mention to Eb how good-looking he was. With his new clothes, haircut, and gold-rimmed glasses, the eagle—and Eb—could hardly believe what they saw.

For years, Eb Wells had acquired a nervous habit of pushing his glasses up his nose. This happened when he was thinking too hard, perturbed, amused, or talking with animation. With his new glasses from the instrument maker in New Haven, Eb kept absentmindedly putting his hand to his face for a gentle nudge up the nose—only to find the glasses sitting squarely where they ought to be. Besides that, Eb's arms were now restrained in a brown tailored wool jacket with sleeves tapering down to a cuff that also sat squarely where it ought to be. It was a miracle how wearing clothes that fit had quieted his body down. His right arm was beginning to get used to this state of affairs. Shedding the nudging-up-the-nose habit did much to augment Eb's poise, as did his new understated sartorial elegance.

Dr. Cabot had also dragged Eb to Mr. Grimes, a Black man who was well-known for cutting the hair of many Yale students. (The choice of barber had also been dictated by John Wells who wanted his brother's haircut to be 'current.' Dr. Cabot's barber would not do.) Mr. Grimes was highly skilled and had worked a miracle, keeping Eb's auburn hair longer in the back, but releasing shorter waves on the sides and even curls on the top with judicious snipping and shaping. The overall effect was that Eb's hair no longer appeared heavy, unkempt, and straggly. Since it was shorter, he did not have to wait for his infrequent bath to wash it—he could keep it clean with soap and hot water in the basin. Eb thought his new haircut made him look more radical and daring. At least I've got a Yale haircut, Eb thought as he grinned at his reflection, if not a Yale education.

When he turned slowly sideways, to the right and to the left, in front of the gilded mirror, Eb began to see how he might present himself to the world—as a man of short stature and slight build but possessing a restrained dignity. As he ran his hands through the liberated curls on the top of his head, it dawned on Eb that he was his own man, not a shorter, inferior version of his older brother. These stolen moments of reflection, standing alone in the dim winter light of the dining room on Elm Street, did much to bolster Eb's confidence. New clothes, new hair, new glasses. "I'm really not so bad looking," he whispered to the eagle who looked down on him with approval. She bent her golden head in accord. Eb Wells was looking good.

CHAPTER 4

Winter Woes

It was a crisp, cold day. The trip to Waterbury went off without a hitch. Eb and Percy traveled alone in a rented carriage to the stagecoach station in New Haven. It was agreed that neither William Lanson nor Dr. Cabot should accompany them. Their presence might give rise to suspicion. Eb was far more nervous than Percy. Percy had to calm Eb down, talking him through what needed to be done.

"Just nod at me when the stagecoach arrives," Percy whispered into Eb's ear, hovering behind him at the station in a servile position. "Don't give me instructions. Just indicate with your eyebrows what I'm supposed to do—load the trunk and sit up on top with the driver. Be more imperious." Eb dried his damp palms on the sides of his new winter coat, wondering where Percy had learned a word like 'imperious.' "You were too polite before when we unloaded the trunk from the carriage," Percy continued. "Men who own slaves don't make polite requests. If you must speak to me, bark orders." Eb worried his pounding heart might fall out of his chest.

Nerves aside, they successfully negotiated their way onto the stagecoach, Eb inside, Percy up on top. By midday, they were met at the Waterbury station by a bewhiskered clergyman who gave Eb a hearty handshake and barked orders at Percy about where to put the trunk. Eb was relieved he no longer needed to sound imperious—a task he was ill-suited for. As soon as they arrived at Reverend Whitson's home, Percy was whisked away. Before he left, Percy gave Eb a formal bow and a lingering look of unspoken appreciation. Eb responded with his own short bow, as if to say, 'you're welcome and good luck.' Eb never saw Percy again. The next morning, after the bird-like Mrs. Whitson had plied him with hot tea, biscuits, cheese, eggs, and bacon, Eb departed by stagecoach for Litchfield, dressed in his ragged student clothes, dragging his new trunk behind him.

Eb had little time to contemplate what he had just accomplished. As soon as he arrived back at school, he was thrown into preparation for his first moot court. In recognition of their rivalry, Oliver Hull and Eb Wells were chosen to argue by the Moot Court Board, a student-run organization. As was the custom, both advocates were handed the moot court question on Tuesday afternoon after Judge Gould's lecture. They had two days to prepare their arguments. The moot was to be held on the Thursday evening of that same week. Both Oliver and Eb went into a paroxysm of preparation, spending most of their waking hours in the law school library, reading cases, and fine-tuning their arguments. Oliver was assigned the role of counsel for Farmer A. Eb was counsel for Farmer C. The problem was this:

Farmer A sold a mare to Farmer B with a disease that was not detectable by observation. Farmer A knew about the disease but did not disclose it to Farmer B. Instead, Farmer A had promised Farmer B that the mare's health was sound. The mare was healthy during Farmer B's short ownership. Farmer B then sold the horse to

Farmer C, making no promises about her health. The mare fell ill and died soon after the sale to Farmer C. Farmer C is aggrieved and sues Farmer A.

The rules of the moot court required the two advocates consult no one—their teachers, fellow law students, anyone in town, or at the female academy. They were permitted to use the law library to prepare their arguments, and nothing more. Eb was disappointed he could not talk to Rebecca Harding, who would have insight into the plight of aggrieved Farmer C. He also had not seen her since the holidays and wanted to discuss the 'Charles and Martha situation.'

More than anything, Eb needed Rebecca to calm him down. He was nervous about the moot but kept repeating Rebecca's mantra: prepare, prepare, prepare. Eb also wanted to practice his argument in front of Charles, amidst the drying herbs and preserved meats hanging from the eaves in his attic room, but he could not do that either. Charles was glad his friend had been chosen to argue in a moot court, although he wished Eb could have represented the poor dead horse. Someone ought to have taken better care of her.

Is a breach of a seller's promise actionable by a second buyer down the chain of distribution? Eb's moral sense told him that Farmer C should win. He was happy to take the high ground on behalf of the remote purchaser. Oliver Hull had the unenviable task of representing the dirty, rotten, lying cheater, Farmer A, a man who sold dying horses to innocent buyers. But Eb also understood by now that his moral sense had no bearing on what the law was or should be. Eb knew that Farmer A had made no promises to Farmer C. There were strong policy reasons for confining the operation of contracts to the parties who had entered into them. His hapless client, Farmer C, also did not know about Farmer A's representations to Farmer B. Farmer C had in no way relied upon them. Equity might not come to the rescue.

Oliver Hull would point out the nature of the goods in question. We're not talking about a man-made article here, Oliver would say, such as a stagecoach that lost a wheel on the road because Farmer A had poorly manufactured it. The 'goods' in this case was a mare— and horses are creatures of nature. They do die, sometimes for reasons having nothing to do with hidden deficiencies. Limits must be imposed on the contractual liabilities of Farmer A horse sellers. As a final refrain, Oliver Hull would sing a chorus of caveat emptor. The Farmer C purchasers ought to be more vigilant in examining the horses they were about to buy. Eb was sure to lose. And he did.

But Eb comported himself well. It was a charged environment, with more than forty law students crammed into the small wooden structure housing the classroom. Although he felt jittery, Eb did not, as Rebecca Harding had so aptly put it, 'stammer, feel woozy, and have to leave the room.' Once he started to plead his client's case, Eb forgot all about his nerves.

Eb felt a surge of outrage for the duped Farmer C. He made Farmer A out to be the man he was, a lying cheat who knowingly put a sick horse into the stream of commerce. Farmer C should not be at the mercy of such a reckless man—not when the animal's illness could not be detected upon inspection. Eb poked holes in caveat emptor by imposing a duty on sellers who have knowledge of latent defects. We ought to bend the rigid rules of privity between makers of a contract to protect innocent purchasers. Eb's argument was morally persuasive, well-structured, and imaginative—but he still lost to Oliver Hull.

Eb already knew this: the law does not like to bend its rules, particularly when those rules protect sellers profiting over duped buyers. Oliver Hull had more in his arsenal than Eb Wells. He too was well-prepared and argued his case with passion and confidence. It came as no surprise when the Moot Court Board declared Oliver Hull the victor. After the argument, Eb and Oliver shook hands. Eb congratulated his opponent, leaning over to whisper to Oliver, "I hope we'll have a rematch."

When Eb and Charles walked home to Mrs. Edwards's that night, Eb was flying higher than a kite. Elated, he could not stop talking. He had not expected to enjoy performing in the moot court. All afternoon leading up to the moot, Eb had been pacing in his attic room, full of dread. Surely, he would freeze or forget his arguments, or fall over in a faint, frothing at the mouth. But once he stood up at the front of the crowded classroom, grabbed the sides of the podium, and began to plead his case, Eb felt a rush of excitement. All eyes were upon him. He registered the murmurs of appreciation when he made a good point or waxed eloquent. Eb felt animated, committed to the plight of Farmer C.

The next day, Eb ate the midday meal with Judge Reeve. The evening before, Judge Reeve had squeezed into the back of the classroom to watch the two stars of this year's class argue. It was a chilly night in early January, but the room was warm and smelled of tobacco and wet wool, packed with young men who had laid bets on the outcome. Judge Reeve was proud of Oliver and Eb. Both were well-prepared and well-spoken. He smiled to himself. The old man had heard this moot court problem argued many times before. It always amused him how, in the murky light of a cold winter evening, the fate of a sick mare could be transformed into a tragedy of such epic proportions.

Eb grumbled to Judge Reeve over the midday meal. He would have won the moot court if Farmer C had been told about Farmer A's promise to Farmer B that the horse was sound. Or if the horse had been a stagecoach. Judge Reeve gently pointed out to Eb: those were not the facts. "That's how it is, being a lawyer." Judge Reeve clapped Eb on the shoulder. "You're stuck with the facts, and you're stuck with your client, even when both undermine you—as they often do."

Eb was disgruntled. To his mind, his only minor victory last night was how professional he had looked, all decked out in his new black wool suit. But looking good did not give him much satisfaction. He would much rather have won the argument. Besides, Oliver Hull too had returned from his holidays in Windsor, sporting a new black wool suit. Still, Eb recognized that he had argued well. He was secretly proud of that.

With moot court, Eb had little time to spend with Charles, who seemed withdrawn, making silent, cameo appearances for lectures and meals at Mrs. Edwards's. Charles told Eb about the letter he had written Martha, cutting off their relationship. Martha had responded with a stony silence. No more chatty, cheerful letters came Charles's way for the rest of the holidays. Now he was back in Litchfield, Charles was terrified of running into Martha. He hoped to postpone the encounter by pretending he was not alive. Miserable as he was, Charles was not even sure he wanted to be.

In the meantime, far away from northwest Connecticut, another event took place that would have a profound impact on the entire Wells family. The conditions in Savannah, Georgia, on the night of January 11, 1820, were perfect for a fire. No rain had fallen in the past few months, and a high northwest wind descended upon the city that night. What should have been a controllable fire, starting in a livery stable behind Mrs. Pratt's boarding house, turned into a hungry beast who devoured most of downtown Savannah.

What made the conflagration so ferocious were the two explosions of gunpowder, illegally stored at the Market Square, scattering flames in all directions. The fire raged on until two in the afternoon the next day. With high winds and exploding gunpowder, the fair city of Savannah was laid bare. By the following afternoon, over four hundred buildings had been burned to the ground. Two out of every three Savannah residents were now homeless—among them John and Eliza Wells, their two daughters, and their dog, Monroe.

"I haven't seen him at all." Martha was tearful. The new term had started up again at Miss Pierce's female academy, and Martha had moved back into the school on North Street after spending the holidays with her family. She had shared Charles's letter with Rebecca. "I heard Charles was back in town." Martha was sniffling. "What about Eb. Have you seen him?"

"I have not." It was evening, and Rebecca was already in her nightgown. Martha had been invited up to Rebecca's room for a visit—for the remainder of her candle. As was true of all the boarders' rooms, her tiny cubbyhole on the third floor was unheated. Both young women were wrapped in woolen shawls. Rebecca had adjusted her blanket to cover their legs. "Eb's been busy." Rebecca knew from the grapevine that immediately upon his return, Eb Wells had been selected to argue in a moot court. This meant he would be knee-deep in preparation and avoiding any substantive conversations. Besides, just as Charles was avoiding Martha, Rebecca was avoiding Eb.

This Rebecca did by staying inside the walls of Miss Pierce's, a strategy the frigid winter weather facilitated. January was brutally cold, the sky perpetually gray, and all the black branches of the trees were silhouetted against the sky. Autumn's colors had been sucked out of the landscape. The puddles in the muddy streets of Litchfield had turned into treacherous black ice. The sun, its light dimmed by clouds, only came out reluctantly in the middle of the day. No one was inclined to go out.

Rebecca's conversation with Miss Mary Pierce had rattled her. What was she seeking from her relationship with Eb? Rebecca was still deeply conflicted. She missed seeing Eb and talking to him, but she did not want to mislead him. It was not that Rebecca could not imagine Eb Wells as a prospective husband. She could. They got along well and had endless things to talk about. They argued amiably about philosophy, law, politics, and human nature. They shared the same values. She had grown fond of Eb's serious nature, the way he fumbled and careened into new situations. He was good-looking, and she liked the way he smelled.

Above all, Eb was kind. Rebecca's father had been a kind man. Eb's solicitude for everyone he encountered was familiar to her—and endearing. Rebecca herself did not acknowledge, or even recognize another potent source of her attraction: Eb depended on her. Rebecca was never happier than when Eb Wells was listening to her sound advice, even when it was unsolicited. It made her feel important and cherished by someone in the world. She was a woman who needed a man who needed her.

But Rebecca Harding was not in the market for a husband of any kind. She had chosen the path of teaching. Society had dictated this to be a narrow path—with room for only one dedicated spinster. But how to approach the subject with Eb—and what to say? Until she had more clarity, it seemed prudent to stay close to the fire in the library at Miss Pierce's.

"I've given your situation some thought." Rebecca shook herself from her reverie. "About Charles's letter."

"Yes?" Under her woolen shawl, Martha too was in her nightclothes and had tied her thick copper-red curls back with a red ribbon that her brother Jack had given her for Christmas. "What are you thinking?"

"That when Charles revealed to his parents his attachment to you, they weren't happy with your difference in station." Rebecca could be forthright with Martha, both being daughters of artisans. Martha would know that her friend was not looking down on her. "It's not unheard of for parents to withhold their consent, particularly wealthy ones, if they feel a match isn't advantageous."

"Does that sound like Charles Godwin to you?" Martha leaned against the wall and maneuvered Rebecca's pillow beneath her lower back. She twirled a lock of red hair around her index finger and looked over at Rebecca. "Truly?"

"No," Rebecca answered with a frown. "It doesn't. Still, we only know the Charles Godwin who goes to the Litchfield Law School, not the Charles Godwin who's the son of a wealthy New Haven shipper." Rebecca remembered her own warm relationship with her mother and father. "We don't know the strength of the bonds with his parents. Although with Charles, I suspect it's more the bond with his mother. I've never heard him talk about the father. He's much older, I believe."

"True. But I wouldn't think my Charles would care more about social status than affection. It's not an attitude I would expect from him."

"I agree. Charles is egalitarian by nature." With both arms reached up over her head, Rebecca was tightening the knot in her own dark hair. "That's probably due to his mother being a Friend," Rebecca added. "She too ought not to be judgmental about social class. You're right. The 'disapproving parents' theory doesn't make much sense, from either of them. Charles or his mother."

"I worry, Rebecca." Martha gave a sad sigh. "Do you think I did something to make Charles think less of me? I know sometimes you and Miss Pierce try to tone down my sense of humor. Even my own mother finds me trying. Sometimes I talk too loud and laugh too much. Maybe he finally got tired of me." Martha had the dejected look of a young woman scanning her deficiencies. "Maybe I'm not sufficiently refined."

"I doubt that." Rebecca gave her friend's arm a gentle squeeze. "From all I've seen, Charles loves your spontaneity and hilarity." Rebecca smiled at Martha. "For that matter, so do I. I know Miss Pierce values your high spirits as well. Don't mind our instruction, Martha." Rebecca smoothed the blanket over their legs, trying to stay warm and comfort her friend. "We teachers don't know what to do with ourselves if we aren't trying to improve someone."

"Maybe he met somebody else?" Martha ignored Rebecca's last comment. "Some woman he met at a brilliant party? Someone prettier? Better educated? An heiress from New Haven who doesn't have freckles?"

"First of all," Rebecca countered, "Charles Godwin wouldn't be caught dead at any party, brilliant or not. He won't even come to tea at Miss Pierce's, so adverse is he to social occasions. And as for the freckles," Rebecca added, "how often does Charles refer to your lovely face and your 'splash of freckles?' Isn't that what he calls them? It gets to be tiresome, how much Charles goes on and on about your beauty. How much he wants to paint you. I'd be shocked if another female face, freckle-less or not, were the reason."

"All right." Martha seemed slightly cheered to hear that Charles went on and on about her beauty. "Then I'm going back to the parental disapproval theory, even though there's something about it that's not quite right."

"You should have a conversation with Charles." Rebecca was thinking about her own situation. "Sit down with him and ask what happened. You deserve to know."

"Easier said than done. With the weather like this, what am I to do, walk over to Mrs. Edwards's boarding house, present myself at her door, and holler up the staircase for Charles?"

Rebecca had wondered the same thing about talking to Eb. The only social event scheduled this month was Miss Pierce's winter ball, hardly conducive to serious conversation. This year, as an assistant teacher, Rebecca was obliged to chaperone the younger students. This entailed her dressing up, but not dancing herself—and certainly not engaging in a tête-á-tête with one of Judge Reeve's law students. "Yes, you're right. Getting access to Charles is a problem. The winter isolates us."

"And ever since Charles came back to Litchfield with that extra trunk, he's been holed up in his room." When Charles Godwin returned from the holidays, he had brought with him a new trunk. This Martha knew from her spies who also lived at Mrs. Edwards's boarding house. It was almost impossible to bring anything new into Litchfield without the entire town speculating about it. "I wonder what Charles brought back. I doubt it's clothes." Martha considered the trunk. "Books?"

"Likely." Rebecca did not give it much thought. "It's a shame the only gathering coming up is Miss Pierce's ball. You can't really talk there."

"It doesn't matter," Martha pointed out. "Charles would never attend a ball, even if things were good between us." She looked down at the blanket with dejection, her eyes filling with tears. "But *I* will attend the ball." Martha's voice was quavering. "I want Charles Godwin to know that I'm not devastated by this. I will not be pitied, Rebecca," she said, the tears beginning to run down her cheeks. "That indignity I couldn't bear."

"And what traits might a young woman look for in a young man?" Miss Pierce was seated at the head of her dining room table, dressed in a beige linen dress, with a high white collar and matching cap, trimmed with a delicate white lace. Miss Pierce was instructing the same students who had been schooled earlier on the minutia of buttering bread. On this frigid January day, the girls were drinking hot tea and practicing polite conversation.

Miss Pierce had chosen a compelling topic. Who at their age was not interested in how to pick a good husband? She also meant to be edifying. Except for Rebecca Harding, who was going to be a teacher, marriage was the destiny of each girl around the table. Sarah Pierce knew full well that, for most of these young women, her life's partner would determine all the circumstances of her future existence. The selection of an ideal marital partner merited thoughtful consideration. Miss Pierce peered down the table at the two giddy sisters from Albany.

"Lydia, what trait would you find most important in a husband?"

Lydia shot a look of utter panic at her sister, startled to be asked the question first. "Handsome, with good legs. What I mean to say is . . ." Lydia faltered, realizing her response had been shallow and inappropriate for polite conversation, particularly with a puritanical, middle-aged spinster and the head mistress of her school.

"Pulchritude." Miss Pierce rescued her stammering student. "It's not an unfair answer, Lydia, for someone your age, although as we have discussed before, we don't mention bodily parts or functions in polite society." Miss Pierce cast her eyes around the table, looking for someone else to query.

"My mother always says not to marry a man with big ears," Martha volunteered, not heeding what Miss Pierce had just said. "She says big ears always show up in the next generation, usually on a girl child's head." Martha slipped a lock of copper hair behind her own ear to indicate she had not been the unfortunate recipient of this gift. Rebecca kicked Martha under the table. "That's what my mother says," Martha mumbled, slinking down in her seat.

"Well, then . . ." Miss Pierce did not miss a beat. "We've established that good legs and small ears are desirable traits, although we're going to resolve not to mention them. Would someone like to offer something more substantive? Katherine?"

"Ambition," Katherine replied. "It's important for a man to have ambition—to choose a profession, work hard, provide for his family—to do well." She was moving her head up and down, her blonde curls quivering on either side of her heart-shaped face, as if agreeing with herself. Katherine tapped her well-manicured nails on the mahogany. "I would value all that over handsomeness. Over pulchritude," she added, demonstrating she had been listening.

"Now that I think on it . . ." From the end of the table, Lydia reentered the conversation, seeking to rehabilitate herself with Miss Pierce. "I think 'handsome enough' would do. And I agree with Katherine. A good provider would be desirable, one lacking in vices. I wouldn't like a man who drinks too much." Lydia rolled her eyes at her sister. Their father in Albany was fond of his whiskey and often fell into a dark, murderous temper with their downtrodden mother. They were happy to be away at school.

"Ambition then, and a good provider." Miss Pierce smiled at the young women around her table. "We're coming up with a better list. Lydia has added temperance to your desire for a professional, hardworking man, Katherine. How do you feel about that?"

"Well, I agree with Lydia. I too would not have a man who drank too much. But I must confess, Miss Pierce," Katherine added, "I don't understand all the fuss over the temperance movement that Reverend Beecher is such a proponent of, and many of the other leaders here in Litchfield. Judge Reeve, for instance. Even yourself." A hush fell over the table. Challenging the temperance movement with Miss Pierce was crossing the line into dangerous territory. "In the South," Katherine continued with confidence, "everyone enjoys alcohol socially. Even a gentlewoman might sip some sherry after supper. We don't understand this puritanical attitude toward alcohol."

"Miss Harding?" Miss Pierce looked over at Rebecca. "What do you think about discussing the pros and cons of the temperance movement at the dining table?" Rebecca's eyebrows shot up. All eyes shifted from Katherine to her.

"Well . . ." Rebecca took a deep breath, fidgeting with the locket around her neck. She had been thinking about Eb Wells, how she liked the way his auburn hair curled slightly over the top of his collar. She was unclear about Miss Pierce's question, leading Rebecca into empty sentences. "We were talking about the qualities of a good husband. Lydia doesn't want a husband who drinks too much. Katherine agreed, pointing out that habits around alcohol consumption can differ. In the South, it seems more common for both men and women to drink, at least in polite society. In moderation, of course." But what question had Miss Pierce asked her? Rebecca was floundering, unnerved by being called upon, wading around in the swamp of words already spoken, trying to pull out the right ones. And failing.

"That wasn't my question, Rebecca." Miss Pierce gave her a forced smile. "I asked you whether Katherine's bringing up the pros and cons of the temperance movement was appropriate for formal dining conversation."

"Ah, yes, I see." Rebecca thought for a few seconds and ventured a more focused response. "Katherine took a leap from Lydia's desire for a husband who didn't drink too much to the subject of legislating for the abolition of alcohol. She moved from a personal preference into the political arena."

"Precisely. And what's the rule about politics at the dining table?"

"Well . . ." Rebecca seemed tentative. "I know what the rule is—politics are not appropriate for dining conversation." Miss Pierce gave an emphatic nod, the lace on her white cap trembling slightly. "But I don't believe it should be a hard and fast rule."

"Go on." Miss Pierce fixed her gaze on Rebecca. She spoke not with harshness, but with caution.

"You have to assess the situation." Rebecca was regaining her confidence. "If your hostess is a teetotaler and a committed member of the Women's Temperance Organization, it would be rude to bring the subject up." Rebecca glanced around the table. All her fellow students were staring at her with disbelief. "But if those at the table wanted to discuss an issue like temperance, with no possibility of giving offense to your hostess, or to others, the rule might be bent." There was silence in the room. Rebecca continued, undaunted. "To be more precise, another rule might come into play. A rule that would permit political debate to be entered into at the table, politely, of course, and in a dispassionate, informed fashion." Rebecca was about to end her diatribe. "So, that's my position. If the atmosphere is conducive to free debate, a civil discussion of politics ought to be permissible at the table. And if a woman jumps into the fray, she ought to know what she's talking about."

"Thank you, Rebecca." Miss Pierce chose her words carefully. "I would like all you girls to write an essay on Miss Harding's well-articulated position. You're free to have your own opinions if you support them with good arguments." Miss Pierce picked up her teacup and took her last sip of tea. "I will reveal my position to you now, so there'll be no pandering. You girls must recognize that Miss Harding is of a different generation than I. She is a modern thinker. I am not. Personally, I prefer the old-fashioned rule. No politics at the table. I see less danger in that." And with that, the older woman dismissed the class and left the room.

The midday meal at Miss Pierce's was not ready yet. The two sisters from Albany had left the table and were giggling with Martha Lewis about how shapely legs and small ears make the man. The other students were milling around the room, complaining about the essay and exchanging information on their dresses for the upcoming ball. Only Katherine and Rebecca remained seated at the table, the latter scribbling furiously in her commonplace book.

"Thank you, Miss Harding," Katherine whispered to Rebecca, "for covering my faux pas. I really hadn't thought of the temperance movement as political."

"Of course it's political." Rebecca looked surprised, momentarily pleased by Katherine's gratitude. "Any time one group of people dictates their morality to others—you've got politics." Rebecca could tell from Katherine's face—she had more to say. "Is there anything else?"

"Well, yes . . ." Katherine replied with a stammer. "I was hoping to ask you about your relationship with Mr. Wells." She looked away for a few seconds, not meeting Rebecca's gaze. Finally, Katherine blurted, "Would you say that you consider him to be your suitor?"

"Would I what?" Rebecca was stunned into silence. She looked down at her commonplace book, trying unsuccessfully to stop a blush from arising on her neck and moving up to her ears and cheeks.

"What I mean to say is . . ." Katherine Montgomery hesitated. "I've had a falling out with Mr. Bradford, and I'm interested in pursuing Mr. Eb Wells. I wouldn't do so if you considered him yours, or in any way laid a claim on him." Katherine seemed relieved that she had made her declaration.

"I lay no claim on any man," Rebecca said in a rush, looking up from her book, not certain what she intended. "Mr. Wells is a valued friend, I will grant you that, but he's a free agent." Rebecca's heart sank at saying these words, even though she knew them to be true. She closed her notebook, jamming her pencil inside its pages. "Romance isn't really in my future, Katherine." Rebecca lowered her gaze again. "I'm pursuing the teaching profession."

"Thank you." Katherine looked less fraught. "I must confess I wasn't certain about the nature of your relationship. I could tell the two of you were friendly, and that Mr. Wells has benefited greatly from your guidance. But I wasn't certain whether there were any romantic aspirations." Rebecca said nothing. Katherine continued, undaunted by her silence. "I'm ashamed to say that I underestimated Mr. Wells. Perhaps I was distracted by another. But you were able to see his potential." She said this with genuine admiration, seeming not to register Rebecca's consternation. "I give you enormous credit for that. Now that Eb's so well-turned-out and performing so brilliantly in the moot court, one of the best law students Judge Reeve has ever seen, or so I heard someone say the other day." Katherine sighed. "I too can see his potential. I believe he might be a brilliant jurist someday."

Rebecca lifted her eyes and considered her competition. Katherine Montgomery sat tall in her chair. Her body, with its ample curves, filled a snugly fitting violet dress, trimmed with expensive grosgrain ribbon of a slightly darker hue. Her blonde hair was beautifully coifed. The shape of her face lent her the look of an intelligent fox. She had a honey-coated Southern accent, impeccable manners, and a stepfather from Charleston who was a wealthy planter. Katherine Montgomery would be a prize for any man from the South.

Rebecca turned her gaze to her own reflection in the round gold federal mirror hanging above Miss Pierce's sideboard. In it, she saw the distorted image of a slight, pale, dark-haired woman of medium height, with a thin, inquisitive face, an austere bun at the nape of her neck, wearing a plain muslin dress, with little sense of style and no money to afford better, the daughter of a cabinet maker, and an orphan. What hurt Rebecca the most—Katherine Montgomery was both intelligent and well-educated. She might be a snob and a social climber, but she was no fluff-headed Southern belle. Katherine's French and Latin were better than Rebecca's. Rebecca could not even claim intellectual superiority. Why would Eb Wells *not* be thrilled to court Katherine Montgomery? And Rebecca Harding was, after all, committed to a teaching career and to having no husband at all. It would be meanspirited and unfair to hold him back.

"Don't consider me an impediment to your pursuit of Mr. Wells," Rebecca said stiffly, with a curt bow.

Miss Pierce rushed into the room, beckoning Rebecca Harding to follow her. There was an urgent need to correspond with a new teacher for next year's French instruction. Mary Pierce was in the school office awaiting her. Rebecca excused herself, leaving Katherine Montgomery at the dining room table, planning her line of attack.

*Letter to Eb Wells from Malinda Wells, Savannah,
January 14, 1820*

Dearest Eb,

You have no doubt heard from the newspapers about the disastrous fire that engulfed Savannah this week. I wanted to write to you promptly. You and Uncle Ebenezer must be so worried. We are all unharmed, although John and Eliza's house on Johnson Square went up in flames. John and Eliza, the girls, their servants, even their terrier, Monroe, were evacuated. Everyone's safe, but the house and its contents were lost. Our house was out of the fire's path. Eliza and the girls are going to her parents' townhouse in Charleston. John put them on a stagecoach today with their servants, and Monroe in his traveling case. John is staying here with us, at least for the time being, to mind the law practice and handle the insurance. All his papers were burned to ashes, but that's true of most of Savannah's businessmen and professionals.

Eb, you simply cannot imagine the destruction. The fire went from Bay to Broughton streets, and from Jefferson Street to Abercorn. Almost everything within that area was burned to the ground or stands in ruin. The United States Bank, Andrew Lowe & Company, the public markets. The entire business part of town has been destroyed. No hardware stores, no saddlers, no apothecaries, hardly any dry goods stores. We don't know how we're going to manage.

Many homes were destroyed. When I walked around the burned-out district this morning, people were rifling through the smoky remains of their homes, picking out items that could be salvaged, piling them up in the squares. John and Eliza's servants were doing the same. Eliza thought she would never find joy in excavated cast-iron skillets. All her worldly possessions were destroyed when their home on Johnson Square finally collapsed. Their furniture, their clothes, their paintings and rugs, her beloved porcelain. Eliza was in tears.

The churches, the city, as well as those merchants who were not burned out, have set up stations to feed and house the fire victims. Our council sent out emissaries to the other towns of Georgia—Augusta, Milledgeville, and Greensboro—to inform them of our suffering. Our mayor too has appealed to the other cities of these United States to inform them that our once beautiful city is standing in ruin. A terrible tragedy has befallen our beloved Savannah.

John is urging me and Mother to leave Savannah during the reconstruction. He wants us to join his family in Eliza's parents' home in Charleston. I suppose it would be lovely to spend time with the girls. The Jackson house is large, even grand. Eliza insists it would be no imposition. At present, only Eliza and the children are in the house. Mr. and Mrs. Jackson are staying out on the plantation. Besides, she says they have plenty of house slaves to tend to our every whim.

But we're both loath to go. What shall I do with myself in Charleston amidst the Southern planters of South Carolina? I'm an old maid of almost thirty whose parents were born in Connecticut—a Yankee by blood who doesn't wish to be waited on by enslaved Africans. Mother feels the same way. John insists that we must acquiesce and be silent about the slaves. I fear John is embarrassed by us, even though he says it's not true.

Mother is adamant. She doesn't want to leave our home in Savannah. Between you and me, Mother cannot abide Eliza's mother. Mrs. Jackson is a silly woman who must dominate every conversation. She likes to remind us at every turn that her daughter has married beneath her station. What's to keep her from joining us in their Charleston townhouse?

A short letter only. I knew you would have heard the news of the fire in Savannah and be worried. Please know that your sister and mother, Susan, and Lottie, are safe, as is our family home. John and his family are safe too, even though their property has been destroyed and they've had to move to Charleston.

Don't be too distressed by this news. Stay the course with Judge Reeve. Keep your nose to the grindstone, my dear Eb. Don't worry about us. Your job is to study hard and make us all proud. Mother, Lottie, and Susan send their love as well.

Much love,

Your old maid sister, Malinda

"Just like that." Thomas Bradford snapped his fingers at Richard McKenzie. It was late January, and they sat in Bradley's Tavern in Bantam, having just finished a loaf of hot bread and a hearty hunk of sharp cheddar cheese. Thomas sat slumped in his chair. "I've been summarily dismissed by Katherine Montgomery."

"What happened?" Richard queried. "Were you indiscreet in some fashion? Another woman perhaps?" A tinge of envy could be heard in his voice. He smoothed down the cowlick on the back of his head with his large hand. "How could I have missed that?"

"You missed nothing, sir," Thomas replied. "It's just that when Katherine came back from Boston, she asked someone from the law school whether I'd been frequenting the tavern in town. They said no."

"That's perfect." Richard's thick lips curled into a smile. He leaned his hefty frame back on the rear two legs of his chair. "You want her to think you're done with the drink."

"No, you haven't heard it all. This person—whoever the spy was—went on to tell Katherine that you and I spent the entire holidays out here at Bradley's." Thomas gestured around the crowded room, full of men from Litchfield and Bantam, mostly farmers and tradesmen. Thomas and Richard were the only law students there. "I don't know how anyone could have found out." Thomas shook his head. "There's no one here to spy on us."

"I imagine it's our transport back and forth on carts of hay at odd hours of the night and day." Richard glanced over at Thomas who was looking disheartened and disheveled, but still rugged. Suffering became him. "You're a tall man and cut a good figure. And I . . ." Richard patted his round stomach. "Well, I'm a man of ample proportion. We're two prosperous, good-looking men from the South. Our comings and goings would not be missed in a small town like Litchfield." Richard picked up his tankard of ale. "What else have they got to talk about?"

"I suppose." Thomas ran his fingers through his thick brown hair. "Katherine didn't give me much time to rehabilitate myself, now did she? She only told me in early November to start studying and give up carousing. Well, I've finally started studying, thanks to those volumes you've introduced me to. I just haven't had time to start on the drink." He took a long swig of his Stone Fence. "It isn't fair at all."

"Did she know that you passed the exams three weeks in a row?" Richard McKenzie and Thomas Bradford had been cramming together on Thursday and Friday evenings from the leather-bound volume of pristine notes they had paid a high price for. During their allotted hours with the volume, Thomas and Richard managed to hastily write down and memorize the most important rules. Richard insisted they only learn the underlined phrases. 'No sense in overdoing things,' Richard advised, as if more than two evenings a week of studying was dangerous to their health. "Acing the oral exams ought to count for something."

"She did know." Thomas sulked. "Katherine said my father would be pleased that I'm passing, but it didn't make up for my spending an entire month drinking in a tavern in Bantam." He shook his head. "It wasn't an entire month, just a few nights each week. What else were we to do over the dreary holidays when no one else was around?" Richard did not contradict Thomas, but the two had been spending at least four nights a week, sharing a bed upstairs at Bradley's, even through January after the lectures had started up again—not that Richard was attending.

"This is why I have difficulties with women." Richard peered into his almost empty tankard. "They're always trying to turn you into something you're not—to improve you." Richard made eye contact with the tavern keeper across the crowded room, wanting another tankard of ale. The air was smoky with tobacco, the room abuzz with men talking about politics, the weather, and the prospects for the upcoming planting season. "You're better off without Katherine Montgomery, that's what I say. Look for a woman who isn't into reform," Richard said laughing, "if there is such a creature."

"But Katherine's so lovely," Thomas moaned. "And rich. And smart."

"There're plenty of other lovely and rich young women in Litchfield." Richard made a harumphing sound. "And what good is a smart woman? If I were you, I'd look for one not so smart. Honestly, you'd spend your whole life trying to please Katherine Montgomery. I guarantee you—your efforts would never suffice. No matter what you did, or did not do, it would never be enough." Richard lifted his tankard to his friend in a salute. "A man has a right to his pleasures, Thomas." He sounded jovial, looking across the table at his dejected friend. "Isn't it better this thing with Katherine ended sooner rather than later? I'm telling you, by spring, she'd be leading you around the front yard at Miss Pierce's with a ring through your nose." Richard clanked his tankard down on the table. "Like a dumb ox."

"I suppose," Thomas conceded reluctantly, not certain such a fate was horrible. "The worst of it is. Well, I heard a rumor. At the ball last Saturday at Catlin's, Katherine spent the entire evening dancing with Eb Wells." Richard's eyebrows shot up. Thomas groaned. "I mean really, Eb Wells? It's bad enough to be dumped by Katherine Montgomery, but to be replaced by the likes of him, that ill-bred shrimp of a man, that socially inept dullard." Thomas took a long swig of his Stone Fence. "That troll." He wiped the foam from his perfectly formed mouth. "It's insulting."

"Wells has gone to a good tailor and gotten new glasses," Richard observed, showing little sensitivity to Thomas's rejection. "And let's be honest, we can say a lot of things about Eb Wells, but he's no dullard. We both heard him argue that contract case. He was every bit the match for Oliver Hull. And with his new clothes and fashionable hair, he even looks the part of a rising star." Thomas grunted. "The truth is"—Richard McKenzie lifted his index finger and shook it at Thomas—"that 'troll,' as you call him, probably has a brilliant future. I could see Katherine Montgomery being interested in him for that. Wells would be putty in her hands. She could mold and bend him to her will."

"How could such a thing have happened? His brother John Wells—well, there's a man fit for rising above his station. But Eb Wells?" Thomas was beside himself. "Why, he's shorter than Katherine. She towers over him."

"Short men can go far if they're powerful or rich." Richard was playing the devil's advocate. "Look at Napoleon. He's barely over five feet. Katherine probably figures Eb's going to be the governor of Georgia or a judge someday. She's making an investment in her future." Richard gave Thomas's shoulder an affectionate slap. "Forget Katherine Montgomery," he exhorted in a drunken drawl. "You're well rid of her. Let Eb Wells become her next project. She can torture *The Troll*."

"Listen, Richard . . ." Thomas wanted to change the subject. "I have a question for you." He leaned forward across the table like a conspirator. "Would it be worth something if I could lay my hands on a volume like the one we've been using—a book that summarizes the first three months of the law school's lectures?"

"You have access to such a volume?" Richard leaned forward too. "Only covering the first three months?"

"That's all this one volume covers right now," Thomas admitted, "but there'll be more coming. It's been compiled by a top law student—number one in his class, or perhaps number two. I was just thinking, we could rent out the first volume to some fellows from the South in next year's class. When the cycle starts up again. Be on the receiving end of the operation, if you know what I mean." Thomas considered his own scheme for a minute. "I'd have to return the volume eventually. This person will need it later on—to study for a bar exam. But in the meantime—"

"You could procure such a volume?" Richard said, interrupting. "Are you certain of its provenance? It's been compiled by someone who's gone to all the lectures, read all the cases, performed well at the oral exams?" Richard seemed to be calculating in his mind how much profit he and Thomas could make from next year's law students. He leaned even closer and whispered, "Is it *The Troll*?"

Thomas started to answer, but Richard put up his hand. "No, no, wait, don't tell me. I don't want to know who it is. Keep that to yourself. It's better I don't know." Richard smacked his lips as he put his empty tankard down on the table. "But yes, I'd be keen to share a piece of that pie. Very keen indeed."

Eb's first snowfall was a marvel. The first winter storm of 1820 began the evening after the moot court. After sunset, Eb bundled up and took a long walk down North Street through the swirling maelstrom of snow. He delighted in tasting the flakes on his tongue and watching them fall thunderously out of the dark sky. Charles Godwin would not join him. 'I'm from Connecticut,' he had rasped to Eb through a crack in his door. 'Snow's no news to me.'

The next morning, with over a foot of snow on the ground, Eb trudged to the law school through the blinding, heavy white stuff. Things improved the next day due to judicious shoveling. Each main thoroughfare in Litchfield had acquired a narrow, winding path that pedestrians were forced to follow. Law students made their way down North Street in single file. The town was silent, except for the crunching sound of boots on snow. After a few days, Eb wondered if he liked the aesthetics of snow more than mucking around in it. His feet were freezing.

On January's full moon, it was tradition, weather permitting, for two of the larger boarding houses, one of them Mrs. Edwards's, to sponsor a sleigh ride. This year, the sleigh ride was scheduled for the week after Miss Pierce's winter ball, where Eb had spent most of that evening dancing with Katherine Montgomery. Thomas Bradford had been 'dismissed' by her for too much carousing. But why Katherine had decided to pursue Eb was a mystery to him.

Eb supposed her interest was due to his new clothes and haircut. His stellar performance at moot court never dawned on him. All he could focus on was his loss to Oliver Hull. Eb did not realize how much his meteoric rise at the law school was being talked about around town—and at the female academy. Eb was also worried. Katherine was a prized flower in Miss Pierce's garden. He was flattered by her attentions, but also anxious. What was he supposed to do now? Eb had no prior romantic experience to draw upon.

But as was her wont, Katherine Montgomery took matters into her own hands. She paid a servant of Miss Pierce's to trudge through the snow with a note for Eb. In it, she wondered whether Eb would invite her to the sleigh ride. Snow was something new for them both. It would be 'fun for two Southern transplants to experience a moonlight sleigh ride together.'

Eb was relieved. All he had to do was write back and make a

reservation with Mrs. Edwards, who was pleased to see Eb foray into romance. The sleigh ride included a trip to an inn near Goshen for a late-night supper, with a promise of shepherd's pie, hot cocoa, cider, ale, and gingerbread. The sleigh would have plenty of lap robes and furs in the wooden piano box, and metal boxes containing hot coals to keep their freezing feet warm.

The sleigh ride was terrifying for Eb. It exposed him to two of his greatest fears: galloping horses and speed. From childhood on, Eb was deathly afraid of horses in motion. Now here he was, several feet away from the massive hind ends of two huge, sweating horses, plowing through the snow, wearing special snowshoes on their churning hooves, breathing heavily and snorting, steam rising from their nostrils. Eb had also assumed that the delicate 'chinking chinking' sound of the sleigh bells was designed for romantic effect. He now saw the bells were a necessary precaution. Their persistent 'chinking, chinking' was a warning for others—an alarm that a sleigh was careening toward them. The wooden sleigh's runners glided effortlessly on top of the smooth white snow, making a barely audible metallic sound, moving the sleigh along at tremendous speed.

A sleigh was not like an oncoming stagecoach, lumbering noisily along poorly maintained roads, bouncing, falling into muddy ruts, hitting rocks, lurching from side to side, the horses' hooves thundering on the ground. No one could mistake its arrival.

But a wooden sleigh was a silent, speeding menace. Eb panicked at the swooping way it glided down a rolling hill. As the horses strained to go up the next hill, his heart would start to pound. He shut his eyes and prayed he would survive the descent. Eb Wells was terrified. Katherine Montgomery was thrilled. She teased Eb for hiding under the lap robe whenever the sleigh reached the top of the hill. Martha Lewis and Oliver Hull sat across from them. They were also in high spirits, laughing and making whooping noises as the sleigh swiftly flew down into the next valley.

Eb fervently wanted to be back in his attic room, reading a book by candlelight in his narrow little bed, sharing a hot brick with Sir Winston. He wondered if he had just been born a little old man. To impress Katherine though, Eb tried to emulate Oliver's masculine, hearty laughter. But his heart was pounding, his palms clammy. Eb reckoned this might be his one and only full-moon sleigh ride.

Eb was also afraid of his proximity to Katherine Montgomery, who had boldly snuggled up against him under the lap robe. Eb had never felt the contours of a woman's body before. Katherine's was soft and curvy. This he could tell even through the layers of their thick winter clothes. He also noticed, once again, that Katherine gave off the familiar scent of gardenias that reminded him of home. Another underlying, musky odor arose from Katherine—one Eb did not recognize but was intensely attracted to.

Under the lap robe, Eb felt warmth, the lure of love and memories of Savannah, but whenever he stuck his nose out to look around, he was smacked in the face with the frigid, crystalline air of a New England winter night. In the endless blackness of the sky, the full moon shone down on the undulating expanses of glittering white snow, indifferent to the hilarity, or the fears, of the young people who rode in the wooden sleigh beneath it. There was beauty there to behold, but Eb was too fraught to see it.

Katherine acted as if their head-to-toe contact was the most natural thing in the world. Once Eb maneuvered Katherine under his arm, he calmed down, discovering that he liked their intimacy. On the way home from the raucous late supper in the tavern, Eb and Katherine, and several of the other couples, disappeared under their furs and lap robes in a pretense of escaping from the cold. Their feet were entwined around the metal boxes, filled with fresh hot coals from the tavern.

Under those coverings, Katherine Montgomery kissed Eb Wells—for that was how it happened—and Eb discovered he liked that too. Needless to say, this was Eb Wells's first kiss. He was certain that he had bumbled his way through it. But the sleigh ride home from Goshen took over an hour. This gave him time to practice. By the time they dropped the young women off at the female academy, Eb was feeling much more confident, and much more interested in Katherine Montgomery. Maybe full-moon sleigh rides were not so bad after all.

Letter to Elizabeth Stafford from Rebecca Harding, Litchfield,
February 10, 1820

Dearest Elizabeth,

Thank you for your letter and *Waverley*. I was able to spend the long, dark, frigid winter nights in the Scottish Highlands. It was my only pleasure. I'm happy to hear your holidays were bright, although I don't envy you all those cups of tea. December was rather bleak for me. Unlike your whirlwind of family gatherings, I was alone most of the time. Miss Pierce offered me a stipend to stay in Litchfield and plow through mind-numbing school correspondence with her sister. It was still better than going to Hartford. I spent Christmas Eve with Martha's family. That was lovely.

Every assistant teacher must do a stint in administration. There's so much business to running a school. This spring, Miss Pierce wants me to become skilled with the accounting. I'll help her sister pay the bills, make deposits at the bank, etc. Since I work on admissions, I'll also sit in when the Miss Pierces and Mr. Brace make up next year's budget. Someday I'll thank her for forcing administration on me, but right now, things seem dreary and dull.

I'm not surprised, Lizzie, that you dismissed Mr. Ruggles, who was demanding a litter of offspring. I confess to disappointment about the medical student. Why has he fallen by the wayside? This Mr. Townsend seems to have captured your heart, which is all well and good, assuming he doesn't break it. I worry he has no profession. Coming from a good family isn't enough. I feel certain your mother has pointed this out to you.

I wrote to you about Katherine Montgomery, the new student from Charleston. She was walking out with Thomas Bradford, a law student, also from the South, but rejected him for spending too much time in the tavern. For all her Southern belle ways, Katherine Montgomery is full of ambition that she'll someday pour into her husband's career. But there was a turn of events I could never have anticipated last fall. You remember I wrote to you about the other new law student from Savannah? Eb Wells? I was so worried he wouldn't take to the law, but I was mistaken. Eb has excelled.

Truthfully, Lizzie, when I first met him, I wondered how this awkward young man could survive the cutthroat competition at the law school. But the answer is: quite well. Eb has turned into one of Judge Reeve's best students, and he excelled last month at the moot court. With new clothes, new glasses, a good haircut, and the confidence success can bring, he's undergone a transformation. Katherine Montgomery has decided quite rightly to set her cap for him. Eb Wells will have a brilliant legal career—and Katherine's going to attach herself to a man with a brilliant career, legal or otherwise.

Here's the part I feel quite sad about. Eb Wells and I spent a great deal of time together in the fall—back before he emerged as a star. I was helping him with study habits, his arguments, and the like. It was pleasurable to be with him. We walked every day with Martha Lewis and Eb's best friend, Charles Godwin, except they truly became a romantic couple. Martha and Charles have since had a falling out—too complicated to explain at present—but the point is Eb and I were seen together so often, we gave the impression we were courting. Miss Mary Pierce asked me about 'my young man.'

Katherine herself asked whether I had staked any romantic claim on Eb before mounting her campaign to win him. I told her I hadn't.

So, I wrote to Eb Wells and broke off our alliance. I informed him that we'd inadvertently created the impression we were a couple. I needed to clarify that we were not. I released him from spending time with me so he might meet others. It seemed only fair. I didn't tell him Katherine Montgomery was waiting in the wings. He would discover that for himself soon enough. Now that Katherine has successfully snared him, she's inherited the task of improving Eb Wells. I'm done.

I can hear you chiding me, Lizzie, for taking the coward's way out. For writing a letter instead of telling him. But I was afraid if we had that conversation, I wouldn't be able to control my emotions. I find myself inexplicably sad about losing this friendship. I didn't realize how often I saved up things to tell Eb—a story, a grievance, a new idea. Now he's gone, except for the most superficial of encounters, I have no one to share them with. He doesn't seem to be missing me much. Whenever I run into him, it's always with Katherine. He looks hearty and prosperous and always greets me with warmth, but we never get to talk. Katherine keeps him on a tight leash.

Through all of this, I'm grateful for Martha Lewis. She has an ongoing flirtation with a law student named Oliver Hull, but it means nothing. Poor Martha. She's nursing a broken heart over Charles. We're like two sad old maids. I've taken to reading *Waverley* aloud to her at night. I'm enjoying it the second time around—almost more than the first. I can attend to the beauty of the words now I'm familiar with the plot.

Poor Lizzie, you must tire of all this. I've gone on too long about my troubles. Things otherwise are going well. I'm done with almost all my exams, finished the wretched journaling project, and am on schedule to get my diploma. It's time to start looking for a teaching position. I think Miss Pierce would keep me on for an extra year if necessary. I keep looking for female academies that emphasize academics over the ornamental arts, but there're few openings this year.

I wish you were here to talk things over. No one knows me as you do. In your next letter to them, please send my love to Penny and Mrs. Johnson and take care of your own gentle heart. I strongly recommend that you dismiss Mr. Townsend. I will write more later.

Yours,

Rebecca

"Charles, you should start coming to lectures again."

The two friends were up in Eb's attic room. Charles was sitting on the chair at the end of Eb's bed, stroking the orange-and-white fur of Sir Winston. Eb was at the other end of the bed, his legs crossed. It was the first week of March. The worst of the winter was over, but it was still bone-chilling cold in the room. Sir Winston shared the hot brick and helped to keep Eb's feet warm. "It's lonely studying alone, and you've missed over a month of oral exams."

"I know, I know." Charles sounded petulant. "Mrs. Edwards is on me too." Charles Godwin had stopped attending lectures at the law school in the early part of February. No one took attendance at the Litchfield Law School. Most law students were diligent, showing up at nine to take their seats on the wooden benches of the classroom. But showing up was not required. Oral exams were. "I've no interest in going," Charles said in a flat voice, "to a law lecture or anywhere else." Sir Winston shook his head, his pointed ears snapping. Charles had been petting him too aggressively. In the middle of a satisfying nap, an unsolicited petting session can be disruptive. Charles should have known that.

"When was the last time you left the boarding house?" Eb looked over at his friend. Charles looked thin and unkempt. His hair had grown greasy and long. His clothes were all rumpled. "And when was the last time you washed up and changed your clothes? Are you on the schedule for a bath?"

"I'll say to you what I said to Mrs. Edwards this morning," Charles replied with a hint of anger. "I'm a grown man and can make my own bathing schedule." Eb did not want to disagree with Charles, given his foul mood, but getting a bath at a boarding house in Litchfield when the two schools were in session was a highly regulated affair. Full baths in tin tubs in the kitchen were a rarity, and no one had his own bathing schedule. "And lots of students skip lectures," Charles added. "Thomas Bradford hardly went to any lectures last term." Charles finally took Sir Winston's hint and stopped petting him.

"Yes, but . . ." Eb searched for nonjudgmental words. "Thomas has been attending lectures these days and showing up for exams. Passing them. He's doing well. More than passably well."

"Good for Thomas." Charles changed the subject, perhaps hoping Eb's love life would divert him from needling him. "Speaking of Thomas Bradford, tell me this. How is it that Katherine Montgomery started out the year being interested in someone like Thomas Bradford, and now she's keeping company with you?" Charles looked at his friend with curiosity. "Two very different suitors. Do you see any inconsistency there?"

"Well, I don't know." Eb felt defensive, although he too was baffled by Katherine's interest in him. "She found Thomas too fond of the drink. Not a serious student." He thought for a few seconds. "Thomas and I are both from Savannah. Maybe that's the common denominator."

"But in the beginning of the year, Katherine Montgomery wouldn't give you the time of day. She wrote you off before you'd even gotten to Litchfield," Charles said, doing some needling of his own. "And now she's led you into her lair."

"I wouldn't say that." Eb bristled. "Let's just say we're spending time together. Katherine admits she underestimated me. Maybe I underestimated her too. She's intelligent, Charles. Her Latin is quite credible. She's fluent in French. Katherine's Southern belle façade is just that—a façade."

"I'll have to take your word for it." Charles did not sound convinced. "And Rebecca? Do you ever see her?"

"Just in passing. I told you about the letter she wrote—shutting me out. We run into her at Miss Pierce's, but she always scurries away, or Katherine finds some inexplicable reason why we must take off. I would love to talk to her." Eb sighed. "There are things I want to tell Rebecca—things only she would understand, but we never get to talk."

"Have you seen Martha at Miss Pierce's?" Charles sounded tentative.

"Hardly at all." Eb lied. He had seen Martha Lewis at Miss Pierce's ball in late January. She had spent most of the evening dancing with a variety of partners, including Oliver Hull. Dressed in a green taffeta gown and with her red hair piled on top of her head, she possessed a beauty Eb had not seen in her before. Eb had also been with Martha and Oliver Hull on that sleigh ride. More recently, he had seen Martha at a tea at Miss Pierce's. There too, she had been in an animated conversation, again with Oliver Hull.

"I miss her so much." Charles looked unutterably sad. The light in the room was dimming, nightfall making its presence known. The dark welcomed the confession.

"I know you do." Eb leaned over to give Charles's shoulder an awkward pat.

"I can't bear knowing I hurt her. She deserved so much better from me."

"I know you're sad," Eb said gently. "But failing at law school isn't going to make things any better. Won't you come to the lecture tomorrow morning with me?"

"No. I've work to do here." Charles lifted his long body from the chair, looking like an under-stuffed scarecrow. Over his shoulder, he said in a thin voice, "Nice to see you, Eb."

After Charles was gone, Eb lay back on his bed, adjusting his feet so as not to disturb the slumbering Sir Winston. He contemplated whether he should study for an hour or go to sleep and get up early. Eb was worried about Charles—and feeling guilty. He had lost track of his friend in the whirlwind of his own tumultuous love life, with the abrupt defection of Rebecca Harding, and the dramatic takeover by Katherine Montgomery.

Katherine had mounted her campaign to win Eb's affections with the precision of a military commander, from an intense flirtation at Miss Pierce's ball to inveigling an invitation to a sleigh ride. What had transpired beneath that woolen blanket had dazzled Eb, and Katherine Montgomery handily won her campaign. Besides, Eb had been feeling vulnerable. He was bruised by Rebecca's sudden rejection. Katherine had deftly created a pathway leading him right to her side. It took almost no effort on Eb's part to become Katherine Montgomery's 'young man.' He had been easy prey.

Eb wondered how things had turned out this way. How had he chosen the rich, calculating Southern planter's daughter, Katherine Montgomery, with her blonde curls and seductive curves, over Rebecca Harding? If this were a novel, Eb declared to himself, he would have stayed true to Rebecca. She should be the heroine, a brown-eyed, slight brunette, fierce, spirited, impoverished—a brainy orphan with integrity. In any good tale, wouldn't a true hero have chosen Rebecca? Besides, Eb and Rebecca were the same height.

But Eb Wells was the first to admit he was not a hero, true or not. He was just a young man who had been short all his life, who had lived under the shadow of a stellar older brother, who had disappointed his father by not being Yale material, who had worn glasses that would not stay on his nose for most of his twenty-two years. After an undistinguished youth and adolescence, Eb finally excelled at something. He had a promising future in the law. His new clothes looked good on him. His hair was waving at the sides, making him look more radical and daring. His glasses were staying up on his nose. Eb had become something he had never dreamed of before— admired. And a beautiful, rich woman was pursuing him. It should not go without saying: Katherine Montgomery was as beautiful and rich as Eliza Jackson Wells, his brother's wife—perhaps even more so. Being admired and the object of feminine pursuit is heady stuff for any young man.

But the truth was, Eb Wells had no choice in the matter. Katherine may have created a pathway for him to pursue her, but Rebecca had put up a stone wall. Eb sensed a conspiracy between them. The timing of Rebecca's letter, banishing him from her company, and Katherine's offensive, presented a suspicious concatenation of events. Eb felt like a pawn but was clueless about the nature of their game. Perhaps he should have probed Charles Godwin's suspicions further, but he had no wish to do so.

Eb yawned and leaned over to extinguish the candle. He slid his feet under the blankets, cautiously maneuvering them around the slumbering cat so he could saddle them up to the sides of the hot brick. Sir Winston lifted his head from the bed and gave Eb a silent greeting. Eb would study in the morning.

Letter to James Montgomery from Katherine Montgomery, Litchfield, March 5, 1820

Dearest James,

Thank you for your last letter. I'm glad to hear you are on the mend. Sickness abounds here too. Everyone at Miss Pierce's is hacking away. Most of the girls carry multiple handkerchiefs to get through the day. I remain in robust health. I know our summers in the South are unhealthy, but nothing could have prepared me for winter in Connecticut. There are rumors that spring is on the way, but I see no sign of it. I find the month of March tumultuous and gray, full of rain and biting winds. Honestly, James, why anyone would choose to live in such a climate is a mystery to me.

My studies go well. I finished my tome on geography. You'll be amused to learn that I am helping the young man I'm seeing, Eb Wells, prepare for his oral exams. Eb claims I have a good mind for the law, for a woman that is. He's always the best in his class, although some claim another young man from Windsor is better. Eb doesn't need to be prodded to study. Still, he fritters away his time. Sometimes he takes my advice and allows me to drill him for his exams. But about how he spends his time—Eb is unyielding. We argue too much, due to his stubborn nature. I suppose that's part of being in a courtship, or a marriage for that matter. His future as a jurist is assured, I promise you that. Eb Wells has talent, works hard, and is gaining a sizable reputation. He just needs guidance.

You think I'm too young to worry about finding a husband, but you're wrong. As you know, the quid pro quo for my coming to Miss Pierce's was finding a suitable match. If I fail, my future is with Morris. I hate to be so frank, my dearest James, but if I'm forced to marry a stepbrother, I would much rather it be you. Things might not work out up here. Just be forewarned. Someday in the future, you may have to step forward and rescue me. My happiness will be at stake. No matter what, I cannot become Morris's wife.

I must go prepare for the geography grilling. Father is foolhardy to insist you go to Isle Pines this summer. Working for a Williamsburg attorney over the break would be more advantageous. You'll acquire new legal skills and make valuable connections. I'll write to him. Father doesn't understand how lawyers are trained, or how they make their reputations. I, on the other hand, am developing some expertise.

Please take care of your health, James.

All my love,

Katherine

"I don't understand why this book is so important." Eb and Katherine were walking briskly under the canopy of oak trees that lined both sides of North Street. The couple was heading for the law school on South Street where the Saturday oral exam would soon begin.

It was late March. Winter was on the wane, but the sky was still a pewter gray. The earth had warmed up enough to make the ground damp, like a wet sponge, but the wind chilled the bones. Eb still wore his winter coat, but Katherine was wrapped in a light, rust-colored cape that came down to her knees. She had a weakness for outerwear, with an ample wardrobe to choose from. This garment was not warm enough, but her blonde hair looked luxurious against the burned orange of the cape. She shivered. Vanity had prevailed.

Katherine was not permitted to attend the oral exams but liked to accompany Eb to the law school before he performed. "Let's forget about the book for now. Why don't you focus on the difference between a fee simple determinable and a fee simple subject to complete divestment?" In their almost three months together, Katherine had taken to helping Eb study. Unlike Rebecca Harding, who gave global advice from afar on how to achieve mastery of any subject, Katherine sank herself down into the legal material itself. With Eb.

Eb did not like the way Katherine settled in, making herself comfortable, right in the middle of his study. He enjoyed sharing the law with Charles. But Katherine had no patience for outside critiques or intriguing tangential wanderings. Instead, Katherine immersed herself in the technical aspects of the material, nailing the details into his skull with a sharp tap, tap, tap of a tack hammer. Her discipline and martinet manner sucked all the joy out of the law.

"It's all right, Katherine," Eb panted. "I feel ready on that one. Even on the notice provisions." He had anticipated her next question. "I'm just so worried about my first volume. It has all the material we've covered since the very beginning, starting with the Law of Baron and Femme all the way to Inns and Innkeepers." Eb was trying valiantly to keep up with Katherine, whose arm was loosely linked in his. She was one step ahead, her legs being longer than Eb's. "Three months of work and study. All gone."

"Well, you aren't covering the Law of Baron and Femme right now, are you?" Her question was rhetorical. "You've already passed that exam. Focus on what's before you this morning. You can look for the book later."

"But I've already looked everywhere," Eb pleaded. "That's what I'm trying to tell you. I've looked high and low. It's missing."

"Where do you normally keep it?" Katherine snapped, giving Eb a sharp look. She took part in the drama of the Saturday oral exam as if she herself were taking it. The couple crossed the intersection of North and South Street, a jagged conjunction, to accommodate the presence of a monumental old tree that no one had the heart to cut down—until it fell over.

"I keep the volume on, well . . ." Eb stammered. "I brought it back from New Haven after the holidays and put it on my bookcase." Eb did not want to confess to Katherine that he lacked a bookcase, or that he had ceremoniously placed his *Volume I-Litchfield Law School Notes* on the windowsill. There he could gaze at the leather-bound book from his bed as a reminder of his hard work. "But when I went to look something up last night, it wasn't there." Eb tried to slow Katherine down by lessening his pace. He felt the impatient pressure of her arm, tugging him across the Green toward South Street.

"Could you have put it in one of your trunks?" Katherine asked off-handedly. "Maybe under the bed?" They passed the grocery store on the edge of the Green, where the proprietor was rearranging some of last fall's apples in a tray. Katherine returned the grocer's warm smile with a preemptory bend of her head, a gesture of noblesse oblige. Eb gave him a friendly, distracted wave.

"Yes, I thought maybe I'd put it away. It's not the law we're covering now." Though still holding on to her arm, Eb continued in Katherine Montgomery's wake. "But it's not there."

"I thought you told me Judge Reeve and Judge Gould mostly recite the law from William Blackstone." The law school was in sight. Eb's fellow law students were standing around outside on South Street, some hunched over their crib sheets, trying to pack in a rule or a definition at the last minute. Others were huddling together in small groups, bragging about how hard they had studied, or more likely, lying about how they had hardly studied at all. "Isn't that what you said? They lecture right out of *Blackstone*?"

"Yes, they do." Eb was relieved the dash to the law school was over. "But my volume has the legal principles written out in my own hand, with all my research from the cases, and answers to any questions that were, or could have been asked, on a Saturday exam."

Eb pulled Katherine to a stop, short of breath. Eb's throat felt tight as if he were close to crying. It had taken him a full month in

New Haven to complete that volume. "The missing book has every-thing in it that I studied or learned in my first three months at law school. I'll need it later to study for a bar exam."

When Katherine heard Eb utter the words 'bar exam,' he finally got her attention. Passing an oral bar exam was a hurdle to be jumped over in Eb's future, giving the lost volume relevance to his career—and to Katherine. "I am sorry, Eb." Katherine pulled Eb toward her, looking down into his flushed face. "I can see you're upset." They were no longer pressed for time, having arrived early for the exam. "I'm sorry. Really, I am." She gave his arm an encouraging squeeze, positioning her ruby lips into a pout. "But you need to gather your-self for today's exam." Her voice swooped down low into a seductive croon, emphasizing her Southern charm. "We can deal with the lost volume later."

"Yes, yes, of course." Whenever Katherine laid on her thick Charleston accent, Eb was a goner. "But I don't want to drill the estates in land right now." He had regained his composure. "I know them."

"Maybe I could find a way to finance a set of *Blackstone* for you." Katherine had a scheming look on her vulpine face. "Then you wouldn't need to copy anything down in your miserable little books."

Katherine Montgomery never understood Eb's compulsion to write everything down. Eb kept three commonplace books in his law study set, one for lecture notes, another for rewritten lecture notes plus cases and comments, and a finalized, leather-bound third tier of formal condensation. But his fourth commonplace book infuriated Katherine. Eb continued to carry around his beloved *The Detritus* in his coat pocket.

Over the years, there had been an endless succession of *The Detritus*, the most recent iteration started in Litchfield. As in his youth, Eb wrote into *The Detritus* poems, random ideas, quotations he liked, and clumsy sketches of Connecticut flowers he cut out and sent to his sister Malinda. Once he began his law studies, Eb instituted a new rule for *The Detritus*—the entries must have nothing whatsoever to do with the law.

What was the value, Katherine complained bitterly to Eb, of a commonplace book dedicated to anything but the law? The law was going to be Eb's life. In her opinion, this was a bad habit that needed to be broken. *The Detritus* was a waste of Eb's time and paper. Katherine was familiar with the compulsion. Her stepbrother James was also hopelessly attached to his commonplace books. In their schoolroom in Charleston, she used to make merciless fun of him.

Katherine herself had an elegant hand, thanks to her two summers with Mr. Mitchell. She took great pride in her writing—so few women could write. At Miss Pierce's as well, writing essays was forced upon her. She was soon to be tested on over thirty pages of geography she had copied verbatim from a text. Katherine also wrote letters. For her, writing should be instrumental, to achieve a task that must be done. But to write things down just for the sake of writing things down, as Eb did, without anyone forcing him to—or anyone else reading them? Katherine did not approve of *The Detritus*. Such a commonplace book, full of Eb's own musings, was foreign to her. And when Katherine Montgomery did not understand something, she had disdain for it—ridiculed it.

Katherine looked down at Eb as they stood in front of the law school on South Street, waiting for the oral exam to begin. "I could always ask my stepfather to purchase a set of *Blackstone* for you." She reached over and stroked his cheek. "That way, you wouldn't even need the volume that's missing."

"Thanks for the offer, Katherine, but buying *Blackstone* won't address the harm." At some time in the future, Eb would purchase a set of *Blackstone*, but it would never replace his own leather-bound books of handwritten law. "I know you mean well." Eb returned Katherine's squeeze, but his heart was heavy. "But this is something you can't fix." Saying goodbye, he went into the law school to take the exam, still distressed about the volume's disappearance.

Eb also felt disquieted. He could not quite put his finger on what was bothering him. It was not just the loss of *Volume I*. It was more that Katherine could not understand what the loss of *Volume I* meant to him. Eb thought gloomily that Rebecca Harding would have understood his despair. Here he was instead, with Katherine Montgomery—by some inexplicable twist of fate he had played no part in—and Rebecca's presence was denied to him. But this feeling of disquiet was fleeting, flushed out by the customary jitters that descended upon him right before an exam.

Eb did well. He enjoyed the section on estates in land and wondered if this was the kind of law his brother practiced. When Eb emerged from the law school a few hours later, the sun had come out. Katherine was waiting for him on a bench in Mrs. Reeve's garden, her golden hair lit up by the pale watery light of the blustery March day. She waved and gave Eb a big smile. Eb waved back. He relished the idea that the other law students pouring out of the law school building would see Katherine—the most beautiful student at Miss Pierce's school—waiting for him on the bench. They would see her waving and smiling. Just at him.

"How was the exam?" Katherine made room for Eb on the bench, gathering up the rust-colored folds of her cape, her full lips curled into a smile. She gave him a flirtatious sidelong glance. "Did you do brilliantly?"

"I'm so worried about him," Martha Lewis explained to Mrs. Edwards. They sat at the large kitchen table in her boarding house. Mrs. Edwards was bent over the bread box, pulling out a loaf wrapped in white muslin. Martha Lewis had just marched over to Mrs. Edwards's, demanding to see Charles Godwin. The older woman looked at her distraught young visitor, trying to decide what to do. She had a strict rule about not letting anyone intrude on her boarders, but she was worried about Charles Godwin too. He had been skipping lectures and missing meals—and had not come down for breakfast.

"I've just heard Charles hasn't been leaving the house at all," Martha said breathlessly. "Eb Wells came over to tell me." Martha tried to take a sip of the tea Mrs. Edwards had poured her. "You know who I am? Martha Lewis? Charles and I were walking out together last term, but then he broke it off."

"Yes, yes, of course. I recognize you." Mrs. Edwards cut off a slice of bread for her. Martha looked pale and undernourished herself. "I used to see the two of you together walking on the Green all the time." Mrs. Edwards did not want to let on how much she already knew. Eb Wells had told her about Charles's situation. It was awkward for poor Mrs. Edwards—to know all the plot lines of the story, and now be sitting in her kitchen, drinking tea with a protagonist who remained in the dark. This was the plight of many older women who received the confessions of the young, often burdened with more of a story than they deserved to be privy to. "I was so sorry to hear you had a falling out," Mrs. Edwards said tactfully. "Charles seemed so happy when he was seeing you."

"We were both happy." Martha looked like a sad lioness, her eyes about to fill with tears. She had practiced for months trying not to cry when talking about Charles Godwin, and she had succeeded for the most part, except with Rebecca. Perhaps Mrs. Edwards's kindness had set her off. "But I really need to know if he's all right." Martha fought back her tears. "Eb tells me he's not well."

Eb Wells had sought her out that morning at Miss Pierce's to tell Martha about the decline in Charles's health. Charles had stopped going to lectures and almost never left his room. He had grown thin, withdrawn, depleted. Martha ought to know the state he was in.

Charles would be angry with him for interfering, Eb knew, but he did not care, alarmed by how poorly Charles was doing.

"Do you think we could check on him?" Martha wiped away a tear and looked directly into the kind old woman's face.

"Well . . ." Mrs. Edwards considered how she should respond. She had meant to ask her servant, Maggie, to knock on his door and offer Charles a tray of food. "Perhaps we ought to both go up and see how he's doing. It's an exception to my rules," Mrs. Edwards said, wanting to make sure Martha understood. "But I too have concern." Martha took a last bite of bread and swig of her tea. The two women went up the stairs, and Mrs. Edwards knocked softly on Charles's door.

"Who is it?" Charles called out, his voice weak.

"Just me, Mrs. Edwards," she replied, quickly adding, "and a visitor. May we come in?" Employing a trick perfected when her own daughters were young, Mrs. Edwards asked for permission at the precise moment she turned the doorknob and pushed open the door. "Oh, my dear," she exclaimed. Charles was lying on the bed, his pallor pasty and white, with beads of sweat glistening on his forehead. "Are you unwell, Charles? Let me look at you." Mrs. Edwards called out over her shoulder. "Martha, go back down to the kitchen and ask Maggie to fetch the doctor. And don't come back up to this room. Not now. I fear Charles is quite ill. We must take care not to expose you." Mrs. Edwards had dealt with ailing students in her boarding house before and had a protocol for preventing contagion.

"Martha?" At the mention of Martha, Charles looked up from the bed, his glassy eyes sunken into his head. "Is Martha here?" he asked feebly, trying to sit up.

"Hush now, Charles," Mrs. Edwards said. "There's plenty of time for you to see Martha. I've called for the doctor. How long have you been like this?"

"Since last night," Charles croaked. "The fever came on me

suddenly. I felt too wretched to come down for breakfast. And I didn't want to make anyone else ill." Mrs. Edwards put her hand on Charles's forehead. He was burning up.

"Maggie will come up and give you a sponge bath. Then I'll change your sheets and get you fresh nightclothes. Once the doctor has come, we're going to have to quarantine you." She laid her hand gently on Charles's arm. "Is there some place in your body where you're feeling pain?"

"No, I just hurt all over, every bone in my body. Even my hair hurts." Charles shook his head, his teeth chattering. "I'm so sorry to be such a bother," he murmured, looking toward the door. "Did you say Martha was here?" Charles tried to sit up again, but could not muster the strength, falling back onto the bed.

"I would say Martha's always here with you, Charles." Mrs. Edwards's voice was full of wonder. She had fallen under a spell. She was staring at a canvas perched on an easel that stood in the corner of the room. With the morning sun's rays pouring through the wobbly glass of the window, the painting was lit up from the side. It was an oil painting, a portrait of a young woman in a green dress, with green eyes to match, her thick coppery red hair piled up on her head, a delicate spray of freckles across her cheeks. She wore an enigmatic smile with an undertone of impishness, as if she were about to tell you a funny story you might not understand. "Did you do that painting?" Mrs. Edwards spoke in a low, reverential voice, staring at the very likeness of Martha Lewis. "It's wonderful. Quite remarkable."

"Yes." Charles gave the kind old woman a weak smile. "Thank you, Mrs. Edwards," he whispered, closing his eyes. "It's my Martha."

"I can see that, Charles, the very likeness." Mrs. Edwards stroked the young man's hot hand. "But you rest now. Before the doctor comes, we'll get you all cleaned up, and I'll bring you some chicken broth." But Charles did not answer. He had fallen back into a feverish sleep.

In his delirium, Charles dreamed of an angel—one who looked and sounded just like Martha Lewis except for a pair of shimmering emerald wings that sprouted from her shoulders. The angel had stood on the threshold of his room. She had been sent to check on him, only to discover he was ill. The angel had left in a whoosh and gone to get help. He hoped that he might live long enough to see her face again—and perhaps to stroke her shiny green wings.

Letter to Eb Wells from John Wells, Savannah,
March 31, 1820

Dear Eb,

I hope this letter finds you well. As you are aware, I let Malinda manage the family correspondence. I'm quite busy, and you both write such good letters. I hear you are excelling in your studies. It surprises me that you should have taken to the law. I was happy to hear you had a good first moot. Don't be too disappointed you didn't win. I didn't win my first moot either. The law is weighted toward the side supporting the status quo. The important thing is to perform well, make a good argument. Be forceful in your position.

Eb, I want to share with you some decisions I have made. I have decided not to rebuild the house on Johnson Square here in Savannah. After I sell the lot, I intend to use the insurance money to purchase a house in Charleston and make a law office on the first floor there. Eliza has been happy enough in Savannah, but the girls are getting closer to school age. Eliza is looking now for a female academy in Charleston that excels in French. She's considering Madame Talvande's. I believe the young woman you are courting, Miss Montgomery, attended the school. Her family is well-spoken of in Charleston, Eliza tells me. An alliance with the Montgomery family would bring our law practice many favorable connections.

The fire has affected Eliza greatly. She experiences life with more timidity than in the past and wants to be closer to her family. It's understandable. The insurance will make us whole, but we'll need to build up from scratch again. These decisions have an impact on you too, should you come, as planned, to do your apprenticeship with me. Our family law practice, and our home, will be in Charleston by the time you finish law school, not in Savannah.

If we were to retain our merchant and shipping clients, Savannah would be the place to be. With the steamboats now coming down the Savannah River, Savannah's port begins to eclipse that of Charleston. But our practice has shifted to land law. Charleston has a larger base of wealth, with more landed gentry. South Carolina produces more cotton than any other state. Charleston offers more educational opportunities for our children. I include in that the children I hope you will have someday. The advantages of the move are many.

I am asking you to persuade Mother and Malinda to move to Charleston with us. You hold more sway with them than I do. Mother has dug in her heels. She flatly refuses to budge. But Savannah is no place at present for two women to be living alone. The city lies in ruins. When it rains here in Savannah, huge pools of water accumulate in the rubble, creating our own urban miasma. They're predicting it will be a bad summer for cholera, malaria, and yellow fever. Indigent people are begging in the streets. Last year, the city was flooded with impoverished Irish immigrants. Savannah doesn't feel safe.

Malinda is just as stubborn, insisting she can't leave Savannah's live oaks and Spanish moss—untenable reasons, in my opinion. I suspect they worry that Eliza's family is served by African slaves. But that was also true of our home in Savannah. Their anti-slavery stance is not sustainable here. Our economy is cotton-based and dependent on slave labor. State and federal laws uphold the institution. I know you admire Judge Reeve and Reverend Beecher, but their abolition-ist leanings are naïve. They're unfamiliar with our Southern ways.

I am greatly unsettled by Mother and Malinda's refusal to move. But these are the facts, Eb. I am moving my family and our law practice to Charleston. Mother and Malinda cannot stay here alone in Savannah. Susan too is invited as Malinda's companion. Lottie would stay behind and watch over the house on East York Street, perhaps take in boarders. She is the only one in favor of the plan.

You and I are the adult men of the family now. The Wells women must do our bidding, but I can't bring myself to force them—and am at a loss to persuade them. I'm counting on you, Eb, to use your newfound skills of advocacy. I'm all out of arguments.

I thank you in anticipation of your cooperation. Study hard.
Your brother,

John Wells

CHAPTER 5

Liberating the Daffodils

"It's a difficult year to find a teaching job." Miss Sarah Pierce poured Rebecca Harding tea from a porcelain pot. The older woman and her mentee sat alone in the administrative office of the Litchfield Female Academy, Mary Pierce having gone down to the bank on the Green. Sarah Pierce wanted to discuss Rebecca's future. By the beginning of summer, Rebecca would have completed her diploma. She was ready to look for a teaching position, and her teacher was putting in her two cents.

"I've heard it's a tough year." Rebecca echoed Miss Pierce.

"You do have options." Miss Pierce picked up her teacup. "We know the Wethersfield Academy is looking for a teacher of English composition and grammar. It's an established school with an excellent reputation. You have connections there. That might make Wethersfield attractive to you. The Morris Academy also has an opening, so I've been told by Rhoda Morris."

"It's my preference to teach at a female academy." Rebecca looked down at her hands, stained with ink from the morning's correspondence. She had misgivings about teaching at the Morris Academy. The school was in South Farms, only a few miles south of Litchfield. The Morris Academy had a radical enrollment policy, letting in almost any student who wanted to attend. The school was also co-educational. It was true Miss Pierce's school educated boys from local families, but by and large, the emphasis was on female education. "I'm not saying I won't consider them"—Rebecca did not want to appear ungrateful—"but neither school would be my first choice."

"Yes, I understand. Wethersfield too will have both young men and women, although I believe they teach them separately." Miss Pierce rapped her fingers on the desk. "A school's admissions policies reflect fiscal necessity, just as its curriculum does, although James Morris is a visionary. An egalitarian. But you can't always cherry-pick your students, Rebecca. You know that."

This conversation was intended to temper a young person's dreams with the realities of making a living, never an easy discussion, no matter the century. Miss Pierce turned her owlish gaze on Rebecca Harding. Her mentee looked thinner, with purple circles under her eyes. Was that any surprise? Purple circles under the eyes were de rigueur for the young women at her school who had just finished their exams. Rebecca had thrown herself into her studies this term, hardly leaving the school building at all, after the fall term when she had shown healthy signs of having a social life. But winter was losing its grip. It was early April. Spring's soft breezes were finally replacing the sharp winds of March. The crocuses had come and gone. The willow trees along the creek were now glowing yellow. Miss Pierce hoped that long walks in the fields with Martha Lewis would bring color back to Rebecca's cheeks.

"Have you heard of any other opportunities?" Rebecca saw that her teacher had been daydreaming.

Miss Pierce surfaced, returning to the conversation. "Well, I believe Catharine's going down to New Haven to teach. She hopes to open her own female academy someday." She was referring to the oldest daughter of Lyman Beecher. "But her school's just an idea for now." Miss Pierce wore the expression of a hard-nosed business-woman, assessing the situation. "I've more faith in Mrs. Willard. At present, her school in Waterford is closing, but she intends to open a new one in Troy, New York. She's going to call it a 'female seminary.' But realistically, it will take at least a year for the start-up. Mrs. Willard will hire our graduates, but her school is simply not ready yet." Miss Pierce settled her teacup back into the saucer. "The spring of 1820 is a tough year to be looking."

"I know." Rebecca sighed. "Just my luck. The school in Troy would be ideal. You know how much I respect Mrs. Willard and her views on female education."

"Well, getting a job with Mrs. Willard in a year or two—whenever it gets going—is certainly within your grasp. You excel at teaching rhetoric and grammar. You're the best at parsing the school has ever seen. You're an able administrator. Your only weakness is in the ornamental arts. Your needlework is lacking. Even that could improve if you'd put in some effort." Sarah Pierce looked slyly over at Rebecca, teasing. "But we both know that isn't going to happen." Miss Pierce too was not known for her stitchery and hired others to teach embroidery.

"Probably not," Rebecca replied curtly, not ready to find humor in her situation.

"Don't worry, at some point, you're going to land a fine job at a female academy." Miss Pierce plowed on, ignoring Rebecca's gloom. "But we must focus on the present. When you finish the course this summer, bad year or not, you'll need a job. One job, that's all."

"But I was so hoping Mrs. Willard might have a position."

"I know, my dear, but she doesn't have one right now. We can't have you mooning over a teaching position that doesn't exist. It takes time to start up a school, so let's focus on your present circumstances." Miss Pierce crossed her arms and looked directly at Rebecca. "You may, of course, stay here as an assistant teacher and help Mary with the administration. But I don't advise it."

"Why not?" Rebecca's eyebrows went up. She had counted on being able to coast for a year at Miss Pierce's if no suitable teaching jobs panned out. Rebecca felt a sudden tightness in her throat, and tears pricked her eyes. She panicked, putting down her teacup with a stumbling crash. How humiliating it would be to weep in front of Miss Pierce. But at that moment, she felt as if Miss Pierce were about to exile her from the Litchfield Female Academy. Rebecca loved her little room on the third floor, her students, her friendship with Martha Lewis—even her dull administrative work with Mary Pierce.

"You've been with us for four years, Rebecca. You need experience outside of the Litchfield Female Academy. A year or two of teaching in a different educational environment will strengthen your application to any school."

"I see." Rebecca could only utter two words, so strong was her desire not to cry.

"That's my considered opinion." Sarah Pierce was confident her professional advice was sound, but when she saw Rebecca's stricken face, she stopped short. Perhaps she needed to reassess the situation. Rebecca Harding was an orphan. The Litchfield Female Academy had become Rebecca's only home. Miss Pierce did not want her to feel even more abandoned. Besides, she was a strong administrator. "Or here's another possibility," Miss Pierce ventured. "You could teach the academic year at either South Farms or Wethersfield, wherever you can find a one or two-year contract." She was making this plan up as she spoke. "Then during the next few summers, you would come to us. Be in our employ. Help Mary out." Rebecca said nothing, surprised at Miss Pierce's suggestion.

Miss Pierce too was silent for a moment, her white cap shaking slightly. She was considering the benefits of this impromptu plan, hatched not from her mind, but from her heart. Her mind concurred. Her overworked sister Mary was always on the verge of hysteria during the summer, admitting the incoming class, arranging for their housing. The cost of Rebecca's stipend, and boarding her for the summer, would be returned many times over in increased revenue. Her presence would also allay her sister's estival distress. It was impossible to place a value on that. And she wanted to do this for Rebecca.

"You could start this summer. We just need to find you a teaching job for next fall, to give you more experience in the classroom." Miss Pierce saw that Rebecca was calming down. "I might add, new female academies and seminaries are being established on the frontier, in the western states. Before you know it, more jobs will be opening for qualified women teachers everywhere. Ohio, Indiana, even further west. Things will be different in a couple of years, I feel certain." The older woman patted Rebecca's hand. "We could hold your room for your use in the summer, if you like."

"Yes, all right." Rebecca felt a flood of relief. She was still needed at Miss Pierce's. If she got a teaching job elsewhere, she had somewhere to return to. Her little room on the third floor of the female academy would be waiting for her. So would her administrative work, and her friends—Martha, Charles, and the Lewis family. "That might work." Rebecca knew Miss Pierce's advice was sound. And knowing she would be returning to Litchfield in the summers—to her only true home—made taking a job elsewhere bearable.

The teapot was empty. It was decided. Rebecca Harding would apply for both vacant positions, one at the Morris Academy and the other at the Wethersfield Academy. Rebecca excused herself to go to her room. She had letters to write.

Charles Godwin had no idea how he ended up in a sick bed in Benjamin Lewis's portrait studio. Delusional from fever, he was too ill to make decisions on his own behalf. Judge Reeve came over to consult with Mrs. Edwards. He still felt responsible for Charles and wanted to notify Charles's parents in New Haven. About that, Charles was adamant, even in his delirium. No one was to write to his parents. Charles was not an infant. A man of more than one-and-twenty was the master of his own destiny. A wise old judge had taught him that.

So, Judge Reeve did not write the letter. The parents would only worry from a distance, the old man reasoned. Worse yet, Mrs. Godwin might try to come up to Litchfield herself. A hysterical mother would in no way improve the situation. The boy was too ill to be transported to New Haven. The trip took a full day, and the roads were muddy this time of year. Charles would have to recover in Litchfield. Everyone agreed that Mrs. Edwards could not nurse Charles. She lacked the staff for such intensive care and should not risk her other boarders. Mrs. Reeve offered to take Charles into their home if they could find no other place for him. She had done so before with other law students who had fallen ill, and she was fond of Charles Godwin. But the Lewis family had also offered to take him. Charles would be well-cared for at their cottage, Mrs. Reeve knew.

Eb Wells's meddling was responsible for getting the Lewis family involved. Once the doctor announced Charles was gravely ill from the grippe, Eb decided to spill all the beans to Martha. He was no longer solicitous of Charles's privacy or integrity, both of which had almost killed him. Before the lecture the next day, Eb once again went to the female academy and told Martha the entire story—about the conversation in December between Charles and her father, Charles's unsuccessful petition to his mother for permission to court her, and Charles's sense of obligation to keep his promises to her father. Eb also described Charles's spiraling downward—physically and emotionally—over losing Martha. Over hurting her.

Predictably, and justifiably, Martha was furious with both Charles and her father. Sitting alone with Eb in Miss Pierce's parlor, she wept copiously—out of anger, out of fear that Charles was going to die, and out of relief that he still loved her, even though the day before, Martha had caught a glimpse of the portrait that Charles had painted of her. More than Eb's assurances, the painting was a testament to Charles's continued devotion.

Rage and fear led Martha to skip classes that day and march out to her parents' home on the edge of town to confront her father. This she did in the presence of her mother and her brother Jack. Sitting around the kitchen table, Benjamin, Ruth, and Jack Lewis listened to Martha's tale and witnessed her anger and tears. Her father sat stiffly at the end of the table, silent and miserable. Charles Godwin was on death's door, and it was all his fault.

"Benjamin." Martha's mother pulled herself away from the table after they had heard from Martha. "I can't believe you would do such a thing." Ruth Lewis got up and went over to her daughter, wrapping her arms around Martha's shoulders. Although Ruth was not a tall woman, she looked down on her husband from what seemed to him a great height. "How could you have put that poor boy in such a position?" She uttered this in a low, hoarse voice. "And how could you have caused our daughter so much pain?"

"I was only trying to protect her." Benjamin Lewis sat hunched over the kitchen table, looking like a bear with a wounded paw. "I didn't want his family forbidding the marriage after she'd given him her heart." Benjamin peeked up at his wife but could not make eye contact with Martha. "I do apologize, Ruth. I'm very fond of Charles. You know that. I didn't mean him any harm, but my girl— our girl—she always comes first."

"It's not me you've got to apologize to." Her voice softened. Ruth had spent many years with this sweet, quiet man. He would never intentionally hurt anyone. But of all their children, Benjamin Lewis loved their only daughter Martha the most. When it came to her, that devotion could cloud his judgment. It had done so in the past. "Martha's due an apology." Ruth looked down at Martha who was seated below her, still sniffling. "And you must apologize to Charles as well. You've done them both a great disservice, Benjamin."

Benjamin Lewis snuck a glance at Martha for the first time. She had pulled back her coppery red hair into a knot and was blowing her nose on the handkerchief that her brother had silently handed her. "Martha . . ." Benjamin considered a way to express himself. Finally, he spoke from the heart. "I'm so sorry, Martha. I meant neither of you any harm. I hope Charles recovers soon."

"Daddy, it was wrong of you not to speak to me before you talked to Charles." Martha spoke in a rush of anger. She glared across the table at her father who cowered in his chair. Being on the other end of feminine Lewis anger was not a place he wished to be. "It's my life the two of you were so cavalier with, treating me as if I were a piece of livestock. What do you think me, a cow? I'm as mad at Charles as I am with you. When he gets better, if he gets better, I'll give him a piece of my mind." Martha collapsed into a new torrent of tears.

"Charles deserves no blame." Benjamin looked her square in the eye. "I was the one who forced his hand. Charles is an honorable man. He was trying to keep promises to me I should never have asked him to make. I'm so sorry." Martha did not respond. A silence fell upon the room. Martha's brother had been watching the scene unfold. It was Jack who finally spoke.

"The fact remains"—Jack sounded crisp and business-like—"Charles is very ill and in need of nursing. Mrs. Edwards and her staff cannot manage. He shouldn't stay there anyhow. Too risky for her other boarders."

"What are you thinking?" Ruth had left the table to prepare tea, setting the iron kettle to hang over the fire to boil water.

"I think we should bring Charles here," Jack continued. "We can put him out in the studio. I'll keep the wood stove going and move one of the brother's old beds into my office. You know, turn it into a sickroom. I'll move in here to work." Jack got up and went to the breadbox where he knew some ginger cookies were stored. "The nursing won't all fall on you, Mother." He reached for a plate to put the cookies on. "Father and I will help out." Jack looked pointedly at his father. "Right?"

"Yes, of course." Benjamin Lewis replied quickly. "It'll be warm enough out there if we keep the stove going." He looked over at Martha who was beginning to cheer up. The ruddiness in her cheeks from the rush of anger had begun to subside. The plan made sense to Benjamin and would show Martha, more than his terse words of apology, he was remorseful. "And if need be," her father added, "Jack and I can take turns sleeping out there on my cot at night. To keep an eye on him." It was a great relief for Benjamin Lewis to have a concrete plan. He was not a man made for extended wading in the waters of emotion.

"It's fine with me," Ruth Lewis called out over her shoulder. "As long as Martha's all right with the arrangement. Remember, we don't have to make this offer. Charles has a place to go already—with the Reeves." She brought the tin of tea to the table. "I want to be absolutely certain that Martha wants Charles here."

"Oh yes, please." Martha's eyes were brimming with tears again, but she reached for a ginger cookie. "That would make me very happy."

And so it was decided. Charles Godwin would recuperate from the grippe—and his bout of melancholy—in Benjamin Lewis's portrait studio. After Jack and his father moved the bed and a nightstand out to Jack's office in the studio, rearranged the room, and stoked up the wood stove, Jack rented a horse and cart.

At the other end, Mrs. Edwards and Eb prepared Charles for transport. Mrs. Edwards packed a bag with clothes, a few books, his easel, and a large wooden box of oil paints. Eb spread straw out on the bed of the cart when it arrived, to cushion the bumpy ride on the winter-worn streets of Litchfield. Jack took the reins, with Eb riding behind in the cart with Charles, trying to keep him warm by obsessively rearranging the blankets Mrs. Edwards had provided. Charles was feverish, oblivious to the whirlwind of activity around him.

When Charles arrived at the Lewis cottage, Jack and his father supported him on either side, helping him out to the studio. Eb followed behind with Charles's belongings. Martha was not there to greet him, having been sent by her mother to Miss Pierce's the day before, back to her tiny room, to her classes, to her map of Connecticut rivers, soon to be entered in Miss Pierce's semi-annual public exhibition—and above all, to the comfort of her best friend, Rebecca Harding.

Mrs. Lewis dictated to Martha with stern maternal authority: she was not welcome home until Charles was on the mend. Martha wrote Charles a quick note which she left on his bed out in the studio—the contents to be shared with no one—and walked back to the female academy. She had studying to do, and a letter to write Oliver Hull.

"Why must you waste so much time going out there?" Katherine's plump lips were fixed in a pronounced pout. Once again, Eb Wells was not taking her advice. "It takes you half an hour to walk there, an hour for a visit, half an hour back—two hours of time wasted that could have been spent on study." Eb had stopped by Miss Pierce's to say hello to Katherine on his way out to see Charles at the Lewis cottage. The law lecture was over.

Eb and Katherine were bickering in front of Miss Pierce's home. Katherine had a habit of standing on the top step of the front porch while Eb remained below on the walkway. This made the difference in their heights the result of architecture and not physical stature. On a break between classes, other students were milling around, moving back and forth between Miss Pierce's first floor and the schoolroom building. After a morning rain, the sun was breaking through the gray clouds. The grass on the side lawn was squishy.

"I'm only wasting one hour," Eb rationalized. "I'm taking with me a list of things to memorize as I walk along." Eb pulled out of his coat pocket a small scrap of paper with definitions scribbled in his tiniest hand. This one was on the law of bailments, how a bailment arose, its different types and duties of care, who the bailee and the bailor might be. "I make up a little poem or a song." Eb smiled. "Then I recite or sing out the elements as I walk."

Eb did the same when Mrs. Edwards led the forced march of her boarders to the Congregational Church on Sunday mornings. He would tuck away a pocketful of law for memorizing during Reverend Beecher's long sermons. Eb did not want to mention that the cheat sheet was Rebecca Harding's idea. Katherine got extra prickly any time he mentioned Rebecca—and she was difficult enough without extra prickles.

"And once Charles gets better, he and I can talk law again," Eb added.

"That makes absolutely no sense." Katherine sniped, exasperated. "Charles Godwin has dropped out of law school altogether. What good is he as a study partner?"

"Charles always has something interesting to say about the law. Besides, he's been so ill." Eb's voice had a determined quality that warned Katherine to back off. "I want to see Charles because he's my dear friend."

"Do as you please," Katherine said with a sniff, signaling defeat. While she had acquired dominion over Eb's behavior in many arenas, she had not yet conquered the unchartered territory of Charles

Godwin. "I just think you'd do better to study with someone your equal in intelligence. Oliver Hull, for example."

"Charles is my superior in intelligence. And Oliver Hull?" Eb laughed aloud. "He wants no more to study with me than I with him. We're matched up again in another moot at the end of the month. That makes him my opponent, not my study partner."

"Another moot?" Katherine had not heard this before, suppressing a momentary flash of anger that Eb was only now informing her. "When?"

"The Moot Court Board just told us." Eb stretched the truth. He had known about the date for several days, but had held off telling Katherine, anticipating she would hatch new plans for him. "We've been given the dates and the partners, although not the topic, of course. But I've been matched with Oliver Hull again."

"That's wonderful news, Eb." Although Katherine and Eb had not been an item during the first moot court match, she had heard about the large crowd and how impressive both advocates had been. Indeed, his moot court success was the genesis of her interest in Eb. She wanted to be part of that success. "We must prepare," Katherine said in a fervent voice.

"There's no 'we' on this one, Katherine." Eb looked meekly up at her. "Once you get the problem, you're not allowed to consult with anyone."

"Oh, I see." Katherine sounded disappointed. "Well, I don't like that at all. Did they give you any inkling of the subject matter? Maybe we could start on background reading?" She clearly had not registered the comment about there being no 'we' for moot court purposes.

"There's no way of knowing in advance." Eb took a deep breath, preparing to tell Katherine what he had learned from a second-year student. "But since it's the last moot of the term, the Board chooses a political issue instead of something more doctrinal. Last year it was on the Missouri Compromise and whether Congress should have the power to regulate slavery, so it won't be that again." Eb paused. "But it could be another issue related to slavery. It's the most divisive issue in the nation today."

"My stepfather—I know I told you this—lobbied in Washington against the admission of Maine as a free state." Katherine shook her head. "People back home feel strongly about these things. I hope the Moot Court Board won't put you in an awkward situation. You're from the South and shouldn't have to argue against slavery."

"The Moot Court Board doesn't care about me." Eb gave her a wry smile. "They relish putting advocates in awkward situations." He had not shared with Katherine his growing commitment to abolitionism, knowing she would not approve. They had enough things to argue about as it was. Several young women had passed them on the front porch, making their way to class. Eb stretched his arms over his head and began to show signs of taking off. "But I've got to get going." His voice was full of false good cheer. "I must be off."

"Don't be too long out there." Katherine leaned over, placing her hand on his arm in a proprietary gesture. The couple had a small audience of young women who were chatting on the soggy lawn. Eb turned and walked down the short walkway to take the Goshen Road out of town. There, on the outskirts of Litchfield, Charles Godwin was slurping a bowl of chicken soup with huge hunks of carrot floating in it.

"Save time for study," Katherine called out after him. Eb lifted his hand in a wave. But he did not turn around to look at her.

In the middle of April 1820, the *Litchfield Republican* published a story about a farmer and two law students who were coming back from Bradley's Tavern in the Bantam area late Friday night. Their cart had veered off the road and gone into a ditch. One of the law students was rendered unconscious from a trauma to his head. The other suffered a broken arm. The farmer was so drunk—the newspaper did not include this in the report—he rolled over into the ditch like a limp rag doll. No harm was done to him. The two injured law students were delivered to the North Street home of Judge James Gould of the Litchfield Law School. Both were recuperating.

Besides the farmer's inebriation, other parts of the story were not recounted. The drunkenness of the two law students was also omitted, as was the fact that the heavy-set law student, the one with the blow to his head, had a leather-bound volume of Litchfield Law School notes and questions from past Saturday oral exams hidden in the breast pocket of his woolen jacket.

Judge Gould and his wife, Sally, were awakened at two in the morning by an insistent knock on the door. It was the constable. He had two inebriated and injured law students stretched out on a cart. Where should he deliver them? The county jail in town had vacant beds, but it seemed inappropriate to incarcerate two such fine gentlemen—clearly two of 'Judge Gould's boys.' Mrs. Gould took over the ministrations, bringing the two drunken young men into her dimly lit front parlor.

Thomas Bradford was too tall for the small chair he was perched upon. He rocked back and forth, holding his left arm at an odd angle. Richard McKenzie was still unconscious and had to be laid out on the settee. Thankfully, the blow had been dealt to his thick forehead, with plenty of bone to protect his brain. Mrs. Gould tended to him with smelling salts, but not before she discovered a rectangular lump in the inside pocket of his jacket. She reached into the pocket and pulled out a leather-bound volume.

"James," Mrs. Gould called out, taking a cold compress from her servant for the goose egg on Richard's forehead. She lifted her eyebrows as she spoke, trying to communicate the importance of what she had found. "You might be interested in this."

Judge James Gould came back into the room with a scowl on his face. He had just sent a servant to fetch the bonesetter for Thomas's arm. James Gould recognized Thomas Bradford. From the South, Thomas had barely attended law school during his first term, but of late had been coming to lectures. Thomas's performance, if not stellar, was more than competent on the Saturday oral exams.

Judge Gould also recognized the heavy-set, unconscious young man. He was another law student, also from the South, who only showed up for oral exams and barely passed. Judge Gould struggled with his partner, Judge Reeve, over the law school's lack of attendance requirements. Law students were adults, Judge Reeve argued. If tuition was paid, it was up to the students if they wanted to waste their father's money. Judge Gould surveyed his front parlor, with two injured, drunken boys draped over his furniture. At two in the morning, they did not look like adults. Changes would be made at the law school next year, after Judge Reeve retired.

His wife was right. What she had discovered in the pocket of Richard McKenzie's jacket was of great interest to James Gould. The proprietors of the Litchfield Law School had never published their lectures. If students had access to a legible version of what was recited during the morning lectures, the law school could never survive. Their system of education was based on sounding the law aloud each day within the walls of the law school. Students obediently wrote down what they had heard. Later they rewrote the notes in their books, with their own refinements, gleaned from reading the cases, debating the issues, and reflecting on the law. If a law student stayed for the full fourteen-month course of study, he would go home with a set of five leather-bound volumes of condensed law, compiled and written by himself.

If students organized to share volumes of notes like these, or if law books could be published affordably, Judge Tapping Reeve and Judge James Gould would no longer be in business. And it *was* a business, Judge Gould kept reminding Judge Reeve. For these reasons, Judge Gould was disconcerted to learn about the volume of annotated Litchfield Law School notes found in Richard McKenzie's coat pocket—with prior exam questions underlined.

Eventually, Thomas Bradford's arm was manipulated, splinted, wrapped, and placed gingerly in a sling, with much cringing and moaning on the patient's part. Afterward, the same servant who had fetched the bonesetter accompanied Thomas up the street to Mrs. Edwards's boarding house. It was long past curfew. Mrs. Edwards too must be roused from her sleep—a second hell to pay. Richard McKenzie needed further observation. Mrs. Gould brought him a pillow and an old quilt to spend the night on their settee.

In the morning, Judge Gould called a groggy Richard McKenzie into his office. Richard thought he would be interrogated about how he and Thomas Bradford had come to be riding on a farmer's cart from Bantam, drunk as skunks, in the middle of the night. But he was wrong. Judge Gould wanted to question him about the leather-bound volume which sat on top of his desk.

Drat, drat, drat, Richard said over and over to himself. Someone must have pulled the book out of his jacket's inner pocket. He had forgotten it was there. He remembered that the volume covered material Judge Gould and Judge Reeve had not yet lectured on—and exam questions were underlined. What was he going to say? His thinking was foggy, to say the least, and his head was throbbing. Richard McKenzie was seriously hungover.

Judge Gould was relentless in his questioning. Was this book his? Was this his hand? How had he managed to copy lecture notes when Richard had not attended any lectures? Some of these notes covered future lectures—how could he explain that? What about the underlining? How did Richard have access to questions to be asked on oral exams that had not yet taken place? How had he procured this volume? Who was its author? Did he pay for the use of this volume? Was he charging others for the use of it? Did Thomas Bradford have anything to do with this book? Did he know where Eb Wells's first volume of notes might be found?

How was Richard McKenzie going to respond to Judge Gould's inquisition? It was a turning point in this young man's life. As is true of many such crossroads, Richard was oblivious to its importance, still too drunk for any analysis of complex moral choices. But Richard figured out one thing. If he answered Judge Gould's questions honestly, he would expose the study group's mastermind, a well-respected senior law student from Augusta. The identity of all the unknown others in the study group might also be revealed. And somehow Judge Gould even knew about the missing volume of Eb Wells—it had been *The Troll*, after all—Thomas Bradford's goose would be cooked as well.

The benefit of telling all, Richard McKenzie also assessed on the spot, was that Judge Gould might cut him some slack. By cooperating, Richard might be able to stay in law school. The others would not. On the other hand, ratting out the others was a terrible idea, with ramifications lasting far longer than any expulsion from law school. Even in his muddled state, Richard McKenzie knew that. As far as he could tell, most of the members of this morally questionable study group were from the South. Richard undoubtedly knew their families.

And their fathers undoubtedly knew each other. They had attended school together. They had traded with one another, hired one another, arranged for marriages with each other's children, bought and sold slaves from one another, banded together as a united force in politics, religion, commerce, and even education. Richard McKenzie was spun into a delicate web of complex Southern social relations. Its members never forgot or forgave any tear in its intricate design. 'Rat' would be carved on his tombstone. All this Richard knew, even though on that April morning, cowering in Judge Gould's office, confronting the stern, impassive face of his inquisitor, he lacked enough firing brain cells to articulate these truths. But Richard had been raised in the Southern tradition of honor among men, even when the enterprise was not so honorable. He knew what he had to do.

He lied. Richard McKenzie protested he knew nothing about the volume. He had no idea how it had ended up in his breast pocket. It was not his. He had not written in it and did not know its author. He had neither paid for its use, nor charged others for its use. He had nothing whatsoever to do with its distribution. He could not explain the underlining, the answers on oral exams that had not yet happened, or the notes on future lectures. He had only squeaked by on the oral exams due to pathetic efforts at studying. Richard McKenzie was also ignorant about the disappearance of Eb Wells's *Volume I*. Richard assured Judge Gould that Thomas Bradford too was clueless about the book sitting on his desk, the book that he, Richard McKenzie, also knew nothing about. Someone must have planted the leather-bound volume on his person. Richard threw in this last theory, thinking that Judge Gould might appreciate an exculpating explanation, one consistent with his innocence.

The next day, following consultation with Judge Reeve, Judge Gould expelled Richard McKenzie from the law school. There would be no refund for his tuition. With suppressed outrage, James Gould explained in a cool, deliberate manner that Richard's barefaced lying was far worse than the crime of possessing the volume. He knew that students copied each other's notes from time to time—to criminal-ize that behavior might implicate half the student body. No, it was Richard's mendacity that rendered him unfit to practice law. His dubious moral character would be of interest to the bar examiners of any county in any state. Richard should immediately book passage to Charleston. His career in law was over.

Richard McKenzie could afford to be gracious about his sen-tence. He was the son of a wealthy cotton merchant in Charleston.

He could sustain this loss, even benefit from it. Richard had joined the study group with his eyes wide open. He had knowingly broken one set of rules while choosing to stay faithful to another. Fair enough, Richard conceded. He had a grudging respect for Judge Gould and his swift manner of dispensing justice.

Richard McKenzie took the remainder of his allowance for the term to purchase passage home. What difference did it make, Richard asked himself, frantically gathering his belongings, fighting a ferocious headache. He had not really taken to the law anyway. Later that week, Richard and his two massive trunks were loaded onto a stagecoach for Boston. Thomas Bradford was unable to bid him farewell, being holed up in his room, on house arrest at Mrs. Edwards's, his arm in a sling, with no access to alcohol.

Three weeks later, Richard McKenzie surprised his parents with his unheralded arrival in Charleston. His family celebrated his premature return. At supper, on his first evening home, Richard informed his parents that the law did not suit him. Richard's father balked at the lost tuition. But law school had not been for naught, Richard argued. He could use what he had learned in the cotton trade. Now Richard knew what he wanted to do—follow in the footsteps of his father.

In the study that night, over a cigar and a glass of whiskey, Richard McKenzie confessed to his father the entire story. His father was angry with his son for his carelessness with the volume, but proud that he had not wavered under interrogation. When pressed, Richard had done the right thing. He had not snitched. His mother would never know what happened to her son's legal career but was glad to have her darling home. Perhaps now they could start with the matchmaking.

News of what happened between Judge Gould and Richard McKenzie, and the latter's sacrifice, did eventually leak to the underground study group. It was decided, at least for a term or two, that the illicit trade in lecture notes and exam questions must go into hibernation. Richard McKenzie's reputation for martyrdom began to take seed, in Litchfield and far beyond. He would benefit from it for the rest of his life. And Eb Wells's *Volume I* was still missing.

But what were Judges Gould and Reeve going to do with Thomas Bradford? This was another matter altogether, Judge Reeve argued. To James Gould, association with Richard McKenzie, and Thomas's inexplicable improvement on the oral exams, provided sufficient evidence of guilt. Judge Reeve disagreed. While Thomas's frequent public intoxication and violation of boarding house rules were subject to sanction, Thomas could not be proven to be linked to the volume. Neither did he seem complicit in its distribution.

Tapping Reeve also believed Thomas Bradford was a young man worth saving. He appeared to be struggling—in school and in life. Judge Reeve clucked sympathetically and shook his head. Thomas had recently demonstrated a fine mind for the law. He had promise, if only he would apply himself, if only he would conquer his bad habits. In this, Judge Reeve was echoing the sentiments of all of Thomas Bradford's former educators. Finally, Judge Reeve argued to his partner, the punishment must be proportionate to the crimes, and tailor-made for Thomas Bradford's rehabilitation.

Judge Gould trusted his colleague on matters of student conduct. Judge Reeve knew the law students better than he. It was also good to let the old man win a round. If James Gould yielded on Thomas Bradford, it would give him leverage on more important matters. Besides, the case against Thomas Bradford was purely circumstantial and difficult to prove. More to the point, Thomas Bradford had not sat across from Judge Gould at his desk that morning, lying through his teeth.

*Letter to Elizabeth Stafford from Rebecca Harding, Litchfield,
April 19, 1820*

Dear Elizabeth,

What churlish behavior on the part of Mr. Townsend! Walking out with two women at the same time. My dear Lizzie—this man is twenty-two years old. His character is set. Some men can't control their romantic impulses. The impetus, I believe, isn't vulnerability to love, but to the thrill of conquest. I fully anticipate Mr. Townsend will lobby to return to your good graces. He'll insist the other woman means nothing to him—that you're all he dreams about. Don't listen to him. What if you had married him? You can't exit a marriage, Lizzie, but you can always leave a courtship with grace. Listen to your mother and your closest friend. Move on.

As you probably know, I've been offered the job at the Wethersfield Academy. I'm still waiting to hear from the Morris Academy, but I'm going to take the position in Wethersfield. I grew up there. My entire family is buried there. The winter weather is much milder than in the Northwest Hills. The Johnsons are there, and your grandmother. Penny's mother wants me to stay with them, but your own mother has an idea more to my liking. I'll live with your Granny Cox. Now that your grandfather has passed, she needs a companion. I'm certain you know all this already. It may have even been your idea. I hope Mrs. Johnson won't be too disappointed. I'll only be staying several houses away and promise to visit her often.

The plan is for me to return to Litchfield during the summers to help bring in the incoming class. I explained this to your mother. Mrs. Cox can come to your parents for the summer months. The long winter nights are her greatest concern. It's an ideal situation. I'm fond of your grandmother, and her house is close to the school. In my mind, I'm already walking the path: Cross the Broad Street

Green, go down Garden a couple of blocks, and there I am, right at the Wethersfield Academy.

You ask how goes the romance between Eb and Katherine. I've little to report. Katherine is deferential to me, but she always finds a pretext to whisk Eb away whenever I come near. Eb and I never have a chance to talk, even superficially. Martha says Katherine's like an eagle. She's sunk her talons into Eb's shoulders and plans to lift him up over the Litchfield Hills and fly him home with her to Charleston. Katherine tells me Eb's brother's home was destroyed in the Savannah fire, and they're moving to Charleston where his wife's family lives. This means Eb will more than likely end up there—near Katherine's home. All very convenient for her. I can almost hear Katherine say how happy she is that Savannah was burned to the ground.

In my four years in Litchfield, I've seen the boys from the North go almost anywhere after Tapping Reeve's. Many even leave for the west, but the boys from the South—they always go home. Savannah, Augusta, Charleston, it's all the same to me. I'm still quite sad about losing Eb. Martha insists a change of scene will be good for me. Maybe she's right. It will be good to be back in Wethersfield.

You asked about the Martha and Charles situation. It's been resolved, although only after Charles fell gravely ill. He dropped out of law school and collapsed into a black mood, never leaving his room. Eb told Martha all that transpired between Charles and her father—did I give you the details? They're now on the road to reconciliation. It seems certain that Charles won't finish law school. He wants to apprentice as a portrait artist with Martha's father and is now living in Benjamin Lewis's studio. His family in New Haven is disappointed, I feel certain.

But it's wonderful to see Martha so happy again. She broke off her flirtation with Oliver Hull who wasn't appropriately heartbroken, I must say. He quickly made another liaison with a second-year student, an heiress from Hartford, of less beauty and spirit than our

Martha. These young men who excel at the law school are hotly pursued by our colleagues at the female academy, even if they look like a toad or a horse. The latter refers to Oliver Hull. I swear to you, his appeal is quite equine. I kept pointing that out to Martha. She worries about the Lewis ears, but I kept telling her the Hull Horse Face is the one to worry about.

Martha and I have finished *Waverley*. I loved it the second time around, and I plan to read it to your grandmother next winter before going to bed, sitting around the fire. I'm always ready to escape to the Scottish Highlands.

Be well, my friend. Don't be too heartbroken by the perfidy of Mr. Townsend. Show him the door.

All my love,

Rebecca

"It would only be for an hour each night." Judge Tapping Reeve and Eb Wells strolled through the garden after the midday meal. It was a sunny day in mid-April. The grass was glowing a bright lime green, with pockets of riotous color where Mrs. Reeve's flowers made a haphazard appearance after their long winter's sleep.

Eb was admiring her bright yellow daffodils, muttering to himself about the need to clean up the garden. Judge Reeve had just asked Eb if he would tutor Thomas Bradford. "He could really benefit from your supervision." The old man tried to appeal to Eb's vanity, adding, "Thomas is not a bad sort of young man, just a weak one."

"You know, Judge Reeve, while we're both from Savannah, we're not really friends." Eb freed up a daffodil from a mat of old leaves. "Thomas doesn't hold me in high regard. I've heard he called me *The Troll* in the tavern."

"Is it over a young woman?" Judge Reeve looked at Eb with his large, liquid eyes that seemed to look right through him. It was his business to read the faces of the young men in his charge. His long silver hair caught glints of sunlight. "Your differences?"

"Well, partly." Eb's ears were turning red. "I'm currently walking out with Miss Montgomery from Miss Pierce's. I believe you're aware of that, sir. Thomas had aspirations regarding her last fall that didn't come to fruition."

"So, he might bear a grudge? Did you steal her heart away from Thomas or were these decisions made by Miss Montgomery?"

"The latter, sir." Eb suppressed a laugh. The thought of Katherine being the victim of such a theft struck him funny. If anyone did any stealing, it was Katherine. What part of him had she made off with, he wondered. Probably not his heart. "The situation is entirely due to her commandeering, I assure you." Eb composed himself. "Miss Montgomery had already dismissed Thomas Bradford before I came onto the scene. She told me so. Thomas spent too much time at the tavern." Eb hesitated. "Katherine has much invested in any young man she attaches herself to." He looked down at the wet leaves in his hands. "Sometimes more than I'd like."

"I see." The judge raised an inquiring eyebrow but decided against a follow-up question. "And what do you think of Thomas's abilities? It's inappropriate for me to ask a fellow student such a question," Judge Reeve added hastily, "but in this instance, your opinion matters."

"I've heard him in the oral exams lately. Thomas Bradford's as intelligent as any man here at the law school. Perhaps more so, but he's never learned how to apply himself." Eb leaned over and relieved a second cluster of yellow daffodils, shedding the shackles of last autumn's leaves. "I think Thomas may have a problem with the drink, sir," Eb said with hesitation, not wanting to speak poorly of another student to their teacher. At the same time, he wanted to give a frank answer.

"Yes, yes." Judge Reeve agreed, a sad expression on his face. "Imbibing too much alcohol is a terrible business. I hate to see someone ruined at his age, with his whole life ahead of him." He shook his head, putting his arms behind his back, gazing down at the bed of daffodils which began to look much improved, thanks to Eb's fussing about. "Apparently, he and that fellow from Charleston had been going out to Bradley's since the holidays, almost every night. Judge Gould and I have put Thomas on probation after the debacle with the farmer's cart."

Eb grunted as he bent over but said nothing. Mrs. Edwards, a fountain of information, had already leaked to him the conditions of the probation: Thomas was to confine his movements to the boarding house and the law school. Thomas was not to frequent any taverns in the vicinity. Thomas was not to imbibe any alcohol for the duration of his remaining tenure at the law school. Thomas was to attend all the lectures and oral exams. If those terms were met, he would be allowed to remain at the law school. With Thomas's permission, Mr. and Mrs. Bradford in Savannah had been informed of the probation by a formal letter from Judge Gould—and the reasons for it.

"There's one more condition I'd like to impose," Judge Reeve said tentatively. "This is where your tutoring him comes in. You both stay with Mrs. Edwards. Thomas can't really leave the boarding house, and you've lost your study partner. I'd like to require Thomas Bradford to spend one hour with you each night reviewing the day's material." Judge Reeve watched Eb put the dead, wet leaves into a mounting pile. "Teaching someone else the material is the very best method of preparation." The judge ignored Eb's silence and increasingly frantic behavior freeing the daffodils. "It would benefit you both and be a great favor to me."

"Well . . ." Eb did not like the proposition one bit. He and Thomas Bradford had history. The scheme deprived him of a precious study hour each night. But Eb could never say 'no' to Judge Reeve.

He adored the old man. "All right, sir," Eb said with a groan, about to right himself. "Thomas and I will try the arrangement for three weeks—if that's all right." He straightened up with a handful of leaves in his hands, peering at Judge Reeve through his glasses. "If it's a disaster, we'll call it a day. And I get to judge its success or failure."

"Of course, Eb." The judge took the wet leaves from the younger man's hands, tossing them onto the makeshift pile. "If the arrangement doesn't work out, we wouldn't want to saddle either of you with it."

"And the week of the moot court." Eb was thinking ahead to his next month's responsibilities. "I won't be available."

"That goes without saying." The old man made a bow of respect. "That week no tutoring."

"And Judge Reeve?" This might be an auspicious time to ask for a favor of his own. "Could you please impress upon Mrs. Reeve the need to rake last fall's leaves?" Eb gave a slight sigh, gesturing to the row he had liberated, and the mound of sodden leaves at the edge of the flower bed. "It's a disservice to the daffodils." This he said under his breath with a tinge of disgust.

"I'll promise to mention it to her." Judge Reeve coughed. "But I can't promise it will be done. There are some things in life I can control, Eb." The old man gave a slight sigh of his own. "And Mrs. Reeve isn't one of them."

"Here's what I'd like to know." Jack Lewis leaned his wiry frame forward. Charles Godwin was sitting up in bed, blowing on a mug of tea. On the mend, Charles was peaceful in Jack's old office, the sickroom crafted for him in Benjamin Lewis's studio. Warmed by the woodstove, he loved waking up each day, looking out the small windowpane at the bank of white pines on the edge of the property.

Jack had come out to the studio for a heart-to-heart conversation. "You're certain, Charles, you don't wish to pursue the law?"

"I am." His illness had clarified how he felt about law school. Charles was tired of trying to please other people. Being dutiful might be the death of him. Worse yet, he might serve a life-sentence to work he had no affinity for—a slower form of spiritual death. "I'm going to be an artist."

"Yes, well . . ." Jack stammered. "That's what I wanted to talk to you about, but I must ask you something first. Of a more delicate nature."

"Ask away." Charles took his first sip of tea. Too hot, he put the mug on the small table next to the bed. He rubbed his thin face with his long fingers, feeling a stubble on his cheeks. "I'm beginning to feel more like myself."

"It's like this. I have an idea for the business here, but it depends on your marrying Martha." Jack cleared his throat nervously. "I don't mean to be blunt. But I guess what I mean to say is—well, what are your intentions toward my sister?"

"As you know, Martha was here last night, giving me a piece of her mind." Charles shook his head. Two weeks had gone by since his illness. Ruth Lewis had finally allowed Martha to visit, a confrontation she now felt Charles had the fortitude for. "I wouldn't say we were on the precipice of matrimony." Charles cringed, remembering shards of their conversation. "I don't know what we were thinking, making deals about Martha behind her back."

"It's hardly unheard of for a man to seek permission to marry a man's daughter." Jack pushed a lock of red hair off his forehead. "Or for a father to put conditions upon his consent."

"I know that, but I was raised in a Quaker home. I was taught to regard women as equals. Martha should have been consulted, or at least informed." Charles echoed some of Martha's wrath from the evening before.

"I agree." Jack nodded. "I thought Father was high-handed too, but he meant well. He can be overprotective of my sister."

"I understand that. He loves Martha. And so do I," Charles added without being prodded. "If that's what you're asking."

"And do you see this love moving toward matrimony?" Jack returned to his business.

"I do want to marry Martha. It's been my wish since the first day I met her." Charles cast his eyes down onto the starburst quilt that covered him. It was red and white, the star partly fashioned from an old calico dress of Martha's. "But I'm not sure how things are going to work out. Whether she can forgive me."

"Don't you worry about that," Jack assured him. "Martha just needs time. She needs to do some huffing and puffing. Give vent to righteous anger." Jack was relying on a lifetime of experience with his sister, a deeper well to draw from than Charles's eight months of infatuation. "Your job here is to keep saying how sorry you are. How much you adore her. After sufficient repentant groveling, Martha will come around, I promise."

"That's good to hear."

"I warn you though, Charles. The siege may last more than a month. My sister learned fury from the master." Jack smiled. "Or should I say, the mistress. My mother can punish my father for at least two months when he's fallen out of line." Jack propped his foot up on the end of Charles's bedframe. "They say it is a redheaded thing, but my theory is—it's a redheaded woman thing. After all, I'm a redhead." Jack ran his fingers through his hair and grinned. "And I'm a docile lamb."

"Does Martha ever give anyone the silent treatment?" Charles's own mother withdrew and fell silent when she was angered. Charles was always fearful when his mother was unhappy with him. Mary Godwin shut him out, making him feel as if he had evaporated into thin air. With Martha, at least Charles was still in the world. She didn't pretend he wasn't there. Charles was the target of her ire. Straight and center.

"Martha? Silent?" Jack guffawed. "My sister doesn't know the meaning of the word 'silent.' If you haven't gathered that much, you really must be in love." Charles too gave a little laugh. "No, I promise you this. If Martha didn't love you, you wouldn't be here. Bringing you home was Martha's way of committing to you. I'm telling you." Jack looked intently at Charles. "She's going to yell and carry on at you for a while—maybe a few months—but she intends to keep you. Whether you like it or not."

"That gives me heart." Charles fingered the quilt absentmindedly. "Thank you for your good counsel, Jack."

"So, let's operate on the assumption Martha's going to cool down. You two resume your courtship, and then maybe after a few years, when Martha's done at Miss Pierce's, you marry." Jack leaned forward. "Would you be interested in forming a business partnership with my father? He'd do the profiles and you the oil paintings? *Lewis & Godwin*, Portrait Artists?"

"Go on." Charles looked over at Jack with guarded interest.

"Well, after I saw your painting of Martha . . . I hope you don't mind, Charles, but Mrs. Edwards let us into your room to pack up more of your belongings. A very nice woman. She offered us a biscuit with jam, very good too, although not as good as Mother's. Eb was with me. But that painting in your room—well, we were both amazed by the likeness of Martha, although I personally don't think she's that pretty." Jack considered his last statement. "I suppose that's because she's my baby sister."

Charles was fascinated by all that had transpired while he had been sick. Listening to Jack's wandering speech also made him miss Martha. "Go on."

"Anyhow, after I saw that portrait, I started to think we could use your talents in the studio. These miniature paintings are popular right now, tiny painted likenesses. Young ladies or gentlemen in love, or mothers, can put them in lockets, or on watch chains or around their necks. Or grieving people. We might even get commissions for larger portraits to hang on walls, like the one you did of Martha," Jack continued. "Maybe we could branch out into those."

"But I'd like to learn profiles from your father," Charles replied. "He sees the outlines of things, and captures character in black and white, without the distraction of color." He shifted slightly in his bed. "And I need time to experiment myself." Charles looked down again at the starburst on the quilt. "I don't want to promise to do portraits with your father from here on out." Charles looked out the window at the pine trees shivering in the wind. "The scenery up here in the hills is magnificent. I might like to paint something other than the human face on command. Trees, mountains, rivers, birds, cows, cats, bears—anything I want to paint. Maybe roam around a bit. You know, see what I can see."

"Oh, I hadn't thought you might have other artistic ambitions." Jack fell silent for a moment. His temperament was by nature mercurial—if his plans were not working out, Jack Lewis would change them. "Perhaps we should approach this incrementally," Jack started up again cautiously. "I wasn't pushing *Lewis & Godwin* until you married Martha anyhow. That could be several years away." He leaned back in his chair. "But you must realize, Charles, I can't sell the partnership idea without your being wed." Jack gave Charles a knowing look, seeking confirmation.

"I understand that." Charles returned the gaze. "Marrying Martha is my wish as well."

"Maybe we do this." Jack Lewis could tell that Charles needed to feel less permanently obligated. He began to see the challenges of dealing with a man raised in a Quaker home—integrity kept getting in the way. "You apprentice with my father for a full year and learn the profile portrait trade from him. Perhaps two years. We can renegotiate the terms after a year. For that work, you'll get room and board and incidental expenses. You pay no apprentice fee. As a bonus, the business will buy your painting supplies and give you time to paint. If a commission comes up for a painted profile or portrait, you'll get a cut of the proceeds." Jack paused. "I'd need to consult with my father about that. Martha's almost nineteen years old. She must, at a minimum, have a second year at Miss Pierce's. Maybe a third. She's doing so well. Mr. Brace has taken a great interest in her maps."

"Maybe Martha's the one who ought to be brought into the business," Charles suggested. "You've already got a budding artist in the family. Many people are enamored of her maps. They too are objects of art."

"Martha? That's an interesting idea." Jack quickly moved the idea of Martha as an artist to the back of his mind. "I'll consider that later, but for now, think on this offer."

"Could I have this room out here to sleep and paint in?" Charles looked around the small room, formerly Jack's office. He relished the privacy of the studio, its roughly hewn walls, and view of the white pines. Charles could not live in the Lewis cottage—let alone paint—in the midst of all that human activity. Working in silence beside Benjamin Lewis all day was one thing, but living in a confined space with Ruth and Jack Lewis, both full of energy and enterprise? That would exhaust him. The two older brothers from Kent dropped by often. Martha too. Everyone in the Lewis family, except for Benjamin, loved to talk. All that chatter, gallons of tea, all those mismatched plates bearing Mrs. Lewis's exceptional baked goods. Lucky begging under the table. Charles needed his solitude, a door to close—and his own roof.

"Yes, you can stay out here." Jack agreed without hesitation. "When we set up this sickroom, I moved my desk and record books into my brother Ben's old room. It's fine. I don't need to be out in the studio for what I do."

"How much time would you give me to paint?" Charles inquired in a steady voice.

"One full workday a week, a day of your choosing. You can also paint all you want at night." Jack tapped the red star on the quilt with his hand decisively. "And if you're painting a portrait for the business, that won't count in your 'Charles's free painting' time. But your day of painting couldn't be the Sabbath. My mother wouldn't stand for that. You'd have to come to church with us."

"All right. That's fair." Charles had attended the Congregationalist Church in Litchfield all autumn with Eb, Rebecca, and Martha. It was tolerable. Lyman Beecher usually had something of interest to say from the pulpit, and if not, Charles could daydream. "And on my one free day of painting . . ." He wanted expectations to be clear. "I'd be free to leave the studio and roam about on my own?"

"Absolutely free, unless you take into account the tethers my sister might put upon you." Jack wore a knowing smile.

"I love the idea of Martha Tethers. Those sound wonderful to me."

"I predict you'll someday need to negotiate the length of those tethers." Jack spoke with the expertise of an older brother. "But from the business's perspective, you could roam at will on your 'Charles's free painting' day."

"I'd like to talk this over with Martha. I hope you're right about her still wanting me. I don't want to make assumptions."

"Let me settle things first with my father and mother, to make sure they're comfortable with our plan." Jack needed to work out the sequencing of the negotiations. Not only must Charles be on board, but his father would be taking on an apprentice and expanding the business to include painted portraits. His mother would also have another mouth to feed, more clothes to wash, and a surrogate son to fuss over. "We'll give Martha more time to calm down. We can approach her after the three of you are agreed."

"All right." Charles reached for his mug of tea. "Give me a few days to think about it. Then you can approach your parents." He took a long sip and looked up at Jack in earnest. "But it must be understood. We can't go forward unless Martha accepts all aspects of the proposal."

"Understood." Jack rose from his chair. "We must not be accused of wheeling and dealing with Martha's future behind her back." Jack gazed down at Charles who suddenly looked pale and exhausted.

"Isn't that what we just did?" Charles moaned, putting his mug down on the table. He gave Jack a worried look as he crawled back under the quilt.

"Maybe." Jack gave Charles a parting grin. "Well . . ." He hesitated. "Yes, of course. That *is* what we just did. But don't you worry." Jack looked over his shoulder while closing the door. "Martha will be fine with this idea."

Charles gave Jack a wan smile. Martha must have absolute veto power, Charles said sternly to himself. I must give her that. Charles settled his head back on the pillow and closed his eyes. I'm thoroughly exhausted, he acknowledged. Time to rest for now. When I wake up, I'll think about Jack's proposal.

Letter to Eb Wells from Malinda Wells, Savannah,
April 27, 1820

Dearest Eb,

Please forgive me for not writing. I've been in such a dither. John has moved his family to Charleston, as you know. Mother is digging in her heels about leaving Savannah. I don't want to go either. But forgive me for regaling you with our woes at the outset. First, thank you for your last two letters. Congratulations on being picked again for a moot court! I know the law wasn't chosen by you, but I'm pleased to see you doing so well. John will be lucky to have you in his practice. About your amorous connections though, Eb, I confess to having reservations. Susan agrees.

I will be frank. I worry about your compatibility with Miss Montgomery. Are you aware how often you complain about her controlling nature? She sounds lovely, and so intelligent, but she also seems intent on having her way. We'll welcome anyone you choose into the family. You know that, Eb. I only want to point out—Miss Montgomery's beauty and brilliance might come at a high price. One's home should be a peaceful shelter, not a battleground.

We were saddened to hear about Charles's illness, but happy to hear that he's on the mend. Do you think he and Miss Lewis will reconcile? His parents must be distressed. I'm relieved, my dear brother, that none of this happened to you—no disaffection for the law, no melancholy, or illness. Besides, if you had to make a living off your drawing, you would surely starve.

Since the fire, living in Savannah has been most challenging. Mother, Susan, Lottie, and I have been working on relief efforts for the poor. So many people are without a home. Many have left altogether. Savannah feels like a ghost town. My heart breaks when I think of all the flowers and bushes in the squares that ought to be in bloom this time of year. Now everything is charred, with no sight of green to be found. The air should be sweet with the perfume of blooming shrubs, magnolias, apple trees, red buds. Instead, there is a rank, smoky miasma hanging over the town. The smell of wet smoke pervades our already gloomy mood. I must confess, living here now is quite discouraging. But neither do we want to move to Charleston.

Our Uncle Ebenezer has written to urge Mother and me, with Susan as my companion, to come up to New Haven for an extended stay. He says the house on Elm Street is large and empty. New Haven would be such an improvement over Charleston. I'm eager to come to Uncle Ebenezer's for a visit but can't convince Mother.

She is fearful of the sea journey. Mother worries the ship will sink in a storm or one of us will fall ill and die onboard. We do hear stories like that. But I keep pointing out—we only hear of the ships that sank, the passengers who perished, not the ones who arrived at their destinations safely.

Mother also doesn't want to leave Lottie. But Lottie says if we go to New Haven, she'll take in boarders. Susan is undecided. I'm putting no pressure on her, but she's my closest friend. My only friend. I would so love her company. I think she'll come. Like me, Susan is eager to see more of the world. Mother's the problem. I would never leave without her, you know that, but I fear she won't budge.

Can you try to persuade Mother to visit Uncle Ebenezer? Maybe you could come down to see us in New Haven? Entice her with an Eb-sighting? John has been so generous. He's been solicitous of our well-being ever since Father died. But his plan to move us to Charleston does not suit.

I wish I had more time to write, but I don't. Please write Mother and describe for her how your sail up north was easy—at least benign. If it wasn't, then lie. Lottie, Susan, and I are taking her out for exercise, to prepare her for the journey. Her grief over our father's death has begun to subside.

Good luck on your second moot court which will have happened by the time this letter arrives. I'll address it to Uncle Ebenezer's in New Haven. You should be there by the middle of May.

All my love, my dearest little brother,

Malinda

"Jack tells me everyone in town is talking about the 'Back to Africa' movement. An ill-fated plan if I ever heard one." Charles

Godwin and Eb Wells sat behind the studio on the rickety bench where Benjamin Lewis usually smoked his pipe. Eb had come to visit Charles who was feeling well enough to cut mats. The smoking bench provided a rare island of privacy. Charles was taking a break. He wanted to visit with Eb, but also to rest, his stamina still wanting. "Jack's scuttlebutt is that Lyman Beecher's been consulting on forming a Connecticut Colonization Society," Charles reported. "As usual, if Reverend Beecher is involved, the whole town's talking about it. Martha too."

"So, you and Martha are conversing like human beings again?" Eb was referring to the month-long *Wrath of Martha* siege. Martha appeared to be running out of steam, and Charles was still standing. "How's the détente going?"

"We're making progress," Charles replied. "On her last visit, we talked about whether to use the Indian name 'the Tunxis' on her river map instead of 'the Farmington,' the radical addition of a candied orange peel in her mother's bread pudding, and her dislike of Katherine Montgomery."

"She dislikes Katherine?" This was news to Eb, who only saw Martha briefly from time to time at the female academy. Miss Pierce insisted on a patina of civility in her home, making authentic exchanges difficult. Besides, Katherine always pulled Eb away from conversations with Martha Lewis, almost as quickly as those with Rebecca Harding. He was not certain why. Perhaps Katherine thought Eb was already wasting enough time on Charles Godwin.

"Martha puts it like this," Charles said. "She doesn't dislike Katherine per se. She just doesn't approve of the partnership of *Wells & Montgomery*." He was scanning the squadron of white pines on the edge of the property with one eye closed, a perspective Charles enjoyed while looking at scenery. It flattened everything out, making the vista look like a painting. "Of course, Martha's loyal to Rebecca."

Eb ignored the reference to Rebecca Harding. "Malinda too

has reservations about me and Katherine, which is ridiculous since Malinda's never even met her."

"Nothing about your sister strikes me as remotely ridiculous. What's Malinda got to say?"

"She says I complain too much about Katherine's controlling nature." Eb knew Malinda could—and did—read his letters with close attention. "That Katherine might be difficult to live with, long-term, if I understand her point."

"And what about that, Eb? Take note, my friend, I don't mean to judge. I've proven myself an absolute dolt in matters of the heart." Charles kept his one eye on the distance. "But does Katherine try to control you too much?"

"Yes." Eb was constitutionally incapable of lying to his friend, perhaps due to Charles's dogged Quaker sincerity. But Eb was still not willing to confess his pleasure at being seen with Katherine Montgomery. The truth was Eb enjoyed being seen with Katherine far more than seeing her. "And I do wish Katherine would let me study on my own." Eb complained under his breath. "It's very distracting to have her stomping around the muddy law of bailments with her expensive, rabbit-fur-lined boots on."

"I'd wager she's more of a taskmaster than I was."

"That's an understatement." Eb chuckled. "But I miss your larger view, Charles. It's important to have someone poking a stick at the law, asking whose interests it serves. Katherine can't do that."

"And how goes it with Thomas Bradford?"

"It goes well, I'm surprised to say. The first week or so was dreadful. Thomas was still in shock from the accident and sick from having no drink. But since then, he's proved an able student." Eb was not certain what brought about the change. Perhaps because Thomas had nothing to do, nowhere to go, and no one to do it with, he had finally settled down to the study of law. "At night, when we meet," Eb added, "Thomas comes up to my room with perfectly reasonable questions, some of them even astute, as if he's given the day's lecture some thought."

"Good. Thomas Bradford deserves a second chance. We all do." Charles was relieved Martha had ceased excoriating him and resumed her amusing, disjointed chatter.

"Judge Reeve's right. Thomas isn't a bad man. There's a sadness about him I can't quite put my finger on." Eb put his hand over one eye and took a long look at the pine trees behind the studio, trying—unsuccessfully—to see what Charles saw. "I fear, like so many of us," Eb continued, "his family puts a great deal of pressure on him. In Thomas's case, he must not only complete Judge Reeve's course, but must marry a rich Southern woman, one with land." Eb shook his head. "No one has bothered to ask Thomas what he might want."

"Speaking of rich women with land, do the two of you ever talk about Katherine? After all, you did step into Bradford's shoes." Charles made an exaggerated look down at Eb's feet which were small, commensurate with his stature. He was about to make a joke about how Eb could swim in Thomas's shoes but decided against it. "Does he ever ask you about her?"

"Not yet." Eb shook his head. "But Thomas has told me about his tyrannical father, a fawning mother who only cares for fashion and status, an older brother who's shut Thomas out of the family business altogether. Thomas was supposed to marry some dour cousin they were foisting off on him—and she rejected him. A great humiliation, I'd say." Eb let out a heartfelt sigh. "Thomas hasn't been supported by those who love him. He's had little guidance about how to be a good person—or a successful one. It's not a happy tale." Eb crossed his arms. "Things haven't gone all that well up here either. Failing at school, Katherine turning him down, the accident, his broken arm, the house arrest. His father is furious with him. No wonder Thomas wants to drink."

"And Sir Winston?" Charles missed Mrs. Edwards's warm kitchen, her strictly rationed cups of tea, chatting idly with the servant Maggie, and the fat, old, orange-and-white cat, posing for him up in Eb's attic room. "How does Thomas get along with our Sir Winston?"

"At first not well." Eb moved his weight from one side to the other on the wobbly bench. "Thomas comes from a hunting tradition where dogs chase foxes and runaway slaves. In his world, a cat is regarded as a barn animal—a ratter. Sir Winston may be the first cat in Thomas's life who leaps onto your bed and demands to be petted." Eb let out a loud laugh. "I wish you could've seen his face the first time Sir Winston waltzed into my room." Eb did an apt imitation of Thomas's first close encounter with the entitled cat. "Now at least, Thomas nervously pats Sir Winston on the head."

"That's progress." Charles nodded. "I feel the need of a cat in the studio. It gets lonely out here at night."

"I could ask Mrs. Edwards if she'd lend you Sir Winston." But Eb knew the old lady would never give up her pet, and Eb did not want to give him up either. "But I doubt she would."

"No, that's all right," Charles said. "I'm already working on taming a stray cat who visits at night. A beautiful brown striped tabby. She's got golden eyes and a little black mask. I've been feeding her scraps. Just last night, she set one paw across my threshold."

"Excellent." Eb took this as a good sign. Charles was feeling better. "What's her name?"

"Midnight. That's when I first saw her. But please, don't breathe a word of this to Martha or anyone else in the Lewis family," Charles added hastily. "Having a cat isn't exactly in my contract. I'm waiting for Midnight to kill a mouse. You know what I mean—to ingratiate herself with Mrs. Lewis."

"Speaking of your contract." Eb set one paw of his own across Charles's emotional threshold. "Have you heard from your mother?" Charles had written his parents a long letter when he was well enough, telling them about his illness, his withdrawal from law school, his apprenticeship, and his courtship, even if at the time Martha was barely speaking to him. Charles had written a few newsy letters since but received no answer back.

"No, she doesn't write." Charles let out a sad sigh. "I don't need their money. I'm supporting myself here on my own." He gestured to the studio behind them. "But I'd love to hear from my mother." Charles lifted his long lanky frame from the wooden bench. "I'm sorry, Eb, but I've got to get back to work." He turned his head toward the sounds coming from Benjamin Lewis's studio. A sawing noise indicated that a frame was in the making. "I do miss my mother. I don't like being on the outs with her."

"She'll write soon," Eb said with unwarranted optimism. "Maybe like Martha, your mother needs some time. But speaking of time, I've got to go too." Eb rose from the bench. "I promised Katherine I wouldn't stay too long."

Charles looked down at his friend and started to say something—but decided against it.

"So, everyone was betting on Oliver Hull's winning." Dr. Cabot and Eb were sitting on the back porch, taking their tea after breakfast. Eb's spring break had just begun. It was a bright, sunny May morning in New Haven. In the backyard, next to the now vacant carriage house, a pink magnolia tree was in full bloom. The air was warm and fresh and sweet. Eb was giving a postmortem on last week's moot court argument. "The odds were strongly in his favor," Eb continued. "Hull had won against me before and had the more popular side to argue."

"So, Congress allocating funds for the American Colonization Society—*this* was the most popular side in Litchfield?" Dr. Cabot pulled on one oversized ear in a gesture of incredulity.

"Lyman Beecher's been consulting with those in Hartford who want to form a Connecticut chapter of the ACS," Eb explained. "The 'Back to Africa' movement is much admired in town. If Reverend Beecher says sending free Blacks back to Africa is a good thing, the idea takes hold."

"That's the danger of giving a man a pulpit." Dr. Cabot put his teacup down with a clatter. "Endless hours to indoctrinate a well-intended, captive audience."

"Yes, well, those good intentions were my greatest obstacle." Eb resumed his account of the moot court argument. "Hull made the American Colonization Society sound so noble. If free Blacks could return to Africa, they could develop their full potential as human beings, as equals in their own society. No need to amalgamate. No more discrimination. That kind of thing."

Eb put down his teacup, straining to see what new bird had landed on the branches of the magnolia. It was bright yellow with black wings and a little black cap. "We have an American Goldfinch," Eb said with excitement. His uncle remained unimpressed, so Eb returned to his story. "Oliver argued how they could return to the land of their fathers. He even threw in the spread of Christianity. How the free Blacks could take the true religion back to Africa and convert the heathens."

"Have I got a surprise for you." A booming voice with the hint of a West Indian accent called out. The back door to the porch flew open and through it walked the dignified Esmeralda, a paisley turban twisted around her head. She wore a gray dress and a fresh, white apron, balancing a tray bearing two large pieces of warm apple pie. Mrs. Potts loved to serve pie after breakfast.

"Thank you, Esmeralda." Eb beamed.

"Mrs. Potts baked this special for you, Eb." The elderly woman put down the tray on the wicker table, pulling two forks out of her apron pocket, handing one to each of them. "It's got the extra cinnamon in it, the way you like."

"Please give her my heartiest thanks. And tell her I'll be in to see her later this morning."

"And get yourself a second piece of pie, I'd wager." Esmeralda handed Dr. Cabot a cloth napkin. "I know your tricks." Eb looked abashed. "She'll be happy to see you, young man." The old woman patted him lightly on the shoulder before disappearing into the house. She too was pleased to have Eb home.

"So, did Oliver Hull talk about slavery at all?" Dr. Cabot was not finished with the discussion. "Did he even put abolition on the agenda?"

"Indirectly," Eb admitted. "He never used the word 'abolition,' but he did say that allowing free Blacks to go back to Africa would prompt a gradual end to slavery." Eb stopped to savor his first bite of apple pie. "That kind of thing goes over well up there. Gradual anything. They like conservative, glacial moves in Litchfield, assuming they veer in a morally righteous direction."

"I don't suppose he mentioned the Southern states legislating against manumission," Dr. Cabot grumbled. "South Carolina is debating a law prohibiting emancipation. Georgia's already done something like that."

"He didn't. And I couldn't really argue that slaves were going to be forced to migrate back to Africa if they bought their freedom. The Society insists it will be voluntary." Eb wiped his mouth with his napkin. "I must stick to their script."

"You and I both know it will end up in forced migration. Free Blacks will be run out of the country, people whose families have been here for a long time." Dr. Cabot gloomily shook his head. "Like Mr. and Mrs. Potts, William Lanson. Our whole neighborhood of free Blacks in New Haven. Such a valuable community." He took his own first bite of pie, relishing its flavor for a moment.

"People like Esmeralda," he added with a tinge of genuine sadness in his voice.

"That may be," Eb replied, "but Judge Reeve says I must confine myself to the facts—or in this instance, not jump to conclusions. I must not second-guess the intentions of the American Colonization Society. Neither may I be aspirational."

"I'm so glad not to be a lawyer," Dr. Cabot said with a shudder. "Why must you recognize both sides to every issue, when one side is so clearly wrong? And why shouldn't you be aspirational?" He waved his fork in the air as if it were a weapon about to be thrust into an invisible beast. "What good is the law if it can't be used to achieve moral results, like the abolition of slavery?"

"The law is just an instrument, Uncle," Eb said, repeating something Charles Godwin had once said to him in the attic. "It can be used to further moral imperatives—or to legislate immorality. It all depends on who's in power and whether the people support them." Eb considered his apple pie. Mrs. Potts must have used the extra tart apples, another ploy of hers.

"I suppose," Dr. Cabot conceded.

Eb started up again. "Then I argued the 'Back to Africa' movement would drain the country of effective anti-slavery advocates. The free Blacks, those who are doing well—like William Lanson—are devoted to freeing their enslaved brethren. Look at the churches they've established. We have free Black ministers holding forth from pulpits, free Black journalists writing in newspapers, organizing others against slavery. They make a mighty noise. If all of them go back to Africa, I argued, who would champion enslaved Africans? The abolition movement would be thwarted." Eb was carried away by his own rhetoric.

"I like that argument." Dr. Cabot had stopped using his fork for emphasis and dug back into his apple pie. "What else did you argue?" The staid physician was infected with Eb's enthusiasm.

"I asked the Board to consider who supports the 'Back to Africa' movement. They're white men like Jefferson, Madison, our president, Monroe—all slave owners from the South. Free Blacks pose a threat to their big plantations. They're afraid of race wars and insurrections—of losing their unpaid labor. The members of the ACS don't really want free Blacks to meet their human potential. They want to keep their brethren locked in the chains of slavery."

"I thought you weren't supposed to second-guess the intentions of the ACS."

"Then I pointed out who's opposed to the 'Back to Africa' movement," Eb continued, ignoring his uncle's astute observation. He was on a roll, returning to his night of glory. "The vast majority of free Blacks oppose the 'Back to Africa' movement. In 1816, the free Black community in Philadelphia unanimously voted against it. I quoted from the Resolution of the Meeting of Free People of Richmond, Virginia, from 1817." Eb sat forward in his seat, reciting this sentence in stentorian tones. "'We prefer being colonized in the most remote corner of the land of our nativity, to being exiled to a foreign country.'"

"You know, Eb, moving them out west—free Blacks and native people—has long been discussed." Dr. Cabot's enthusiasm temporarily receded. "As a means of getting rid of them. You don't want to appear to support a forced migration."

"I know, I know." Eb winced. "I thought about that later." He felt a little deflated, hoping his uncle would have been impressed by the quotation. "Anyhow, I put slavery front and center. We couldn't consider the 'Back to Africa' movement without putting it in context—against the backdrop of the morally corrupt institution of slavery."

"So, tell me . . ." Dr. Cabot looked over at his nephew with a new appreciation as Eb shoveled another bite of apple pie into his mouth. "Did you start from an anti-slavery position?"

"No, I started from a position of natural law—from our own Declaration of Independence. That all men are created equal. How white society does not truly accept that proposition. How free Blacks are discriminated against because of the widespread belief, as Jefferson suggests, that Blacks are biologically inferior." Eb took a break for more pie. "It seemed best to start with a critique of the so-called 'science' that justifies slavery. That's where I used your Dr. Rush." He wiped his mouth. "The only weak spot in my argument—I didn't want to suggest Congress lacked the power to regulate slavery. But that was okay. Oliver didn't want to litigate that either. The extent of federal power is a real hot potato up in Litchfield. Best to leave it in the fire." Eb scraped his plate of the last bit of pie. "I finished with an argument about how impractical the whole 'Back to Africa' scheme is." He was winding down. "You know, an appeal to prudential people."

"Splendid, Eb. So, who won this debate?" Dr. Cabot had been waiting for the punchline.

"Oliver Hull." Eb shrugged. His voice lacked even a note of dejection. "I knew he would. My arguments were too progressive for my audience. I was in Litchfield, in a hot, stuffy room full of aspiring, conservative future lawyers. A full quarter of the members of the Moot Court Board are from the South. My opponent was prepared and argued well. I knew Oliver would win. Again."

"You're taking your loss well." Dr. Cabot observed. "I remember how disappointed you were when you lost that first moot court. The one about the duped farmer with the dead horse."

"My friend Charles Godwin says it's sometimes better just to take a stand, even if, on this occasion, you're bound to lose." Eb looked over at his uncle with affection. "I always listen to what Charles has to say. And you too, Uncle." Eb did not mention that his presence in the dark, hidden room behind William Lanson's stable had changed his life forever. The recurring image of Percy's ravaged back loomed large in his dreams, and sometimes his daydreams, even half a year later.

"Does your brother know about this moot court argument?" Dr. Cabot suddenly realized Eb's public stance on abolition would not be well-received in Savannah or Charleston.

"Not yet." Eb groaned. "But he will. Once John catches word of it, my return to the South will become more difficult. I'm already persona non grata with the Southern law students. Most of them won't even speak to me now. Katherine Montgomery was none too pleased with me either."

"That's the young woman from Charleston you've been walking out with?" Dr. Cabot knew about Katherine Montgomery from Malinda's letters. It was a family difficult to keep secrets from. "The one whose stepfather owns a large plantation off the coast of South Carolina? Like John's wife?"

"Yes. We had a ferocious row after the moot court, right before the break. Katherine worries that news of the moot court, and my views, will travel down South in letters home. She's right about that. News does travel fast. She thought I should do something to mitigate the damage—write home that day and assure my family that I was just saying those things to win the moot court." Eb shook his head. "Winning is something Katherine understands, but the cruelty of slavery? That she does not."

"And what did you say to her?" Dr. Cabot wanted to tread lightly.

"I was honest with her. That for me, opposing slavery is not just an intellectual exercise, or a moot court puzzle, but a moral stance." Eb loosened the top button of his shirt which felt too tight. "That's when we had our row. Katherine claimed my views were an indictment of her father, her family, their livelihood, and entire way of life, and of my own brother's family as well. She went on to say her father treats his slaves with kindness. He tries to keep families together. He provides food, housing, and clothing for them. She considers

Lulu, her own personal slave, a friend. She even taught Lulu her letters." Eb continued to describe her tirade. "Katherine claims slavery's not always cruel and heartless. Plus, the cotton economy has brought prosperity to both the South and the North—a prosperity that has sent me to law school and purchased all my fancy clothes. She accused me of being a hypocrite."

Eb did not look at his uncle while he recounted Katherine's long litany of objections. Finally, he admitted the truth. "It wasn't pleasant, being the object of her anger. Katherine argues as well as any student who ever set foot in Judge Reeve's law school." Eb let out a long sigh. "And there's truth to what she says. My legal education, my nice clothes, my room and board, money for travel—my brother has provided me with all of that. Indirectly, I benefit from the enslavement of other human beings."

"Did you and this young woman break it off?"

"No." Eb looked over at his uncle. "But I'm waiting for my letter of dismissal. That's how my friend Thomas Bradford puts it. I call it my *Notice of Eviction*." Eb gave out a low chuckle. "Katherine is in Boston for the month, but I feel certain she'll soon give me my marching orders. That's her modus operandi. I hope you don't mind. I gave her your address here in New Haven."

"No problem at all." Dr. Cabot tried to look like he did not care. "Well, I'm proud of you, Eb, for taking a stand. To my mind, you won this moot court."

"To mine as well, Uncle." Eb leaned over to stack his empty pie plate on top of his uncle's. "And now I'm off to the library to work." Over the spring break, Eb was hoping to finish *Volume II*, and start with *Volume III*, despite still missing *Volume I*.

"Oh, Eb," Dr. Cabot said as he got up, checking his pocket watch to see the time. "We must talk tonight. We need to get your mother and sister out of Savannah. Malinda's having a terrible time persuading her to come north."

"The thing of it is, I'm in a bit of a pickle." Eb picked up the tray with the two empty plates and forks to take to Esmeralda. "Malinda wrote to ask me to convince Mother to come up to New Haven, and John wrote to ask me to convince Mother to go to Charleston. I'm paralyzed."

"I figured as much. I'll get this." Dr. Cabot took the tray from Eb's hands. "We must put our heads together and sort this out."

The two men separated, one to heal the sick and the other to copy his notes into leather-bound volumes. Dr. Cabot passed the tray of dirty dishes to Esmeralda, who had just emerged from the house.

Letter to Eb Wells from Katherine Montgomery, Boston,
May 20, 1820

Dear Eb,

I have given our conversation serious consideration. Upon reflection, I cannot countenance the views you put forth during the moot court—views you purport to believe in. My friend Lucy in Boston urges me to be patient with you. Sometimes young men who come up from the South are swayed by the influence of others—by men in authority they respect. It's a passing phase, Lucy promises. Maybe that Quaker Charles Godwin has turned your head, or you seek to emulate Judge Reeve or Lyman Beecher. You've fallen under their collective thrall. But Lucy doesn't know you as I do. Your stubborn streak will be your undoing, Eb. If you get it into your head to do or believe in something—no matter how ill-considered—there's no talking you out of it.

You'll hold to this radical stance, no matter how kindly we treat our slaves, no matter how much you personally have benefited from their labor in the cotton trade. With your public affirmation of abolitionist views, our courtship is unimaginable. My father will not countenance our alliance. And how can your brother John take you into his law practice? You'll bring ruin upon your family and shame upon those who care for you. I don't wish to stand by your side and watch you espouse these dangerous ideas.

My stepbrother James has advised me to cut off our relations. I'm going to do as he bids me. It's for the best we stop seeing one another. I have my own reputation to protect, even if you care nothing for your own. Please accept my judgment as final in this matter.

Respectfully yours,

Katherine Montgomery

"Does Charles know you've come?" Charles's mother, Mary Godwin, sat in her morning room in her home in New Haven. She had been reading alone, the men of the house having breakfasted and gone down to the wharf.

It was late May. Mary Godwin had asked her servant to raise the double-hung windows. A soft spring breeze blew in from Church Street. Around her shoulders, she wore a light shawl of yellow—homespun, dyed in dandelions—that matched the walls of the morning room. She faced a short young man, wearing a white shirt, brocaded vest, brown pants and gold-rimmed glasses, his auburn hair tucked behind his ears. Mary handed him a teacup and saucer.

"No, Charles doesn't know I'm here." Eb Wells had taken a big chance, stopping in at the Godwin home without an appointment. The last time he had taken such a leap, dire circumstances had justified the intervention. Charles had been on death's door. Eb had rushed over to Miss Pierce's to tell Martha what had transpired between Charles and her father. But no such emergency loomed today. When last seen, Charles was on the mend and learning how to cut profiles. "I didn't tell Charles I was coming." Eb picked up the delicate teacup from its matching saucer. It was trimmed in gold and painted with pink roses, just like his sister-in-law's old set that was ruined in the fire. "I came without his permission."

"And how is his health? Judge Reeve wrote that Charles was much better when he refunded the tuition. That we shouldn't concern ourselves about his condition." Mary Godwin turned her head, looking down at the pine floor. "Charles says the same in his letters, but I've been worried sick."

"He's much better, madam, although he was ill in March with a winter fever. The grippe, the doctor said. Very ill indeed."

"Yes, I learned that later." Mary Godwin made brief eye contact with Eb. It was the first time Eb had looked straight-on at her elegant face. He found the ghost of Charles around her eyes and mouth. Another influence had invaded the center of his face, but Charles bore many of his mother's features, her length, her tapering fingers, her reserved demeanor—at least with strangers. "I wish someone had let us know he was so ill," Mary Godwin added with a note of complaint. "I would have come up to Litchfield."

Eb tried to soften the blow. "Judge Reeve wanted to write you immediately. But Charles didn't want you to know. He knew you'd worry."

"Worry is a mother's prerogative." Mary Godwin gave Eb a faint smile. "Charles wrote us later, telling us of his plans, but his father was so angry about his dropping out of law school, taking on an apprenticeship, courting this Martha—well, Mr. Godwin asked me not to write back." She paused. "I haven't answered his letters."

"Charles has been waiting to hear from you. He's missing his mother terribly." Even if it veered slightly from the truth, Eb added hastily, "He misses all of you. You, his father, his brothers."

"It's difficult for me to disobey my husband." Mary Godwin

looked down at the floor again. "You must understand, Mr. Wells. I promised Mr. Godwin I wouldn't write, and I must keep my word. Charles has been very disobedient. His father isn't ready to forgive him. Charles must understand this as well."

Eb did not know how to reply, so he launched off on another topic. "I wish you could meet Martha Lewis." Eb decided to gloss over the period of the *Wrath of Martha* since relations had been restored. "She's a splendid girl, intelligent, lively—spirited even—and an expert at drawing maps." Eb did not know what else to say. Did Mary Godwin want to hear about her mane of coppery red hair, her splash of freckles, and Martha's irrepressible sense of humor? Looking over at Charles's pale, stately mother, the epitome of feminine restraint, Eb decided he should not promote Martha too much. Eb was a great Martha fan, but she might not fit easily within the bare, pale yellow walls and tall ceilings of Mary Godwin's refined morning room. "And she adores your son." This was truly Martha's greatest selling point with Charles's mother. "His whole family does. They've nursed him back to health."

"Charles writes that he's living in the studio behind their house." Mary Godwin said, ignoring Eb's comments about Martha and her family. "Is it warm enough out there for someone of his delicate constitution?"

"There's a woodburning stove in the studio, and the Lewis family is vigilant about providing Charles with enough wood." Eb was making some of this up. Charles had never complained of the cold, only that he wanted a cat at his feet. "Charles likes the privacy of the studio. He paints out there on his off-hours." Eb ventured carefully into these waters, hoping to stay in the shallows, not thrashing around in the deep end, his feet no longer touching the bottom. "Charles is doing remarkable portraits. He did one of Martha and has started on one of Judge Reeve's wife."

"Charles always was good at art. We were just set on him studying the law, that's all." She pursed her lips. "The shipping business could have used a lawyer, and it was never clear what Charles's calling in life was meant to be. We all thought law was a good fit."

"Charles did very well at the law, madam." Eb did not have to stretch the truth here. "But it doesn't suit him. He doesn't like to speak in public. The law has a performative aspect to it, as you know. Charles hates to perform. And he disdains competition. In the law, winning matters. Charles doesn't seem to care about who wins anything." Eb continued to summarize why he thought Charles Godwin was not suited to the law. "More to the point, Mrs. Godwin, Charles doesn't want to be a lawyer. He wants to be an artist, and he wants to marry Martha Lewis." Eb spoke rapidly through this last set of proclamations, fearing that if he hesitated, he might not finish what he had to say.

"Yes, Mr. Wells. I'm beginning to see the inevitability of both those things." She sighed, finally picking up her cup of tea. "We must resign ourselves to the life he's chosen. I keep telling that to my husband. Charles is an adult now, supporting himself. We no longer have control over him." Eb said nothing for a moment, letting the silence resound in the room. "It's just going to take some time for his father to accept that," Mary Godwin added quietly. "Mr. Godwin is much older. He's set in his ways, not quick to change his mind. Charles must be patient with him. I must be as well."

"Yes, of course. I do understand." Eb took his last sip of tea. "I have a family of my own to disappoint," he added with a forced laugh. Mary Godwin gave him a wan smile. "But I must go." Eb gingerly placed his empty teacup into its delicate saucer. "I will say this, Mrs. Godwin, if you were to come up to Litchfield for a visit, I could make you a reservation at the United States Hotel. Martha Lewis has entered her map of Connecticut rivers in Miss Pierce's public exhibition next month. It runs from June 20th to the 23rd. The prizes are given out at a reception on the first afternoon. Martha's sure to win a prize." Eb stood up, getting ready to leave the room. "It might be a good time for you to come and see Charles. You could make the acquaintance of Martha and the Lewis family."

"I'll give it some thought, Mr. Wells. I think it's unlikely though, given how my husband feels. But we shall see. I'll speak to him." She got up and extended her hand to Eb. "Thank you for coming to see me this morning. I'm relieved to hear Charles is well, and grateful he has such a good friend. I don't expect you'll tell Charles you were here." Eb said nothing. "But if he becomes ill again, or is in any way wanting," she added, looking Eb directly in the eye, "would you please let me know? Even if Charles forbids it?"

Eb nodded a vague affirmation, feeling awkward and shy. He wondered if a silent nod constituted an enforceable promise. He backed out of the morning room on Church Street, bowing to Mary Godwin. Saying his farewell, Eb felt a pang of homesickness. Charles was not the only one who missed his mother. How long had it been since he'd heard his own mother's sweet voice?

CHAPTER 6

Lids and Pots

Eb Wells loved Savannah in the spring. Spring in Savannah was glorious. The whole city was redolent with a heady fragrance, resplendent with blooming flowers, shrubs and trees with waxy green leaves and exploding colors—pale pink, orange, yellow, coral, scarlet—a tropical paradise. Migrating songbirds abounded. Eb's favorite bird, the Painted Bunting, came through each year—a fusion of blue, green, yellow, and red. Eb was even fond of Savannah's autumn and winter, predictably gray and often wet, but the air was mild and fresh and good for sleeping. The marshes around town took on the glowing hues of golden wheat. The White Ibis, Snowy Egret, and Brown Pelican came to roost. The city's palette was muted and subdued.

But summer in Savannah? Eb had nothing good to say about it. The weather was miserably hot and humid. Summer in Savannah was also risky. It brought stagnant air, dangerous swamp miasmas, hurricanes, aggressive mosquitoes, cockroaches the size of mice, ticks, predictable rounds of summer fevers, malaria, yellow fever, diarrhea, and a feeling of deep lassitude and fatigue. Summer in Savannah could even be fatal. Those who could afford it left the coastal area and retreated to the interior of the state, to higher elevations, perhaps to summer homes in the mountains. But Eb's family had no place to go. His mother would close the shutters of their house on East York Street, and the family tried to stay cool inside its dark rooms. Summer in Savannah was something to be endured.

"So, Charles, that's why I love summer in Connecticut." Eb and Charles were walking along the Goshen Road from the Lewis cottage to Miss Pierce's. It was late June. Today was the first day of the public exhibition of student ornamental artwork at the Litchfield Female Academy.

The opening drew people from all over the county. Town leaders and faculty from both schools would be present, and most of their students. Refreshments would be served. A student pianist would be hard at work, dressed in her best frock, providing a soothing background from the pianoforte for the enjoyment of samplers, botanical watercolors, landscapes, maps from all over the world, embroidered scenes, miniatures, and mourning pictures. The judges would announce the winners at the afternoon reception. Mrs. Beecher and Mrs. Reeve were on the panel of judges. Miss Pierce herself never judged, wanting to remain impartial.

Eb had walked out to the Lewis cottage to fetch Charles. The two had vowed to attend the event together—for moral support. Eb had not set foot in Miss Pierce's since his *Notice of Eviction* from Katherine Montgomery the month before. He was afraid of their first encounter.

Charles too was apprehensive. Eb had been successful in luring Charles's mother to come up to Litchfield, ostensibly to see Martha Lewis's maps, but more to make amends to her darling Charles and meet the Lewis family. Mary Godwin was already ensconced in the United States Hotel. Charles was excited about seeing her, but anxious. He had bristled at Eb's meddling, but his eagerness to reconcile with his mother had diluted his ire. Charles's father had not come.

"It's my favorite time of year." Charles stopped to peer up into a canopy of maple trees. Everything around them was lush and green. The grass along the dry-stacked rock fence was tall, punctuated with staunch yellow dandelions. The hum of insects could be heard in the background. The sun was warm, and its rays, filtering through the maple leaves, made dappled patterns of light and dark on the road. On the horizon, white wispy clouds were etched across the cornflower blue sky. It was a stunning June day in northwest Connecticut. "But it's even better up here." Charles looked down at the shifting patterns of light cast by the verdant canopy above. "Litchfield has a quality of light in mid-summer I cannot put my finger on."

"I wonder . . ." Eb was contemplating. "Perhaps this day's glory has something to do with the miserable, cold winter we've had to endure." Poor Eb was still in shock over the New England winter he had just survived—his first encounter with snow, ice, and deep, bone-chilling cold. He had never experienced such discomfort for so long—short day after short day, and the longest nights of his existence. It was true, January brought brief, brilliant days of bright sun when the snow glistened and crunched beneath his boots, the sky a cobalt blue. But even on those days, Eb was freezing. The law school was not heated, the library was not heated, his room was not heated.

At night, Mrs. Edwards sent Maggie up with a piping hot brick, heated by the kitchen fire and wrapped in a thick cotton cloth, to warm the bottom of Eb's bed. This gesture was more out of solicitude for the old cat than for her boarder, Eb suspected. He had grown accustomed to having Sir Winston at the bottom of his bed. The hot brick allowed Eb's pale feet to thaw out and gave Sir Winston something sturdy to wrap around. This provided Eb's lower extremities with much-needed freedom from the weight of the old cat and several heavy woolen blankets. Even though warm in bed, Eb could still see his breath when he got up to use the chamber pot. "Do you think this splendid summer day would mean as much to us," Eb mused, "if our bodies didn't remember February?"

"It was a bad winter, I'll admit. But nothing like the winter four years ago. And in 1817, it was even colder. The crops were so bad that year due to the harsh winter, farmers in Connecticut went hungry. A lot of them left for Ohio."

"I can't imagine a harsher winter than this last one." Eb shuddered. "But what do you think of my idea—that spring seems so lovely because we're still in shock from winter?"

"Yes." Charles gave the subject thought. "There's something to that. Death does the same thing for life. This very day we're having, this perfect day . . ." Charles breathed in the summer smells of hay, grass, and abundant growth. "It's even more beautiful because we know it won't last forever. Autumn will return. Leaves will fall, the sun's light and warmth will wane, the cold Arctic air will descend from Canada again. This lovely summer day is ephemeral, as are we. Death gives the whole experience meaning."

"Goodness, Charles," Eb muttered under his breath. "I just meant how cold my feet were." Ever since his illness, Charles was ready to invite death into almost every conversation. It was getting annoying.

"Not to worry." Charles was cheerful. "I was just pointing out how your theory echoes mine. We need winter to enjoy summer. Death to appreciate life." The two men walked along in amiable silence for a while.

"Do you ever wonder, Charles," Eb abruptly said, "whether it will mean anything to anyone that you lived a life? You know, will it matter there was once a short, nearsighted man named Eb Wells who was here on this earth for a little while?"

"I do wonder about that," Charles responded without hesitation. "It's one reason I paint. I want to make my mark. Leave behind some part of me. Like you say, evidence that Charles Godwin was once alive and saw beauty in an old woman's hands." Charles was obsessed with his current portrait of Mrs. Reeve, who would have balked at being called an 'old woman.'

"You're so lucky to be an artist, Charles. Martha too. Just look at her splendid maps and botanical watercolors. She'll be dead in a hundred years—as dead as you and I will be—but you both will have left something behind for posterity. A painting. A map that captured the contours of Connecticut and its waterways in the early part of the century." Eb hurled a rock from the roadway over a stone fence to keep a cart's wheel from encountering it. "But what do I leave behind to show that I was here?"

"It's early to say, Eb, but you may have children and grand-children. They count toward your immortality. And what about the fruits of your labors?" Charles continued, again without hesitation. "You'll use your legal skills to help people. Your efforts on behalf of others may help change the course of history." Eb strode on silently, his hands behind his back, listening to his friend. He appreciated that Charles was slowing his pace, enabling Eb's much shorter legs to keep up with the long Godwin stride. "Take that slave you helped transport to Waterbury last winter. What was his name?"

"Percy." Despite Dr. Cabot's strict orders of secrecy, Eb had shared with Charles how he had helped William Lanson transport Percy to Waterbury. He was incapable of keeping a secret from his friend.

"That act alone," Charles said, making a sweeping gesture with his hand, "is testament to the fact that Eb Wells was once here. You helped make it possible for Percy's children and grandchildren to be born out of slavery."

"I guess so. On that theory, I might just as well die today." Eb laughed. "I've made my mark, although no one will ever know. All history will know is this. Ebenezer Wells did not go to Yale and lost the moot court—twice—at the Litchfield Law School."

"I guess that means you can't die today." Charles gave Eb a nervous grin. "Please don't. I need you to help smooth things over with my mother. And act as a buffer with Martha." The two walked along in silence for another minute or two. "Are you nervous about seeing Katherine again?"

"I am." For weeks, Eb had imagined how it would be when he and Katherine Montgomery first met after their breakup. In his mind's eye, Katherine would come up to him in the parlor of Miss Pierce's, pulling herself up to her full height, towering over him, her blonde curls shaking with rage from side to side, her talons extended. She would castigate him, excoriate him, demolish him—all in front of the gaping crowd assembled at the ornamental arts exhibition. He would wither under her verbal assault and melt into a puddle on the floor. Mr. Anscombe, the caretaker at Miss Pierce's, would have to bring a bucket of soap and hot water to mop up the greasy remnants of Eb Wells, the Wretched Abolitionist. "Don't leave my side, Charles, when we get there." Charles and Eb had made a pact to stay together for the day, no matter which of the two awkward social situations they were attending to.

"Don't worry. I'll protect you from the furious raptor, Katherine Montgomery. But you must assure me Martha and my mother won't tear each other apart."

"I'll do my best." Eb and Charles were approaching Miss Pierce's on North Street. The judges would soon be announcing the winners of the exhibition. They stepped up their pace.

From a distance, Eb could see the tall figure of Katherine Montgomery on the front lawn of the female academy, arm in arm with a tall man, gazing up at him with a coquettish smile. A tall man with a horsey face. Oliver Hull.

Letter to Elizabeth Stafford from Rebecca Harding, Litchfield,
June 28, 1820

Dearest Elizabeth,

This will be a short letter. Thank you for sending me *Guy Man-nering* from the 'author of *Waverley*.' Martha and I have already started it. The endless summer days allow for more reading. No need to ration candles. Martha loves the part about the gypsy telling the baby boy's fortune. She comes from a superstitious family. They all believe in ghosts and diviners at the Lewis cottage.

I've accepted the job in Wethersfield—a one-year contract as a tutoress. Your grandmother and I have come to terms on my board-ing. I'll be teaching in the upper female division at the Wethers-field Academy, rhetoric, composition, and grammar. Mrs. Johnson understood about my staying with Mrs. Cox, but I've promised to take a meal with them once a week. I believe Penny has finished her course at Miss Patten's and is coming home. I'll relish her com-pany. (Although I wish it were yours as well.) Mrs. Johnson reports Penny has been courting an apprentice doctor from Hartford. He'll be coming to Wethersfield for a visit in September. I'm to join them for his welcoming dinner. The meeting will entail, no doubt, intense scrutiny of his background and demeanor. Mrs. Johnson will proba-bly check for cleanliness behind the poor man's ears.

You were silent about your romantic life. What should I infer from your reticence?

You ask for news of Martha. She just won a big award for her map of Connecticut rivers. She and Charles Godwin have settled back into their romance as if nothing ever happened. Charles's mother came up from New Haven to see the exhibition, to meet the Lewis family, and repair relations with her son. I predict Mrs. God-win will come around on Martha. She can't fail to see that Martha adores her son. What more can a mother ask for?

No one has seen hide nor hair of Eb Wells since Katherine Montgomery dismissed him. He made a brief appearance at the exhibition, but disappeared before I had a chance to say hello—all I could do was give him a half-hearted wave across the room. Katherine has taken up with Oliver Hull, another star from the law school. Oliver dumped the heiress from Hartford for the privilege of having the tall Southern beauty from Charleston on his arm. Another doomed romance, I fear. Katherine's third this year. Oliver Hull is not, I feel certain, moving to the South.

I feel sorry for Katherine. Her search for a husband has a frantic quality. The man she seeks must meet her exacting standards. If he doesn't, Katherine is determined to mold him to her liking. I suspect Eb was not that pliable. Eb is often unsure of himself but determined to make his own way. One day before class, I heard Katherine make merciless fun of Eb's commonplace book, *The Detritus*. It took my breath away. How could she purport to love the man and yet deride *The Detritus*? Everything surprising and funny about Eb Wells is inside that book.

I must go. Mary Pierce and I are up to our ears with letters of acceptance, answering questions about dance and music lessons, placing young women in various boarding houses. Sometimes I wish I had no flair for administration. I'm good at it but dislike the work.

More later, and good luck with your exams. Missing you.
All my love,

Rebecca

"I'm grateful you took such good care of Charles when he was ill, Mrs. Lewis." Mary Godwin and Ruth Lewis were alone in the kitchen of the Lewis cottage. Ruth tended a simmering beef stew in a huge copper pot hanging above the fire. A basket of corn muffins was cooling on the table. She had also just brewed a fresh pot of tea for her visitor. Charles had rented a carriage from the hotel to transport his mother out to the Lewis cottage. He had wanted to stay in the kitchen, but Ruth pushed him out the door. She was determined to meet with Mary Godwin alone.

Charles and Benjamin Lewis were out in the studio, working on a large order of silhouettes for an entire family in Kent. Charles had been experimenting with staining the wood frames instead of painting them black, but Benjamin had not liked the effect. The black resonates with the profiles, he insisted. Charles was discouraged, but Mr. Lewis was right. Now they were contemplating putting the family's portraits inside a single frame, another innovation of Charles's. Benjamin was bemoaning that there were only three children instead of four. It was ruining the symmetry. Charles wondered if a profile of the beloved family dog might suffice—to even out the portrait. An expansion on the concept of family.

"We weren't even told Charles was ill until he was on the mend." Mary Godwin regarded the pretty, redheaded woman who had just sat down at the table. Ruth Lewis was dressed in a plain house frock and apron. "Apparently, Charles didn't want us to know."

"I know." Ruth put the teapot down on a woolen crocheted mat, a childhood art project of Martha's. Ruth looked across the table at Mary Godwin. Charles's mother was dressed in a tailored gray morning dress, with a matching gray and maroon paisley shawl tied loosely around her narrow shoulders. "I heard that later," Ruth said. "Charles wouldn't let Judge Reeve write you." Ruth offered Mary Godwin cream for her tea. Mary raised a long, delicate hand and shook her head. "I didn't agree with that," Ruth continued. "Judge Reeve ought to have overruled Charles. He wasn't in his right mind from the fever. You should have been told directly. If one of my lads had taken ill, or my Martha, I'd want to know."

"Precisely." Mary took her first sip of tea. The tea was well-brewed, although she noticed the two teacups they used did not match. The teapot itself came from a different tribe altogether. "Charles and I quarreled when he came home over the break. You know, about dropping out of law school." Mary Godwin continued with hesitation. "And working with your husband."

"And wanting to be with our Martha too, I imagine." Ruth Lewis decided to help the tall, shy woman overcome the high conversational hurdle. Mary Godwin could not bring herself to reply. "Do you know, Mrs. Godwin, about the foolish deal your son and my husband concocted over Charles wanting to court Martha? How my Benjamin insisted that Charles get the approval of both you and your husband? And if he failed, Charles had to break it off and couldn't tell Martha why?" Ruth got up from the table on a mission.

"Yes, I know all that now. Charles told me everything last night." The evening before, Charles and his mother had eaten supper alone at the United States Hotel. Charles had poured his heart out to his mother—about his ill-fated bargain with Benjamin Lewis, the letter to Martha, dropping out of law school, his inability to get out of bed in the morning, painting Martha's portrait, his illness—and brush with death. "I didn't know all that at the time, or I wouldn't have been so harsh," Mary added wistfully, "or so dismissive."

"It wasn't your fault." Ruth rummaged around in the bread box. "It's my Benjamin who should take the blame here. I would say Charles too, but he's so trusting and naïve. Charles loves Martha so much, he couldn't imagine you wouldn't love her too, even though you'd never met her." Ruth's arm almost disappeared inside the bread box. "And I suppose, through your eyes, his knowing the Lewis family put a stop to his legal studies." Ruth seemed pleased, having unearthed the covered plate in the back of the box, hidden from her men. "Benjamin set Charles up in a most unfair way." Ruth carefully lifted the plate out. "My husband can be so unreasonable if he thinks he's protecting Martha. A pig-headed mule."

"I am familiar with unreasonable husbands." Mary Godwin gave Ruth a wan smile. "I tried to get my husband to come up to Litchfield with me, to see Charles and meet Martha and all of you, but he refused." Mary was ordinarily a reticent person, but something about Ruth Lewis gave her the courage to be frank. Ruth set the plate down on the table, yet again from a different china pattern. It was laden with a small mountain of shortbread.

"Husbands." Ruth Lewis shook her head in commiseration.

"It's been a blow to George," Mary Godwin continued, "Charles's dropping out of law school. He didn't stick it out at Yale either." She picked up a piece of shortbread and took a delicate bite. "We were running out of things for Charles to do."

"That's not the way I see it." Ruth sat back down and poured her own cup of tea. Even though Mary Godwin looked like a pale, delicate bird, a gray mourning dove perhaps, Ruth was determined not to treat her too lightly. "Charles is going to be fine," Ruth stated in a forthright manner. "He's earning a living now and learning a trade. And I promise you, Benjamin will teach him well. Charles has found something he wants to do. He's got an artistic gift."

"You're probably right." Mary Godwin leaned back in her chair, taking in the cozy cottage, the warm, crackling fire with its pot of beef stew slowly simmering, this kind woman about her own age, offering her the best shortbread she had ever tasted. "But it's going to take time to convince my husband. You're not the only one married to a pig-headed mule." Mary hesitated. "But I'll have to say this. George is making an effort. My own parents were opposed to our marriage for religious reasons. It was stressful, for both of us. Anyhow, even though my husband refused to come to Litchfield with me, he wanted me to come up and present Charles with an offer. An offer of compromise." Ruth Lewis was closely scrutinizing Mary Godwin's face. "We would let Charles court Martha. He could work on Saturdays and holidays with your husband, but in return, Charles must agree to return to the law school to finish up the course—do an apprenticeship, get admitted to a bar at least." Mary Godwin peered tentatively over at Ruth Lewis. "What do you think about that?"

"It doesn't matter what I think," Ruth responded without hesitation. "Charles's opinion is what matters." Ruth Lewis said this as if it were a proclamation. She also wanted to quarrel with the phrase, 'we would let Charles court Martha,' but decided against it. "Does Charles know about your husband's offer?"

"I tried the idea out on him last night, but Charles said an emphatic 'no.' He doesn't like the law, he insists. He wants to be an artist, or an artisan—whatever you call what he does out there with your husband. And his love for Martha is non-negotiable. He's clear on that. Now that I've met her . . ." Mary gave Martha's mother a warm smile. "Well, I understand better his loyalty."

"I'd say you've got your answer then—from Charles at least." Ruth Lewis was secretly pleased her daughter had passed Mary Godwin's muster. "Charles never much enjoyed the law, as far as I could tell. Even if he hadn't met Martha and Benjamin. It didn't suit him."

"That's what Eb Wells told me too." Mary Godwin took her second piece of shortbread. "My husband doesn't understand the attitude of these young men—like our Charles—who think an occupation must 'suit' them. Charles has always been searching for something he 'likes to do.' George just keeps saying, what does it matter if you 'like to do' it? It's your work." Mary Godwin shook her head. "For him, that's the end of the discussion. If it's your work, you do it. That's how a man provides for his family."

Ruth Lewis contemplated a response but opted for silence. Her own husband had followed his passion in choosing his work. Ruth had long ago accepted their lot in life. Still, she looked longingly at Mary Godwin's shawl with its delicately woven paisley pattern, swimming with little maroon teardrop shapes. Benjamin's decision to be an artisan had landed her in a cottage on the edge of Litch-field, with mismatching china. Ruth Lewis had only three dresses in her wardrobe. They were scrimping to pay Martha's tuition at Miss Pierce's, even with help from her brothers.

But something else was bothering Ruth Lewis. "I wonder, Mrs. Godwin . . ." Ruth put her chin in her hand, considering all that Mary Godwin had just told her. "Does my Martha know about this offer of compromise from your husband?"

"I don't know. I doubt it. I saw no indication the matter was going any further. Not from Charles's response. The law isn't what he wants to do. He was adamant."

"I'm just asking." Ruth Lewis folded her hands on the table. "I'm worried. We've all of us made a lot of plans for Charles and Martha. I know Martha's felt left out. She feels like everyone's plot-ting her course without asking her." Ruth looked down. "Martha's right, really. Even I've been part of those schemes." She was thinking about the recent negotiations with Jack about Charles joining the business.

"It's so difficult being a parent." Mary Godwin gave her a look of sympathy. "And even more difficult to be a young woman. I remem-ber how Martha feels. My own parents thought they had a stake in my future. I'd like to believe things are better for young women these days, but I'm not certain it's true."

"Would you mind, Mrs. Godwin, if I mentioned to Martha this offer of compromise from your husband—about courting her, being a part-time apprentice with Benjamin, in exchange for returning to his legal studies? An apprenticeship? Passing a bar exam?"

"Of course not," Mary Godwin responded with alacrity. "That would only be proper. More than any of us, Martha has an interest in what Charles does for a living, or so it seems to me. It would be her livelihood as well—if . . ." She paused, and then said with deliberation, "When they marry." A silence hung between the two women for a few seconds. Mary Godwin looked up at Mrs. Lewis shyly. "And please, Mrs. Lewis, won't you call me 'Mary'?"

"That would be lovely." Ruth Lewis gave her a smile. "And you must call me 'Ruth.'" Thinking it was time to change the subject, Ruth asked, "What did you think about the exhibition yesterday?"

"I was most impressed by Martha's map." Mary seemed relieved the difficult part of the conversation was over. "She certainly deserved that award."

The day before, Martha had won first prize for her Connecticut rivers map and an honorable mention for a watercolor, a still life of glistening, purple grapes. Charles had stood by Martha's side during the reception, beaming with pride, his mother on his arm. Martha was excited about winning first prize. She was radiant in a new pale pink cotton dress her mother had stitched. Her father, mother, and brother Jack had also attended the ceremony. Benjamin Lewis was over the moon about his daughter's Connecticut rivers map.

"I was amazed myself. I'll tell you that," Ruth Lewis admitted. "She's my own girl and all, but I never knew Martha had any artistic talent." Ruth cocked her head in the studio's direction. "It must come from her father. I can't even draw a stick figure."

"Probably so. I envy you having a daughter." Mary chewed thoughtfully on her shortbread. "I raised three boys, two from my husband's earlier marriage, and Charles, but I'm often lonely in a household full of men."

"I'll have to admit. When Martha arrived, I was thrilled. We had the three boys too." Ruth blushed slightly. "To tell you the truth, Martha came to us late in life. She was a complete surprise. Benjamin and I thought we were done."

Mary Godwin flushed slightly at Ruth's confession, but at the same time she was happy to be in her confidence. "Martha seems like such a lively girl. Spirited, so it seems."

"Oh, she's spirited all right." Ruth Lewis let out a sudden guffaw. She tilted the plate in Mary Godwin's direction and offered her another piece of shortbread. Mary could not help herself, picking up a third piece with her long, thin fingers. Ruth Lewis leaned back in her chair and smoothed back an errant lock of red hair. "Let me tell you how spirited my Martha can be."

An hour or so later, Benjamin Lewis and Charles Godwin appeared at the back door of the cottage, looking for the midday meal. Jack Lewis too was hungry, having emerged from his office for *Lewis Portraits.* Much to their surprise, Ruth Lewis and Mary Godwin were still sitting at the table, chatting freely, next to an empty teapot and a plate that had once shouldered a mountain of shortbread. A mountain no more—and no meal yet on the table. But the beef stew was ready, Ruth Lewis told her hungry men standing at the threshold of the kitchen, the corn bread as well.

"Just give me ten minutes to set the table." Ruth shooed them away. "We're expecting Charles and Mary to join us for the meal." Charles looked at his mother with raised eyebrows. She gave him a wink and a warm smile.

"We'd love to stay." Mary Godwin got up from her seat. "Let me help you with the table."

The year 1820 was a terrible year for the city of Savannah—and for the Wells family. First, the devastating fire in January, and then a yellow fever epidemic in the summer and fall. The former destroyed the home of John and Eliza Wells. The latter resulted in the death of Abigail Cabot Wells, aged fifty-three years—the mother of John, Malinda, and Eb Wells.

No one really knew how yellow fever was transmitted. Some believed that deadly miasmas, vapors from the eastern winds containing decomposing substances, harbored the infection. Others theorized the fever was carried by slaves from the west coast of Africa or the West Indies. To be on the safe side, strangers were to be avoided at all costs, particularly if they had just disembarked from a ship.

Deaths by yellow fever were horrific, marked by distinct and grotesque symptoms—spiking and recurring fevers, discharges of bile, severe body pains, hemorrhaging noses and bowels, spongy gums, flushed cheeks and lips, furry tongues, delirium, a liver under siege causing jaundice in the head and shoulders, and finally vomiting of a black matter that looked something like dark coffee grounds. It was a violent and swift way to die, with its victims usually perishing within a week. The yellow fever epidemic of 1820 eventually claimed almost 700 lives—over ten percent of the population of Savannah. Abigail Cabot Wells was among them.

How was it that Eb's mother and sister were still living in Savannah during the fever season of 1820? In the late spring, rumors of deaths from yellow fever were already whispered, although confined to the northeast quadrant of the city, near the Washington Square area, home to many recent Irish immigrants. The leaders of Savannah did not want to admit publicly that this year's summer illness was yellow fever. When the telltale black vomit began to appear—the reason for calling the illness 'Black Jack'—the Mayor of Savannah continued to insist the disease was confined to the one section of town, mostly full of 'strangers and people of intemperate, dissolute habits.'

It was not until middle September, after so many deaths had occurred, that the Board of Health was forced to acknowledge the presence of yellow fever in Savannah. The Board advised people to leave the city. Anyone who could afford to—over seventy percent of the residents— had already left town. Savannah was a deserted ghost town. From a population of around seven thousand five hundred, only one thousand five hundred remained in town. Abigail and Malinda Wells were among them, as well as their housekeeper,

Lottie, and her daughter, Susan. Abigail Wells was determined to stay put, despite desperate pleas from family members to flee either to Charleston or New Haven. As her older son put it, Abigail Wells refused to budge, and because Abigail Wells refused to budge, Eb's sister Malinda was stuck in Savannah too. She would never leave her mother's side.

From Abigail Wells's point of view, riding the epidemic out at home seemed reasonable. This was not the first yellow fever outbreak in Savannah. It would not be the last. Just fourteen years earlier, when Eb was eight, yellow fever had decimated the city. Yet no one in the family had fallen ill. They had avoided any exposure to strangers, rarely leaving the house except for bare necessities. Yellow fever had returned almost every year during the fever season, but the number of cases was low, with only Africans or Irishmen as its victims. Based on that experience, Abigail Wells felt safe. She had escaped the clutches of 'Black Jack' before. She and her family would do so again. By the middle of July, she, Malinda, Lottie, and Susan had hunkered down in the house once more until the season of sickness was over. 'Black Jack' would pass them by.

Abigail Wells was relieved. The yellow fever epidemic gave her an excuse to shutter the house and stay inside her own four walls. Home was where Abigail wanted to be. Home was where she felt safe. She felt besieged by entreaties from everyone—her sons, her brother, her daughter, Susan, Lottie—to flee Savannah, first from the fire and now from yellow fever. But Abigail Wells did not want to sleep in any bed but her own. She did not want to eat meals at any table but her own. She did not want to read a book in any parlor but her own. Now that sickness had descended upon the city, Abigail had an excuse to stay home, right where she wanted to be, following prudent advice never to go out.

The strategy worked well, until it did not. Whatever the mechanism of transmission, in the middle of August, yellow fever made its way through the walls of the clapboard house on East York Street and overtook Abigail Wells. Oddly enough, no other members of the household were affected. Malinda, Susan, and Lottie took turns nursing Abigail with no apparent risk of infection. But they failed to keep her alive. All the doctor could do was to give her laudanum to keep her comfortable, as she drifted unaware through a nether world. Abigail died the fourth day of the illness, after vomiting up dark matter for several hours. It was a horrible way to die, and worse yet to witness. Malinda was heartbroken, watching her mother suffer, and devastated when Abigail fell back upon her pillow, yellow-skinned, perspiring, wracked with fever, and took her last agonizing, rattling breath.

But death acted as an arbiter. The conflict was resolved. Abigail Cabot Wells would stay put in Savannah—and die there. Over thirty years before, when she was just twenty years old, she had come to Savannah to make a new life with her husband. She had died in the same bed where she had given birth to their five children. She had remained in the same house, and the same city, where she and William had raised three of those children and buried the other two. Savannah was her home. Unrelenting to the end, Abigail Cabot Wells had gotten her way.

Malinda took over the sad task of writing to her brothers and Dr. Cabot. John came promptly down from Charleston to ensure their mother was properly buried next to their father and two sisters in the Old Cemetery on South Broad Street. With so many dead in the city, bodies were being carried over to the Old Cemetery on carts. Later that fall, a mass grave had to be dug. A private grave was not guaranteed unless a family member pressed for one. John Wells did his duty by his mother, but his heart was heavy. Somehow, he felt he had let her down. But John's guilt was misplaced. There had been no persuading Abigail Cabot Wells to leave Savannah.

Eb had just returned to Litchfield from New Haven when he got Malinda's letter. The news of his mother's death hit him hard.

Losing his father when Eb was off at college had saddened him, but in an almost abstract way. His father's bouts of recurrent fever had often put William Wells on death's door. At least to his children, if not to his hopelessly optimistic wife, the death of William Wells was a well-rehearsed event. And Eb had a more complicated relationship with his father. They had not been close.

Losing his mother was another matter altogether. Not only was her death unexpected, but the loss was also far greater. Next to Malinda, Eb was closest to his mother. She was his caretaker, nurturer, educator and helpmate, his greatest champion and avid listener to stories in which Eb was always the hero, the interpreter of all his triumphs and disasters, minor and major. She was his mother. Eb had already been separated from her for almost a year. He could not bring himself to imagine that he would never see her again.

Eb had never mourned before. He stumbled around the boarding house, the law school, and the town of Litchfield in a daze, oblivious to the peak of the Connecticut summer and to every social interaction. Like an automaton, he took notes during the lectures, copied them, ate, studied, slept, and did it all over again the next day. Every time Eb thought about his mother, he would choke up and start to cry. He was afraid to let that happen. What if he started to cry—Eb was in a panic—and couldn't stop?

Eb shied away from feeling anything at all, disturbed by the flood of emotions that were backing up within him. It felt like being pulled along by the rushing waters of the Niagara River, approaching the precipitous drop at the top of the Horseshoe Falls that Eb had heard so much about. Eb feared that if he acknowledged the sadness in his heart, it would be like tumbling over those falls in a rickety barrel. He would fall and fall and fall into a deafening wall of white mist, only to drown in the churning green pool below.

Charles Godwin and Martha Lewis tried to soothe him. Ruth Lewis tried to soothe him. Mrs. Edwards tried to soothe him. Betsey

Reeve tried to soothe him. Judge Reeve tried to soothe him. Even Thomas Bradford tried to soothe him—all to no avail. Eb just kept telling everyone he was fine, thank you, and threw himself into his studies. Rebecca Harding wrote him a note of condolence.

Eb Wells was past the middle of his course of study at the Litchfield Law School. He was determined to remain at the top of his class. Eb's response to everyone's solicitude was 'I must study, I must study, I must study.' By giving Eb permission to ignore his grief, the study of law kept him sane. The situation could not last forever, but for now, studying kept Eb Wells from drowning. The law was keeping him dry.

"I don't know how you're going to paint such a dried-up old grape." Martha sat at the worktable on a high stool in the studio, watching Charles Godwin sketch. Her father had gone into the Lewis cottage. "She's practically a raisin."

It was a Saturday in early August, not Ruth Lewis's usual baking day, but she had made a peach pie for Martha. Benjamin wanted to have a chat with Jack about their travel schedule in the fall. He also wanted to give the couple privacy. Martha had come home from Miss Pierce's to spend the night, to visit her family and see Charles. Jack had procured Charles his first commission for an oil portrait of a rich old lady on South Street. Charles was now working on preliminary sketches.

"It's my job to find the beauty in her." Charles was not paying much attention to Martha. "She's a very nice woman." The day before, Charles Godwin and Jack Lewis had gone over to the patroness's gracious federal style home across from the law school for her first sitting. The old woman had offered them tea and told Charles about the early years of her life in Canaan when there were still lots of native people living in Litchfield County. "She has spirit too."

"I'm glad you're doing this and not me." Martha yawned. "Painting an old woman. I like flowers when they're in bloom, not when they're all withered up and dying."

"I like flowers when they're in bloom—*and* when they're all withered up and dying." Charles was sketching in wrinkles on the old woman's face. "You should be glad of that, Martha. It means I'll find you beautiful when you're an old lady—if I'm lucky enough to still be around."

"That's very romantic of you." Martha could not imagine she too would have wrinkles someday. More freckles, yes, but wrinkles never. Growing old was out of the question. Martha put her elbows on the table and leaned forward. "I've been thinking about something. Do you think Eb and Rebecca will ever become a couple?"

"I don't know." Charles had tried many times to get his best friend to discuss his feelings for Rebecca Harding, but Eb was always evasive. Now after the death of his mother, Charles could hardly get Eb to talk about any feelings at all. "I hope so. Rebecca thinks she can't marry because of her teaching profession, but I think they're well-suited for one another."

"I do too," Martha said. "My mother always says there's a lid for every pot, but it seems to me some people have more unusual pot shapes than others. Rebecca's an odd pot. So is Eb. Lids for them are much harder to come by."

"I agree." Charles had sunk back into his most recent sketch, wondering whether it had been wise to insist his patroness wear her lacy white cap. "Unusual pots, both of them," he repeated, without giving it much thought.

"Do you think I'm an unusual pot, Charles?" Martha cocked her head. She had the distinct impression Charles was paying more attention to his sketchbook than to her. Her mother had warned her not to visit the studio when Charles was working. Her advice was based on several decades of marriage to Benjamin Lewis. Martha may as well stay inside and talk to her mother.

"Hmmm."

"Are you even listening to me?" Martha said, her voice rising.

"I'm sorry, Martha." Always on the alert for Martha's temper, Charles heard the flicker of irritation in her voice. He promptly put his sketch pad down on the worktable, giving her his full attention. "What did you ask me?"

"I asked if I was an unusually shaped pot." Martha was pleased to have him look at her. "Requiring an unusual lid?" Charles leaned over and gave Martha a quick, soft kiss. She reached up to stroke his cheek and scruffy sideburns.

"You're the most unique and beautiful pot I've ever encountered, my love." Charles smiled down at Martha and ran his hand over her coppery red hair. "And I am your most willing lid, if you'll have me." Charles gave her another kiss, this one more perfunctory, on the top of her head. "I will mold myself to whatever unusual pot shape you offer me."

"That's sweet, Charles." Martha inched to the edge of the stool, moving back to her original question. "But I'm going to insist Rebecca meet up with Eb before she leaves for Wethersfield. I hope you'll do the same with Eb. Encourage him, won't you?" She leaned into Charles's arm. "We've got to get them together."

"Yes, my love," Charles said absentmindedly, having returned to his sketch.

"And Charles . . ." Martha said tentatively. "There's something else I want to talk to you about."

"Maybe the white cap on this old lady is a good addition. I wonder if she'd lend me the cap for a week so I could work on the detail in the lace."

"Charles, are you listening to me?"

"Yes, yes. I am." Charles kept his eyes on the sketch.

"My mother informed me that your father offered you a compromise, and that you turned it down. Back in June." Martha turned her gaze to the worktable, not looking up at Charles. "The way I heard it, your father was willing to consent to our courtship, and a part-time apprenticeship with my father, but you had to finish your studies with Judge Reeve, do an apprenticeship, get admitted to a bar."

"Yes, that's true." Charles put down his piece of charcoal on the worktable, his eyebrows raised. Martha certainly had his attention now. "How did your mother find out about my father's offer? I didn't tell anyone about it—not even Eb. Who told her?"

"Your mother told my mother that day she came out to the cottage. Then your mother said it was all right if my mother told me," Martha replied with growing annoyance. "No one figured you were going to tell *me* about it." Her lower lip was beginning to extend into an emerging pout. "And they were right."

"I didn't mention it to you, Martha"—Charles went on the defensive—"because I turned down his offer. The law is not what I want to do. It's what Judge Gould calls a moot point."

"And why would you assume I had no interest in your answer to him?" Martha was trying to remain composed, but she could feel her temper getting the better of her. Charles could feel its heat too.

"Well, whether I finish up at Judge Reeve's or not seemed like my decision to make." Charles's voice had a studied calm, not wanting the spat to escalate into another siege of the *Wrath of Martha*.

"I see," Martha snapped back. "Just like you becoming a full-time apprentice with my father, and maybe his partner someday, is your decision to make?" Martha had caught wind of the negotiations—no surprise in a chatty family, ill-equipped to keep secrets. "Have I no say in anything that happens to us, Charles?" Her voice was beginning to fill up with righteous indignation.

"All those plans, Martha . . ." Charles protested. "That's all they are. Plans. Jack wanted to clear things first with your parents before we spoke to you. It made sense. Don't you see? Your father would be taking me on. Your mother would have to feed me, do extra laundry. Jack was going to ask how you felt about it once we'd hammered things out." Charles opened his palms in supplication. "I've just assumed he's still working on it."

"But why couldn't I be part of the hammering?" Martha's eyes were beginning to fill up with tears, something she was not expecting. Martha was better suited for rage than sorrow.

"You were going to be, my love." Charles saw the imminent tears but did not alter his even tone of voice. "I told Jack. You must have absolute veto power over the entire scheme. And he agreed."

"So, at the very last minute, you and Jack were going to present me with a fait accompli?" Martha had just learned this expression at Miss Pierce's and felt a certain smugness for using it. "And how do you think I could say no when everyone else I love in the world wants me to agree? You, my mother, my father, Jack. I'm surprised you didn't consult with Lucky before you mentioned the scheme to me."

"We didn't want to get you riled up until the terms were decided upon," Charles replied. "Why upset you if the whole thing wasn't going to work out?"

"Well, you upset me more by excluding me." Martha began to shift back to her wrathful mode, so much more comfortable than tears. "I don't know why you and Jack imagined I shouldn't be consulted in what you do for a living. If we are to marry, my whole future—and that of our children—will depend on you and your ability to provide." Martha was trying hard to hold back her anger. Rebecca had been working with her on how to use reason with Charles instead of losing her temper. Martha's part of this conversation had been well-rehearsed on the third floor of Miss Pierce's. "This isn't just your decision, Charles. It's *our* future, not just yours. And what you 'want to do,' as you put it, while important, is not necessarily the determining factor."

"I see." Charles raised his eyebrows again.

"I think your father's compromise was fair." Martha had already ripped apart the peace between them—she may as well get everything off her chest. "He's sanctioned our courtship. He approves of your working part-time with my father. And he's not saying 'no' to your being an artist. He just thinks you'd be better positioned in life if you finished up your course with Judge Reeve, did your practicum, and got yourself admitted." Martha took a deep breath. "And so do I."

"You do?" Charles flinched at her words.

"I support your working with my father," Martha continued. "You're a wonderful artist, Charles. I hope you'll develop your talent and be wildly successful. But having the law to fall back upon would give our family more security. That's what I think." Martha was just about to run out of steam but wanted to finish what she had to say. "If there was an economic downturn, like last year's Panic—my father says we're still feeling its effects—no one would be able to afford a portrait. Or God forbid, what if something happened to my father? What would we do? How would we eat—you, me, our children?" Martha shuddered at the thought of her father's mortality and her starving children. "Or my mother?" She added her starving mother to the list.

"Doesn't it matter I don't like the law?" Charles's voice was quavering.

"You don't have to be the same kind of lawyer as Eb." Martha had thought this out. "Eb's a natural orator. He loves to speak in public. But not all lawyers are like that. I see other lawyers in town, strolling to their offices. Or practicing law in a room off their parlors. They sit peacefully at their desks all day, writing wills, drafting contracts, helping people buy and sell property. They hardly go to court at all."

"I suppose that's true."

"You could find a quiet corner to practice law, one with less public speaking and competition." Martha felt breathless. "You might think you don't like the law, Charles, but you're good enough at it. Everyone says you give excellent advice, even now." There was a long silence after Martha had finished. At the very end, she added, "And you could still pursue your art."

Charles finally spoke. "I'll have to give this some thought." He drilled his long fingers on the worktable. "I'm going to need to discuss matters with Jack and your father some more. Consult with Eb." Charles added quietly, "And perhaps with Judge Reeve."

Martha did not want to disturb the waters by saying anything else. She could not wait to tell Rebecca how well her new, more rational approach was working. Martha intended to use those 'determining factors' another time.

Charles closed his sketchbook, deciding not to work on the old lady's portrait anymore that day. He owed it to Martha to mull over what she had just said. He moved closer to her, leaning over to be in nuzzleable range. "Do you really think we're going to marry and have children?" His cheeks were flushed with color. "Really, Martha?"

"I do, Charles." Martha reached up to Charles and gave him a kiss, a long, proper kiss. "Really I do." He gathered her in his arms. They lingered in their embrace for a while. Then Martha whispered into his ear, "My mother's peach pie is probably out of the oven. Shall we go and get a piece?" In a seductive tone, she added, "With fresh whipped cream?"

"You go on in, Martha. I'll be in shortly." And with that, Martha left the studio to go into the cottage. Charles wanted some time to regain his composure. Martha had surprised him with her request that he accept his father's offer. He had never considered how his decision to quit law school might deprive his hypothetical children of food on the table. And no one had ever before suggested to Charles

Godwin that 'what he wanted to do' was not of the utmost—and sole—importance. This was a novel concept for him. Although perhaps not truly novel. Charles had heard his father say this before, but that did not count. This time it was Martha's suggestion—the woman he loved, his fiancée, the mother of his future children, the lid to his own peculiarly shaped pot.

Charles had to laugh to himself. He could feel the influence of Rebecca Harding in her request. Martha would never have resorted to 'determining factors' without coaching. Charles was beginning to see the virtue—and the downside perhaps—of giving a young woman an education. He put his sketchbook away and began to make his way into the cottage—toward warm peach pie, fresh whipped cream, Ruth bustling about, Benjamin and Jack waiting expectantly, Lucky hiding under the table, and his dear Martha, waving him into the kitchen, urging him to sit down next to her.

Charles shut the door to the studio. Maybe he should ask the old lady to sit for her portrait in a different cap? A plain, white one, perhaps? One without so much lace?

"Yes, I've heard of Ned Haines. A Yale man, I believe." The morning lecture was over. Judge Reeve and Eb were seated on a wooden bench, leaning up against the Reeves's house, facing the garden. Mrs. Reeve's marigolds were going strong. The day was muggy, threatening rain. It was the end of August, only weeks after Eb had received news of his mother's death. Eb was discussing his future with his mentor. He had received an offer to do his practicum in New Haven with Ned Haines, his father's old friend from apprenticeship days. Haines was also his uncle's colleague from Yale.

"I'd have to ask Judge Gould," the old man said, "but I feel certain we've had other young men from the law school go work for

Mr. Haines. I used to remember these things. Now I must count on James to do so." Judge Reeve knocked on his head as if it were a wooden door, trying to cheer up the glum young man. "You would live with your uncle in New Haven for the duration?"

"Yes, he's asked me to. My sister Malinda is probably sailing north to live with our uncle, at least for a while. My being there would be a comfort to her. She's grieving after our mother's passing." Eb looked away, focusing his eyes on the bright tangerine color of the flowers. He almost never mentioned his mother's death. "My brother and I are trying to get Malinda out of Savannah. It's not safe for her there now. Yellow fever's ravaging the city."

"Yes, yes, I see." The old man pondered the situation. "She must leave, of course. And I'm in favor of your not lodging in the home of your master. Those old-style arrangements where the apprentice lives under the same roof as the practitioner are no good. The young assistant's too available night and day." Judge Reeve leaned back against the house and crossed his legs. He too was enjoying the hardy little marigolds whose bright orange color defied the gray light of the day. "But what about your plans to go back home and practice law with your brother?"

Ever since his arrival in Litchfield, it was common knowledge that Eb Wells would return to Savannah to join the family law practice. But the dual catastrophes in Savannah that year—the devastating fire and the yellow fever epidemic—had changed everything. By moving to Charleston, his brother had left behind his father's mercantile clientele. Their mother was dead from yellow fever. Changes in Eb had also taken place, not so catastrophic or visible, but for him personally, tectonic. Eb had formed his abolitionist views—and expressed them in a public arena. This was not going to sit well in Charleston, particularly not with his brother's clients.

"I don't know what to do. I respect my brother John. He could teach me a lot. And it would be wonderful to be in a family practice—to become *Wells & Wells* again." Eb blew out air as if he were putting out a fire of his own. "But John's clients in Charleston all own slaves. For that matter, John owns slaves. His wife's father owns lots of them. The practice has shifted almost entirely to property law for rich plantation owners. There's no way to keep my hands clean, morally speaking."

"Anything else bothering you?" Judge Reeve suspected Eb was opening the box marked 'Eb's Future' in front of another person for the first time. The old man wanted Eb to cautiously pick out its contents by himself. The box might shelter hidden explosives.

"I would have to muzzle myself," Eb went on. "In the middle of this cotton boom, with the need for more free labor, the illegal slave trade in Charleston is growing. Thomas Bradford has been talking to some of the law students from Charleston. That's what he tells me. I'd have to stand by and watch other human beings being bought and sold in the Old Exchange Building—and say nothing."

"And why would that be?" Judge Reeve asked. "Why would you have to say nothing?"

"Because if I were down there in Charleston and spoke out, it would threaten the status quo. And the livelihood of John's clients. They would cease to hire him. If John lost business, his family would suffer. My sister-in-law, my little nieces." After stating these obvious facts, Eb did not speak for a moment. "It's always been a problem in our family," he continued. "I've tried explaining this to Charles before. Even back in the day, my father wouldn't permit my mother, or any of us, to make public anti-slavery remarks, even though he limited his practice to merchants who didn't deal in human cargo."

"And how do you feel about muzzling yourself?" Judge Reeve gently probed. "I assume you did once abide by your father's wishes. Back then, you must have held your tongue. Could you do so now?"

"I couldn't," Eb said quietly. "I've come to another way of thinking up here. From Charles, my uncle, my readings, exposure to the free Black community in New Haven, from my own experience. And from you, sir." Eb gave the old man a look of respect. "I can't stay quiet about my views on slavery." Eb let out a weak little laugh, making his first feeble attempt at being amusing since his mother died. "I fear I'm no longer muzzleable."

Judge Reeve smiled. "Anything else? What about the nature of the practice itself?"

"There's that too. Mr. Haines has a large commercial practice in New Haven. Another lawyer works with him, his son I believe, and a senior apprentice. The law office handles all kinds of matters—contracts, wills and estates, shipping, debtor's law, some minor criminal cases, some conveyancing. But mostly commercial matters." Eb was staring at the sturdy marigolds. A sudden image of his mother's treasured pale pink Noisette Roses in their backyard in Savannah flickered across Eb's mind. They often bloomed late in the summer. Would Lottie remember to tend to them? Eb looked around. Mrs. Reeve had no roses in her garden, which was just as well. Roses were too high maintenance. Mrs. Reeve should stick to self-sufficient marigolds. "My brother John's practice in Charleston is more limited." Eb resumed his train of thought. "I might gain a deeper knowledge of property law, but I'd rather be exposed to a wide range of legal issues. At least for now." Eb crossed his arms. "I truthfully don't know what to do with my Litchfield Law School education. No offense, sir."

"None taken. That's to be expected at this stage of your career. You've got to get out there and muck around in the law for a while, see what's going on in a day-to-day practice." Judge Reeve gave Eb's knee an avuncular pat. "I guarantee you, something will capture your imagination. You'd be surprised. Our top student from a few years ago was hell-bent on commercial law. Now he's got his own practice in New Milford, drafting wills for old ladies, assisting in the buying and selling of farms. He wrote to me last month. Says he likes helping farmers more than making money in the city. He often gets paid in chickens." Judge Reeve took a breath, wondering if he was done giving advice. Living inside his peculiar mind, Tapping Reeve had learned that sometimes he had to wait for his own words to come to a stop—all of their own accord. They had not. "So, you've got to give things a try. Practice the law. That's how you'll find your niche, Eb. Not by studying the law in the abstract."

"All right." Eb considered Judge Reeve's advice. "So, you think I should do my apprenticeship in New Haven?"

"It doesn't matter what I think." The old man leaned his head back up against the house. "This is your life, Eb. You've got to make this decision, not me."

"That's what Charles says too." Eb sighed. "I just don't know what to say to my brother." Eb looked over at Judge Reeve who had closed his eyes. To his surprise, Tapping Reeve looked suddenly quite old and tired. "Has Charles Godwin spoken to you recently?"

"Yes, he has." The old man opened his eyes, looking more like himself. "Charles is returning to his studies next term."

"That's my understanding, but I'm not sure his heart's in it." Eb sounded worried. "This is more Martha's idea than Charles's."

"Ah, yes," Judge Reeve replied. "That's undoubtedly the case. But his young woman strikes me as sensible. Her arguments have merit. Being an artist full-time might not be steady employ. She's already acting like a ferocious mama bear, protecting her future children."

Judge Reeve poked Eb with his elbow. "Charles will be fine. He's choosing to do this to please the woman he loves. Not his father." The old man shook his head. "I'm telling you, Eb, it's a world of difference." He smiled secretly to himself and looked out at the marigolds. "The rewards are far greater."

"Studying the law for love, eh?" Eb smiled at his mentor, remembering that Tapping Reeve had once been forced by his first wife's uncle to prove his professional mettle.

"Worse things have happened before." The old man rested his arms across his ample front. "Charles will start up with your class this term. He missed the whole summer, so he'll have to wait to take that portion when the subjects come around again. But the second half of the spring term—he can study that on his own and take the exams. We've already mapped things out for him, Judge Gould and I." Tapping Reeve gave Eb an inquiring look. "We were hoping you could help Charles catch up."

"Of course." Eb and Charles had already discussed how in the upcoming term they would spend the afternoons together in the library, along with Thomas Bradford. Charles would work with Benjamin Lewis in the evenings, and on Saturday afternoons after the exams. Eb and Thomas would continue to study in Eb's attic room at night, but Charles would not join them. He would be living in his cozy room in Benjamin Lewis's portrait studio. "I'll be happy to help Charles. Thomas says he'll help too. He attended all the lectures this spring—the ones Charles missed. His volume of notes is almost as good as mine."

"Good. The two young men can help each other." The old man looked satisfied. "Thomas too has oral exams to make up—from last fall when he was failing. Since I'll no longer be lecturing, James and I have agreed. Thomas will be retaking those exams with me. I'm also to give Charles the oral exams on what he missed last spring, along with another student who fell ill in the middle of the term. It's all set." Mrs. Reeve's bell for the midday meal could be heard loud and clear. Judge Reeve's grandson T.B. rounded the corner.

"Grandfather . . ." The little boy was breathless, having run around the grounds looking for Judge Reeve. "I've been sent to fetch you for the midday meal." T.B. sidled up to his grandfather who put his arm around him and gave him a sideways hug.

"And how was Miss Pierce's this morning, T.B.?" The old man peered down at his grandson. At first T.B. did not answer, staring up at Eb with the undisguised fascination of a child.

"All right." T.B. shook his head morosely. "Except for math. I don't like math, Grandfather. I don't want to study numbers anymore."

"Ah, well." Judge Reeve gave his grandson another squeeze of the shoulders. "I never liked math much myself. But we must do as Mr. Brace bids us, no?" He tweaked T.B. on the nose. "Mr. Brace is the teacher, and you, Tapping Burr Reeve, are his pupil. That's how it works, my dear boy." He looked down fondly at his grandson with his large, liquid dark eyes. "Your job is to obey." The old man reached over and stroked T.B.'s soft, downy cheek with a shaking hand.

"Your meal is ready." The husky voice of Betsey Reeve hollered out the dining room window.

"Speaking of obedience." Judge Reeve looked over at Eb with a knowing look. "Let's go inside and eat, shall we? She's been baking all morning." Judge Reeve braced his hands on either side in preparation to hoist himself from the bench. He teetered slightly, suffering from the gout. "I'm looking forward to a piece of Betsey Reeve's hot bread, with a slab of freshly churned butter. Maybe some strawberry preserves." He took the hand of his grandson, and the two disappeared around the corner.

The smell of fresh bread wafted in on a slight breeze that brought with it a few drops of rain. Like Judge Reeve, Eb's interest too had shifted to the meal. He followed the old man and his grandson around the corner. Eb could feel a subtle change in the atmosphere. Even though there was no chill in the air, a certain slant to the light hinted that summer was almost over. Fall would soon arrive, with winter on its heels. Oh well, Eb thought, not wanting to contemplate the cold again. One of these days, Mrs. Reeve would be serving hot soup.

"You have to see him before you leave." Martha and Rebecca walked along the Goshen Road, arm in arm. They were making their way back to Miss Pierce's. It was late August. The humidity had finally lifted. The sky was blue, the sun warm, and the bees were busy buzzing in their languorous, late summer dance. Martha and Rebecca had been out to the Lewis cottage for a meal. Rebecca had a reservation for a stagecoach on Friday, and she wanted to bid adieu to Charles and the Lewis family before taking off for Wethersfield. Rebecca had not seen Charles since the art exhibition.

Charles Godwin had been happy in the interim, sleeping out in the studio, working with Benjamin Lewis, secretly sharing his quarters at night with Midnight. He had also been smuggling food for the little cat from the kitchen table. Each morning, the brown-and-wheat-colored tabby, an entitled queen with a cunning black mask, could be found at Charles's feet, staring up at him the long distance of his body, lifting her terracotta nose in the air, inquiring when her next meal might appear. Charles desperately wanted Midnight to conquer her first mouse, to justify her presence with Mrs. Lewis.

But otherwise, for Charles, things hummed along. He was learning how to cut profiles. Martha came home at the end of each week for a visit. His health was almost restored. Ruth Lewis had fattened him up with delicious food, far better than the sparse fare at Mrs. Edwards's. His father had insisted on paying the Lewis family an ample boarding fee. Charles was resigned to starting up law school again. Rebecca's visit had gone well, and she was pleased to see Charles in such fine fettle.

Martha continued her campaign. "You won't feel right about things if you don't say goodbye to Eb. You need to tell him how sad you were to hear about his mother." Martha caught a stray bit of hair and maneuvered it back up into her casual bun. It was a warm day. Both young women had tossed their hair up onto their heads, under their sun hats, anything to get it off their necks. Martha's face was pinkened by the sun and ablaze with freckles. Even Rebecca had a rosy glow from their many walks in the fields on the long summer afternoons.

"I suppose so." Rebecca sounded half-hearted. "I did write him a note of condolence." Rebecca had shed private tears for Eb when she found out his mother had died, knowing how much he loved his mother. His loss made her think of her own mother's death in childbirth, and a few years later, her father's death from blood poisoning. She hated that Eb had to endure those sorrows too. Now both Eb Wells and Rebecca Harding were orphans. "It's all I could muster."

"That's one of your few failings, Rebecca." Martha patted her elbow. "You always write a letter when it would be so much better to talk to someone. You should go and find Eb. Tell him goodbye."

"Elizabeth made the same observation in her last letter." Rebecca frowned. "But I lack your courage, Martha. You know how to storm into a situation and state your mind. I hate any kind of confrontation."

"But sometimes you must confront things. If you just stay in your room and read books and write letters all day, you might neglect to lead a life."

"Hmmm." Rebecca's answer was noncommittal. "The truth is . . ." Rebecca started up again with hesitation. "I don't know how I feel about Eb. I gave him up readily to Katherine because I knew we could never have a courtship. Courtships lead to marriage, and I'm not going to marry. It didn't seem fair to lay claim to him." Martha was uncharacteristically quiet, perhaps sensing if she said anything, Rebecca might stop talking. "But then later," Rebecca continued softly, looking out on the hazy horizon and the rolling Litchfield hills, "I regretted doing that. I missed him, and I didn't like seeing him with Katherine."

"Well, we both know Katherine Montgomery wasn't a very good idea. I imagine Oliver Hull's discovering that too." Martha scoffed at the idea of Katherine with Oliver Hull. She had not been that interested in him, but it rankled her to see Oliver strutting around town with a doting Katherine on his arm. It had taken Oliver an insultingly brief time to get over her, not to mention the heiress from Hartford. "But I don't understand, Rebecca, why you're so certain you can never marry. I really don't get that."

"You must understand, Martha, I intend to be a teacher. A husband would rule that out."

"Who says so?" Martha's tone was defiant.

"It's just the way things are. Look at Miss Pierce. Look at any of the women who teach in the female academies, or even at a school like Wethersfield. They're all unmarried." Rebecca was starting to assume her teacher's voice with her friend, guaranteed to annoy Martha. "Husbands are an impediment."

"Well, you know what Charles would say." Martha slipped her arm out of Rebecca's, stopping at the side of the road to admire a marvelous purple foxglove. It was unusual to see one blooming this late in the summer. Its hardiness suggested human intervention, possibly an herbalist woman. She turned to face Rebecca. "Charles would say that just because things *are* a certain way doesn't mean that's how they *ought* to be."

"I admire Charles greatly. You know that, but it's easy for him to rewrite the rules. Charles is a white gentleman. He comes from money, with all its attendant privileges. He's got status, education, the freedom to craft his own future. I've had none of those advantages. I've worked hard for this education, for my right to become a teacher. I won't casually throw it away for a romance." When Rebecca tossed her head in a gesture of defiance, her hat fell off, and her dark hair fell to her shoulders. She caught her hat deftly. "Charles Godwin can afford to be an idealist. I can't." Rebecca made this declaration with more determination than she felt, swept away by the thrill of her critique.

"All right." Martha wanted to stroke the foxglove but knew she should not. She linked her arm back into that of her friend. "I'm just trying to pry your mind open a little." Martha spoke gently, not sounding like a teacher at all. "In my opinion, you ought to talk to Eb before you leave. You'll feel so much better. I promise you."

"I'll think about it." The two women continued walking along the road in silence for a while, arm in arm. "Just so you know, Elizabeth says the same thing. That I ought to meet up with Eb before I go."

"I'm sure she does. Elizabeth Stafford has known you since you were eight years old." The two women had reached the end of North Street and were almost at Miss Pierce's. "No one knows you better than Lizzie." Martha nudged Rebecca gently in the ribs. "You should listen to her good counsel."

Letter to Eb Wells from Malinda Wells, Savannah,
August 25, 1820

Dearest Eb,

This letter will be short. I wanted you to know first. I've decided to come up to New Haven to stay with Uncle Ebenezer. John doesn't know yet. I want to choose the right time to tell him. It's better he hears it from me. Susan is coming too. I need your support in making it clear to everyone, including Esmeralda, that Susan comes as my companion, not as a servant. Once I inform John, I'm certain he'll work out the details.

I believe Uncle Ebenezer is going to stay in his current quarters, his father's old room. When you come in December, he intends to put you into our grandmother's room—the two of you will share a suite, a masculine snuggery. The plan is for me to take our mother's old bedroom. Susan will take Uncle Ebenezer's childhood bedroom. Uncle Ebenezer has invited us to assist in the clinic. We both stand ready to pitch in with the housekeeping. I don't wish our presence to be a burden.

Lottie intends to stay here in Savannah and take in boarders in our home. John will be amenable to that, I'm certain. We need your approval too since the East York Street house belongs to the three of us. I'm not in favor of selling it now. My intention is to first come up to New Haven for an extended visit. I want to see how we like it up there. Keeping the house in Savannah gives us all flexibility. The house will be safer if Lottie continues to live there in our absence, at no cost to her, of course. That's my opinion at least. We owe her so much.

I'm beginning to make travel arrangements. Staying busy keeps me from dwelling on Mother. The house is so empty without her. I keep thinking she'll show up any time, at the kitchen table, by the fireplace when it's time to read. Having a change of scene will be good for both me and Susan. We hardly go out at all, not with yellow fever everywhere. Lottie has been ordering our groceries to be delivered. Our lives are rather small right now—and sad. I'm looking forward to seeing New Haven and being with you and Uncle Ebenezer. I'm even looking forward to a journey at sea. Susan too is excited. Our first foray out of Georgia!

I wholeheartedly support your decision to apprentice with Ned Haines. Our father was very fond of him. Frankly, Eb, your abolitionist stance wouldn't sit well with our brother, or his clients. I'm somewhat selfish in this, I'll admit. I love the idea of the two of us living together in New Haven with Uncle Ebenezer.

I must confess, now the dust has settled, I can say this. I wasn't saddened to hear about your rupture with Katherine Montgomery. She wasn't the woman for you. It's not clear to me why you no longer mention Rebecca Harding. Why is that? I can imagine Katherine wouldn't have countenanced your having a friendship with another woman. But to my mind, Rebecca Harding sounded like a far better match for you. We can talk about it later when I'm once again in your presence. You can explain all. One year apart, my dear little brother! I'm so looking forward to your coming down to New Haven. I can hardly wait to see you again.

All my love,

Your owl of a sister, Malinda

"Eb?" Thomas Bradford's long legs were extended, his bare feet crossed on Eb's bed, next to the slumbering Sir Winston. "Do you think I have any talent for the law?"

Thomas was putting in his mandated hour of study as per his probation. The two young men had been meeting after supper like this for months, but Thomas often stayed longer than an hour. Something akin to a friendship was slowly developing between them. Once Thomas had achieved sobriety, a much nicer, somewhat apprehensive person showed up in Eb's attic room. Eb found himself looking forward to their study time. No one could replace Charles, Eb repeated often to himself, but Thomas had his merits.

The truth was both Eb Wells and Thomas Bradford were lonely. Thomas no longer went to the tavern, divorcing himself from the fashionable drinking set from the South. No true friends had been among them anyhow. Only a love of drinking, status, shared background, and a false sense of Southern honor had bound them together. Richard McKenzie, his only true confidant at the law school, was at home in Charleston, learning the cotton trade. Thomas had no one else to talk to.

Eb too had cut himself off from almost everyone during Katherine's reign. Charles had moved into the Lewis cottage. Being at the top of his class in law school had brought Eb his fair share of admiration and envy, but no new friends. Besides, Eb had imposed upon himself an even more rigorous study schedule since the death of his mother. He had little time to socialize, and little inclination.

"Yes, I do think you have legal talent." Eb sounded strained by virtue of his upside-down posture. He was stretching at the other end of the bed, his legs in the air, his feet settled on the attic rafters between two large sprigs of drying lavender. "I wouldn't have said so a year ago when we first met, but now we've been studying together, I can say with certainty that you, Thomas Bradford, have legal talent."

Eb did not want to state the obvious. Thomas had a future in the law because he now attended lectures, looked up cases in the library, studied, and had started filling in his own leather-bound volumes. Eb appreciated that Thomas Bradford was intelligent, and in his own way, talented. But Eb also knew intelligence and talent alone would not suffice. For the law, dedication and hard work were required as well.

"My friend Richard—the one who was expelled—told me no matter how hard I studied, I could never do as well as you." Thomas thought back to those hazy, drunken winter days in Bradley's Tavern in Bantam. They were all a blur, but he could still see Richard's face before him, his thick lips and ham-like hands, lifting his tankard of ale to his mouth. "Richard said you were talented, and we—mere mortals—were not. I found that rather disheartening."

"Well . . ." Eb swung his legs down from the rafter, avoiding a collision with Thomas and Sir Winston. "I witnessed Richard McKenzie do a few oral exams, and I would agree with him." Eb chuckled. "He is a mere mortal. He doesn't have much talent. But you, Thomas?" Eb saw that his face seemed troubled. "You do have legal talent. A different talent from mine, but legal talent just the same. All your own."

Eb was not exaggerating to make Thomas feel good. Because of his classic good looks, with his shock of thick brown hair and Roman coin face, Eb had underestimated Thomas Bradford. Eb was learning to question his first impressions. He had assumed that men and women who possessed beauty could not also be intelligent. But he was wrong. Thomas Bradford was intelligent, as was Katherine Montgomery. It might be an unfair allocation of resources by whatever deity had crafted them, but the conjunction of beauty and intelligence was possible. Eb also pondered some of the other pretty young women at Miss Pierce's. A few might be flighty. He was thinking about the giddy sisters from Albany. But even those two had their own version of practical wisdom—they were far more skillful at navigating emotions than Eb was. Eb's whole concept of what it meant to 'be smart' had expanded since he came to Litchfield.

Thomas Bradford demonstrated a practical bent Eb lacked. Thomas kept bothering Eb with questions such as, 'What should the innkeeper say to her, if he knew this woman of ill-repute was selling her favors in his tavern?' Thomas had known many innkeepers. He could imagine being sought out for advice. A perplexed innkeeper with burly arms, leaning over a roughly hewn tavern table, wiping his hands on a damp white apron, asking his lawyer friend, Thomas Bradford, what he should do.

'How would you advise your client in this situation?' This was Thomas Bradford's favorite question. His approach was not unlike his brother John's, Eb suspected. Once Thomas had a grasp of the principles, rules, and exceptions, he did not linger in the upper realms of conceptual thought. Rather, Thomas liked to descend into the messy, human world, to see how the law might play out in real life. This maneuver—to test one's understanding of the law by pondering its applicability—was foreign to Eb.

And to his other study partner, Charles Godwin. While Eb preferred to stay always in the stratosphere of legal theory, Charles tended to drift in outer space, outside the pull of earth's gravity and the law altogether, always thinking about social justice, morality, even theology. Law for Charles was just one piece of the puzzle, often a piece he showed minimal interest in. Neither Charles nor Eb had ever given much thought to the practical worries of an innkeeper with burly arms.

"Thomas, do you know where you'll do your practicum?" This topic was on the minds of all the students who had started at the law school a year ago—where to apprentice after law school for practical experience.

"I'm not sure yet. But I'm going back home, of course." Thomas only gave the matter two seconds' thought. "Aren't you?"

"I may do my practicum up here with a friend of the family," Eb said, trying to sound casual. "In New Haven."

"Not with John Wells? I thought it was all settled. You were going to practice law with your brother." Thomas sounded confused. "Maybe the practice is in Charleston now, but I still thought you'd be going with him."

"I don't think it's such a good idea anymore." Eb and Thomas had built their version of friendship on a foundation of silence over certain subjects. There were three in fact: 1) slavery; 2) Thomas's problem with the drink; and 3) Katherine Montgomery.

Eb was now infamous for his abolitionist views after the moot court argument. Except for Thomas, he was shunned by the other law students from the South. Even though his father was a plantation owner, Thomas Bradford had allowed Eb the freedom to hold his own views—as Katherine Montgomery and others had not. But neither Thomas nor Eb wanted to burden their nascent friendship with any frank discussions about slavery.

"I haven't told my brother yet," Eb confessed. "But I was wondering how you'd feel if I recommended you for the position."

"You would do that?" Thomas turned his head away to look out the tiny attic window. "I'd be honored to work with John Wells, but I fear I'm not worthy of him."

"You are, Thomas, I promise you, if you keep working hard and stay off the drink." Eb caught himself short. He had blurted out the last part of that sentence, straying off the path of safe conversation. Still, Eb had wanted to bring the subject up but was undecided where it fit on the agenda. "I couldn't recommend you to John unless I had your assurance you've stopped drinking."

"I have, Eb." Thomas was still looking out the window. "It's been almost five months. I haven't had a drink since the accident. I feel much better for it, at least after those first horrible weeks." He shook his head solemnly. "I would never want to go through that again. To feel that sick. I'm done. No more drink."

Eb said nothing for a moment. "It would mean a move to Charleston. And I can't give any guarantees about what John would say. But I wanted to ask you first before I wrote the letter."

"Thank you." Thomas's voice broke slightly. "But I have something I want to tell you first." His tone was confessional.

"What?" Eb could not imagine what Thomas had to unburden.

"I took your first volume, the one that went missing. The one that you did on the first unit of law we covered." Thomas turned to look directly at Eb, wanting to look him straight in the eye. "I'm so sorry, Eb. It was a terrible thing to do. Richard McKenzie and I were involved in a dubious scheme to rent out volumes written by top students. There's a market for them, you know. Other law students who don't want to do the work. I came upstairs one afternoon while you were at the library and took your volume from right here." Thomas tapped the windowsill with his fingers. "I've got the volume hidden in my trunk downstairs. I'll bring it up to you tomorrow." Thomas continued to look Eb in the eye. "I always meant to return it. I knew you'd need it to pass a bar exam." Thomas now looked down at the floor. "But I know that doesn't matter. It was still a dishonorable thing to do." Thomas moved his gaze from the floor to his feet, propped up on the bed. He could not bring himself to look at Eb again. "Truly, I'm so sorry. You've been so kind to me. I can't forgive myself."

Eb stared for a moment at Thomas Bradford, not entirely in disbelief. When the Richard McKenzie drama was unfolding last spring, Eb realized his missing volume had value. Their rooms at the boarding house were not locked. His book could have been taken by anyone at Mrs. Edwards's, to be leased out or sold on the academic black market. Eb also knew that Thomas Bradford and Richard McKenzie had been close friends. Thomas had started to perform well on his oral exams during a highly suspicious time. Under the circumstances, Eb was not surprised by Thomas's confession. But he did not know what to say now.

"I know you'll feel obliged to inform Judge Gould and Judge Reeve." Thomas looked over at Eb with solemnity. "I'd understand that. I wouldn't blame you. It's only right." He removed his gaze and started to look out the window again. Eb suspected that Thomas was fighting back tears.

"No." Eb shook his head. "I won't do that." He only had a split second to make up his mind, but his decision came easily. Eb felt a sudden pang of sadness for Thomas who had been through a difficult year. He did not have the heart to add to Thomas's woes. If he told Judges Reeve and Gould about the theft, Thomas would be expelled from the law school. Of that, there was no doubt. But Thomas was studying hard. He was off the drink. He was going to make a fine lawyer. For Eb, the apology and Thomas's remorse were enough— and getting his *Volume I* back. "No one ever needs to know about your borrowing the book. I won't mention what you did to my brother either."

"You won't?" Tears were finally rolling down Thomas's face. "Thank you, Eb." Thomas stifled a sob. "You're very kind."

"But, Thomas," Eb said hesitantly, "I must be frank with my brother." Eb had given this some thought. "I feel duty bound to mention your history with the drink and your probation."

"I accept that. It's better he be fully informed." Thomas wiped the tears away with the sleeve of his shirt. "Let's face it. John Wells probably knows already. Little happens here in Litchfield that's not talked about in Savannah. Plus, your brother is aware of my reputation. It's almost certain my father has told him why my own brother deems me unworthy to work at Mary Mount." Thomas let out a heartfelt sigh. "That's one thing I can count on in life. My father's vocal and public disapproval."

"All right, then." Eb noted to himself that moving out of Savannah might be good for Thomas Bradford. "I'll mention your interest in the position to John and provide him with some background information. Apprise him of the situation." Thomas Bradford bowed his head. "But what I'd really like to know about . . ." Eb's voice took on a lighter, more playful tone. He had moved back into his stretching position, lying flat on his back on the bed, lifting his legs up into the air and placing them gingerly on the crowded rafter. "Well, it's this. I'd really like to know about your stint with Katherine Montgomery." Eb gave his lower back a tremendous stretch and giggled. "What was it like for you? Did she try to make you over?"

"Oh, my goodness." Thomas wiped one last errant tear from his cheek. "If you only knew. I was Katherine's most unsuccessful project." He let out a hearty laugh. "And she had a lot to work on, that's for sure. But what could she have ever found about you to redeem?"

To Thomas, Eb Wells was a perfect suitor for Katherine—smart, sober, hardworking, ambitious, from the South, and these days, well-turned-out. There was the undeniable fact that Eb was too short, something he could do nothing about, although Thomas did not put it past Katherine Montgomery to command Eb to grow a few inches or two. But Thomas also knew Eb's abolitionist views were impossible for Katherine to countenance, or for anyone who belonged to their universe of Southern plantation owners.

"Oh, just let me tell you about Katherine Montgomery's campaign for the improvement of Ebenezer Wells." Eb was on the verge of hilarity. "I don't even know where to start." The two young men talked for an hour or more. Mrs. Edwards had to send her servant Maggie upstairs to the attic to ask Eb and Thomas to turn their laughter down to a dull roar. Others in the boarding house were trying to sleep. Eb and Thomas apologized but went on talking, even in the dark when their candle ran out. And their conversation had nothing whatsoever to do with an innkeeper or his liability for public nuisance.

Letter to John Wells from Eb Wells, Litchfield,
September 1, 1820

Dear John,

Thank you for your letter about our mother's burial. It's proper Mother should rest beside our father and two sisters. I'm grateful for your efforts. I'm still in shock over her death. I can't imagine we'll never see her again. It was a shame Mother refused to leave Savannah, but that can't be undone. You must not blame yourself. In the end, Mother just wanted to stay home. We can't fault her for that.

I have given your offer to apprentice with your law practice in Charleston a great deal of thought. I hope this won't distress you, John, but I am going to take a position up here in New Haven with our father's old colleague, Ned Haines. You may remember Father and Ned Haines were apprentices together. Mr. Haines has a thriving commercial practice. Uncle Ebenezer has invited me to live with him until I take a bar exam, and if Malinda comes north, I can help her get acclimated too.

You have heard—this I know from my friend Thomas Bradford—about my last moot court. My abolitionist views have developed over my time here in Connecticut. I cannot disavow them. I fear my reputation as an abolitionist would cause problems for your law practice. I wouldn't want to compromise your livelihood in any way, or your family's security. My stance on slavery would do just that.

I feel sad about these circumstances. You have financed my education with Judge Reeve. I intend to pay you back as soon as I am able. I'll be able to support myself from here on out with the money from the estate, and from my own employment as well. You may be disappointed by my decision, but you may also be relieved.

If you're looking for a young lawyer for your practice, I can heartily recommend Thomas Bradford. I must warn you. Thomas had a difficult beginning at law school. In an accident coming home from a tavern, Thomas broke his arm. Judges Reeve and Gould put him on strict probation. As you may already know from Savannah's gossip mill, Thomas Bradford has struggled with the drink. But he has been without alcohol since April and pledges not to return to it. For almost five months, we've studied together each night. I can attest to his legal acumen and diligence. Thomas shares a practical bent with you. He would be an excellent replacement for your somewhat impractical brother. If you're interested, you may write to him here at the same address as my own. No pressure. It's my hope that you might give him a chance, but the decision is entirely yours. Judges Reeve and Gould too stand ready to write Thomas a favorable—and frank—reference.

We'll be in touch soon, I suspect, over Malinda's trip to New Haven. I hope she'll come. I think the change of scene will do her good and perhaps relieve some of her mourning. We must support her in this, I think, John. The loss of our mother is felt acutely by Malinda who dutifully stayed at home by the hearth to take care of her. Uncle Ebenezer is in favor of Susan accompanying her. Shouldn't the family pay her a stipend as well? We also need to make clear that Susan comes north as a companion, and not a servant. Let me know about the arrangements, and I'll bear my fair share. Lottie wants to stay in the house on East York Street and take in boarders. This is also fine with me. I agree with Malinda—we shouldn't charge her rent. I know there are other matters in our mother's estate to be dealt with. Let me know if I can help.

John, I hope this letter doesn't distress you in any way. I have nothing but the utmost affection and respect for you. But I also have no desire to disrupt our cordial family relations. I fear that my coming back to the South would do them much harm. Please give my love to Eliza and the girls—and to my old friend Monroe.

Your devoted brother,

Eb

"I was glad to get your note." Eb Wells and Rebecca Harding sat on a wooden bench, under a shady oak in Mrs. Edwards's garden. The spot was hidden, far from the view of others. Rebecca had written Eb a short letter asking to meet with him before she left. Eb just needed to let her know when and where.

Charles had suggested that Eb ask Mrs. Edwards for the use of her garden out behind her house. Normally, her garden was off limits to boarders, but Mrs. Edwards could never say 'no' to Eb Wells. Besides, Martha Lewis had dropped by the day before, to explain the importance of the interview. Mrs. Edwards was a hopeless romantic and understood the value of privacy, a rare commodity for young couples in Litchfield.

"Charles told me you were leaving for Wethersfield, but I wasn't sure if you wanted to see me." Eb gave Rebecca a look of appreciation. Her dark brown hair was caught up in its customary knot at the nape of her neck. She was wearing a simple, indigo-colored muslin dress, with a light blue cotton shawl (borrowed from Martha) tied around her shoulders. Rebecca had gotten some sun on her face. She looked more rested than when he had caught a glimpse of her at the art exhibition in June. The circles under her eyes were gone. She looks so pretty, Eb thought. You can tell her exams are over.

Rebecca was fidgeting nervously with the gold locket around her neck. "Well, I did." She seemed hesitant. "Want to see you, that is. My reservation for travel is this Friday. I wouldn't feel right if I left town without saying goodbye."

"Aside from superficial encounters, Rebecca, we haven't spoken to each other since December," Eb said, gently reminding her. "At your insistence, I might add." He was still hurt that Rebecca had slammed the door on their friendship. There was an awkward silence. Rebecca was kicking herself for yielding to Martha's insistence they meet. "You're taking the position in Wethersfield, I believe." Eb already knew, having followed her employment saga via the Rebecca-to-Martha-to-Charles-to-Eb pipeline all summer, but he wanted to stay on neutral ground.

"Yes, I am. I'll also be the companion for my friend Elizabeth's grandmother, Mrs. Cox, a few doors down from the Johnsons." Rebecca tried to sound as matter-of-fact as she could muster, but her heart was pounding. "You remember Elizabeth, I know. I told you about the dame school she and I attended in Wethersfield for four years, with Mrs. Johnson and her daughter Penny."

"I do remember," Eb replied. "Penny, the daughter who didn't like to read but who could embroider like an artist. And Elizabeth, the great reader." Eb remembered all the details of Rebecca's years in Wethersfield and Hartford, just as she knew everything about his youth in Savannah and Athens. The two had shared so much during their intense four months of friendship, few gaps of knowledge in their personal histories existed.

Rebecca took note of how much of her past Eb had remembered. "Penny's coming home from her Hartford female academy later this month with a young doctor in tow."

"Does he know about her skill with healing herbs?" Eb wondered how open-minded a medical doctor might be. "She could be helpful to him."

"I don't know. I've never met him. But Mrs. Johnson has invited me to his first meal at the Johnsons' where he'll be on display. The poor man. Penny's the only child of older, doting parents. He'll have a series of tests to pass," Rebecca added, growing quiet. "I was so sad to hear about your own mother's death." She kept her gaze to the ground. "I know how close you were to her. Malinda must be grieving as well."

"My poor sister." Eb felt the familiar clutching feeling creep up on him, a tightness in his throat, an irrepressible urge to sob—or horrors, to weep. "I'm the most worried about Malinda. She and my mother spent every waking moment together. She feels lost. I know that."

"Charles tells me the plan is for Malinda to come up north to stay with your uncle. Is that still happening?"

"Yes, at least for a while." Eb could still feel the tightness in his throat. He did not feel sure of his voice. "She sails at the end of the month."

"And does Susan come too—the daughter of your mother's housekeeper?""

"Yes." Eb did not mean to be so monosyllabic, but he did not trust himself to speak.

"And how are you feeling, Eb?" Rebecca asked, leaning over to give his arm a squeeze. "This must be hard for you, losing your mother so suddenly like that, without warning. And being so far away."

"Being so far away is the worst part." Eb steadfastly gazed away from Rebecca. His eyes began to fill up with tears, and he feared there was no holding them back. "I hate that she suffered so much, and I wasn't there to comfort her." A sob welled up from the bottom of his lungs. "I wasn't there to tell her how much I loved her or to help my poor sister." The sob finally erupted. The tears could not be stopped and started to pour down his face. Before Rebecca knew it, Eb Wells was weeping inconsolably. "I know she didn't die alone." Eb tried to speak, amidst the shorter, shallower sobs that followed. "But I wasn't there for her."

"That must be a terrible feeling." Rebecca reached into the breast pocket of his vest for his clean, white handkerchief. "I can't even imagine." This was the truth. Rebecca too had lost both her parents, but she had been at their deathbeds, holding their hands and soothing them, even though she had only been a child at the time. She had never received news from afar that one of her parents had died—without her being there to give comfort. "I'm so sorry, Eb." She had not yet handed him the handkerchief. He was still sobbing, but Rebecca did not want the weeping to end prematurely. Without being told, she understood that Eb had not yet shed tears over his mother. These unleashed tears were his first, and much needed.

"It was so horrible for Malinda. Susan wrote that Mother had been so very ill the last day, she was vomiting up a black material. Like coffee grounds. It must have been a terrible thing to see her suffer so. For Malinda to witness that." Eb shuddered and gave a deep sob. "To bear that alone."

"But like you said, Malinda wasn't alone," Rebecca interjected. "She had Susan and Lottie there with her, and the doctor at hand. Your mother understood why you couldn't be there. I feel certain."

Rebecca finally handed Eb his handkerchief. Tears were still rolling down his cheeks, but his sobbing was slowing down. "She was so proud of you, Eb, and how well you were doing in law school."

"I know." Eb took the handkerchief Rebecca offered him and blew his nose. He had been swimming in a torrent of tears. His glasses too were all fogged over. He lay the handkerchief down on his knee, took off his glasses and rubbed them on the sleeve of his clean white shirt. "You're right, of course, but I still feel terrible I wasn't there. There's nothing to be done about it now. What's done is done."

"I understand that. Of course you feel that way. I know how much you loved your mother." Rebecca did not move or say anything while Eb cried a bit more, this time with silent tears. He wiped them away with his handkerchief. His tears began to abate.

"I haven't cried before," Eb said in a faint voice, beginning to collect himself. "About my mother. I've been afraid to cry."

"Why is that?" Rebecca herself was stingy with tears, although Martha was giving her instruction. Martha was a great fan of a good cry and had been giving Rebecca lessons on how to give vent to one's emotions. The campaign had limited success, due to Rebecca's reserved nature, but she was working on it. "Do the tears make you feel afraid?"

"They do." Eb gave his nose another blow. "It's irrational, I suppose, but I was afraid if I started to cry about my mother, I would never be able to stop."

"Martha's encouraging me to cry more." Rebecca gave a little hollow laugh, trying to steer the conversation away from Eb's grief to give him more time to recover. "She says tears never last that long and afterward you feel so much better." Rebecca settled back into the bench and fingered the light blue shawl. "She's probably right. Sitting on one's grief is like tamping down a live volcano."

"That's a nice turn of phrase." Eb reached into his jacket pocket and pulled out *The Detritus*, his portable hodgepodge common-place book. With the stubby end of a pencil, also scrounged from the depths of his jacket pocket, Eb scribbled, 'Sept. 6, 1820, Sitting on one's grief is like tamping down a live volcano. R. H.' Rebecca watched him write this down with amusement.

"You're still writing things down, Eb."

"It's been a long time since R.H. had an entry in *The Detritus*. Almost eight months." Eb thumbed through its pages. "Although from last September through the end of December, this old book is replete with R.H.'s pearls of wisdom." Eb pointed to a page from the middle of October. The book was full of things Rebecca had said to him. Observations that had amused, puzzled, disarmed, or otherwise pleased him.

"And what about the Montgomery Era?" Rebecca was surprised to see how many entries bore her initials. "Are there many entries?"

"Nothing." Eb looked forward through the pages from January through May. "Honestly, Katherine rarely said things that interested me. Mostly she just suggested how I might become someone else." Eb glanced over at Rebecca who was studying the ground. "I don't know what I was thinking, Rebecca," Eb confessed. "Spending time with Katherine Montgomery. The writing was on the wall early on. She and I were never going to make a good match. I can't even remember now what prompted me to walk out with her."

"Katherine's beautiful. She's intelligent and well-educated. She's from the South. That's familiar to you. Perhaps more to the point, she was interested in you." Rebecca could imagine a whole host of other reasons why Katherine Montgomery might have seemed desirable but did not want to list them. "It was worth a try," Rebecca added with a slight shrug.

"It was my vanity. Katherine is admired by all the fellows at school. I wanted everyone to know that I'd captured her—or that I could." Eb lifted his legs and examined his boots. "But honestly, I was too short for her, not up to her stature and standards—in oh so many ways." Rebecca said nothing. "And I didn't enjoy Katherine's company the way I enjoy yours." Eb's voice was faltering. "You will never know how much I've missed you, Rebecca."

"I've missed you too." Rebecca still would not make eye contact. "I didn't anticipate how much I would miss you when I wrote that letter."

"That letter was cruel." Eb's hurt from the letter boiled up inside him. His tears over his mother had engineered an avenue for other emotions. "I didn't understand why you turned your back on me the way you did."

"I thought it was for the best. Katherine Montgomery came to me after your first moot court and asked me if we were a couple. If not, she wanted to pursue you." Rebecca had firmly decided before their meeting that she was not going to reveal this part of the story. But the words came tumbling out. "I didn't see how we could become a couple since I want to be a teacher. I thought I had to let you go. For your sake."

"You and Katherine orchestrated this whole thing? This changing of the guard? The two of you, without my even knowing?" Eb was sputtering. He had always wondered about the timing of these events—the letter from Rebecca cutting things off and the launch of Katherine's campaign. He had been right to feel like a pawn. "You 'let me go'—is that what you said? You gave up jurisdiction over me?" he said with some rancor, shaking his head.

"I did." Rebecca understood exactly what he was saying. "You might say I withdrew my petition so you could entertain other petitioners." She continued to look down at the ground. "Honestly, Eb, when I did it, I wasn't sure how I felt. It wasn't until later, when I got into the 'missing you' part, that I realized I'd made a terrible mistake. But by then, it was too late. Katherine had sunk her talons in you, as Martha puts it."

"I'm amazed." Eb shook his head, feeling both mystified and outraged at the same time. "I truly don't understand how you women think. I doubt I ever will." Rebecca said nothing. "Why didn't you just come out and ask me how I felt?" Eb added with a rush of feeling. "Wouldn't that have been the kind and prudent thing to do? About you and me courting, instead of assuming you knew?"

Rebecca flushed, angered by his outrage. "It didn't matter what you felt. Or what I felt either. You know how much I want to be a teacher. The fact is I was *not* available. It didn't seem fair to hold you back from finding someone more suitable." Rebecca stopped short, considering how ill-matched Eb and Katherine had proved to be. "Or at least someone more available. I wasn't in a position to go forward."

"I don't see why you have to accept this truism that women teachers can't marry," Eb said bluntly. "Charles has explained to me your position. We're both puzzled by your passive acceptance of society's restrictions."

"That's easy for you and Charles to say." Rebecca's rebuke was sharp. She did not feel that either Charles or Eb understood her circumstances. "Those are the rules, and at least at this stage of my life, a courtship and a marriage would put an end to my teaching. What Eb Wells and Charles Godwin think about that won't change things."

"And when you say, 'at least at this stage of my life . . .'" Eb had picked up on that qualification, his legal mind ever in search of an exception to the rule. "Does that imply a different outcome at a later stage?"

"I really don't know, Eb." Rebecca responded with a heartfelt sigh. "It's just too soon to tell. Things are moving so fast in female education. Martha points out that Emma Willard is married, but she was already an established educator. Miss Pierce says that within five years, the country will be full of female academies. It's impossible to say how the rules might change."

"I see." Eb tried to absorb what Rebecca said. "So, just to clarify, if the only impediment to our being a couple was this supposed rule that female teachers cannot marry—if that impediment were removed, would you want to . . . Well, could you, uh, well, would you want to be, or at least consider, being in a coupleship with me?" Eb was struggling to find the right word, and when he could not, he made one up.

"I'm honestly not certain." Rebecca finally looked up at Eb. "I've never had a male friend before, so I have no basis for judgment. What do I know about love? I only know that I love to be with you. I love talking to you. I save up things to tell you every day, even during those long bleak months of the Montgomery Regime. I think about you all the time. I feel sad now that I'm moving to another part of the state where I won't get to see your face every day. Not that I've seen it much this year." Feeling dizzy from this rush of words, Rebecca abruptly stopped talking.

"And with all that . . ." Eb pondered all she had said. "With all those factors?" Eb was into arguing factors at this stage in his study of the law. "You don't see a persuasive argument that you and I would make a fine couple?"

"I only see my side of the argument," Rebecca said bitterly. "I don't even know how you feel." She felt anger rising in her again. "And I hate your 'factors,' as you call them. I don't like you talking about my feelings as if they were part of a legal argument. Sometimes you go too far, Eb. You don't recognize where the law ends, and your life begins." Rebecca stopped her tirade and spoke softly. "I don't like being part of a calculation. It hurts my feelings."

"I'm sorry, Rebecca." Perhaps he was being too analytical. Eb could not help himself. He was deep into the study of law. Lawyers have this problem in their personal lives: they analyze, they categorize, they argue pro and con, they wallow in factors, they qualify their conclusions, they pontificate—in short, they are often clumsy and hurtful in love. It is an occupational hazard that must be understood, accepted, and forgiven by their partners.

"I don't mean to make a legal argument out of this." Eb felt some contrition. "Listen, Rebecca, I love talking to you too. I also save up things to tell you, every day. It was even worse during my time with Katherine. The contrast was sharp." Eb considered this fact for a moment. "It was a good thing to have those months with Katherine after our time together. It gave me a basis for judgment. Here's my assessment."

Without any hesitation, Eb suddenly leaned over, took Rebecca's face in his hands, and kissed her on the mouth. Rebecca was startled but did not resist. It was not an awkward kiss, as she might have expected from Eb Wells, but a sweet, gentle, thoughtful kiss. It was also Rebecca's first kiss. She liked it. Eb then pulled back and looked at Rebecca's face, flushed, perturbed, but smiling. He stroked her cheek. "So, there it is, Rebecca Harding."

If this were one of her novels, Rebecca Harding thought, this kiss would have been the end of the book. But it was not one of her novels, just two young people on a wooden bench in Mrs. Edwards's backyard in Litchfield, trying to find a way to be together amidst the pressure of finishing law school, a demanding apprenticeship in New Haven, a disappointed brother, a dead mother, a grieving sister, a lonely uncle, a first teaching job in Wethersfield, a little old lady wanting to be read to, a stagecoach journey taking her to the center of the state, another stagecoach journey in December, taking him to the southern part of the state—and their own respective difficult natures.

Eb, on the other hand, was thinking how grateful he was to have practiced kissing. That had been part of the problem before, something he would never admit to Rebecca. Eb had not known what to do in the kissing department. And even though theirs was not a kiss to end a book—not quite yet—it was a kiss to alter the nature of their relationship forever. From here on out, things between Eb Wells and Rebecca Harding would become more complicated.

Rebecca Harding left at the end of the week for her first teaching position in Wethersfield. Mr. Anscombe, the caretaker at the female academy, had wheeled her trunk down North Street on a wooden hand truck to the stagecoach station. Martha Lewis and the two Miss Pierces had come down to the Green to say goodbye. Eb Wells and Charles Godwin had snuck out of Judge Gould's lecture to do the same. Eb gave Rebecca a lingering kiss on the cheek, making her flustered and pleased. Everyone else looked tactfully away. Rebecca waved at them all from the stagecoach window. The driver climbed onto his perch on top, clicked at the horses, and slapped them with the reins.

Soon Rebecca Harding was on her way in a cloud of dust. The stagecoach started to rock from side to side, continuing its journey to Hartford where she would change coaches for Wethersfield. She settled back into the weathered leather seat, pulled her shawl around her shoulders, and heaved a great sigh of relief. She was going to her first job as a teacher.

Above her, lashed onto the stagecoach's roof, was her trunk. In that trunk, nestled among her books and clothes, was Rebecca's commonplace book. On a fresh page, she had entered the addresses of Mrs. Edwards's boarding house and Dr. Ebenezer Cabot's house on Elm Street in New Haven. Standing there on the Green in Litchfield, as the stagecoach disappeared, Eb patted his jacket pocket and felt the contours of *The Detritus*. Eb too had written the address of Mrs. Cox's brick home on Broad Street in Wethersfield.

Rebecca Harding and Eb Wells had finally hacked out an almost imperceptible pathway to each other through the dense and tangled weeds of their ambivalence. As is true of so many couples of their day, forced to endure prolonged periods of absence, their letters would soon turn this narrow, still overgrown pathway into a well-worn thoroughfare. Although where that thoroughfare was going might still not be clear.

Charles and Martha walked back home for the midday meal at the Lewis cottage. Her two brothers from Kent were passing through on grocery business. Ruth Lewis had baked a Strawberry Rhubarb Brown Betty in the stone oven for a treat. These two brothers were great talkers—like all the members of the Lewis family, except their father. They would report on family news and town gossip, praise their mother's cooking, and tease their younger sister. The midday meal at the Lewis cottage would be noisy and cheerful.

But walking along the Goshen Road with Charles, Martha was teary-eyed about Rebecca's departure. She would be lonely at Miss Pierce's. At least Rebecca would be back in Litchfield the next summer, and they intended to write. Martha had also promised to visit Rebecca in Wethersfield for the December break, assuming Mrs. Cox was amenable. This meant Martha would miss the holidays at home, but she was excited about her first foray out of Litchfield. Ruth Lewis insisted that Martha make the journey. She would sew her daughter a couple of new dresses for the visit and embroider some dish towels for Mrs. Cox as a hostess present.

As they walked along the road to the cottage, Charles cradled his hand beneath Martha's arm in their customary fashion. Charles was still thinking about the old lady he was painting. The white cap was not going well. Perhaps he should dispense with the cap altogether. Could his patroness manage the stress? Settling on a hair style might throw her into a dither. She already complained how thin her hair had become with age. Perhaps he could paint a younger version of her, one with thicker hair? What was a commissioned portrait any-how—a picture of who the sitter really was, or who she wanted to be? Or once had been? He would have to discuss all this with Jack. Charles was also contemplating when to tell Martha about Midnight, who had finally caught her first mouse. Martha was good at strategizing. She would know how to approach her mother. Charles suspected Benjamin Lewis already knew about the cat. The striped tigress entered a room with a sense of entitlement. No one would ever accuse Midnight of being discreet.

Eb had been invited to the Lewis cottage for the midday meal but declined. He had already committed to Mrs. Reeve. The air was crisp and cool this morning. Autumn was signaling its arrival. Yesterday, Mrs. Reeve had mentioned something about her first fall soup. Eb was looking forward to asking questions of Judge Reeve about Judge Gould's lecture on the difference between law and equity. Thomas Bradford would be there too.

Eb wanted to show Thomas how to sneak a piece of chicken from the soup for Sir Winston without Mrs. Reeve knowing. Eb fully expected this inaugural broth to include tidbits of chicken, having cast a glance into the Reeves's kitchen this morning before the lecture. The old cat loved his chicken. Eb had developed a method of wrapping the meat in a lettuce leaf, filched from Mrs. Reeve's vegetable garden. When he unfurled the contraband chicken later, much to Sir Winston's delight, Eb's pocket would not be tainted with even a hint of grease. He must remember to show Thomas this trick.

As Eb made his way down South Street, he thought about how sad he was to see Rebecca depart. But he also had a strange feeling in the pit of his stomach, a mixture of excitement and anticipation. He was unfamiliar with this feeling, but it made him sing a little reedy song to himself—a song nobody but Eb could hear, which was just as well. Eb Wells sang about as well as he sketched, poorly but with enthusiasm.

I wonder, Eb thought, smiling to himself, if this is what it feels like to be happy? Or maybe he was in love? How does one tell when one is in love? Eb would have to discuss this with Charles. He had more experience in these matters. But about this, Eb was certain—he had been happy all week, sitting on the back bench in the law school, with Charles Godwin on one side of him, and Thomas Bradford on the other.

Eb was planning the rest of his day. He would eat with Judge Reeve and Thomas, and afterward go to the library, even though the term had barely begun. Perhaps he would write Rebecca a letter there. When exactly would be the optimum time in his study schedule to write her a letter? In the middle of the day, as a break from his studies? Or would thoughts of Rebecca derail him, distract him, and muddle his mind for the evening session with Thomas? Or maybe it would be best to write to her early in the morning, before he perused his notes for the lecture? To get the task done early and clear the agenda? Or perhaps it would be better to write a letter to Rebecca at the end of the day, after his studying was over? Eb was stumped. Maybe writing to her was like dessert—like the Strawberry Rhubarb Brown Betty he was missing at the Lewis cottage.

This is the new frontier, Eb thought, having a woman in his life—this time one he cared for. It was going to be far trickier than pacifying Katherine Montgomery, even if Rebecca lived far away. But the luxury of having such a problem made him giddy. No matter what time he settled upon in his busy schedule, Eb was looking forward to writing Rebecca Harding.

Eb continued to ponder as he arrived at the Reeves's house on South Street. Now what should I say in my first letter to Rebecca? He could smell the chicken as he approached the side door into the dining area. Mrs. Reeve grinned at him as he walked in, a tureen between her able hands. He returned her greeting and took his customary seat next to Thomas Bradford. I've never written such a letter before, Eb mused. Does this letter count as a love letter? What are the elemental parts of a love letter? I must ask Charles. Or Thomas tonight. He often has good advice.

Judge Reeve came tottering into the room and took his seat at the head of the table, with Eb Wells on his right hand, Thomas Bradford one seat down, and a dozen or so other law students. The table was more crowded than usual. The new law students were being introduced all around. Judge Reeve held forth with animation about the history of the equity court in England. How it had given relief to all those harmed by the strict requirements of the common law. Eb, Thomas, and the other law students leaned forward to hear his whisper, asking questions now and then, dipping their slices of warm bread into their soup. Afterward, the room became noisy with chatter—about the rigors of law school, which boarding house was the best, and the new young women who had just arrived at the female academy, observed just the day before, drifting about on the Litchfield Green in fine dresses, arms linked together in feminine solidarity.

When Eb Wells surreptitiously slid a piece of chicken into his lap beneath the table, Judge Reeve's eyes widened, and he smiled kindly at the young man. What could Eb Wells possibly be up to, stealing that piece of chicken and placing it in his lap? Is that a lettuce leaf I see? The old man was curious but kept silent. Instinctively, this much Tapping Reeve did know—he must not mention this maneuver to his wife.

THE END

Author's Note

What prompted me to write this book, or this series of books? Proximity played a huge part. I live in the Litchfield Hills in northwest Connecticut. And because I taught law, I was interested in the history of legal education, having written an article in 2008 about the Litchfield Law School in the *Legal Studies Forum*. All my visitors from out of town must visit the Tapping Reeve House and Law School in Litchfield, and then go to Bantam for Arethusa ice cream.

Litchfield is a short distance from my home. I take walks there frequently. The sleepy town retains much of its late eighteenth and early nineteenth century charm, with its iconic white Congregational Church, county courthouse, and public green. But in the early 1800s, Litchfield was a far more important town than it is today, ranking fourth in the state in population, after New Haven, Hartford, and Middletown. It was easy to get to by public transportation, a stagecoach station on the main routes between Hartford and Albany, New York and Boston. After the Revolution, many lawyers, merchants, and important political families settled in Litchfield, bringing with them considerable wealth, witnessed by the elegant federal homes, designed by famous architects of the day. It was a busy hub of commerce and industry—a perfect location to establish two schools of such renown, the Litchfield Law School and the Litchfield Female Academy.

Tapping Reeve was an innovator in legal education. His idea of giving lectures, national in scope, on the law, over a period of many months, was radical for its day, as were the law school's trappings—a committed student body, a free-standing building, a law library, oral exams, and moot courts. The Litchfield Law School represented a leap forward from the haphazard, hodgepodge apprenticeship system which not only failed to properly educate the bar, but also exploited young men seeking to join the profession. But Tapping Reeve's idea lost traction by the 1830s, with the establishment of law schools within universities and the ability to publish law books cheaply. Students no longer needed to have *Blackstone* dictated to them or to create their own set of handwritten leather volumes.

But we should celebrate the Litchfield Law School's contribution to the leadership of the New Republic. More than a thousand men were educated there from 1792 to 1833. The law school trained two vice-presidents, 101 members of the House of Congress, 28 Senators, 6 cabinet members, 3 justices of the Supreme Court, 14 state governors, and 13 chief justices of state supreme courts. It must have been an exciting place to study in its heyday, and if you are in the area, I urge you to visit the Tapping Reeve House and Law School in Litchfield.

Unfortunately, no equivalent house and school museum exist to educate the public about the Litchfield Female Academy, founded by the innovative Sarah Pierce. None of the academy buildings have survived, its location marked by a plaque on North Street that only a pedestrian could read. That is a shame. Sarah Pierce's contribution to female education is not as well-known as Tapping Reeve's contribution to legal education. But in many ways, Sarah Pierce and the female academy movement had more impact, laying the groundwork for educating young women for the rest of the century.

In the early 1800s, female academies confined themselves to teaching the 'ornamental arts,' embroidery, music, painting, singing, dance, and perhaps some rudiments of composition. Sarah Pierce expected more of her students. Her academic curriculum was expansive for its time, being one of the first schools to offer women an opportunity to learn ancient and European history, geography, mathematics, rhetoric and composition, logic, chemistry and botany. She cleverly united the ornamental arts with these substantive courses, with her students making maps, and embroidering subjects from poetry, literature, mythology, and the Bible. Natural history, such as botany, was learned through painting watercolors. Sarah Pierce had the vision to imagine young women engaging in intellectual endeavors, of becoming teachers, writers, suffragettes, abolitionists—of taking their place in public life. Over three thousand young women attended her female academy, from 1791 to 1833, attracting students from over 15 states, Canada, Ireland, and the West Indies. Many, like the fictional Rebecca Harding and the historical figure, Catharine Beecher, went on to teach.

With Litchfield's strong culture of history and preservation, it is possible to roam the streets of this small town and still feel the presence of the young men who studied at the Litchfield Law School and the young women who studied at Miss Pierce's. When I sit on a bench on the Litchfield Green, I can imagine them promenading, the young women walking arm-in-arm, in flowing dresses and capes with matching bonnets. I can also envision the young men standing around in clumps, leaning up against trees, trying to impress, or at least make eye-contact. Romance was in the air—as was the pressure from their families to make a 'suitable' match.

The Tapping Reeve House and Law School Museum is open to the public, and I often slide onto a bench in the back row and pretend that I am taking notes. That is where I first conjured up Eb Wells, Charles Godwin, and Thomas Bradford, who sat in that same back row. Thomas, an aimless, arrogant, alcoholic Southern dandy who found his way to sobriety, friendship, and competence in the law. Charles, the ne'er do well son of a New Haven shipper, an artist who struggled with law school and depression, but conquered both through love. And Eb Wells, our protagonist, also from the South, a brilliant nerd, striving to meet his family's expectations and clueless in love. He conquered law school, but it was not so clear that he had, or could, conquer love.

I felt a kinship with these young men, despite the almost two hundred years between us. I too was once a reluctant, misplaced, confused first-year law student. I too was fearful of the competition of law school. I too overachieved to compensate, pressured by my family to stay the course, and saddened by having the poetry beaten out of me. Those feelings, I know from teaching law for thirty years, transcend time.

The problems that plagued Eb, Charles, and Thomas, as early nineteenth-century law students, are still experienced by law students today, possibly all over the world. Legal education is demanding, difficult, and coercive. Hating law school is not only common, but to my mind, a sign of mental health. And the law can also be seductive, as Eb discovered. The best secret, and one he eventually learns, is that if you can survive your legal education with your integrity intact, you can use the law to combat society's injustices. Charles Godwin understood this, way before Eb did. But Eb was a young man who flopped around a lot, professionally and in his personal life. I understood him.

Once these young men introduced themselves, I began to wonder about their love lives. Before I knew it, Rebecca Harding, Martha Lewis, and Katherine Montgomery, all three students at Miss Pierce's academy, showed up. Martha, an irrepressible local girl, whose artistic talents went unrecognized by her artist father, and Katherine Montgomery, a faux Southern belle, sent to Litchfield to find a husband, with no one at home aware of, or interested in, her intellectual gifts. Both these young women were open to love, but Rebecca Harding was a tougher nut to crack. Her drive to become a teacher meant that she could not marry, rendering courtship moot. That made her an awkward romantic figure for Eb Wells who was already clumsy in love's arena.

If you want to know how their romance turns out, you will have to read the next three books. This is a series. *The Education of Ebenezer Wells* is only the first of four books, under the rubric *The Litchfield*

Chronicles. The others are *The Apprenticeship of Ebenezer Wells*, *The Trial of Ebenezer Wells*, and *The Education of Johanna Wells*, a story about the next generation, although Eb and Rebecca still feature prominently in the book, as do Charles and Martha Godwin.

Whenever I read a novel written in a historical period, I leap to the author's note to discover what characters really existed. **Here are the people who actually lived in Litchfield, Connecticut or elsewhere who are featured in the book**: Judge Tapping Reeve, his second wife, Betsey Reeve, his grandson, T.B. Reeve, Judge James Gould and his wife Sally, Miss Sarah Pierce, her half-sister Mary Pierce, her nephew John Pierce Brace, the landlady Mrs. Edwards, and by reference, Reverend Lyman Beecher, his daughters, Catharine Beecher and her sister Harriet (later Harriet Beecher Stowe), Aaron Burr, Sally Burr Reeve, William Grimes, Moses Brown, Venture Smith, and Benjamin Rush. There are first-hand accounts of many of the Litchfield historical figures, in particular Judge Reeve, Judge Gould, Betsey Reeve, Sarah and Mary Pierce, and Mrs. Edwards. I have relied on sources to imagine how they might have comported themselves in the world. All the conversations, however, are fictional.

Many of these people are buried in Litchfield, and I visit their graves often. Tapping Reeve is buried in the East Cemetery next to his first wife, Sally Burr Reeve, and his second wife, Betsey Reeve. On the other side of his grave is his beloved grandson, T.B. Reeve, who sadly died at Yale in his twentieth year. The Pierce family are buried in the West Burying Grounds. The graves of Sarah and her half-sister Mary are side-by-side. Their nephew, John Pierce Brace, who later moved to Hartford to serve for fifteen years as the principal of Catharine Beecher's female seminary, is buried in Hartford's Old North Cemetery.

In the portion of the book that takes place in New Haven, the only actual historical figure was William Lanson, the free Black engineer and entrepreneur. Everyone should know about William Lanson, an 'African king' or 'governor' of the free Blacks in New Haven, an accomplished individual who paid dearly for his success. Lanson challenged voting laws prohibiting free Blacks from voting, was active in what became the Underground Railroad, and helped to create independent religious institutions for the free Black community. He was also an innovative engineer, working on the Long Wharf and the Farmington Canal, changing forever the future of New Haven. William Lanson's success posed a threat to the dominant white society. His unraveling is a stain on Connecticut's history.

I have attached a bibliography that includes most of my resources. I offer it for anyone who wants to dig deeper, not as evidence of my seriousness as a scholar. I did try to be accurate about the two schools in Litchfield, and the historical backdrop, to the degree possible. Sometimes sources were not consistent, or there were gaps in knowledge. Sometimes, I filled in the blanks or made minor changes.

For example, sources state that the law school breaks tended to be from mid-May to mid-June, and then again for most of October. I altered that second break to take place over the winter holidays—to suit the flow of my narrative. I found no historical evidence of cheating at the law school, so I made that part up, on the theory that cheating exists on the underbelly of any institution and might not make it into the annals of history. I also took liberties with the postal system, assuming letters would arrive in a timely fashion, e.g., Eb learns about the Savannah fire, and his mother's death, just a week or so after their occurrence. This is probably historically inaccurate. The mail was slower than that, and not always dependable. Again, I stretched things here to keep the narrative moving along. More characters have better teeth than is probable, given the state of dentistry at the time. Harriet Beecher Stowe praised the loveliness of Betsey Reeve's garden, but I needed it to be messy to illustrate something annoying about Eb Wells's personality. I hope Mrs. Reeve will forgive me. The idea for the opening scene came from the excellent film that is shown at the Tapping Reeve House and Law School as an orientation.

Which brings me to my final point. I apologize for any historical mistakes that I have made. I am not a historian, merely a writer of historical fiction. Fiction is not the same thing as history, but I did try to accurately portray how these two schools operated. I hope that I have succeeded, but if some of the details are not quite right, I am sorry about that.

I would like to express my thanks to the staff of the Oliver Wolcott Library, the Torrington Library, and the Litchfield Historical Society, in particular, for the kind assistance of its Executive Director, Jessica D. Jenkins. I am also grateful to Sharon Rutland, my editor, and Professor Emeritus James R. Elkins of West Virginia University College of Law, the former editor of the *Legal Studies Forum*, who published my first article about the Litchfield Law School, and several other works that would never have seen the light of day, were it not for him. And of course, I am always indebted to Avrom, Nan, Kate, and Jo, and my beloved cats.

Bibliography

American Revolution Bicentennial Commission of Connecticut (1976). *The Underground Railroad in Connecticut.* https://prod.ctda. dgicloud.com/node/281031

Appel, A. (2014, February 27). "King of the Colored Race" of New Haven Revealed. *New Haven Independent.* https://www.newhavenindependent.org/article/willian_lanson_revealed

Beck, K. (1999). One Step at a Time: The Research Value of Law School Notebooks. *Law Library Journal, 91*(1). https://works.bepress.com/aallcallforpapers/33/

Boonshoft, M. (2014, Winter) The Litchfield Network: Education, Social Capital, and the Rise and Fall of a Political Dynasty, 1784–1833. *Journal of the Early Republic, 34* (4), 561-595. https://www.jstor.org/stable/24486661

Bryant, J. (2015, March 19). Before Ebola, there was Yellow Fever. *We're History.* http://werehistory.org/before-ebola/

Bryson, W.H. (1979). The History of Legal Education in Virginia. *U. Rich. L, Rev., 14* (1). https://scholarship.richmond.edu/lawreview/vol14/iss1/9/

Bulkeley, A.T. (1907) *Historic Litchfield, 1721-1907; being a short account of the history of the old houses of Litchfield.* Hartford Press. https://www.loc.gov/item/07029605/

Bukkuri, A. (2016). The history of malaria in the United States: how it spread, how it was treated, and public responses. *MOJ Anatomy and Physiology, 2* (3), 82-87. https://medcraveonline.com/MOJAP/MOJAP-02-00048.pdf

Burr, N.R. (1942, Spring). The Quakers in Connecticut: A Neglected Phase of History. *Bulletin of Friends' Historical Association, 31* (1), 11-26. https://muse.jhu.edu/article/395496

Butler, N. (2017, April 7). A Woman's Progress in Early South Carolina, Part I. Charleston County Public Library. https://www.ccpl.org/charleston-time-machine/womans-progress-early-south-carolina-part-1

Clark, G. L. (1914). *A History of Connecticut: Its People and Institutions*. G.P. Putnam Sons.

Close, S. (2021, Winter). *William Lanson Shaped New Haven*. National Endowment for the Humanities, 42 (1). https://www.nps.gov/articles/connecticut-abolitionists.htm#:~:text=Abolitionists%20Lewis%20Tappan%2C%20Joshua%20Leavitt,living%20expenses%20throughout%20the%20trial.

Collier, C. (2003, Summer). Why the First Law School in the United States was Established in Connecticut. *Int. J. Legal Info., 31* (2), 205-210. https://doi.org/10.1017/S0731126500010568

Coulter, E. M. (1939, March). The Great Savannah Fire of 1820. *The Georgia Historical Quarterly, 23* (1), 1-27. https://www.jstor.org/stable/40576606

Coulter, E. M. (1950, September). Franklin College as a Name for the University of Georgia. *The Georgia Historical Quarterly, 34* (3),189-194. *https://www.jstor.org/stable/40577234*

Custer, L.B. (1993, Spring/Summer). The Litchfield Law School: Educating Southern Lawyers in Connecticut. *Georgia Journal of Southern Legal History, I & II* (1 & 2).

DeLuca, R. (2011). *Post Roads & Iron Horses: Transportation in Connecticut from Colonial Times to the Age of Steam*. Wesleyan University Press.

Eichner, S. (1988, July). Medicine in the Revolutionary War. *Tredyffrin Easttown Historical Society History Quarterly Digital Archives, 26* (3). 90-104. https://tehistory.org/hqda/html/v26/v26n3p090.html

Gallman, J.M. (1984, Winter). Relative Ages of Colonial Marriages. *The Journal of Interdisciplinary History, 14* (3). https://www.jstor.org/stable/203726

Gilder Lehrman Center for the Study of Slavery, Resistance, and Abolition. The Emergence of Free Black Communities in Connecticut, 1800-1830. *CitizensAll African Americans in Connecticut, 1700-1850.* https://gradebuddy.com/doc/2416607/the-emergence-of-free-black-communities-in-connecticut/

Grant, S. (2002, March 3). Sisters Trace Black Ancestors to 1700s in Litchfield County. *The Hartford Courant.* https://www.courant.com/2002/03/03/sisters-trace-black-ancestors-to-1700s-in-litchfield-county/

Griffen, S.G. (1980). *The History of Keene, New Hampshire.* Heritage Books (1980).

Hardman, R. (2019, July 5). War on Campus: Papers Reveal Life at Yale During The American Revolution. *Connecticut Public Radio.* https://www.ctpublic.org/news/2019-07-05/war-on-campus-papers-reveal-life-at-yale-during-the-american-revolution

Harmon, L. (2008). The Lawyer Scribe: The Litchfield Law School, Laptops, and the Metaphysics of Soul-Searching. Legal Studies Forum, 32. https://digitalcommons.tourolaw.edu/scholarlyworks/64/

Havens, E. (2001). *Commonplace Books: A History of Manuscripts and Printed Books from Antiquity to the Twentieth Century.* Beinecke Rare Books & First Editions.

Hicks, P.D. (2019). *The Litchfield Law School: Guiding the New Nation.* Prospecta Press.

Huber, C., & Huber, S., & Schloeler, S. & Lansing, A.K., & Andersen, J. (2011). *With Needle and Brush: Schoolgirls' Embroidery from the Connecticut River Valley, 1740-1840.* Wesleyan University Press.

Kelley, M. (2008). *Learning to Stand and Speak: Women, Education, ad Public Life in America's Republic*. The Umohundro Institute of Early American History and Culture and The University of North Carolina Press.

Kenslea, T. (2006). *The Sedgewicks in Love: Courtship, Engagement, and Marriage in the Early Republic*. Northeastern University Press.

Kilbourne, P.K. (1859). *Sketches and Chronicles of the Town of Litchfield, Connecticut.* Case, Lockwood & Co.

Klebaner, B. J. (1955). American Manumission Laws and the Responsibility for Supporting Slaves. *The Virginia Magazine of History and Biography*, 63(4), 443–453. http://www.jstor.org/stable/4246165

Land, J. (2009). Lyman Beecher: Conservative Abolitionist, Theologian and Father. *Madison Historical Review*, 6(2). https://commons.lib.jmu.edu/mhr/vol6/iss1/2/

Langbein, J.H. (2004). Blackstone, Litchfield, and Yale: The Founding of the Yale Law School. In A.T. Kronman (Ed.), *History of the Yale Law School: The Tercentennial Lectures* (pp.17-52). Yale University Press.

Langbein, J.H. (2004). Law School in a University: Yale's Distinctive Path in the Later Nineteenth Century. In A.T. Kronman (Ed.), *History of the Yale Law School: The Tercentennial Lectures* (pp. 53-74). Yale University Press.

Larkin, J. (1989). *The Reshaping of Everyday Life, 1790-1840*. Harper Perennial.

Litchfield Historical Society (n.d*.). The Ledger: A Database of Students of the Litchfield Law School and the Litchfield Female Academy.* https://ledger.litchfieldhistoricalsociety.org/ledger/

Lockley, T. (2012, Fall). Survival Strategies of Poor White Women in Savannah, 1800-1860. *Journal of the Early Republic (32)*, 415-435. https://warwick.ac.uk/fac/arts/cas/staff/lockley/jer_lockley.pdf

Lomask, M. (1979). *Aaron Burr: The Years from Princeton to Vice-President, 1756-1805*. Farrar Straus & Giroux.

Magoffin, D.S. (1938). A Georgian Planter and His Plantations, 1837-1861. *The North Carolina Historical Review, 15* (4), 354-377. https://www.jstor.org/stable/23513832

Mansfield, E.D. (1879). *Personal Memories, Social, Political and Literary Sketches of Many Noted People, 1803-1843*. R. Clarke & Co.

Marsh, B. (2012, January). Planting families: Intent and outcome in the development of colonial Georgia. *History of the Family, 2* (2), 104-115. https://www.tandfonline.com/doi/abs/10.1016/j.hisfam.2007.08.003?tab=permissions&scroll=top

May, I.B. (n.d.). Religious Society of Friends (Quakers). *The Encyclopedia of Greater Philadelphia*. https://philadelphiaencyclopedia.org/essays/religious-society-of-friends-quakers/

McKenna, M. C. (1986). *Tapping Reeve and the Litchfield Law School*. Oceana Publications.

McKirdy, C.R. (1976). The Lawyer as Apprentice: Legal Education in Eighteenth Century Massachusetts. *J. Legal Educ., 28* (2), 124-136.

Mead, S. E. (1940, September). Lyman Beecher and Connecticut Orthodoxy's Campaign against the Unitarians. *Church History, 9* (3), 218-234. https://doi.org/10.2307/3160433

Melhorn, D.F. (1995). A Moot Court Exercise: Debating Judicial Review Prior to Marbury v. Madison. *Constitutional Commentary, 12)*. https://scholarship.law.umn.edu/concomm/272

Moline, B.J. (2002-2003). Early American Legal Education. *Washington L. J., 42*. https://heinonline.org/HOL/LandingPage?handle=hein.journals/wasbur42&div=44&id=&page=

Moss, H.J. (2006, Spring). Education's Inequity: Opposition to Black Higher Education in Antebellum Connecticut. *History of Education Quarterly, 46* (1). https://www.jstor.org/stable/20462029

Muney, L. (2014). *Silhouettes in History*. Silhouettes in History. https://www.silhouettesbyhand.com/history

National Park Service (2012, November 12). *Connecticut Abolitionists*. https://www.nps.gov/articles/connecticut-abolitionists.htm#:~:-text=Abolitionists%20Lewis%20Tappan%2C%20Joshua%20 Leavitt,living%20expenses%20throughout%20the%20trial.

Nelson, M.K. (2002, Fall). The Landscape of Disease: Swamps and Medical Discourse in the American Southeast, 1800-1880. *The Mississippi Quarterly, 55* (4), 535-567. https://www.jstor.org/stable/26476658

Pressly, P.M. (2003, Summer). The Northern Roots of Savannah's Antebellum Elite, 1780s-1850s. *The Georgia Historical Quarterly, 87* (2), 157-199. https://www.jstor.org/stable/40584669

Rodabaugh, W.J. (1979, September 29). A Nation of Sots: When Drinking was a Public Duty. *The New Republic.*

Rothman, E. (1984). *Hands and Hearts: A History of Courtship in America*. Basic Books.

Russell, P., & Hines, B. (1992). *Savannah: A History of Her People Since 1733*. Frederick C. Beil.

Sagafi-nejad, N. B. (2011). *Friends at the Bar: A Quaker View of Law, Conflict Resolution, and Legal Reform*. State University of New York Press.

Sandman, G. (1992). *Quaker Artists*. Kishwaukee Press.

Seeley, S. (2016, March). Beyond the American Colonization Society. *History Compass, 14* (3), 93-104. https://www.researchgate.net/publication/297616376_Beyond_the_American_Colonization_Society

Siegel, A. M. (1998). "To Learn and Make Respectable Hereafter:" The Litchfield Law School in Cultural Context. *N.Y. U. L. Rev., 73*. https://digitalcommons.law.seattleu.edu/faculty/644

Sizer, T. & N., Schwager, S., & Brickley, L., & Krueger, G. (1993). *To Ornament Their Mind: Sarah Pierce's Litchfield Female Academy, 1792-1833*. Litchfield Historical Society.

Smith, D.C. (1976, July). *Quinine and Fever: The Development of the Effective Dosage*. Journal of the History of Medicine and Allied Sciences, 31 (3), 343-367. *https://doi.org/10.1093/jhmas/XXXI.3.343*

Spooner, M. (2014). 'I Know this Scheme is from God:' Toward a Reconsideration of the Origins of the American Colonization Society. *Slavery and Abolition, 35* (4). https://doi.org/10.1080/0144039X.2013.847223

Strong, B. N. (1976). *The Morris Academy: Pioneer in Coeducation*. Morris Bicentennial Committee.

Tawa, N. E. (1975). The Performance of Parlor Songs in America, 1790-1860. *Anuario Interamericano de Investigacion Musical, 11*, 65-8. https://www.jstor.org/stable/779885

Terada, Y. (2023, March 17). Why the 100-Point Grading Scale is a Stacked Deck. *Edutopia*. https://www.edutopia.org/article/why-the-100-point-grading-scale-is-a-stacked-deck

Thompson, J.E. (1973, March). Lyman Beecher's Long Road to Conservative Abolitionism. *Church History, 2* (1), 89-109. https://www.jstor.org/stable/3165048

Thornton, T.P. (1996). *Handwriting in America*. Yale University Press.

Trainor, S. (2014, January 20). The Racially Fraught History of the American Beard. *The Atlantic*. https://www.everand.com/article/387554625/The-Racially-Fraught-History-Of-The-American-Beard

Tucker, L. L. (1974). *Connecticut's Seminary of Sedition: Yale College*. Pequot Press.

Tyson, R. (2011, Spring.) "Our First Friends, the Early Quakers." *Pennsylvania Historical & Museum Commission, 37* (2), 26-33. http://www.phmc.state.pa.us/portal/communities/ pa-heritage/our-first-friends-early-quakers.html.

Vanderpoel, E. N. (1903). *Chronicles of a Pioneer School from 1792-1833, Being the History of Miss Sarah Pierce and her Litchfield School.* Cambridge University Press.

Vermilyea, P. C. (2014). *Hidden History of Litchfield County.* The History Press.

Warren, C. (1911). *A History of the American Bar.* Little Brown & Co. http://www.minnesotalegalhistoryproject.org/assets/Warren%20History%20of%20Am.%20Bar%20(1911).pdf

Waring, J. I. (1968, December). The Yellow Fever Epidemic of Savannah in 1820, with a Sketch of Dr. William Coffee Daniell. *Georgia Historical Quarterly, 52* (4), 398-404. https://www.jstor.org/stable/40578899

Wethersfield Historical Society (n.d.) *History.* https://www.wethersfieldhistory.org/history/

Westfield, K. (2018). *The Enslaved Members of the Davenport Household: Geography, Mobility, and Pre-Davenport House Lived Experiences.* Georgia Southern University Department of History Public History Graduate Project Reports. https://digitalcommons.georgiasouthern.edu/history-grad-internship/1/

Winans, R. B. (1975, Winter). The Growth of a Novel-Reading Public in Late 18th Century America. *Early American Literature, 9* (3), 267-275. https://www.jstor.org/stable/25070682

White, A. C. (1920). *The History of the Town of Litchfield, Connecticut, 1720-1920.* Enquirer Print.

Woodruff, G. C. (1845). *History of the Town of Litchfield, Connecticut.* Library of Congress.

About the Author

Louise Harmon is a retired law professor, with a JD, a gratuitous PhD in philosophy, and two master's degrees. She has written numerous scholarly writings and published short stories with *The Legal Studies Forum,* including one on the history of the Litchfield Law School. Her two published books are: *Fragments on the Death-watch*, Beacon Press; *Cultivating Intelligence: Law, Power, and the Politics of Teaching* with Deborah Post, New York University Press. She lives in northwest Connecticut and frequently visits the graves of Tapping Reeve and Sarah Pierce, the two innovative educators who made Litchfield a center of learning during the years of the Early Republic.

www.ingramcontent.com/pod-product-compliance
Lightning Source LLC
Chambersburg PA
CBHW032346310726
48973CB00007B/1871